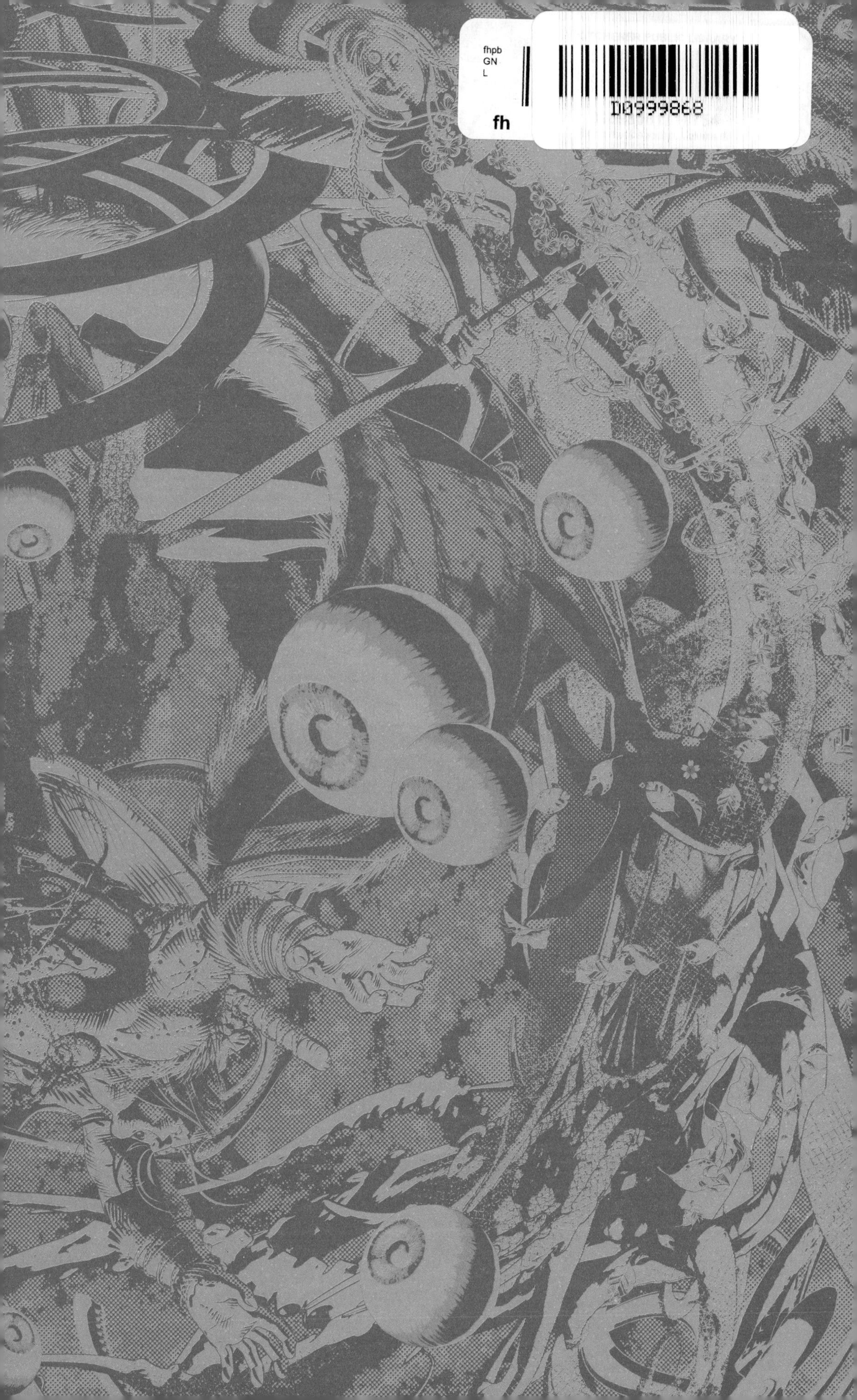

BERSERKER™ UNBOUND

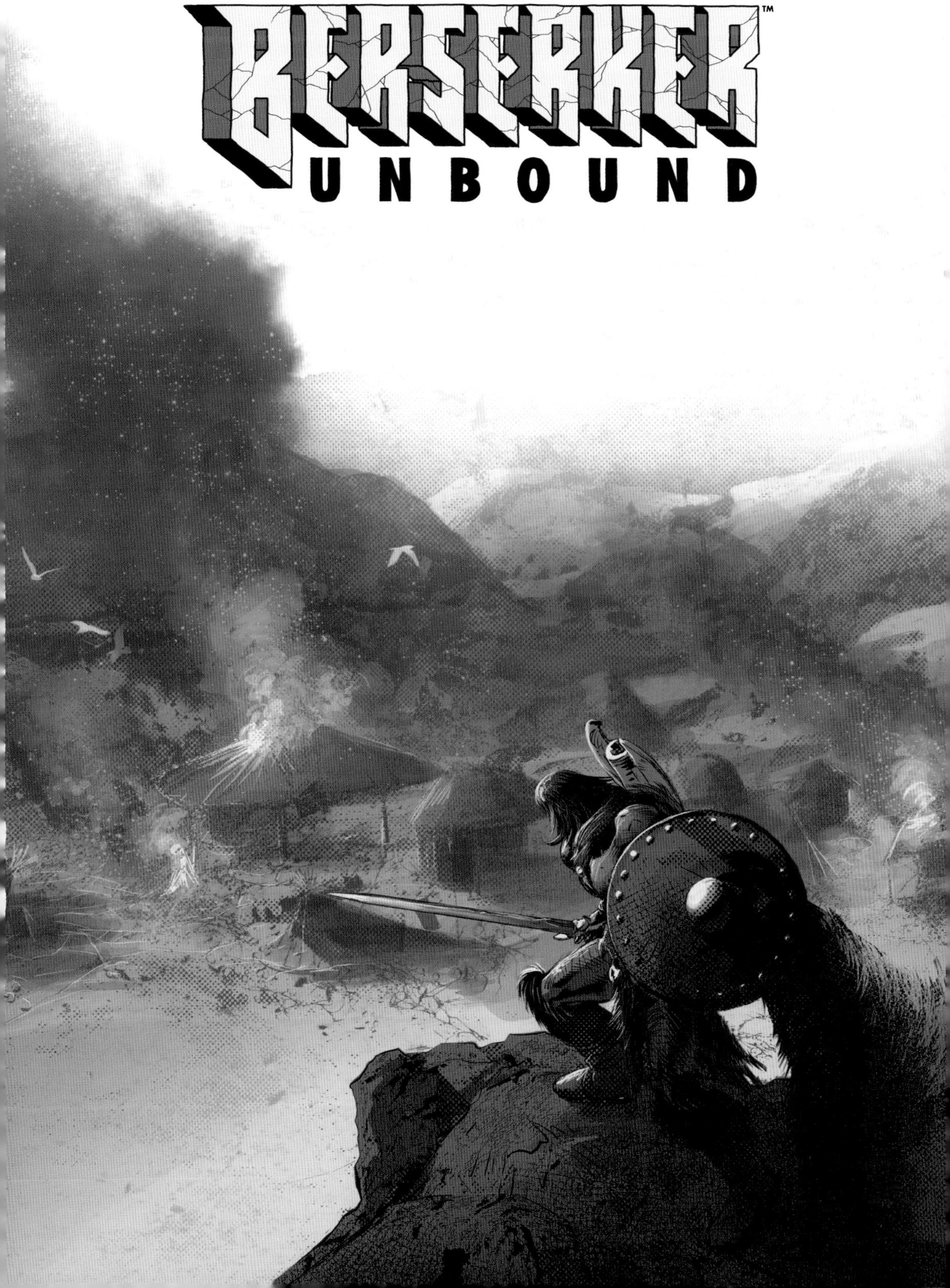

BERSERKER™ UNBOUND

VOLUME 1

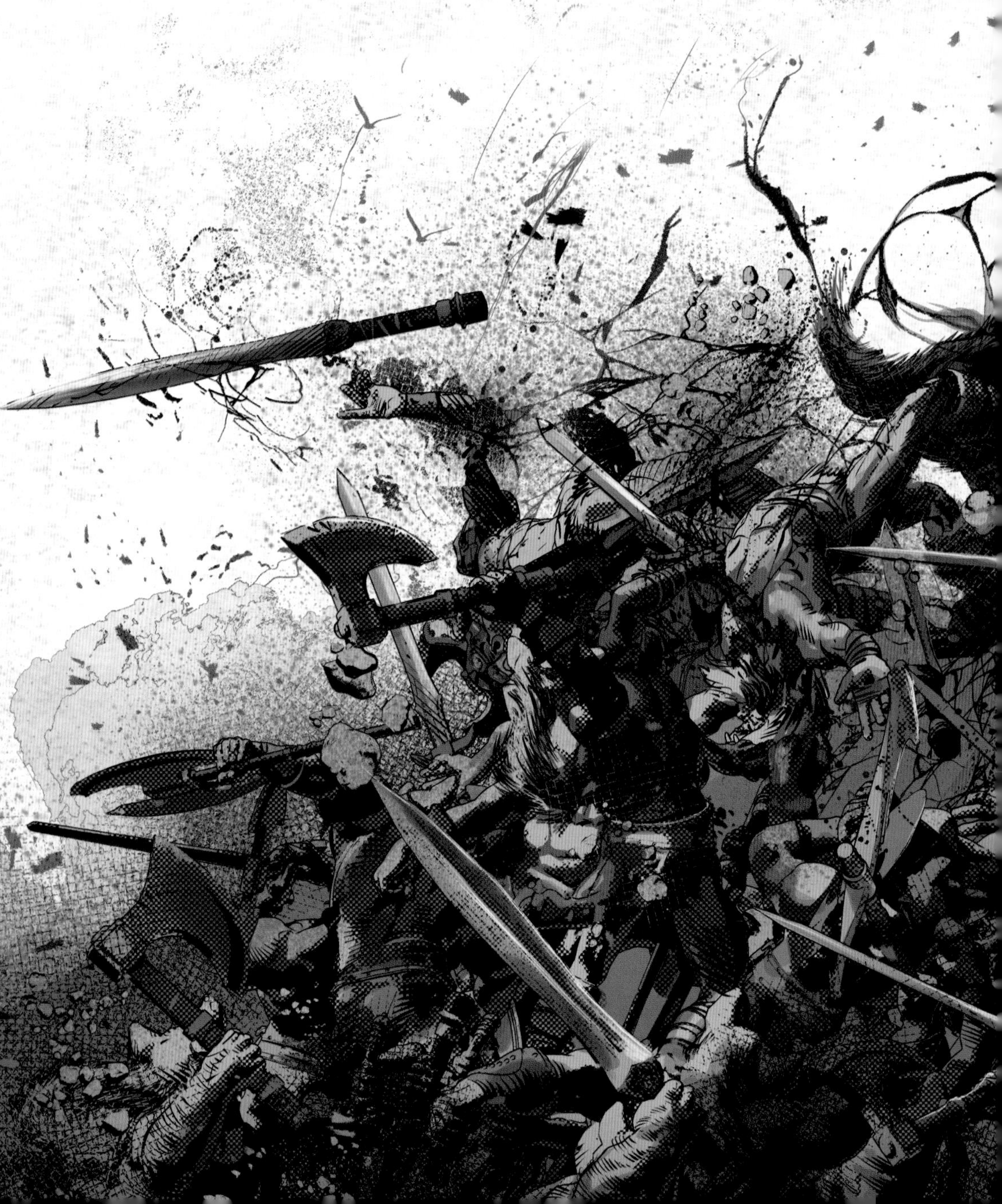

WRITER **JEFF LEMIRE**

ARTIST **MIKE DEODATO JR.**

COLORIST **FRANK MARTIN**

LETTERER **STEVE WANDS**

COVER AND CHAPTER BREAKS BY

MIKE DEODATO JR. AND **FRANK MARTIN**

DARK HORSE BOOKS

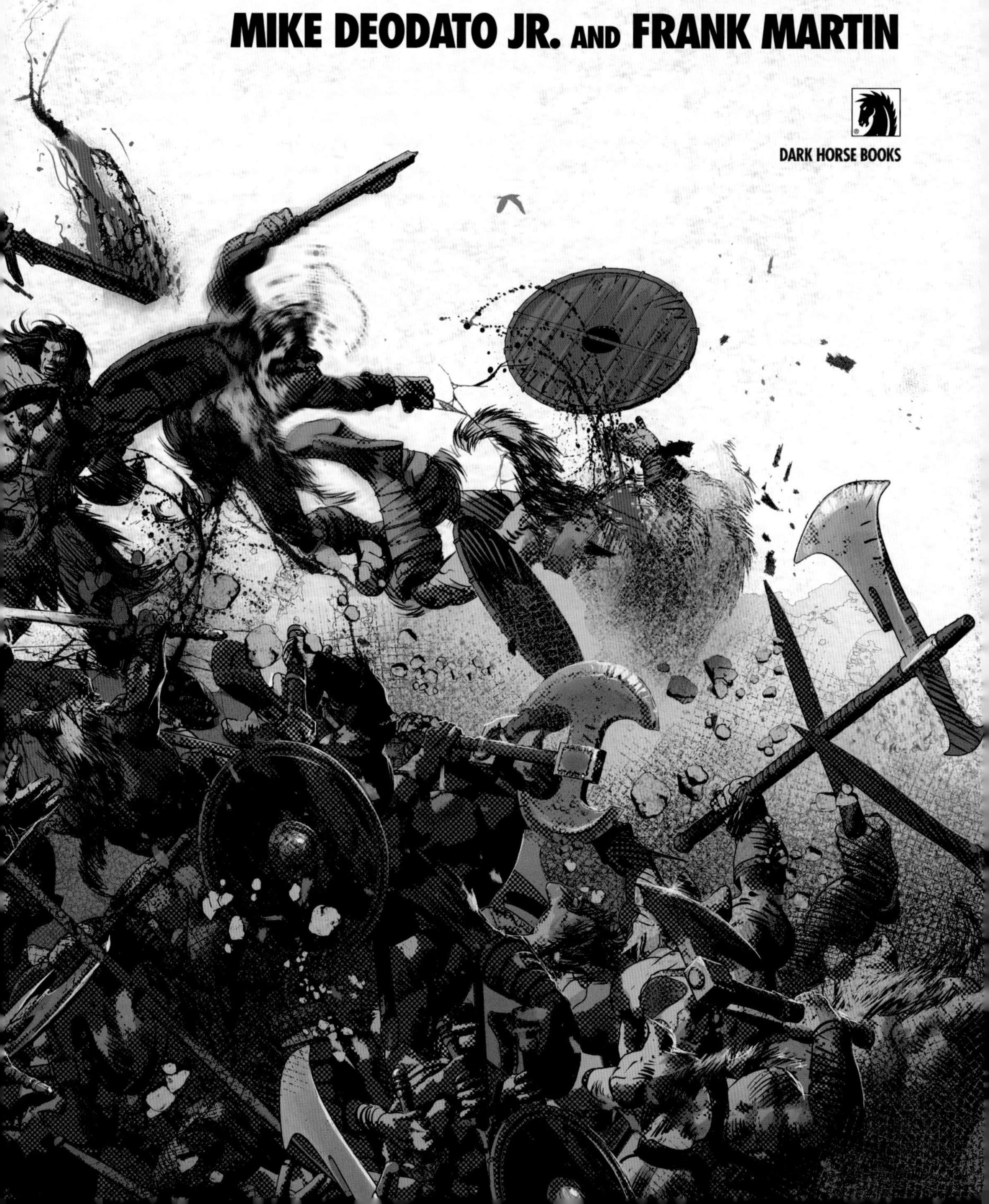

PUBLISHER **MIKE RICHARDSON**

EDITOR **DANIEL CHABON**

ASSISTANT EDITORS **CHUCK HOWITT, BRETT ISRAEL**

DESIGN **SCOTT ERWERT**

DIGITAL ART TECHNICIAN **JOSIE CHRISTENSEN**

BERSERKER UNBOUND VOL. 1
Berserker Unbound™ © 171 Studios, Inc., and Mike Deodato. All rights reserved. Dark Horse Books® and the Dark Horse logo are registered trademarks of Dark Horse Comics LLC. All rights reserved. No portion of this publication may be reproduced or transmitted, in any form or by any means, without the express written permission of Dark Horse Comics LLC. Names, characters, places, and incidents featured in this publication either are the product of the author's imagination or are used fictitiously. Any resemblance to actual persons (living or dead), events, institutions, or locales, without satiric intent, is coincidental.

Collects issues #1–#4 of *Berserker Unbound*.

Published by Dark Horse Books | A division of Dark Horse Comics LLC | 10956 SE Main Street | Milwaukie, OR 97222
DarkHorse.com | To find a comics shop in your area, visit comicshoplocator.com | First edition: February 2020 | ISBN 978-1-50671-337-3
10 9 8 7 6 5 4 3 2 1
Printed in China

NEIL HANKERSON Executive Vice President TOM WEDDLE Chief Financial Officer RANDY STRADLEY Vice President of Publishing NICK MCWHORTER Chief Business Development Officer
DALE LAFOUNTAIN Chief Information Officer MATT PARKINSON Vice President of Marketing CARA NIECE Vice President of Production and Scheduling MARK BERNARDI Vice President
of Book Trade and Digital Sales KEN LIZZI General Counsel DAVE MARSHALL Editor in Chief DAVEY ESTRADA Editorial Director CHRIS WARNER Senior Books Editor CARY GRAZZINI
Director of Specialty Projects LIA RIBACCHI Art Director VANESSA TODD-HOLMES Director of Print Purchasing MATT DRYER Director of Digital Art and Prepress MICHAEL GOMBOS
Senior Director of Licensed Publications KARI YADRO Director of Custom Programs KARI TORSON Director of International Licensing SEAN BRICE Director of Trade Sales
Library of Congress Cataloging-in-Publication Data

Names: Lemire, Jeff, writer. | Deodato, Mike, artist. | Martin, Frank, 1981
  September- colourist. | Wands, Steve, letterer.
Title: Berserker unbound / writer, Jeff Lemire ; artist, Mike Deodato ;
  colorist, Frank Martin ; letterer, Steve Wands.
Description: First edition. | Milwaukie, OR : Dark Horse Comics, 2020- | v.
  1: "Collects the Dark Horse Comics series Berserker Unbound #1-#4"
Identifiers: LCCN 2019039191 (print) | LCCN 2019039192 (ebook) | ISBN
  9781506713373 (v. 1 : hardcover) | ISBN 9781506713380 (v. 1 : ebook)
Subjects: LCSH: Comic books, strips, etc.
Classification: LCC PN6728.B435 L46 2020 (print) | LCC PN6728.B435
  (ebook) | DDC 741.5/973--dc23
LC record available at https://lccn.loc.gov/2019039191
LC ebook record available at https://lccn.loc.gov/2019039192

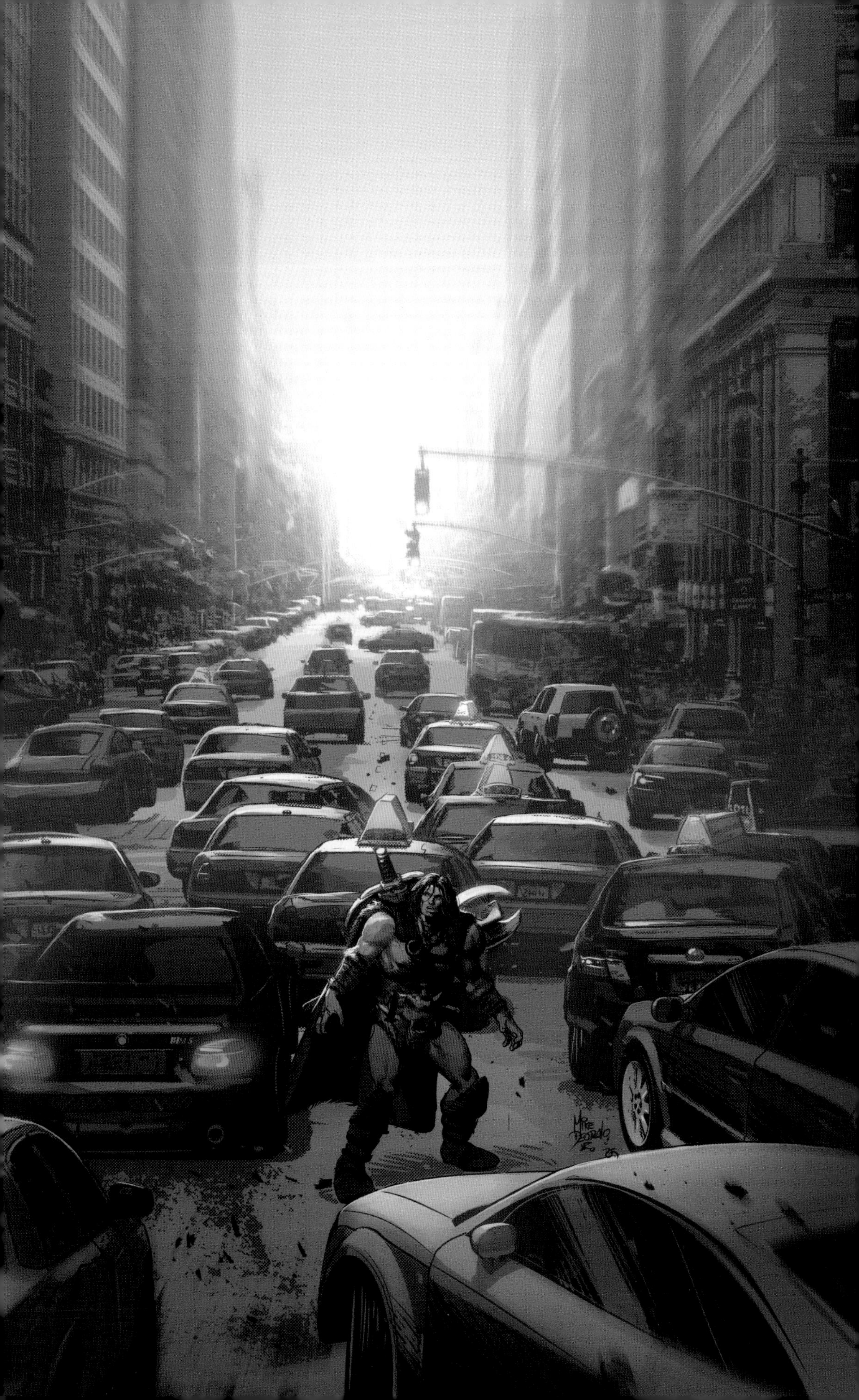

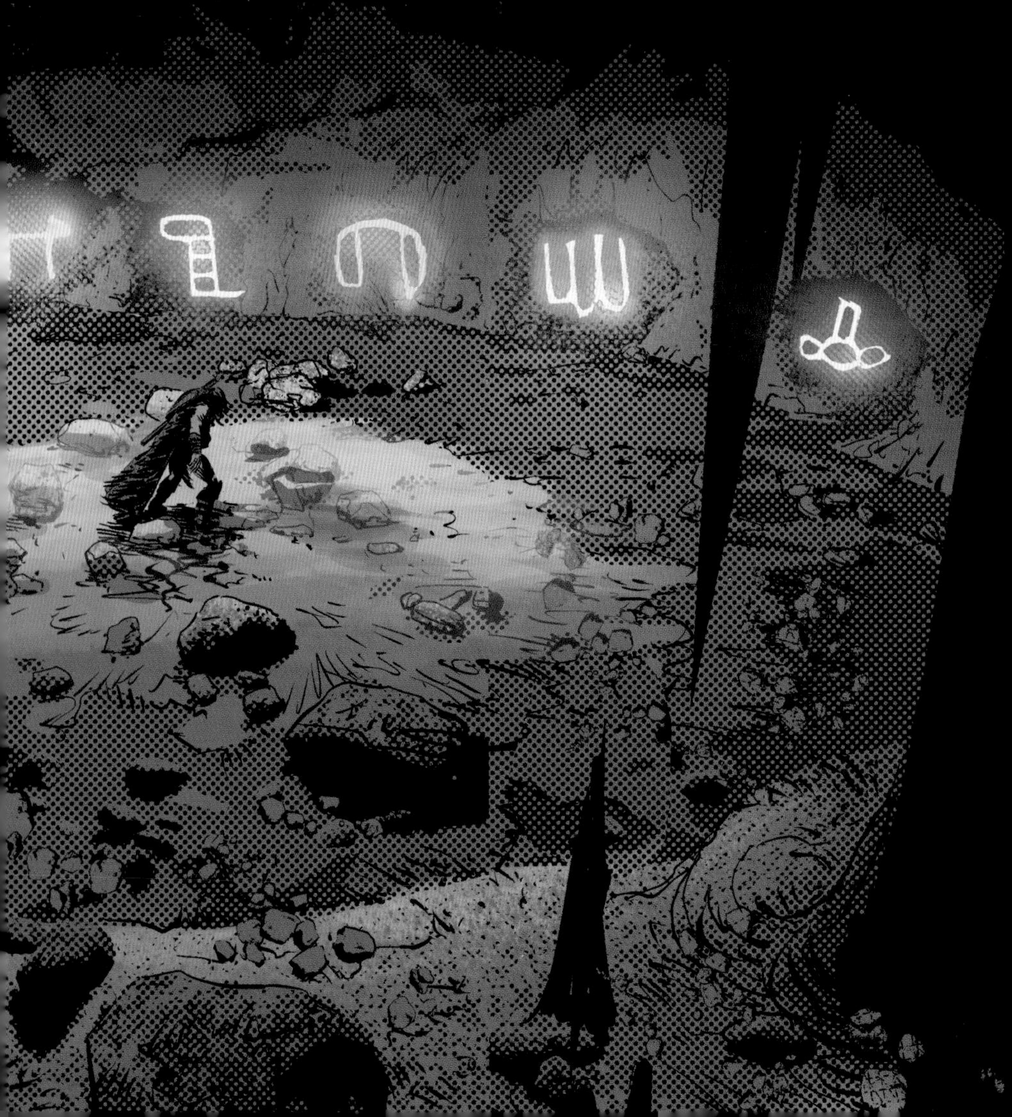

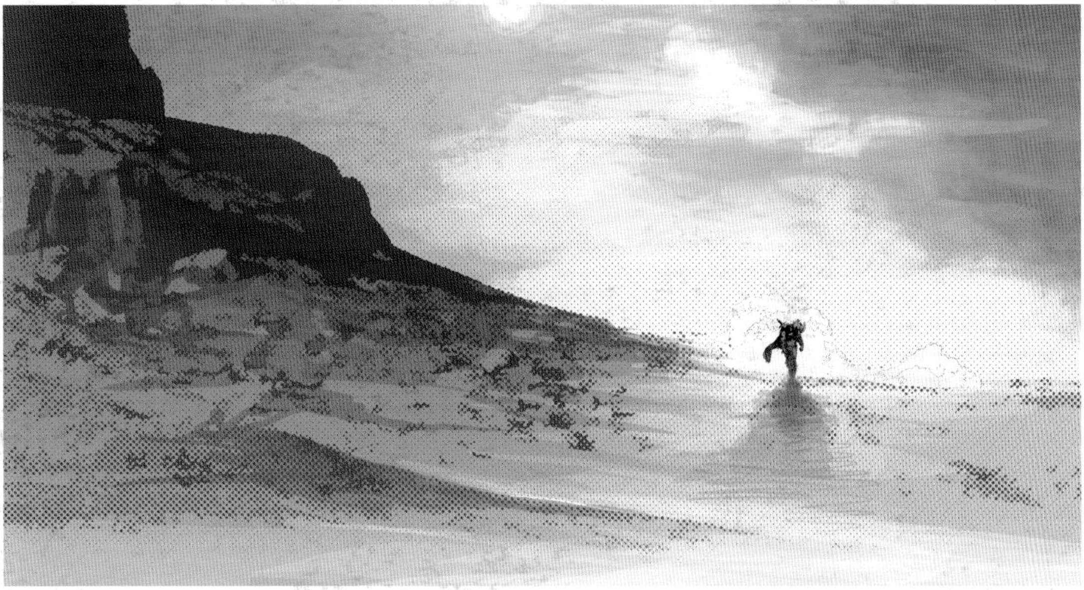

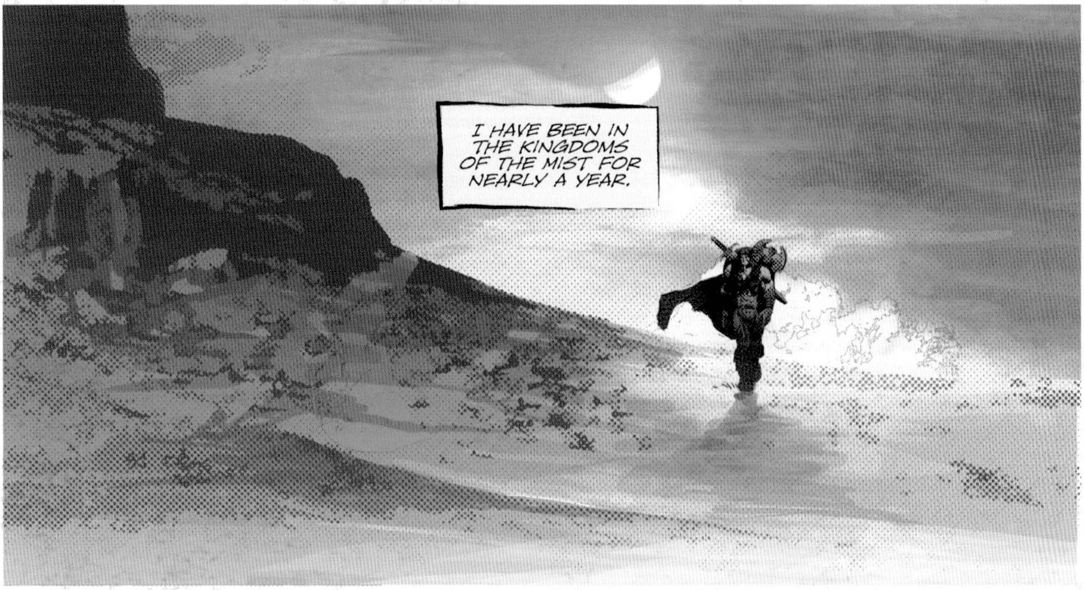
I HAVE BEEN IN THE KINGDOMS OF THE MIST FOR NEARLY A YEAR.

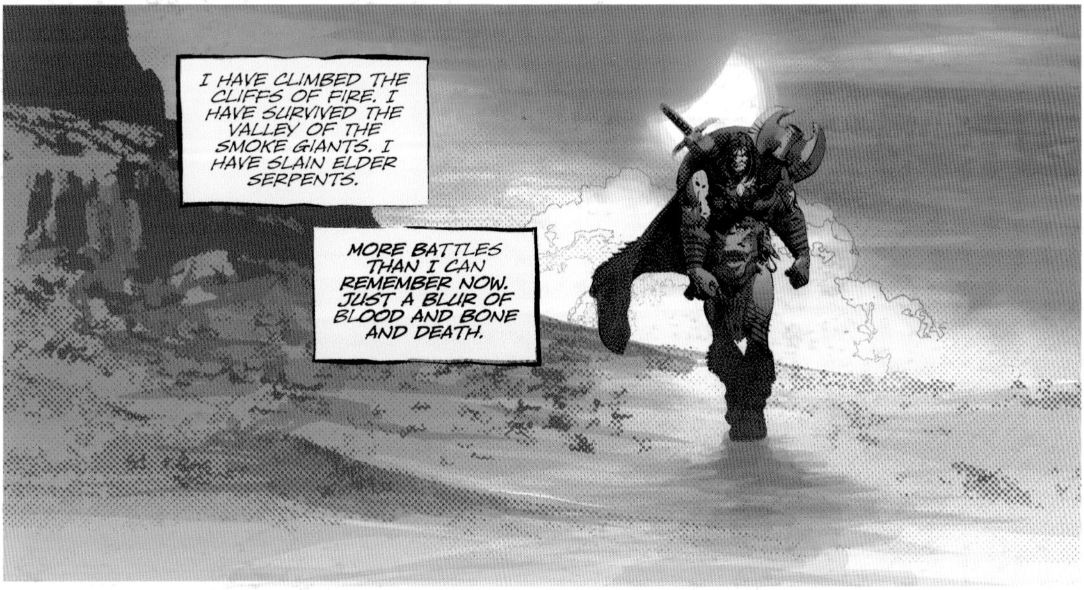
I HAVE CLIMBED THE CLIFFS OF FIRE. I HAVE SURVIVED THE VALLEY OF THE SMOKE GIANTS. I HAVE SLAIN ELDER SERPENTS.
MORE BATTLES THAN I CAN REMEMBER NOW. JUST A BLUR OF BLOOD AND BONE AND DEATH.

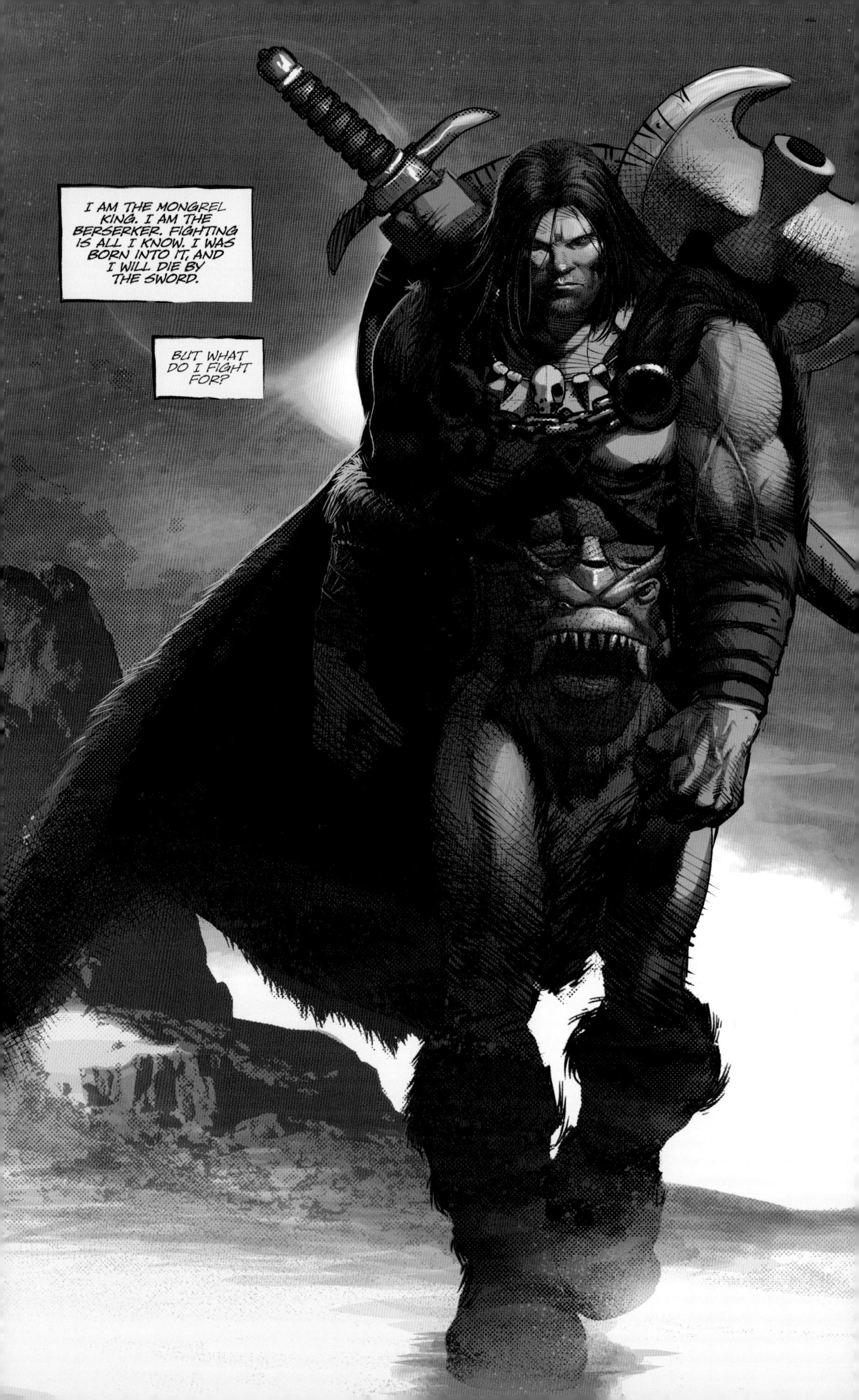
I AM THE MONGREL KING. I AM THE BERSERKER. FIGHTING IS ALL I KNOW. I WAS BORN INTO IT, AND I WILL DIE BY THE SWORD.
BUT WHAT DO I FIGHT FOR?

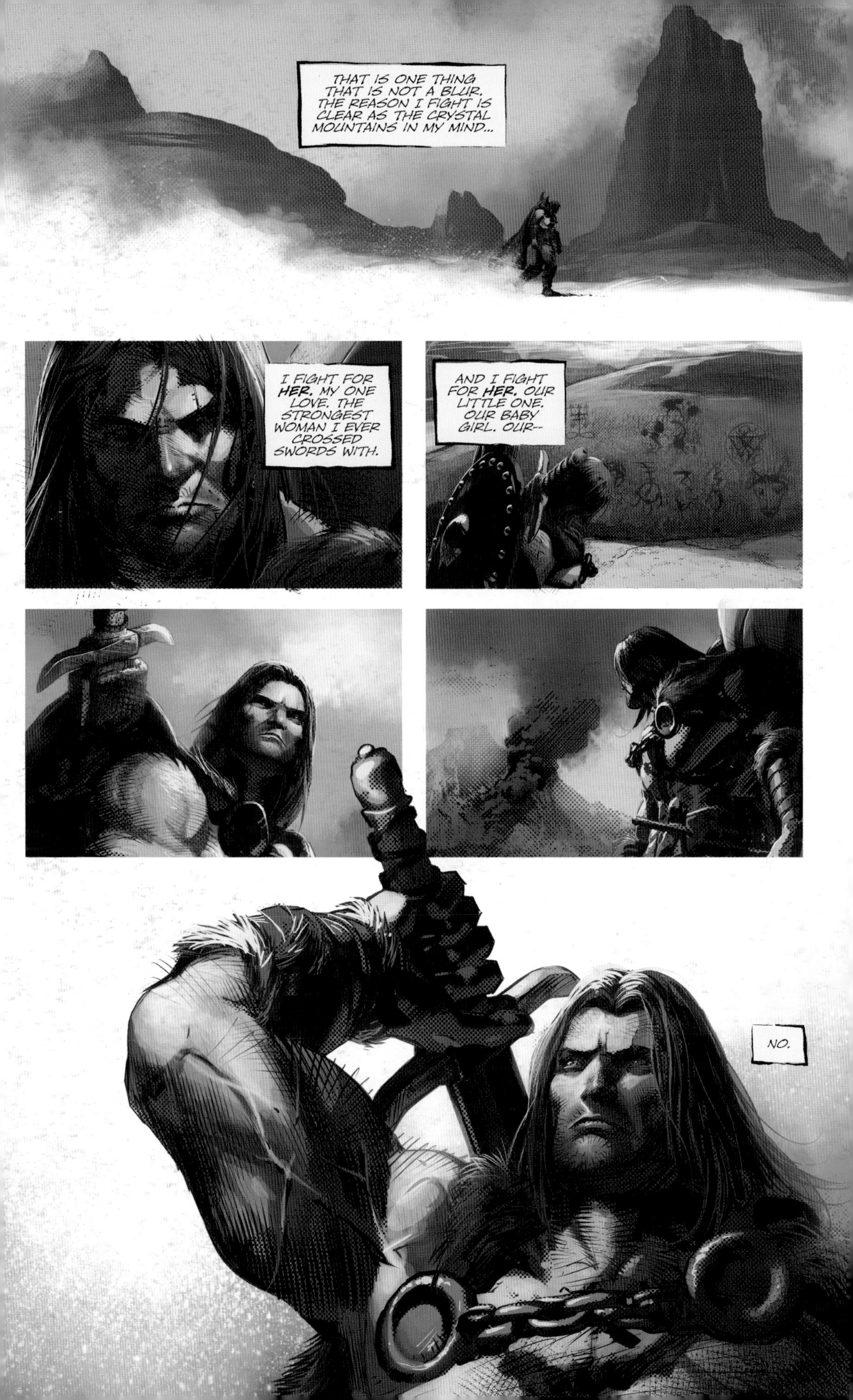
THAT IS ONE THING THAT IS NOT A BLUR. THE REASON I FIGHT IS CLEAR AS THE CRYSTAL MOUNTAINS IN MY MIND...
I FIGHT FOR HER. MY ONE LOVE. THE STRONGEST WOMAN I EVER CROSSED SWORDS WITH.
AND I FIGHT FOR HER. OUR LITTLE ONE. OUR BABY GIRL. OUR--
NO.

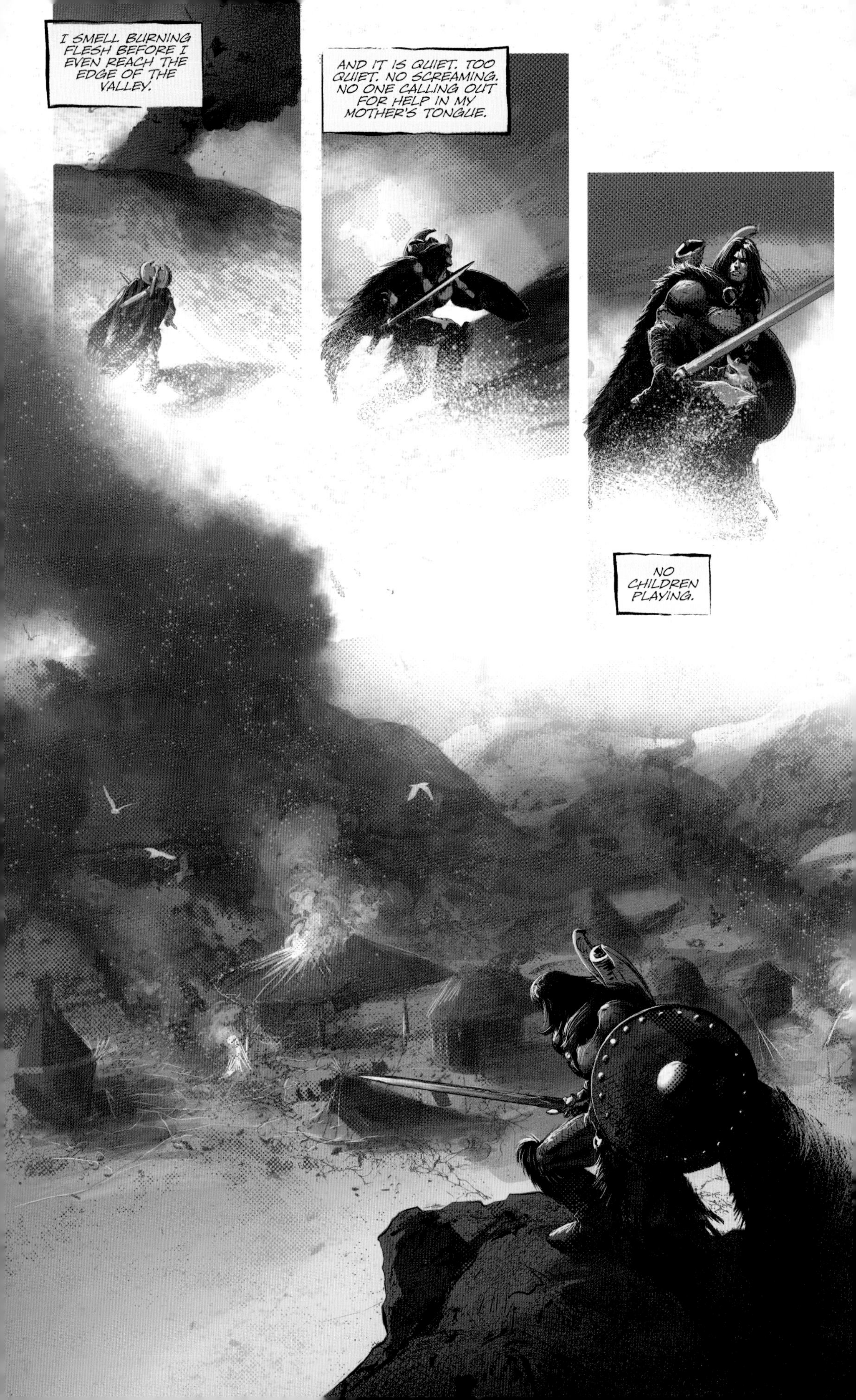
I SMELL BURNING FLESH BEFORE I EVEN REACH THE EDGE OF THE VALLEY.
AND IT IS QUIET. TOO QUIET. NO SCREAMING. NO ONE CALLING OUT FOR HELP IN MY MOTHER'S TONGUE.
NO CHILDREN PLAYING.

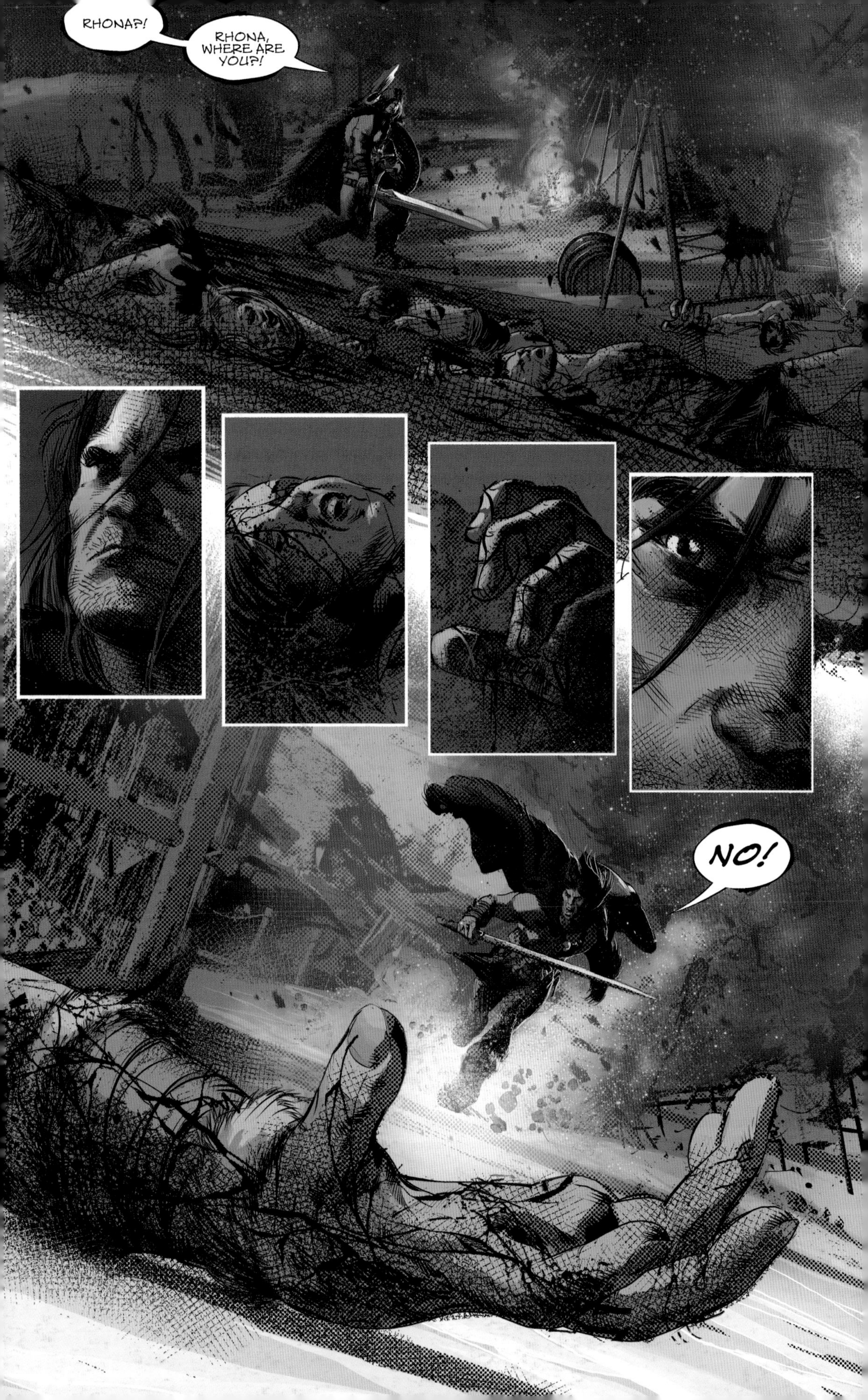
RHONA?!
RHONA, WHERE ARE YOU?!
NO!

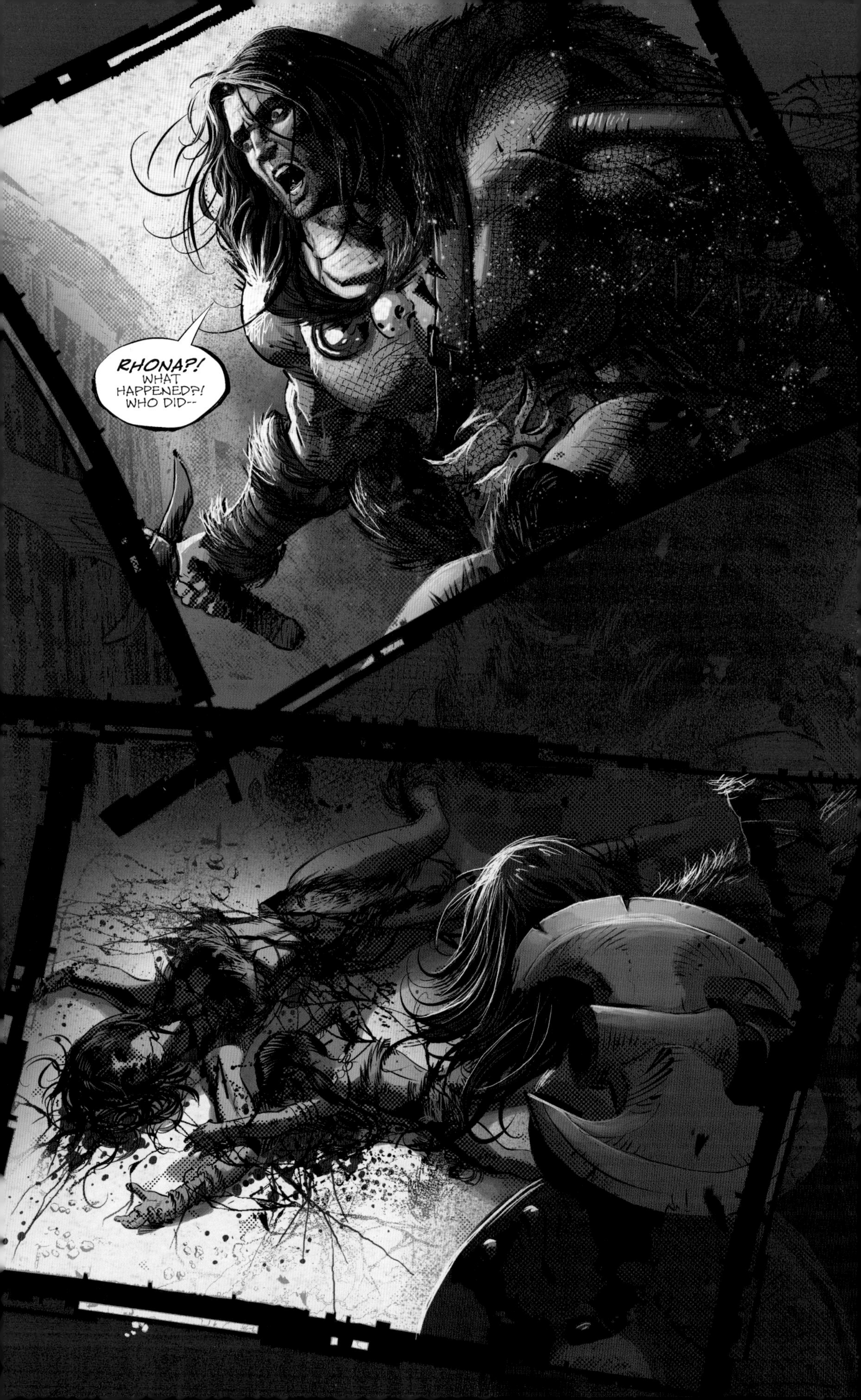
RHONA?! WHAT HAPPENED?! WHO DID--

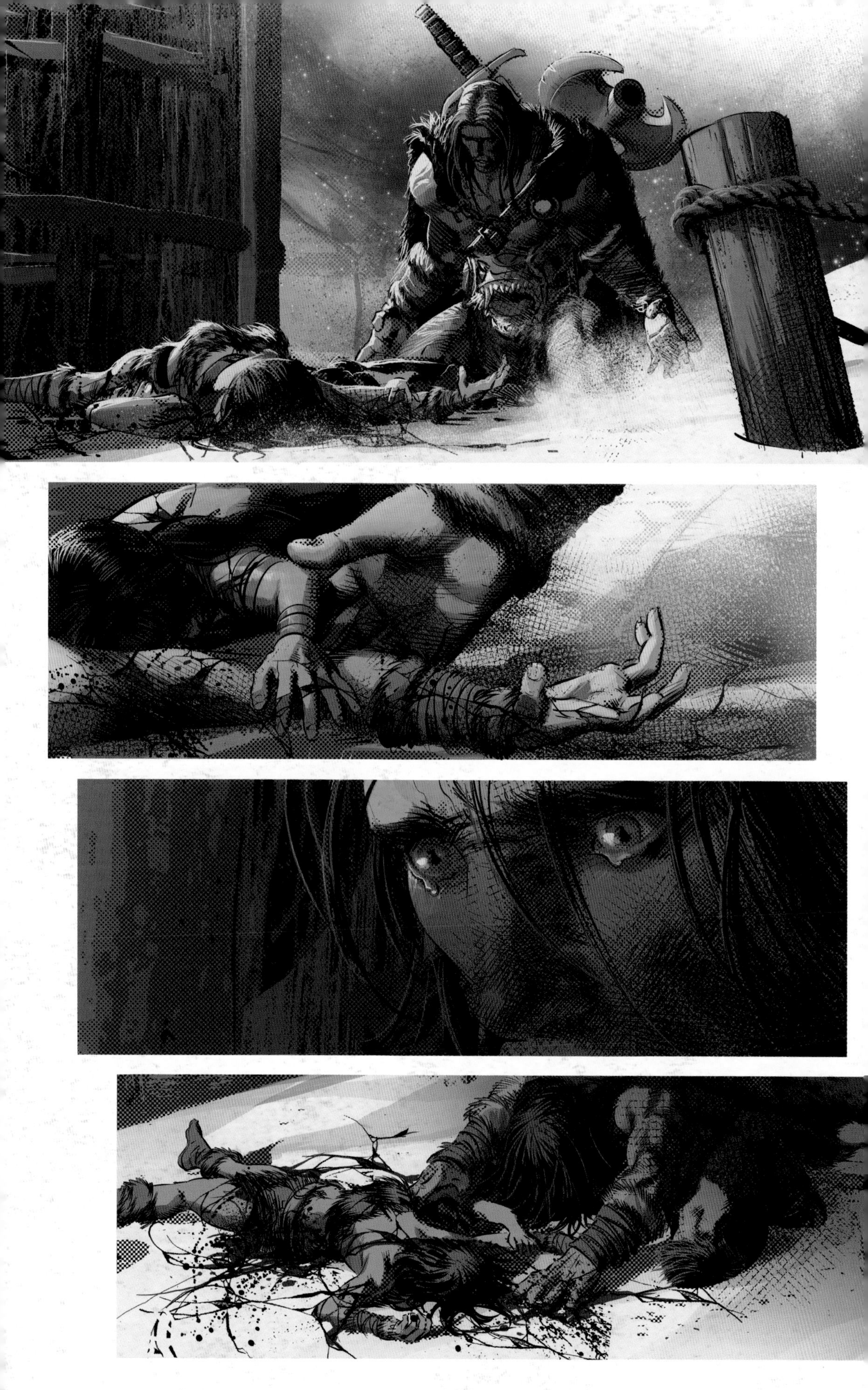

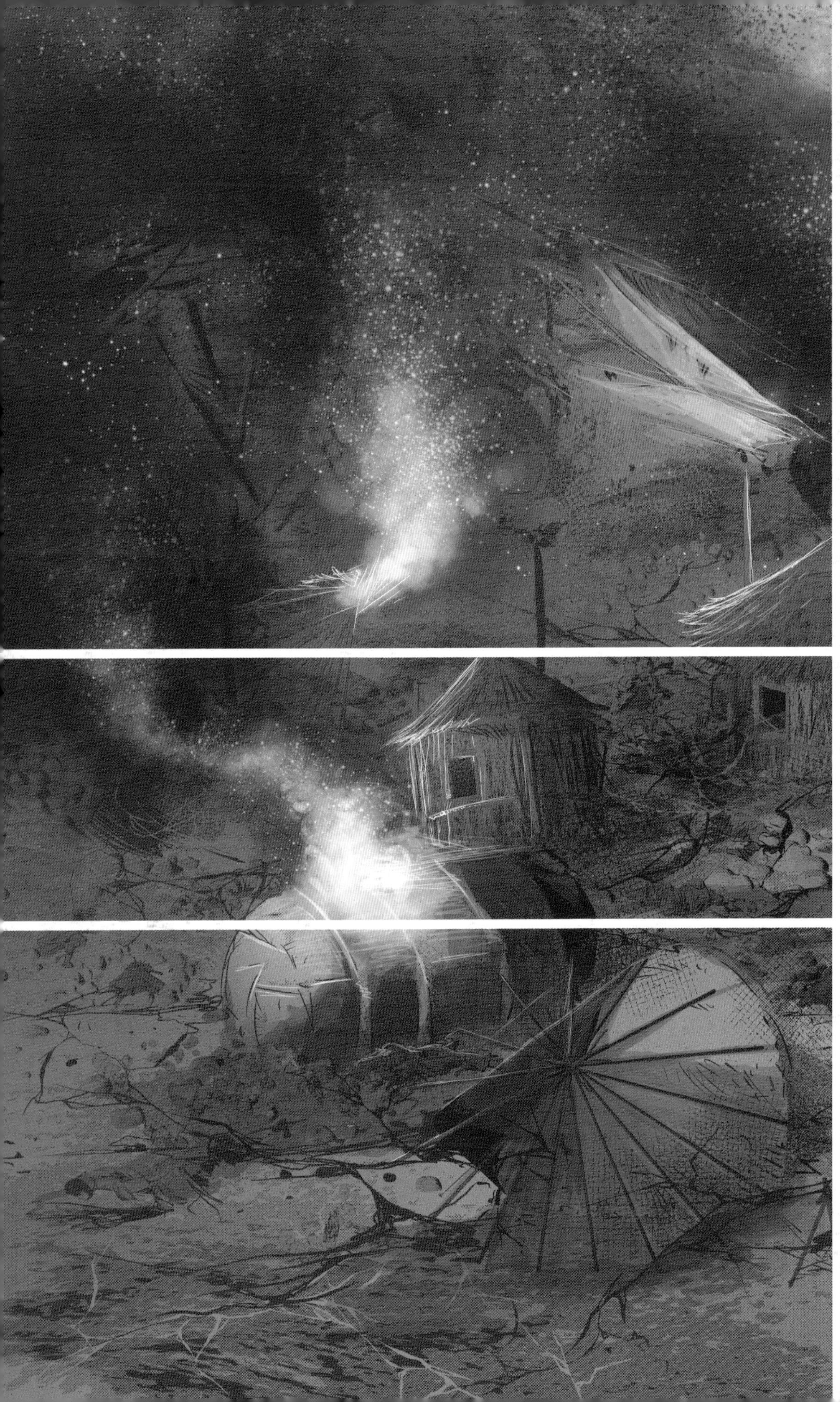

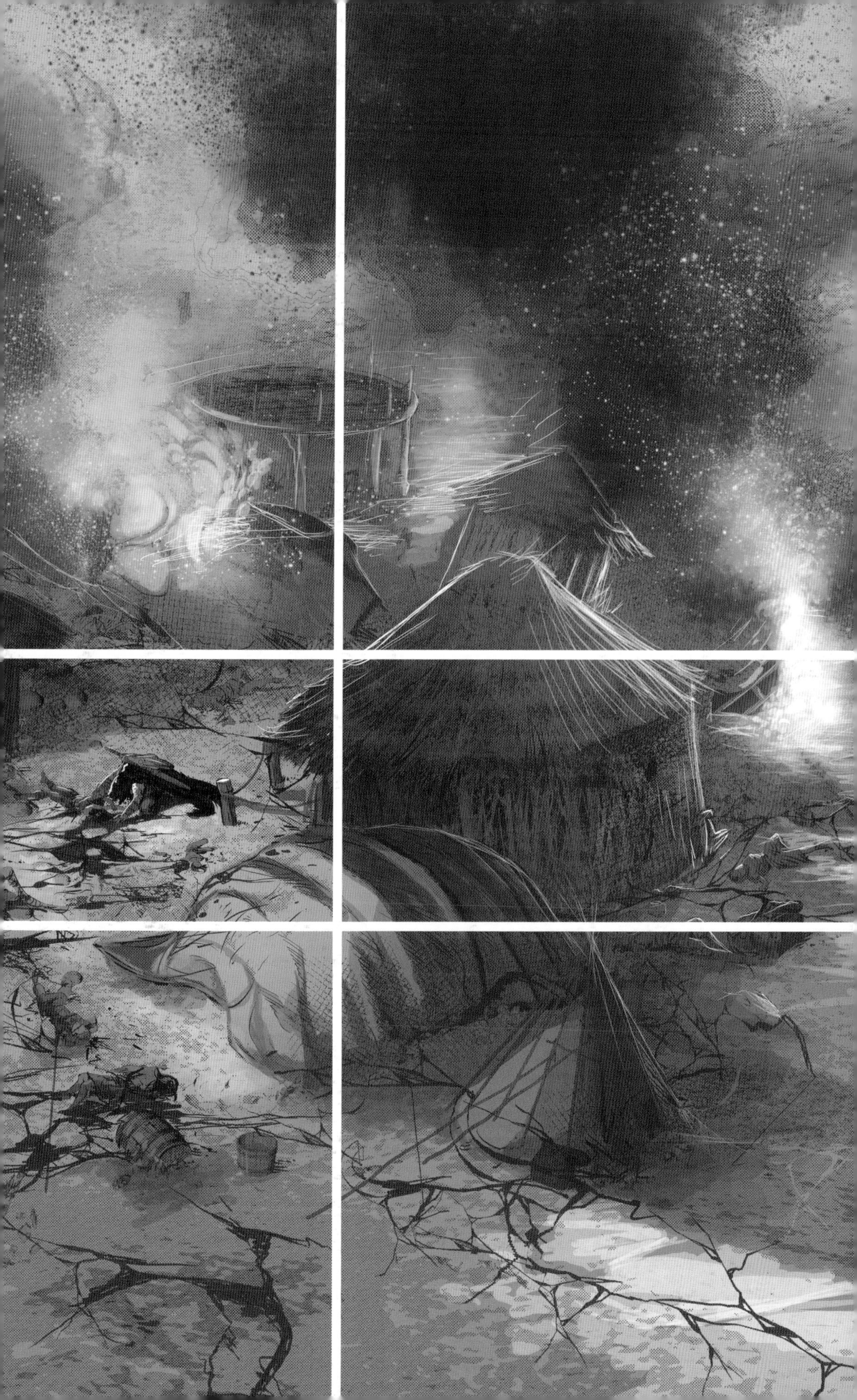

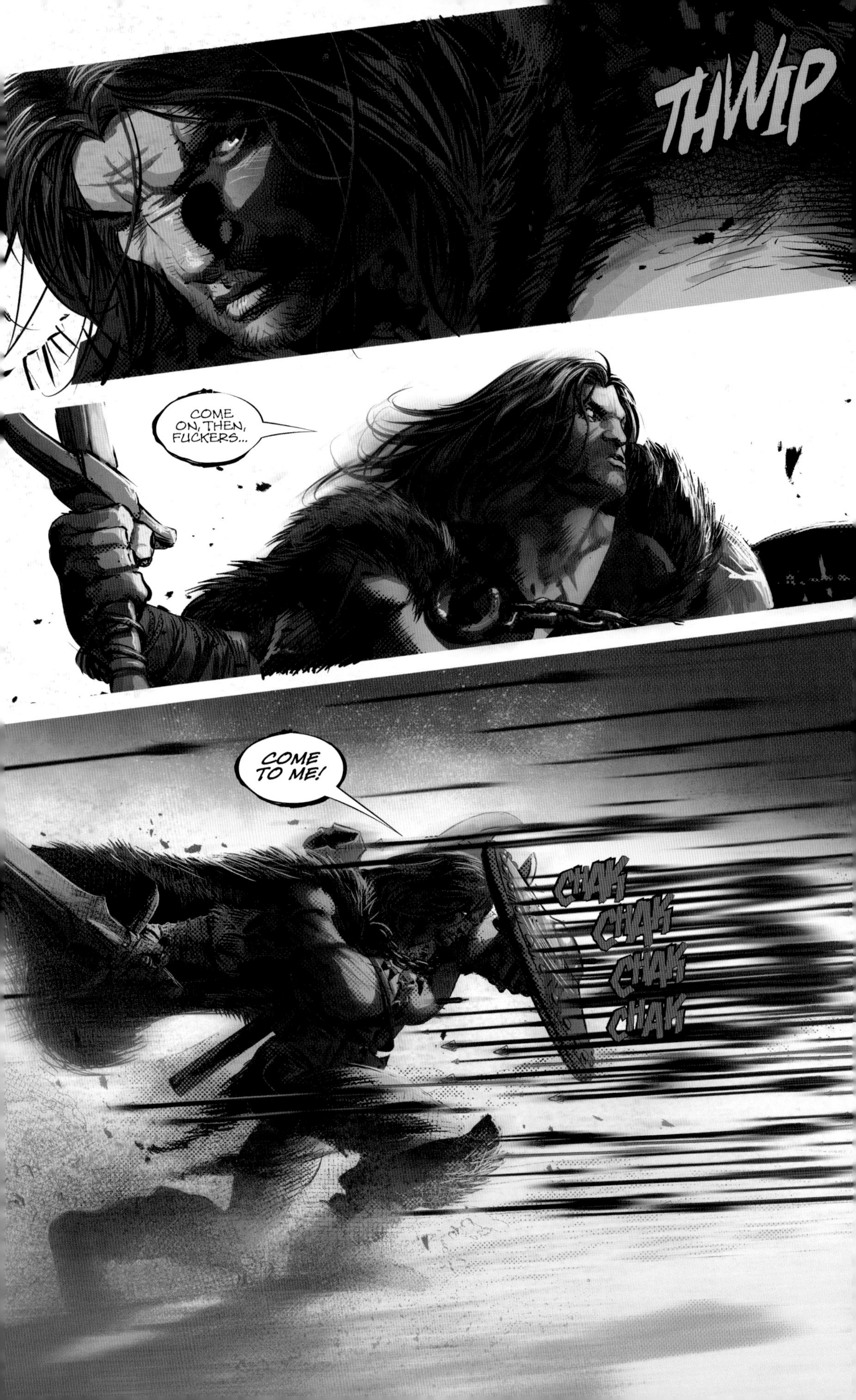
THWIP
COME ON, THEN, FUCKERS...
COME TO ME!
CHAK
CHAK
CHAK
CHAK

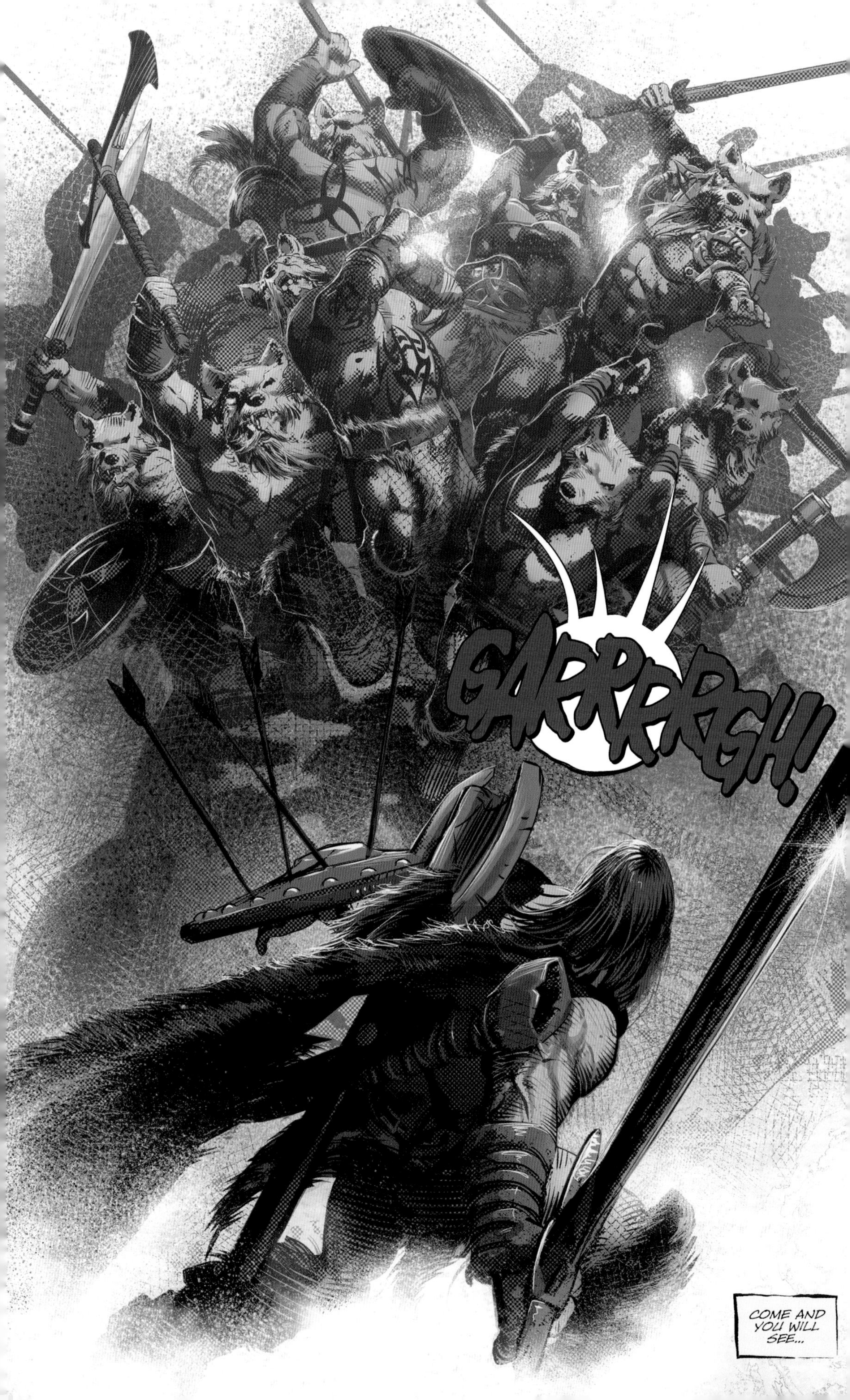
GARRRRGH!
COME AND YOU WILL SEE...

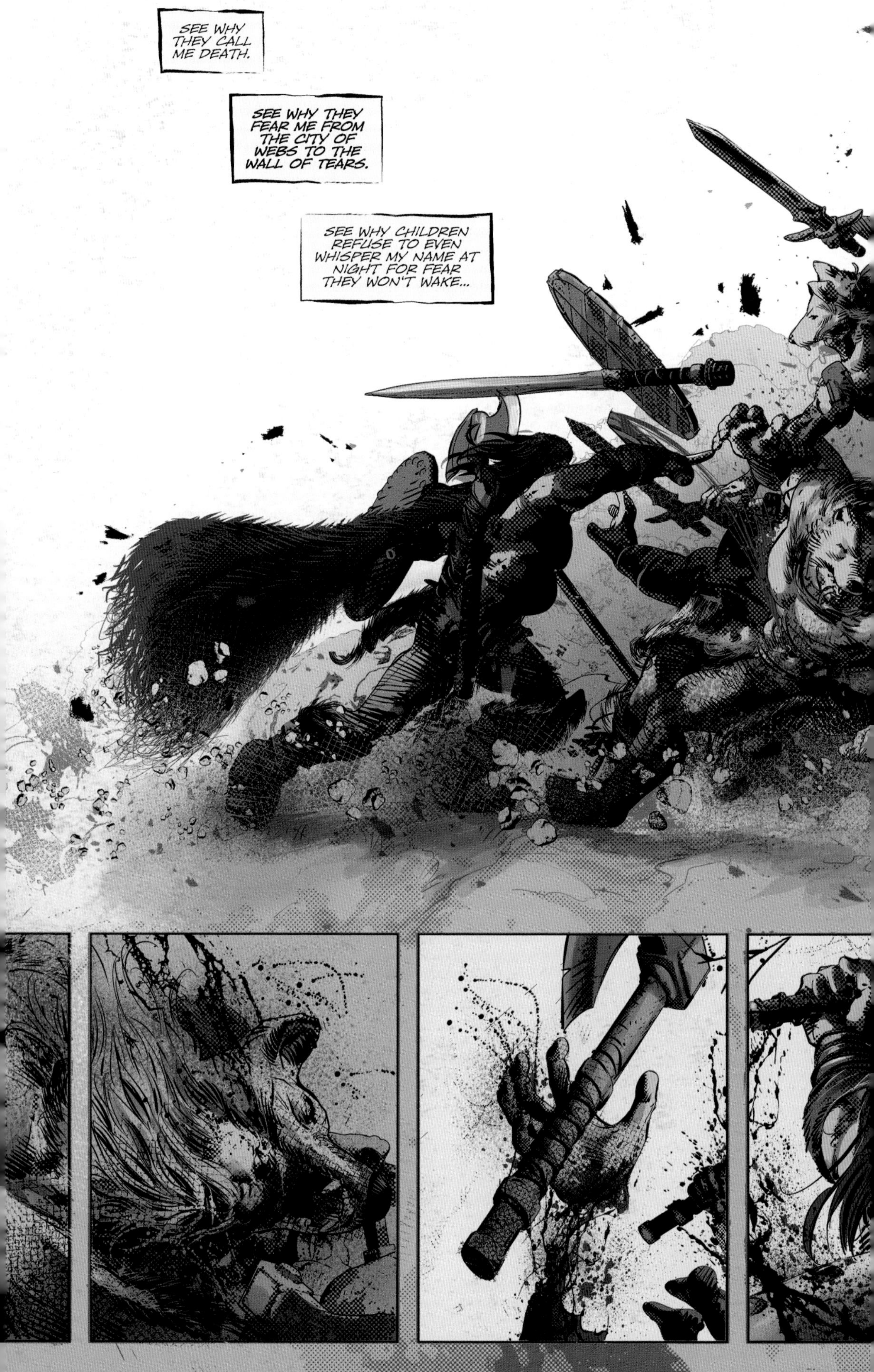
SEE WHY THEY CALL ME DEATH.
SEE WHY THEY FEAR ME FROM THE CITY OF WEBS TO THE WALL OF TEARS.
SEE WHY CHILDREN REFUSE TO EVEN WHISPER MY NAME AT NIGHT FOR FEAR THEY WON'T WAKE...

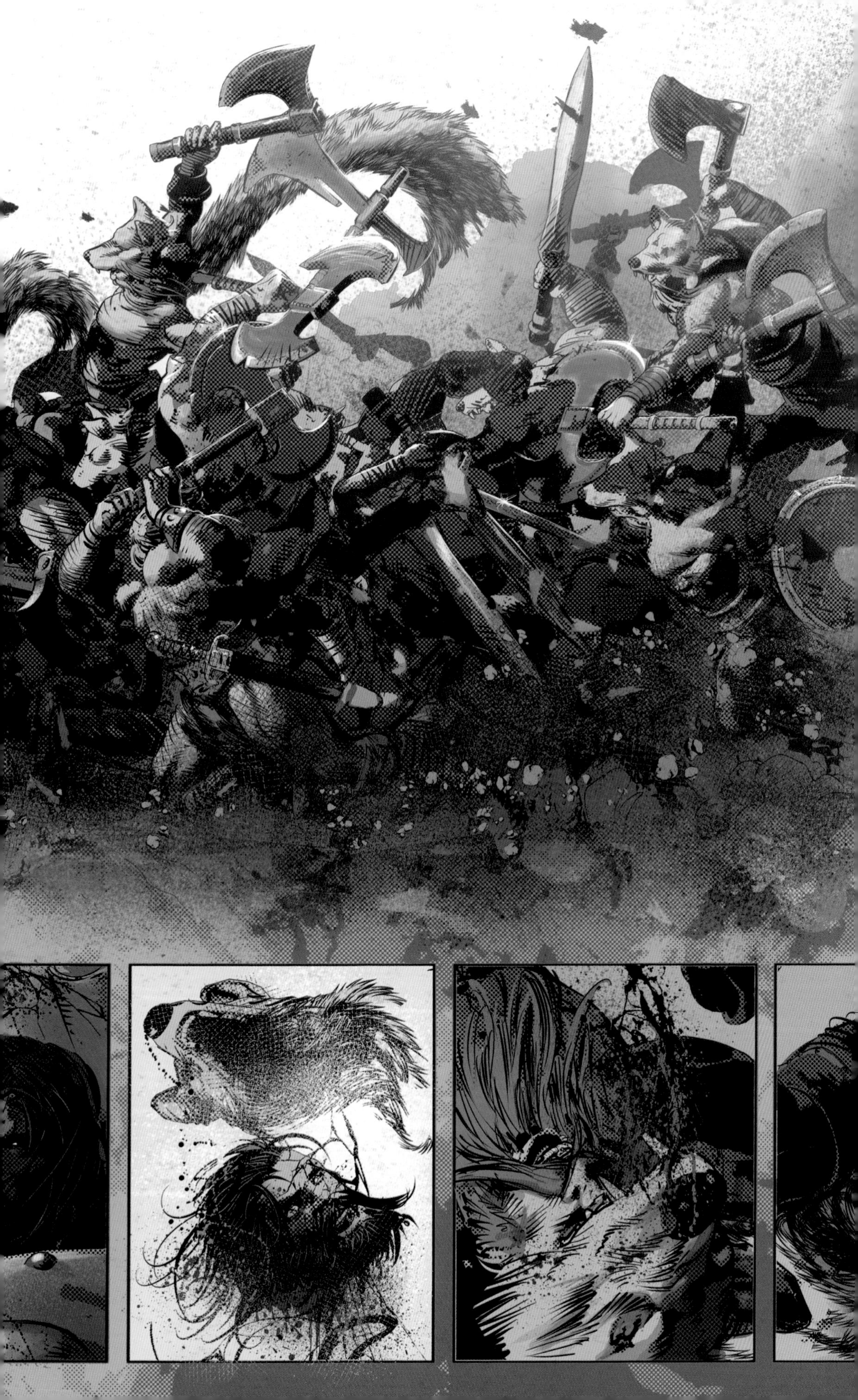

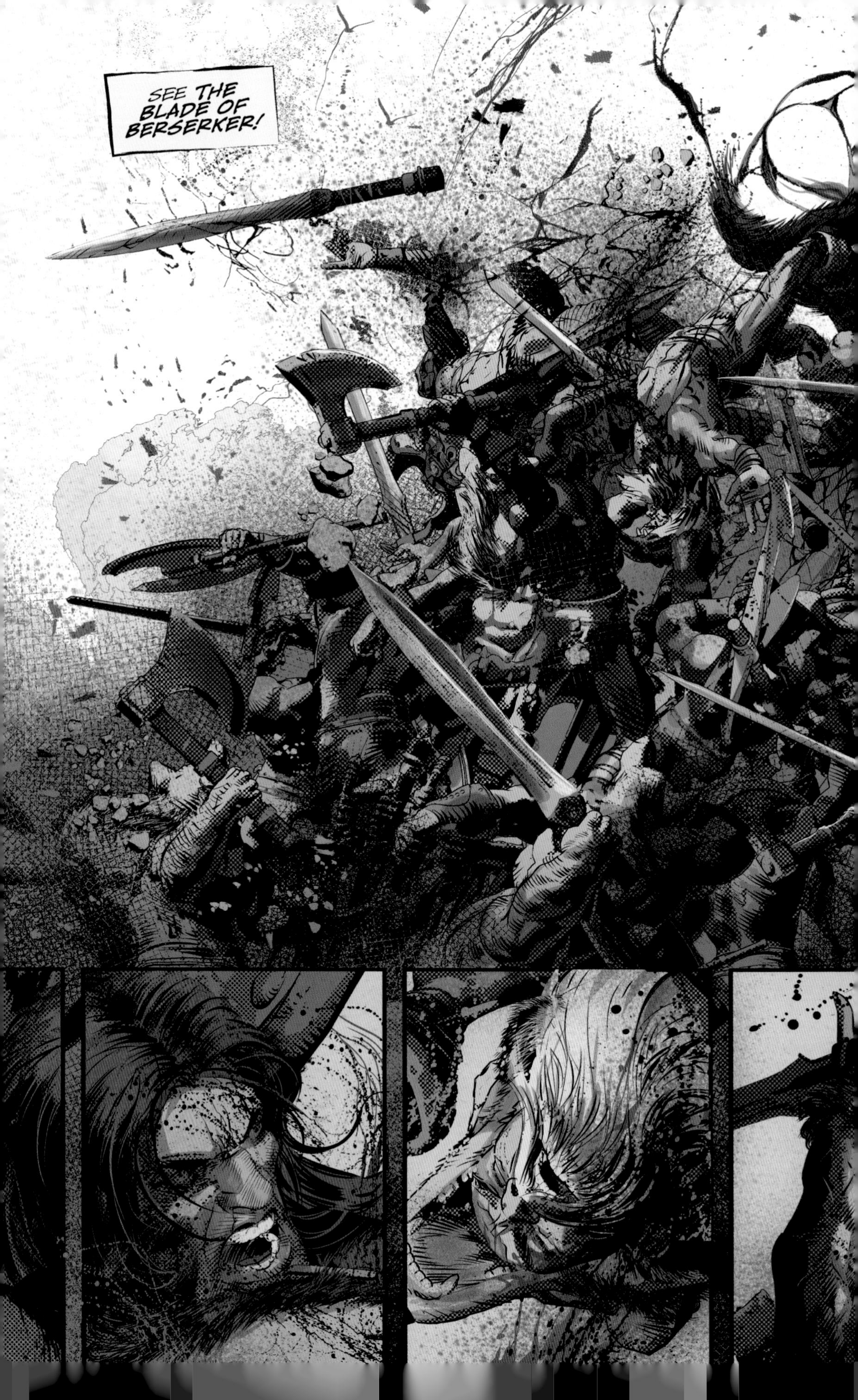
SEE THE BLADE OF BERSERKER!

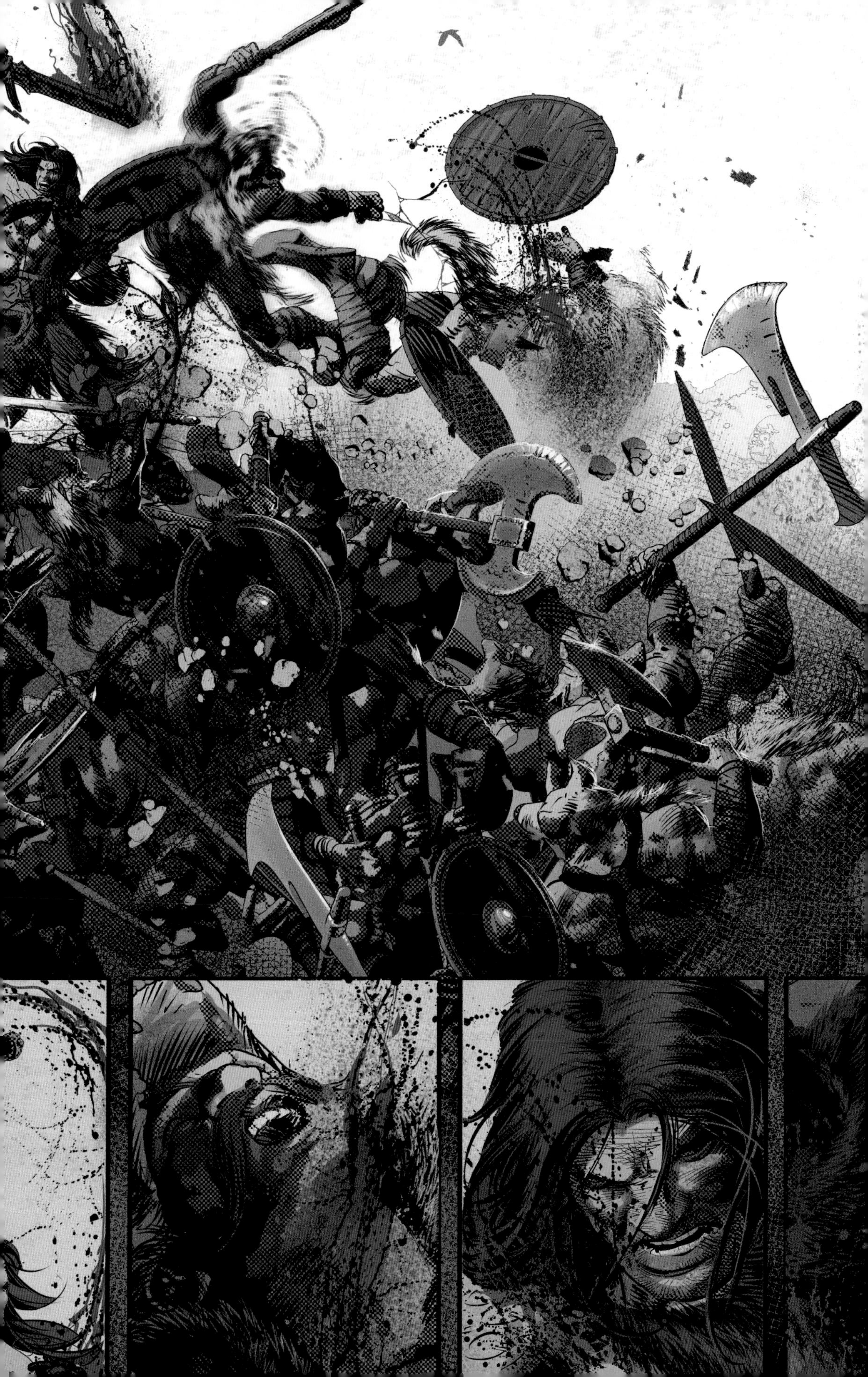

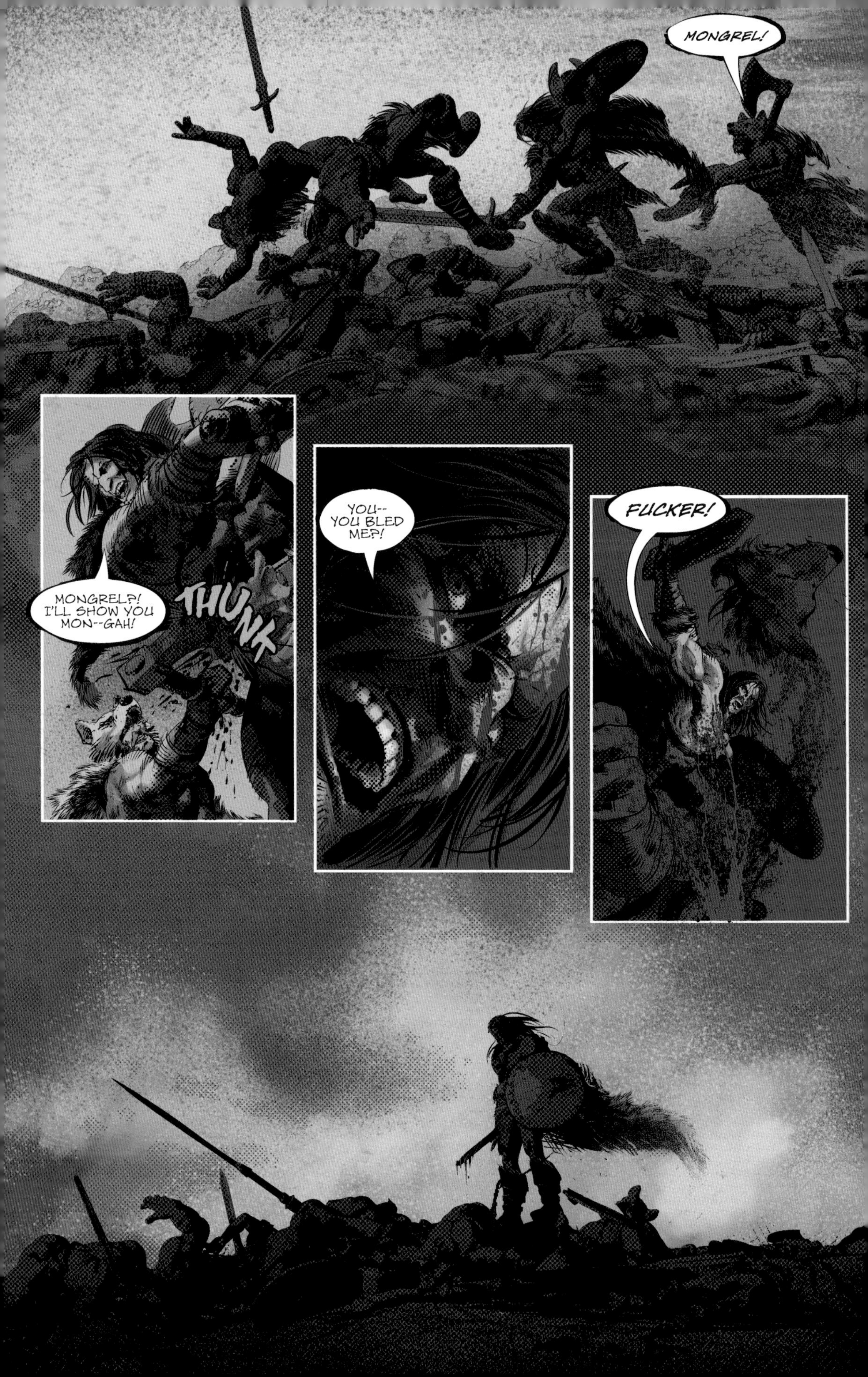
MONGREL!
MONGREL?! I'LL SHOW YOU MON--GAH!
THUNK
YOU-- YOU BLED ME?!
FUCKER!

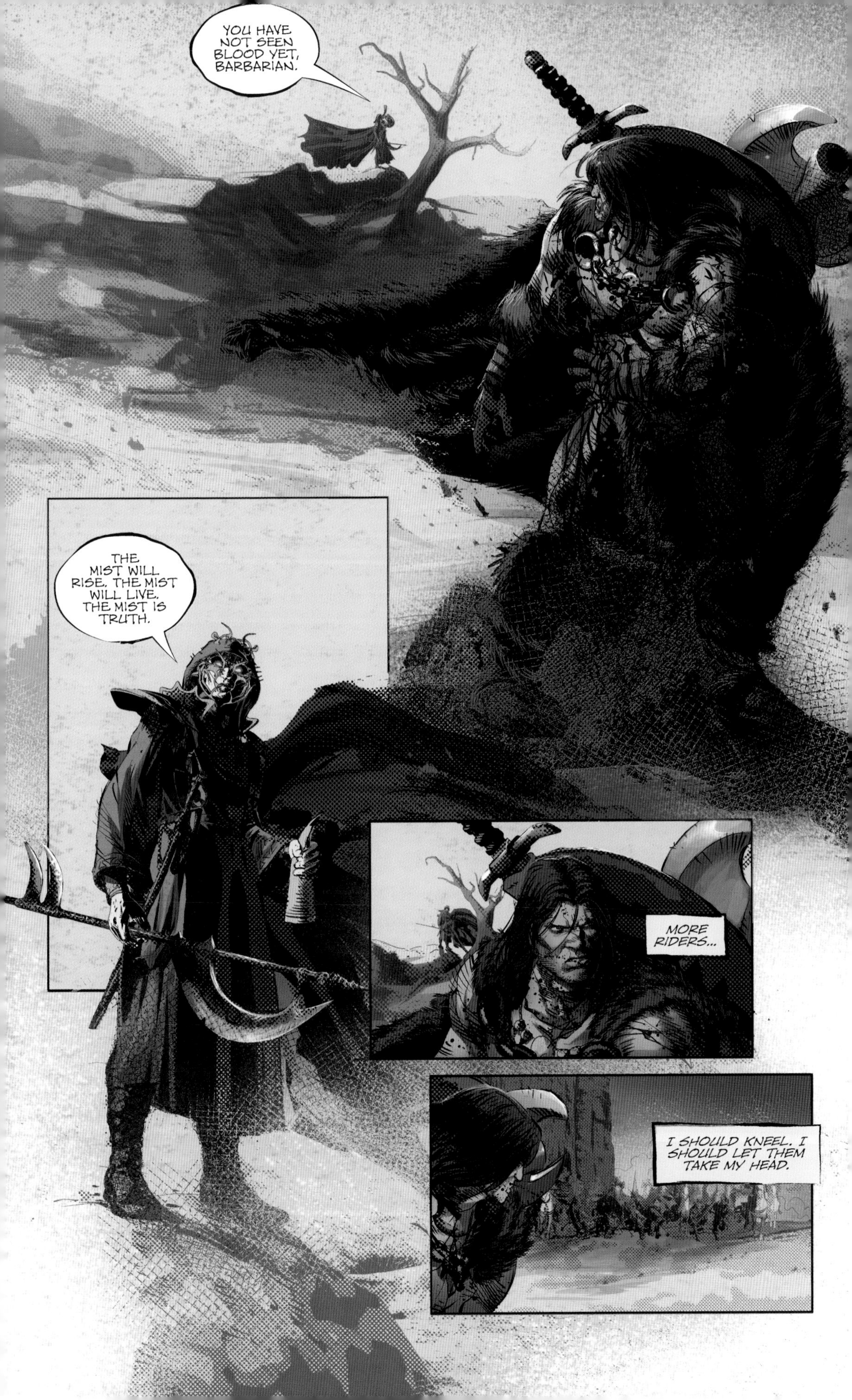
YOU HAVE NOT SEEN BLOOD YET, BARBARIAN.
THE MIST WILL RISE. THE MIST WILL LIVE. THE MIST IS TRUTH.
MORE RIDERS...
I SHOULD KNEEL. I SHOULD LET THEM TAKE MY HEAD.

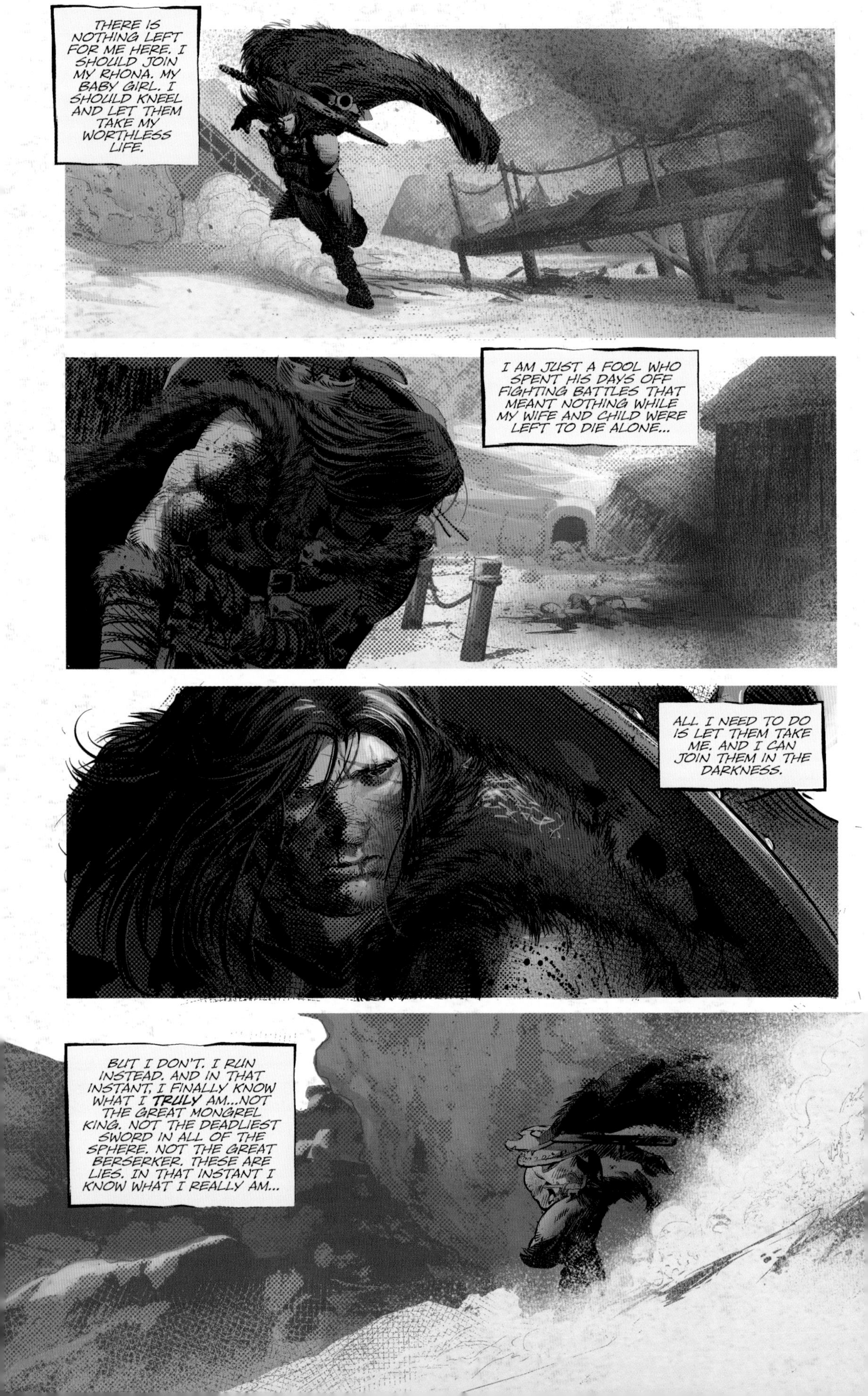
THERE IS NOTHING LEFT FOR ME HERE. I SHOULD JOIN MY RHONA. MY BABY GIRL. I SHOULD KNEEL AND LET THEM TAKE MY WORTHLESS LIFE.
I AM JUST A FOOL WHO SPENT HIS DAYS OFF FIGHTING BATTLES THAT MEANT NOTHING WHILE MY WIFE AND CHILD WERE LEFT TO DIE ALONE...
ALL I NEED TO DO IS LET THEM TAKE ME. AND I CAN JOIN THEM IN THE DARKNESS.
BUT I DON'T. I RUN INSTEAD. AND IN THAT INSTANT, I FINALLY KNOW WHAT I **TRULY** AM...NOT THE GREAT MONGREL KING. NOT THE DEADLIEST SWORD IN ALL OF THE SPHERE. NOT THE GREAT BERSERKER. THESE ARE LIES. IN THAT INSTANT I KNOW WHAT I REALLY AM...

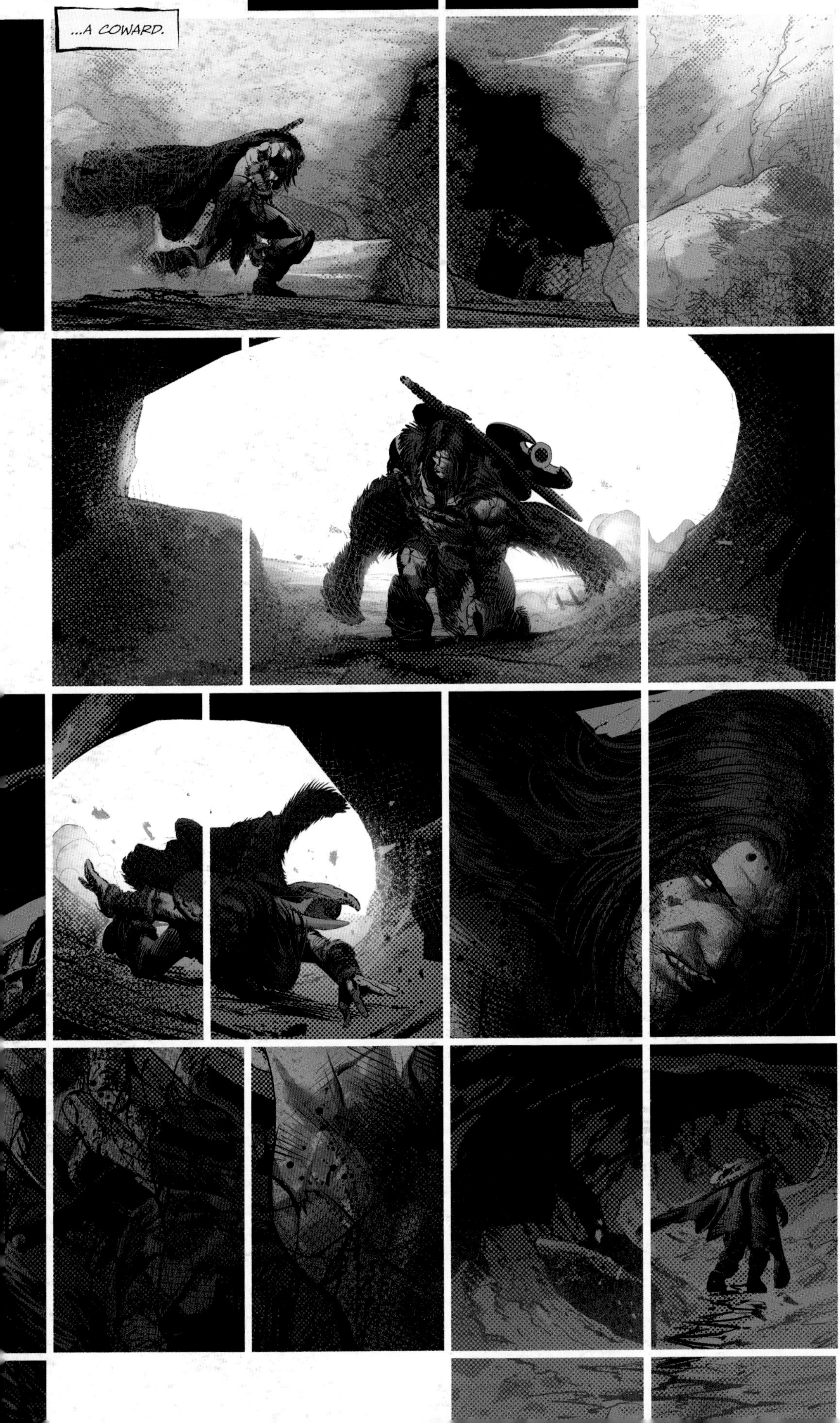
...A COWARD.

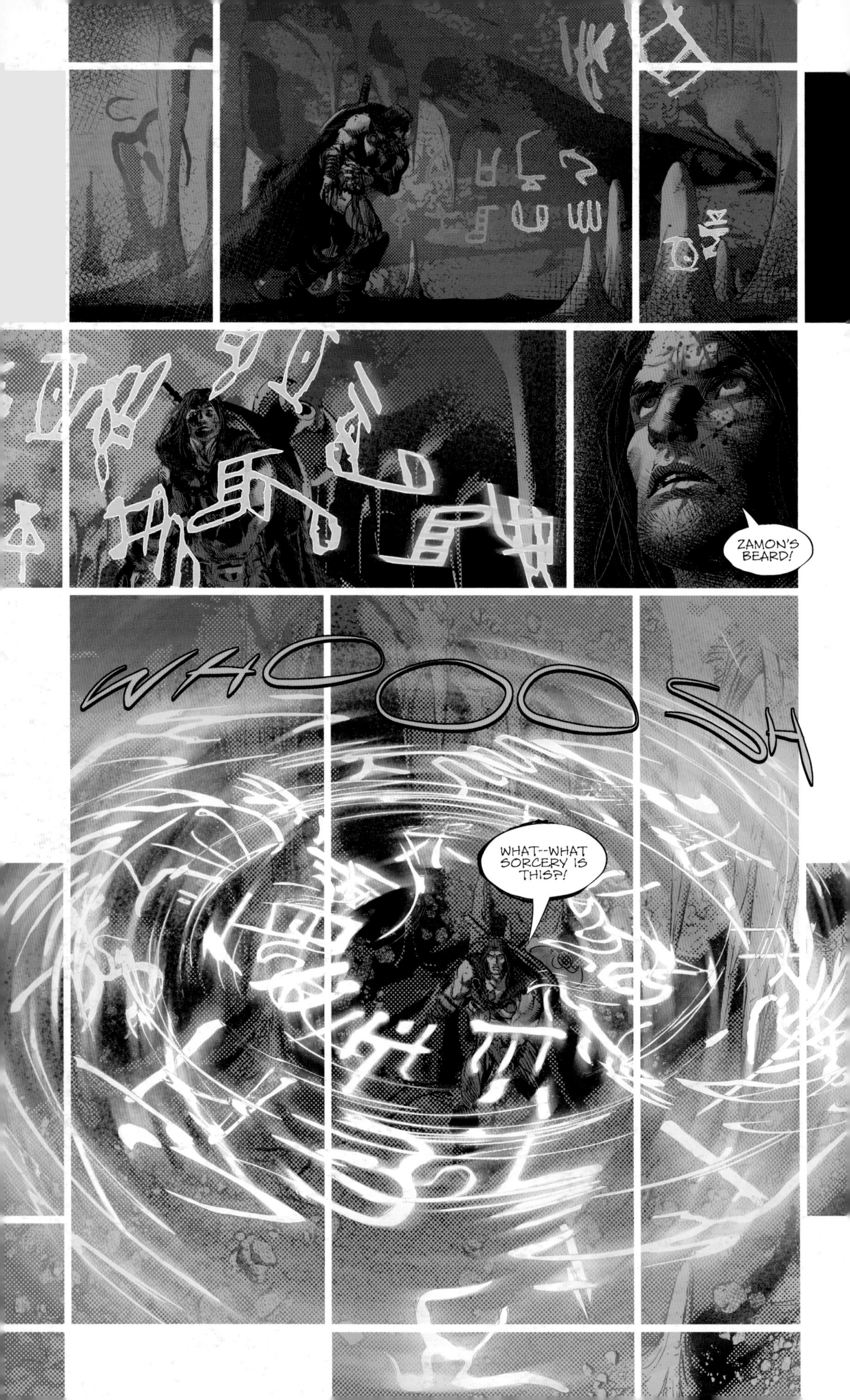
ZAMON'S BEARD!
WHOOOOSH
WHAT--WHAT SORCERY IS THIS?!

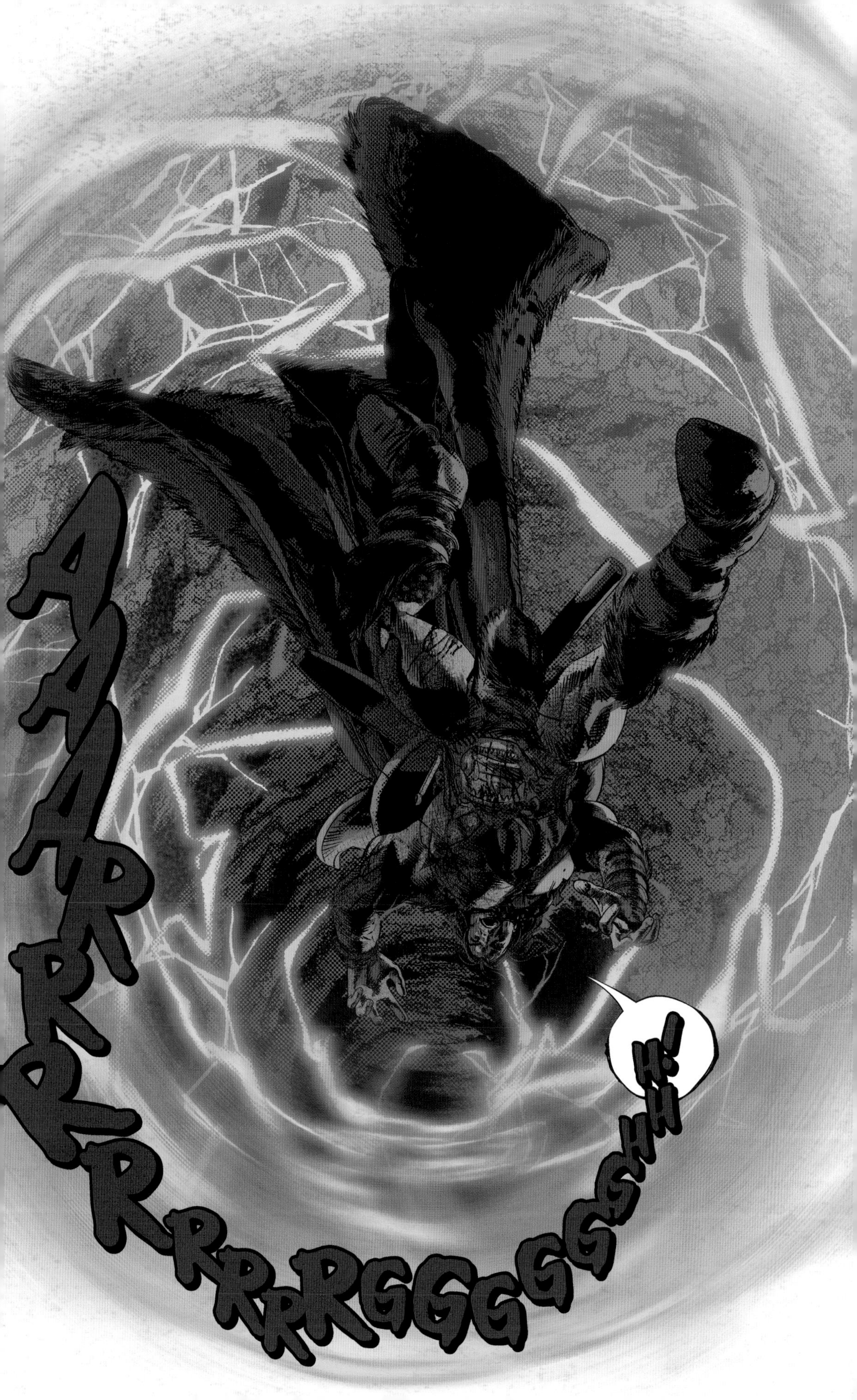
AAARRRRRRRRRGGGGGGSHHH!

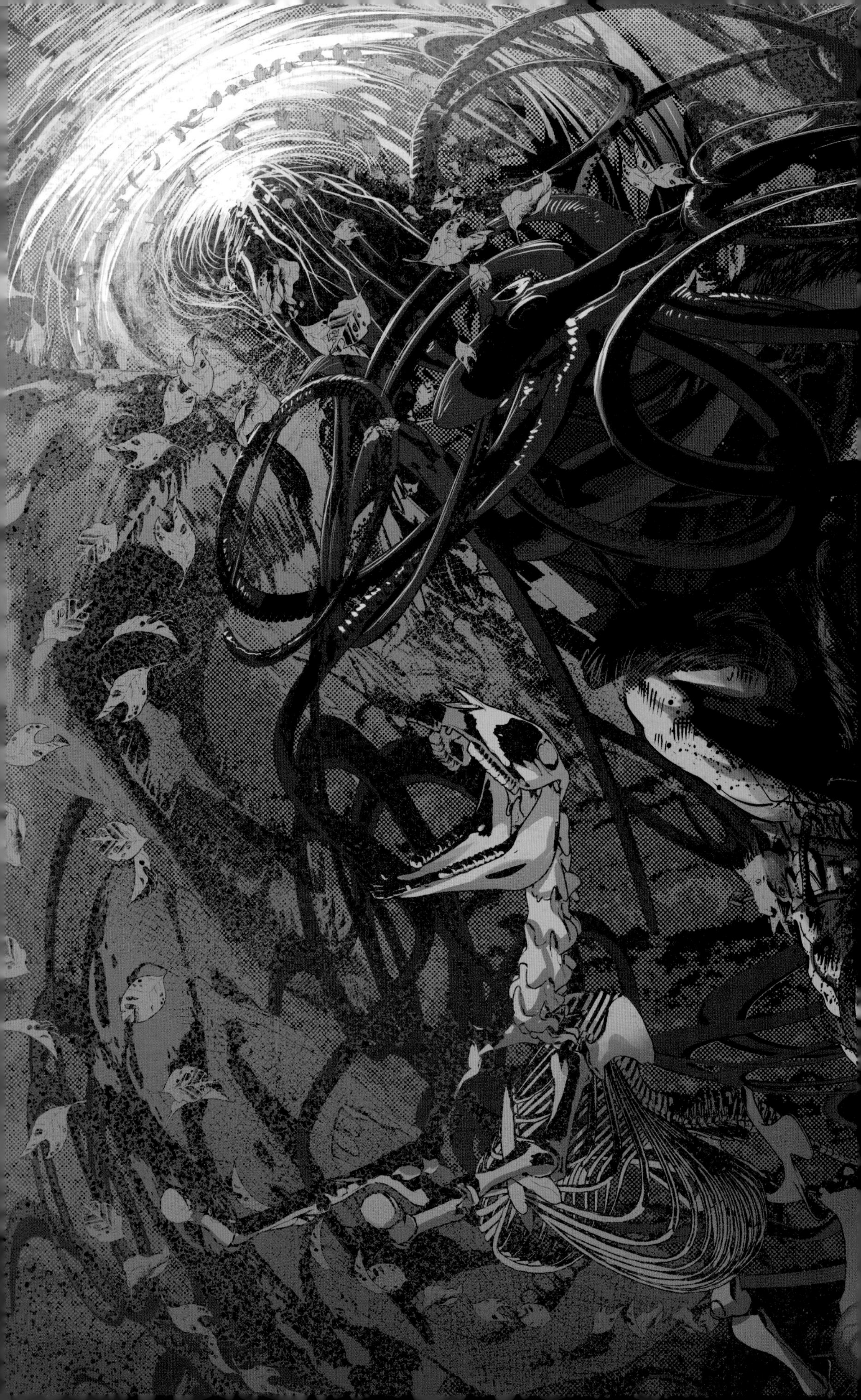

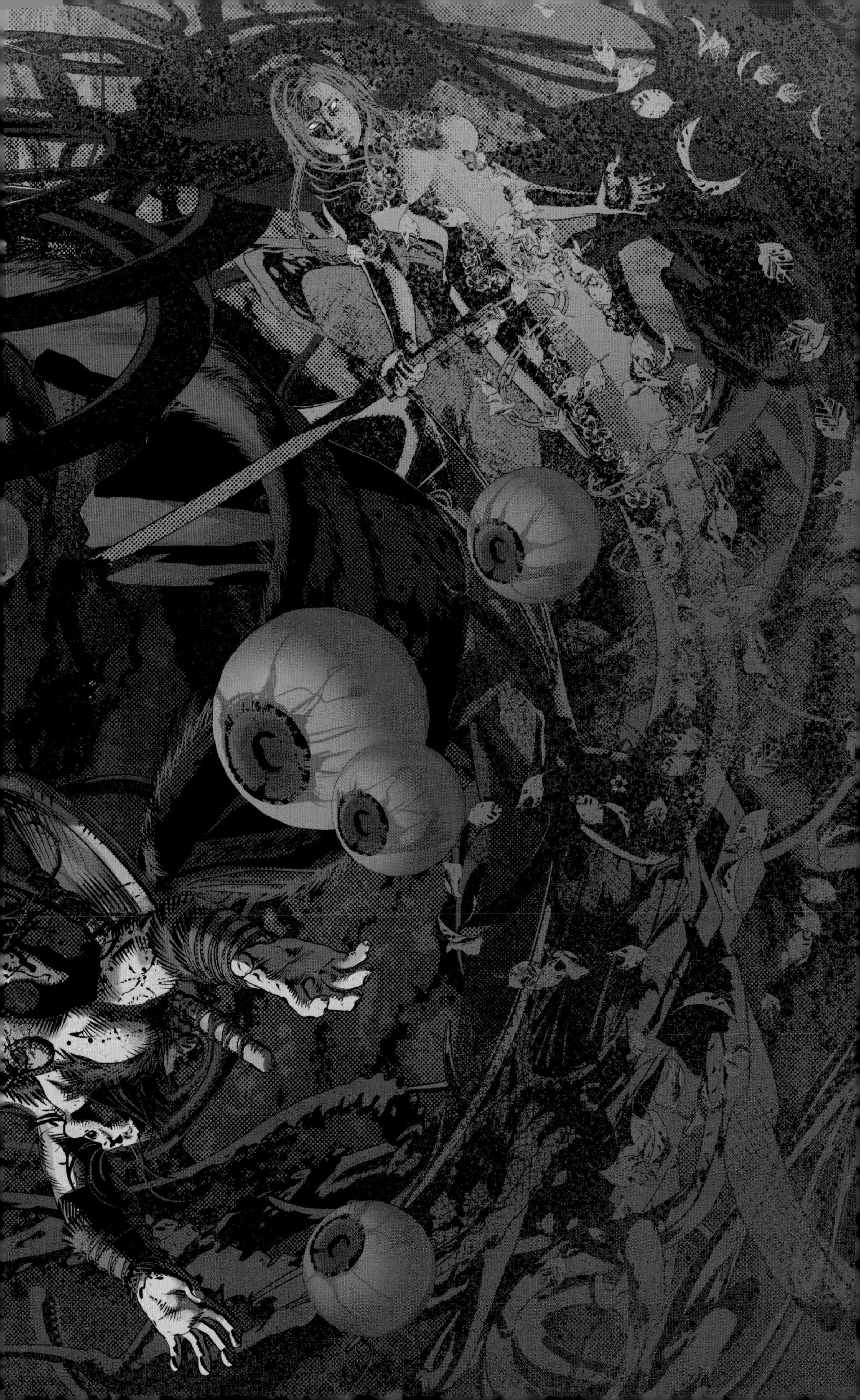

BOOM

MAYBE--

UNGH!

--MAYBE I DID DIE? MAYBE THIS IS WHERE I CHOOSE WHICH PIT OF HELL I DESERVE TO SQUIRM IN?

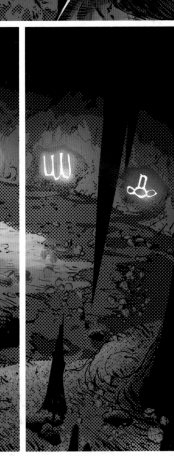

WHAT DOES IT MATTER NOW? WHAT DOES ANYTHING MATTER?

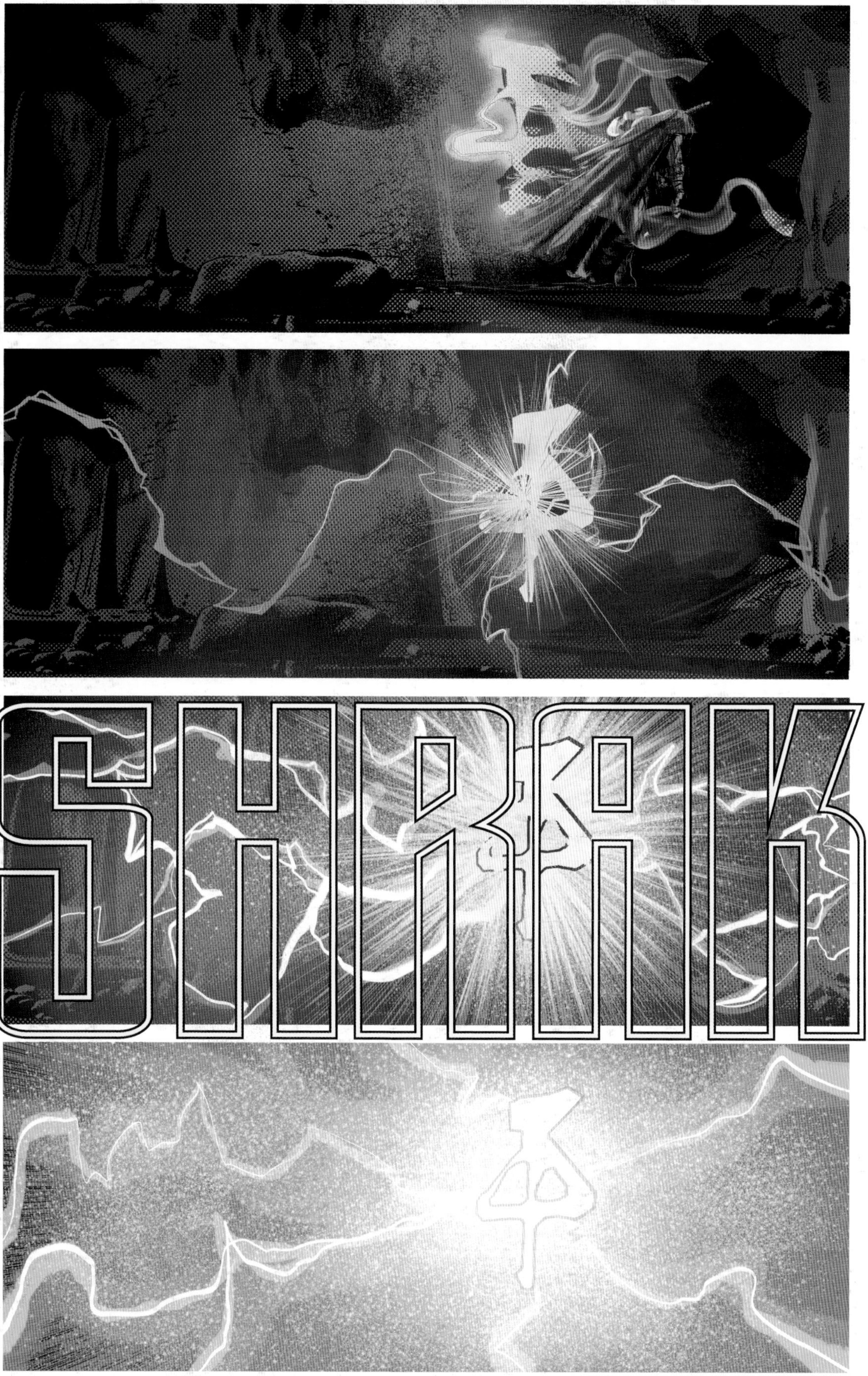
SHRAK

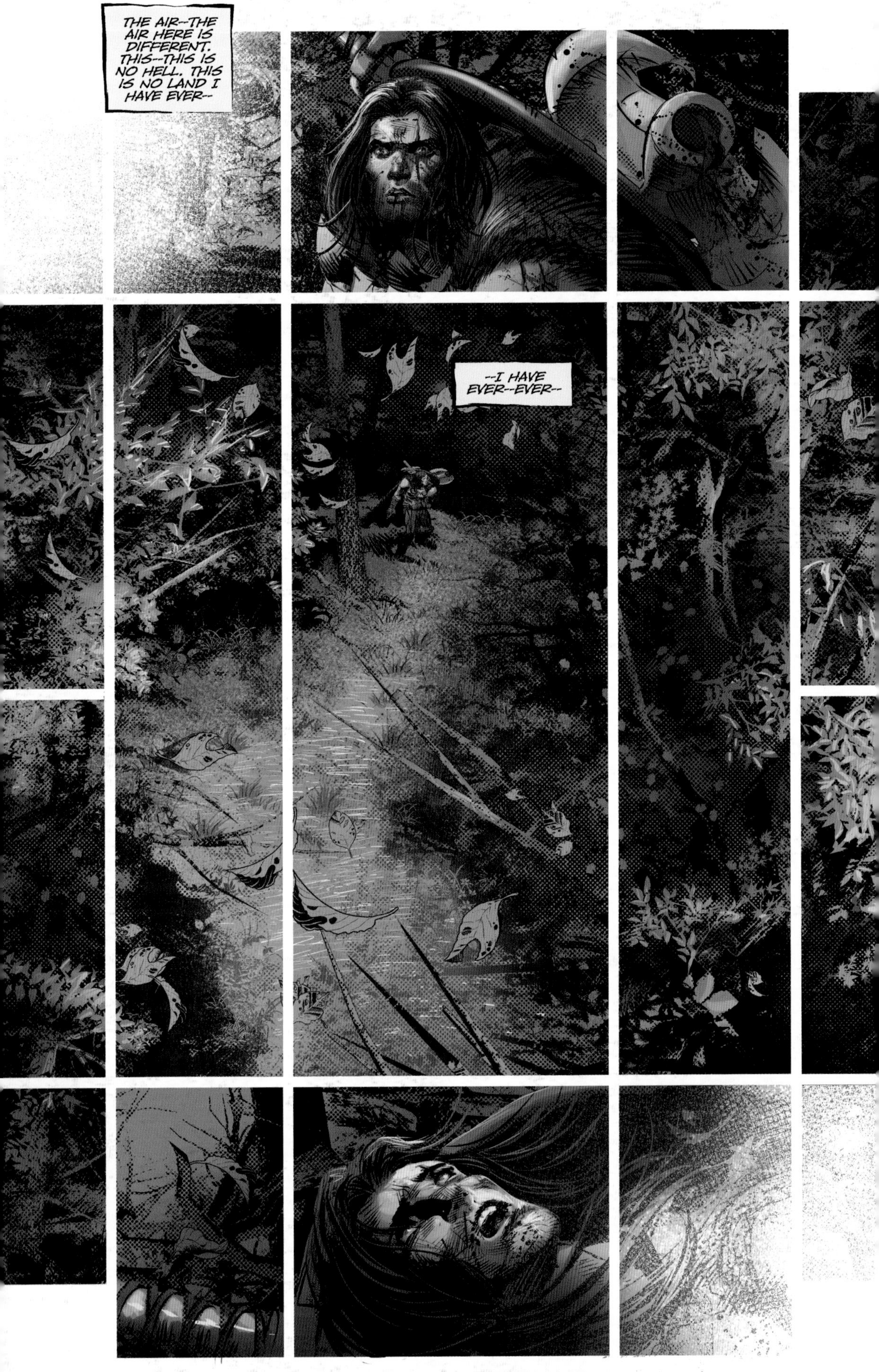
THE AIR--THE AIR HERE IS DIFFERENT. THIS--THIS IS NO HELL. THIS IS NO LAND I HAVE EVER--
--I HAVE EVER--EVER--

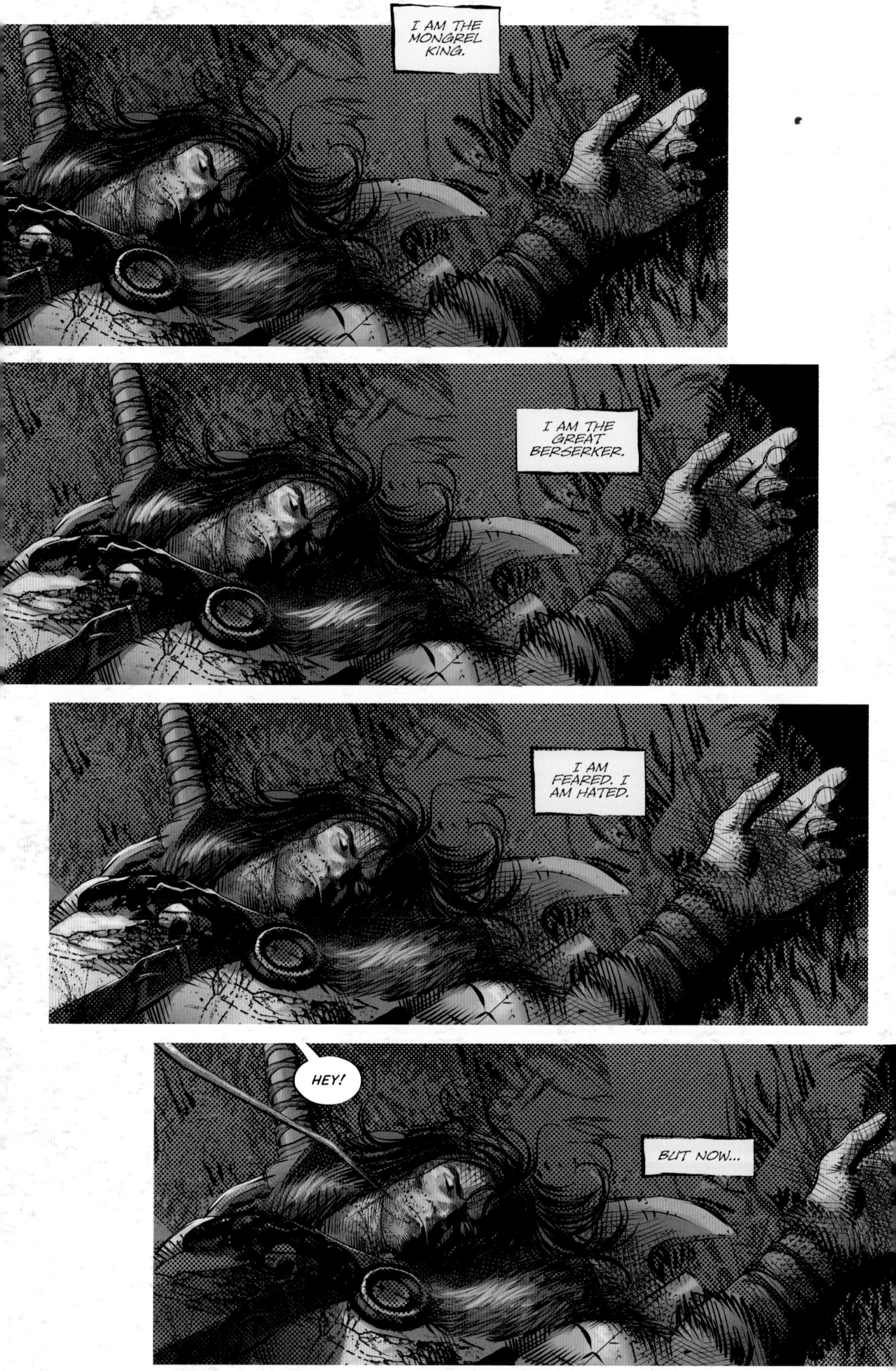
I AM THE MONGREL KING.
I AM THE GREAT BERSERKER.
I AM FEARED. I AM HATED.
HEY!
BUT NOW...

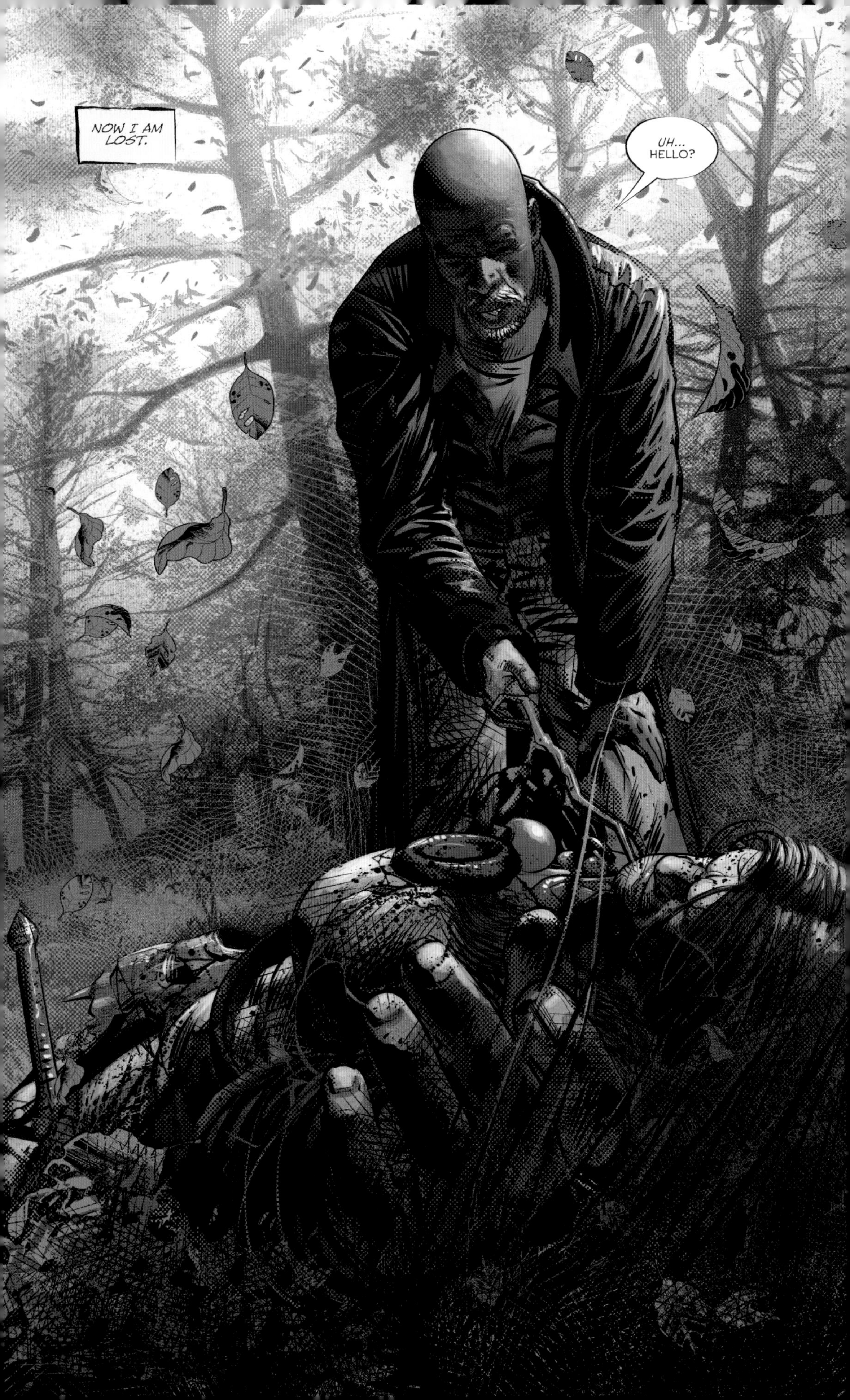
NOW I AM LOST.
UH... HELLO?

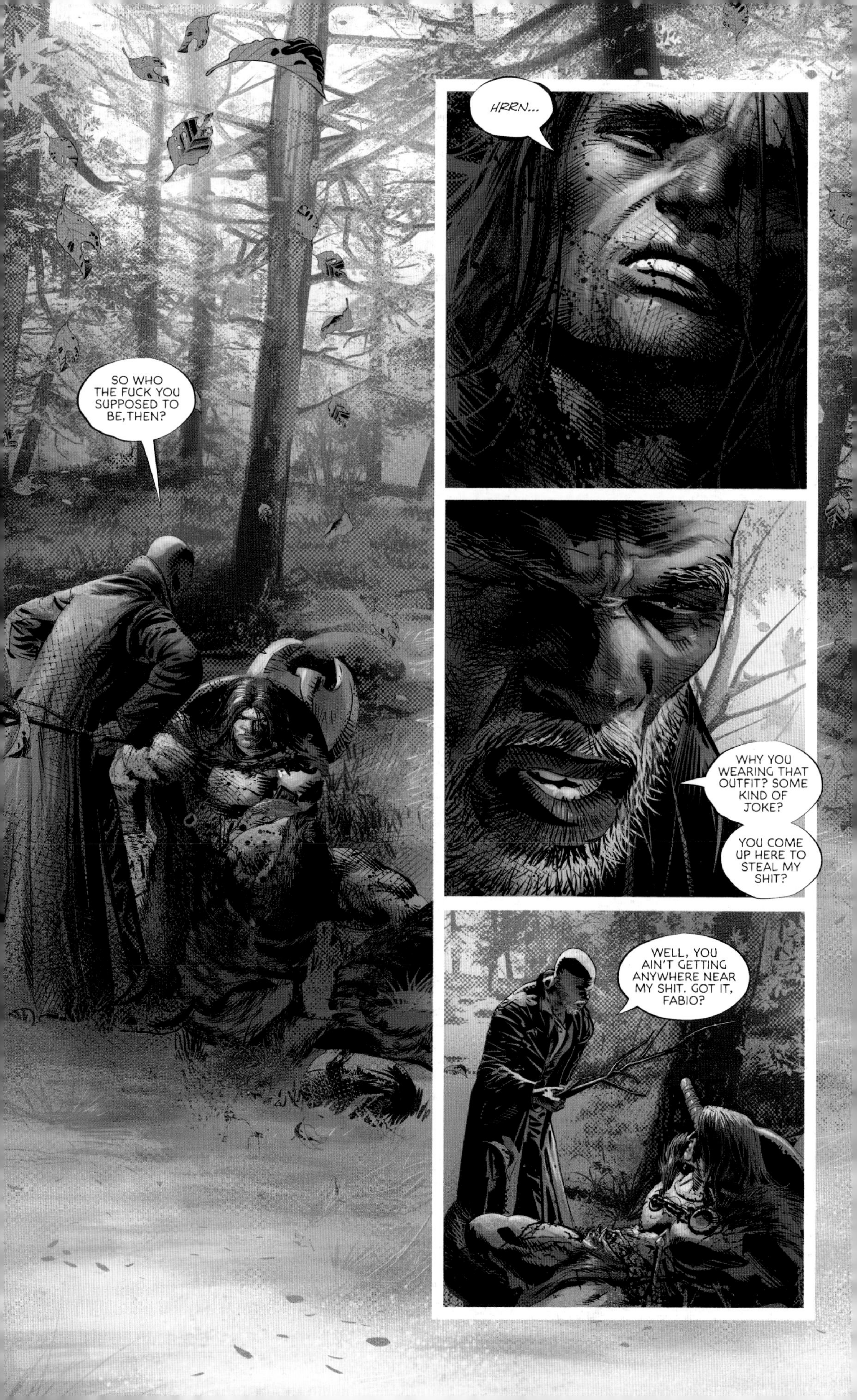
HRRN...
SO WHO THE FUCK YOU SUPPOSED TO BE, THEN?
WHY YOU WEARING THAT OUTFIT? SOME KIND OF JOKE?
YOU COME UP HERE TO STEAL MY SHIT?
WELL, YOU AIN'T GETTING ANYWHERE NEAR MY SHIT. GOT IT, FABIO?

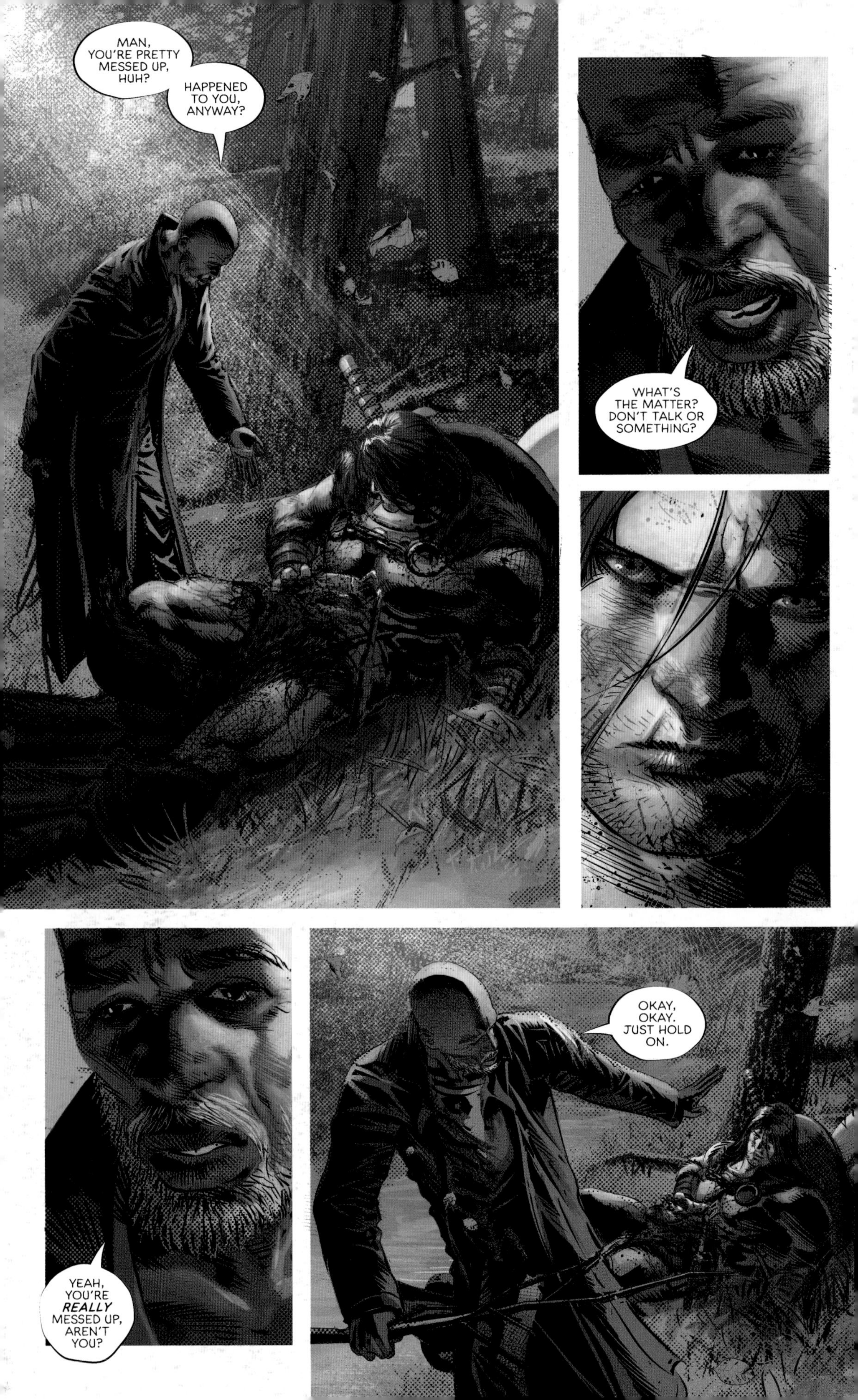
MAN, YOU'RE PRETTY MESSED UP, HUH?
HAPPENED TO YOU, ANYWAY?
WHAT'S THE MATTER? DON'T TALK OR SOMETHING?
YEAH, YOU'RE *REALLY* MESSED UP, AREN'T YOU?
OKAY, OKAY. JUST HOLD ON.

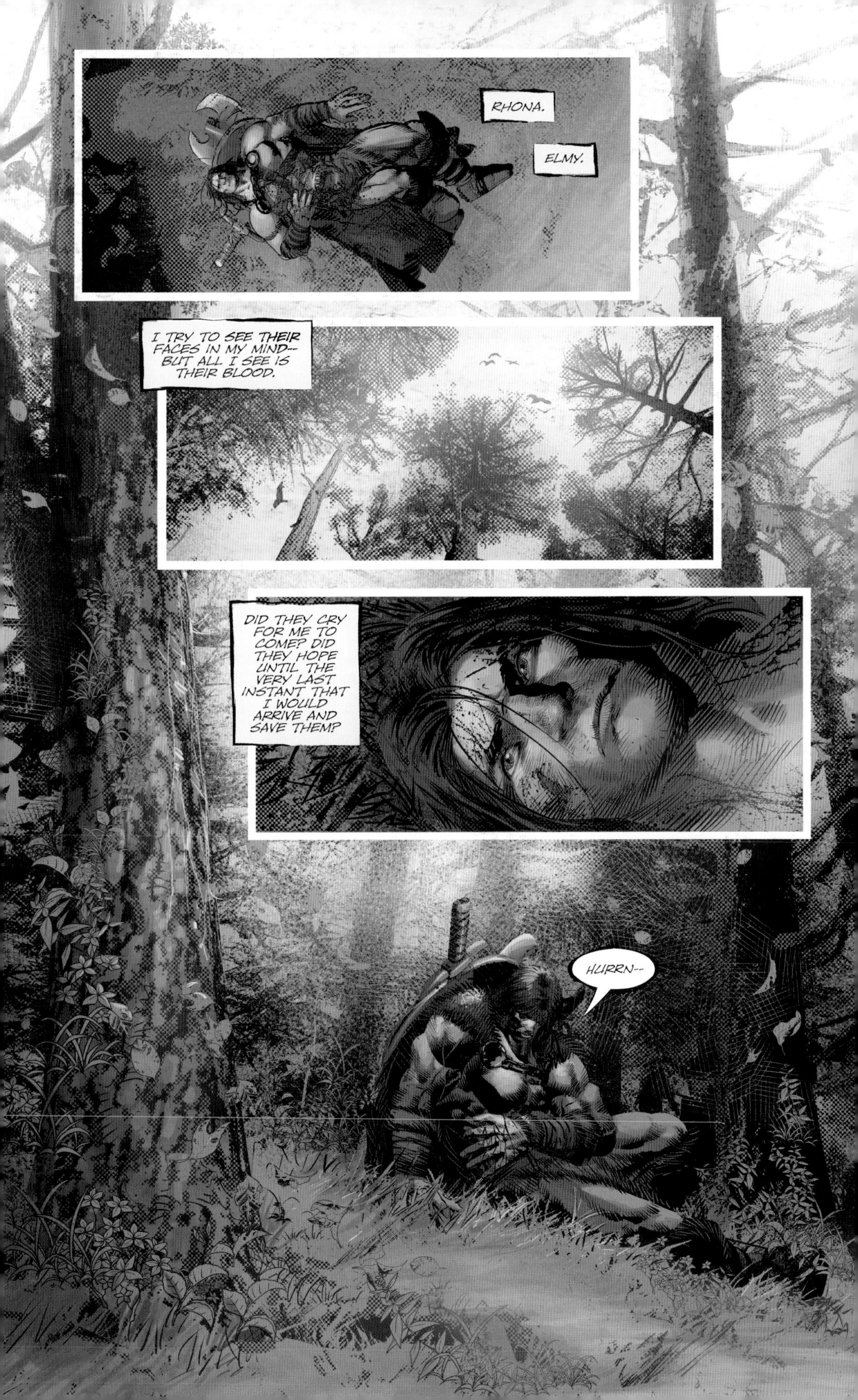
RHONA.
ELMY.
I TRY TO SEE THEIR FACES IN MY MIND-- BUT ALL I SEE IS THEIR BLOOD.
DID THEY CRY FOR ME TO COME? DID THEY HOPE UNTIL THE VERY LAST INSTANT THAT I WOULD ARRIVE AND SAVE THEM?
HURRN--

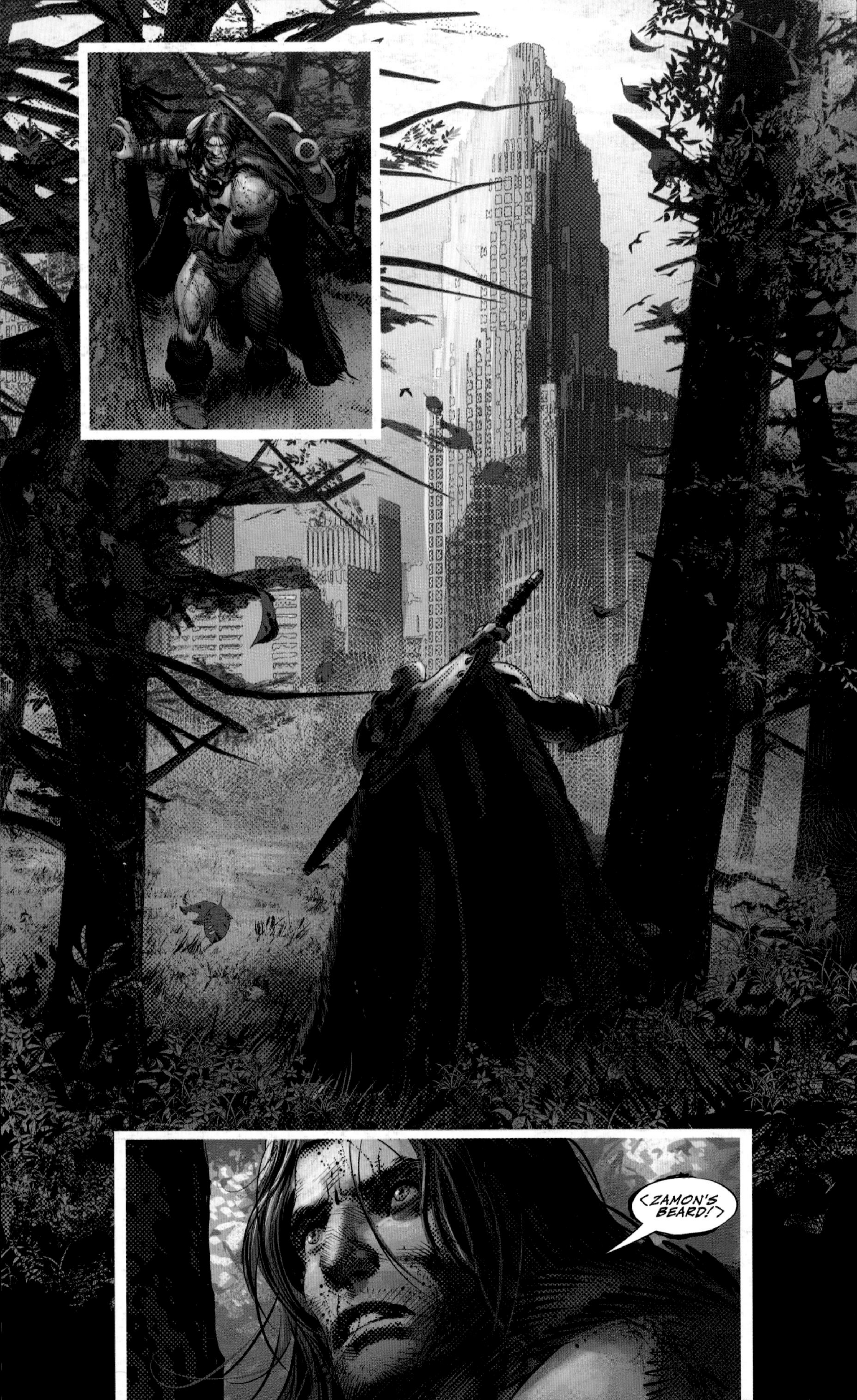
<ZAMON'S BEARD!>

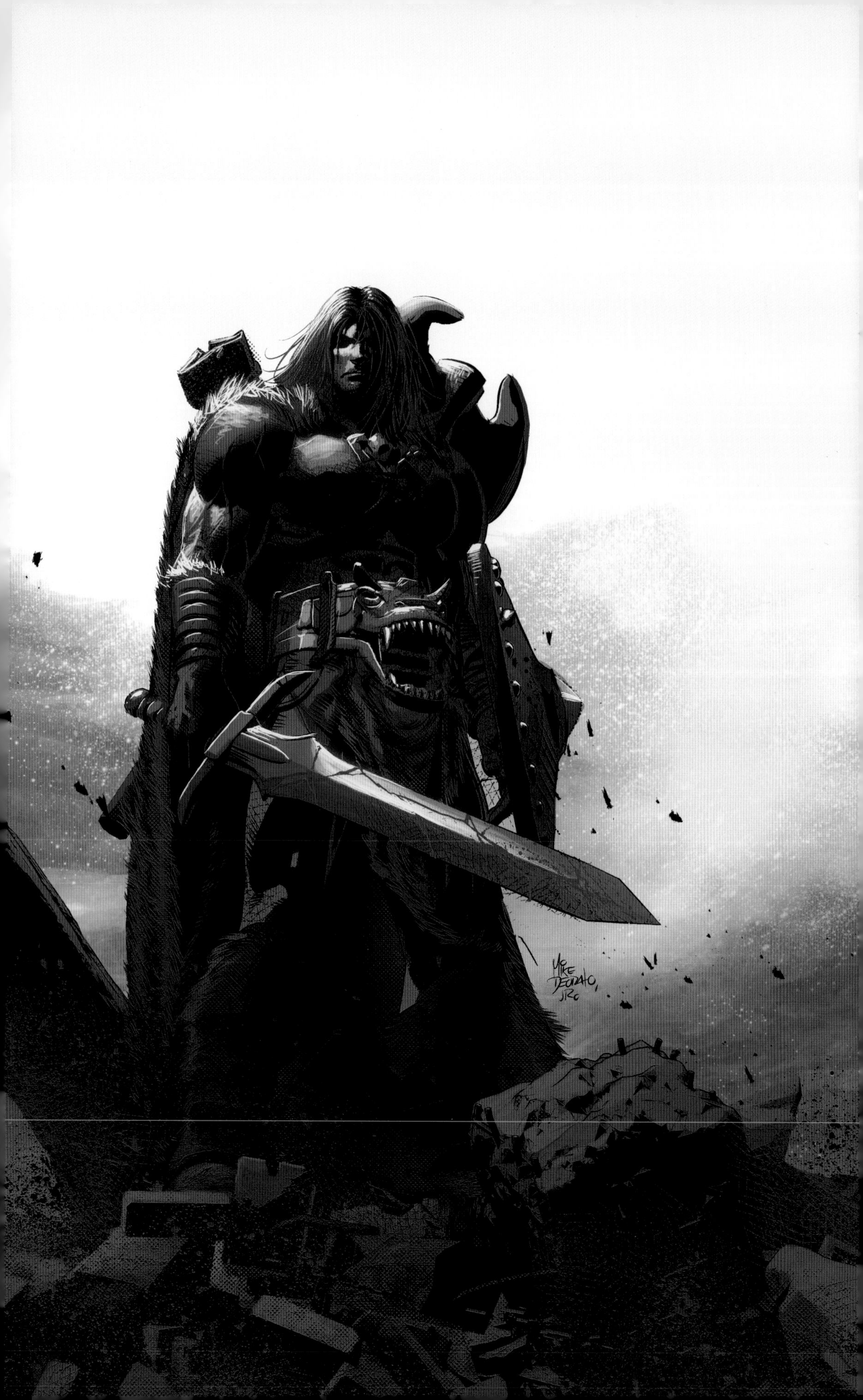
MIKE DEODATO, JR.

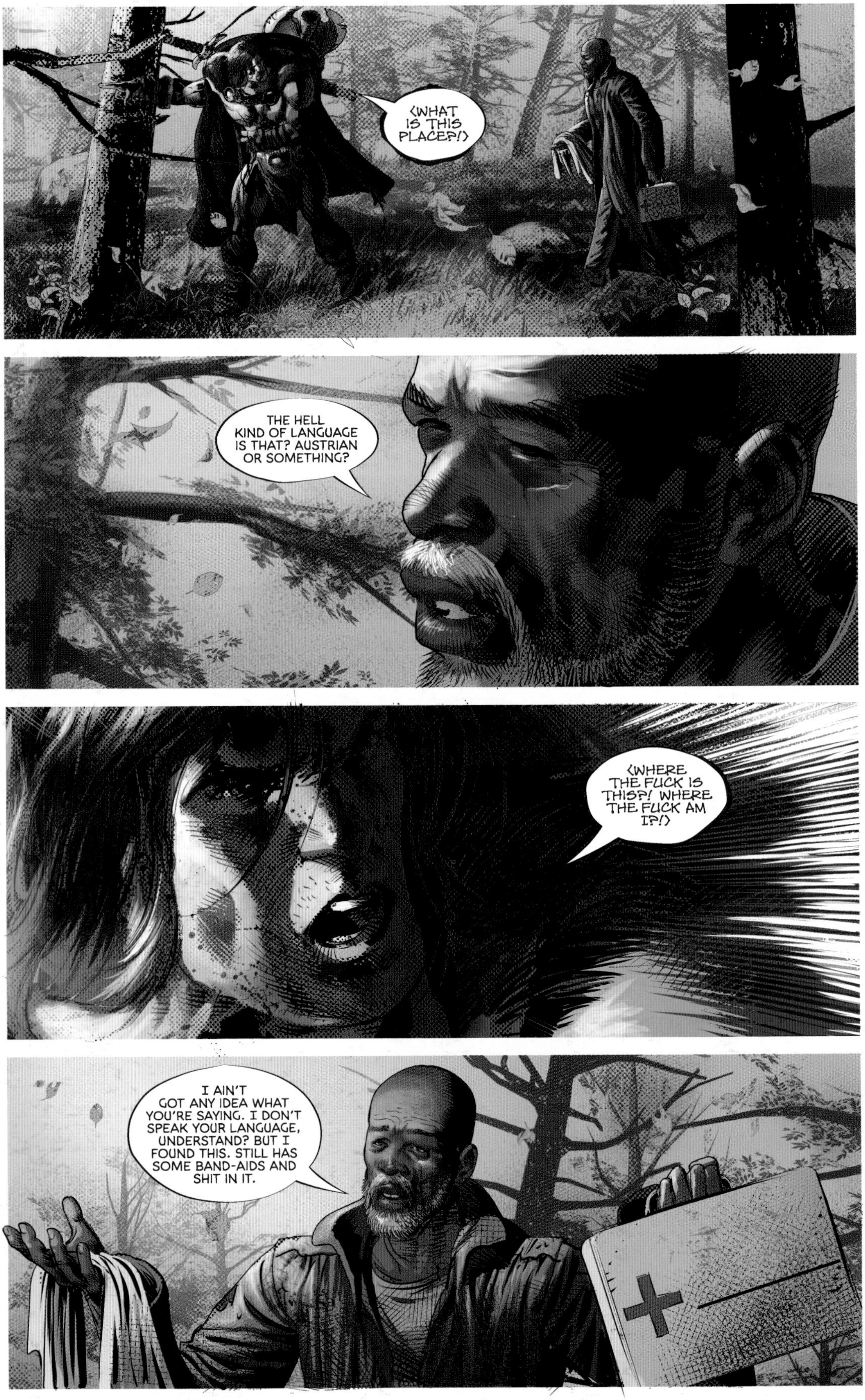

<WHAT IS THIS PLACE?!>
THE HELL KIND OF LANGUAGE IS THAT? AUSTRIAN OR SOMETHING?
<WHERE THE FUCK IS THIS?! WHERE THE FUCK AM I?!>
I AIN'T GOT ANY IDEA WHAT YOU'RE SAYING. I DON'T SPEAK YOUR LANGUAGE, UNDERSTAND? BUT I FOUND THIS. STILL HAS SOME BAND-AIDS AND SHIT IN IT.

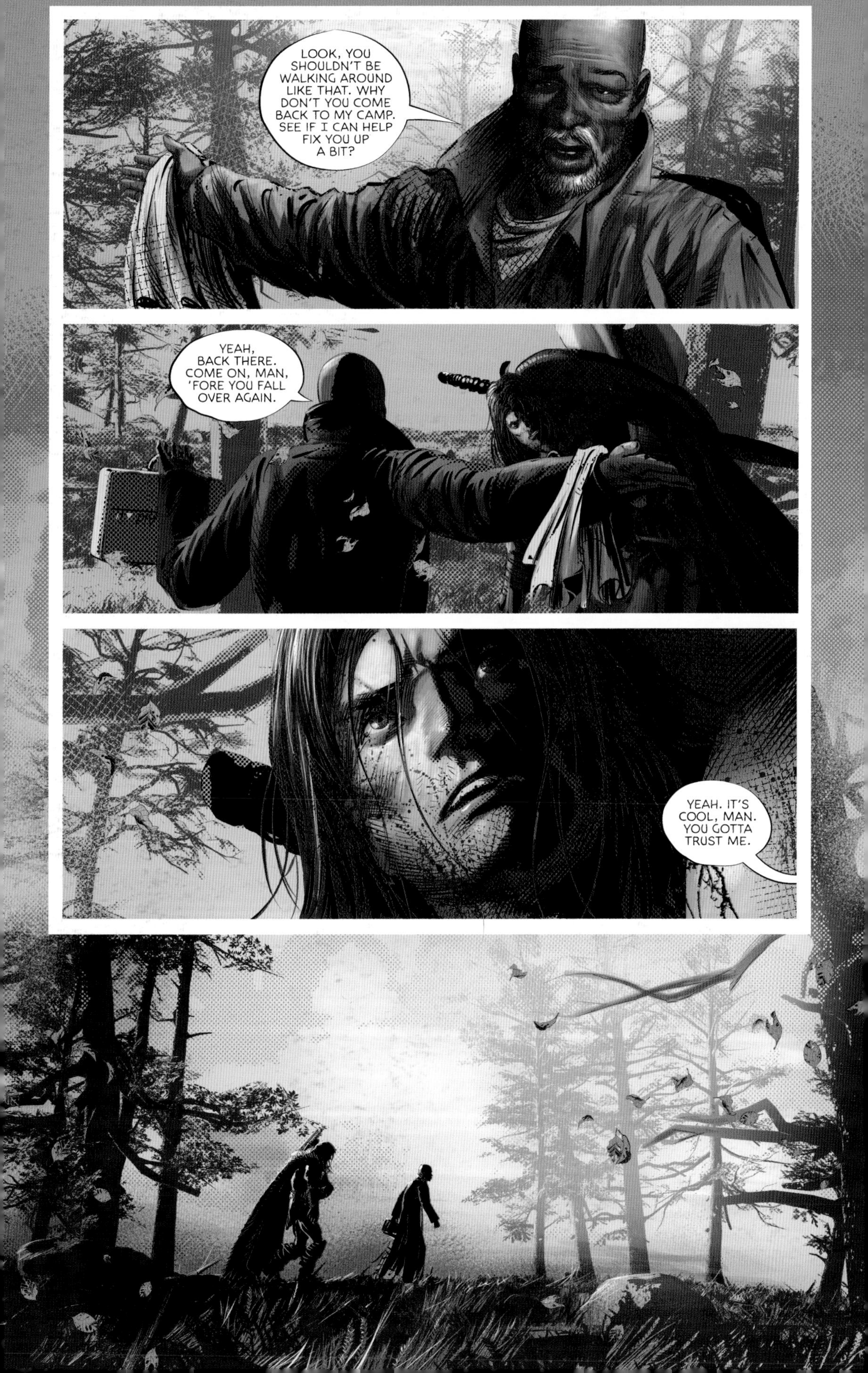
LOOK, YOU SHOULDN'T BE WALKING AROUND LIKE THAT. WHY DON'T YOU COME BACK TO MY CAMP. SEE IF I CAN HELP FIX YOU UP A BIT?
YEAH, BACK THERE. COME ON, MAN, 'FORE YOU FALL OVER AGAIN.
YEAH. IT'S COOL, MAN. YOU GOTTA TRUST ME.

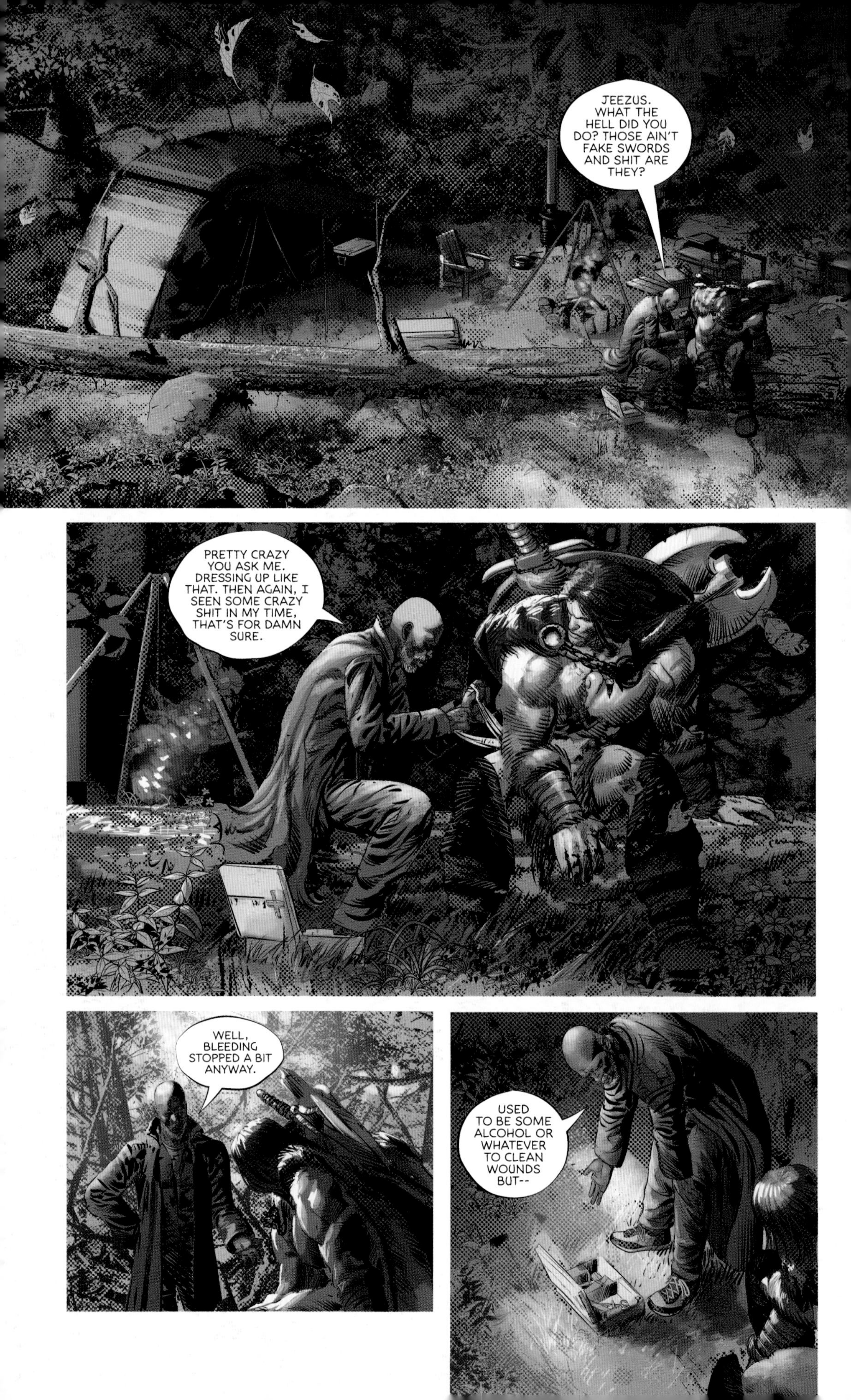
JEEZUS. WHAT THE HELL DID YOU DO? THOSE AIN'T FAKE SWORDS AND SHIT ARE THEY?
PRETTY CRAZY YOU ASK ME. DRESSING UP LIKE THAT. THEN AGAIN, I SEEN SOME CRAZY SHIT IN MY TIME, THAT'S FOR DAMN SURE.
WELL, BLEEDING STOPPED A BIT ANYWAY.
USED TO BE SOME ALCOHOL OR WHATEVER TO CLEAN WOUNDS BUT--

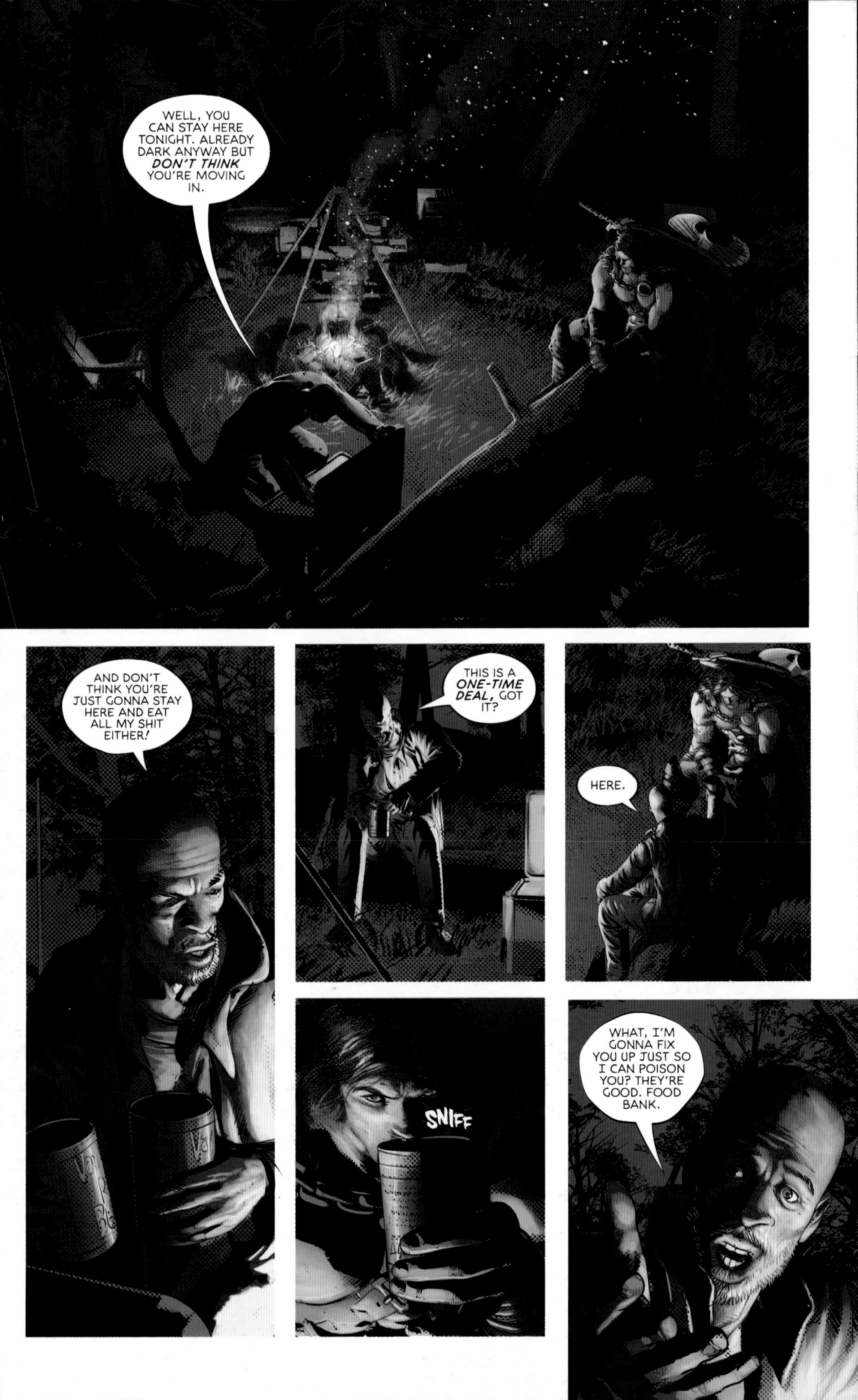
WELL, YOU CAN STAY HERE TONIGHT. ALREADY DARK ANYWAY BUT *DON'T THINK* YOU'RE MOVING IN.
AND DON'T THINK YOU'RE JUST GONNA STAY HERE AND EAT ALL MY SHIT EITHER!
THIS IS A *ONE-TIME DEAL,* GOT IT?
HERE.
SNIFF
WHAT, I'M GONNA FIX YOU UP JUST SO I CAN POISON YOU? THEY'RE GOOD. FOOD BANK.

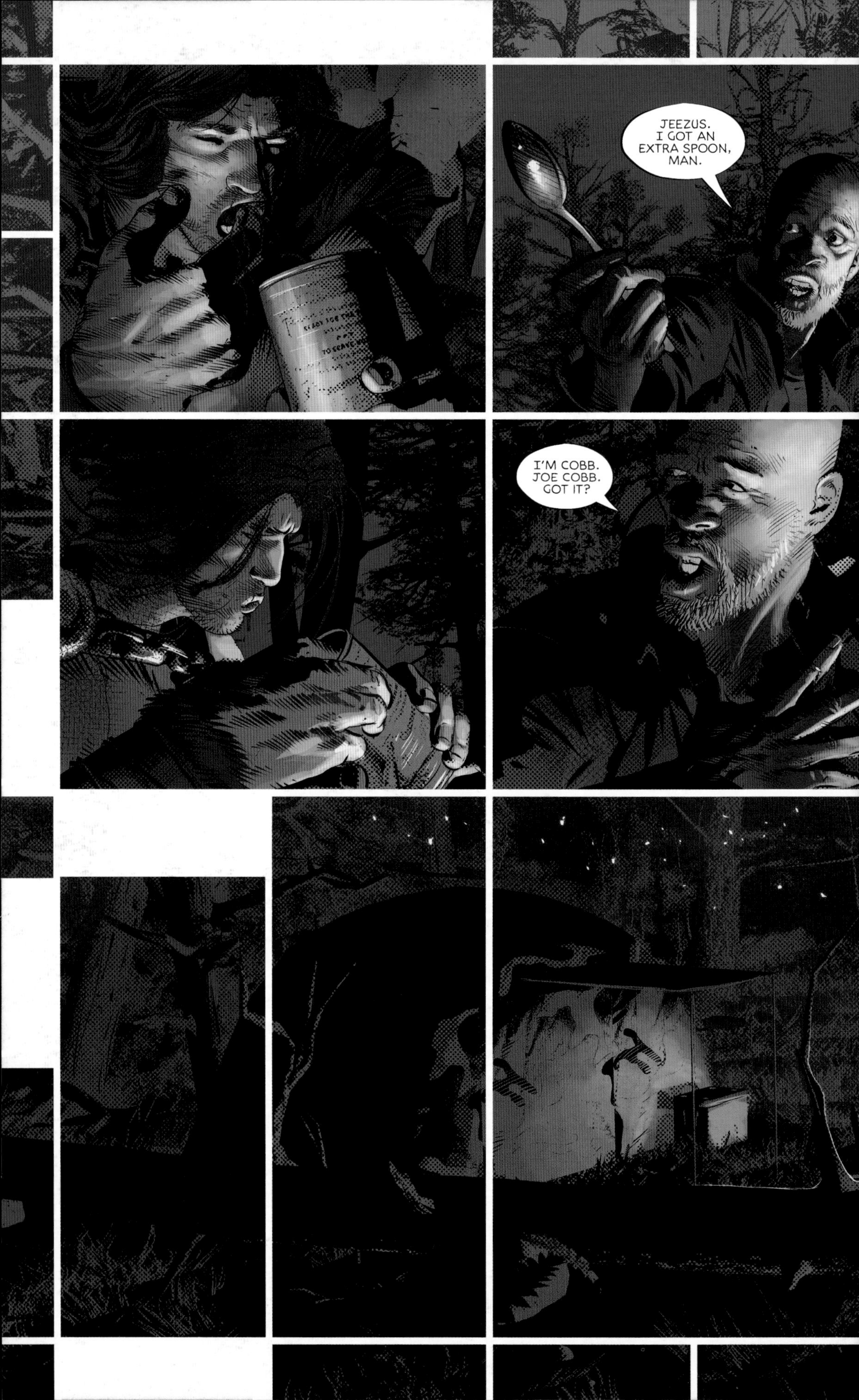
JEEZUS. I GOT AN EXTRA SPOON, MAN.
I'M COBB. JOE COBB. GOT IT?

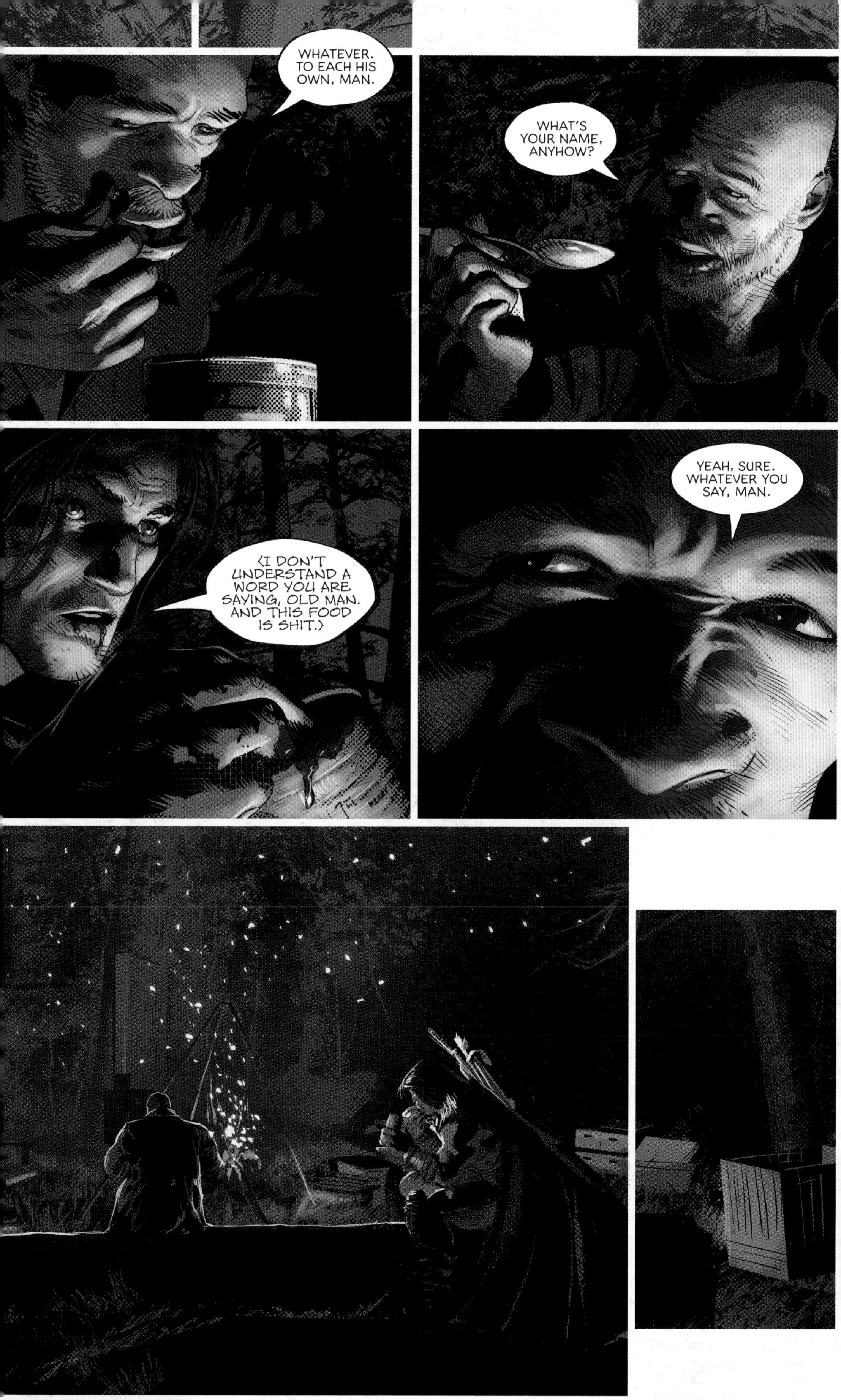
WHATEVER. TO EACH HIS OWN, MAN.
WHAT'S YOUR NAME, ANYHOW?
‹I DON'T UNDERSTAND A WORD YOU ARE SAYING, OLD MAN. AND THIS FOOD IS SHIT.›
YEAH, SURE. WHATEVER YOU SAY, MAN.

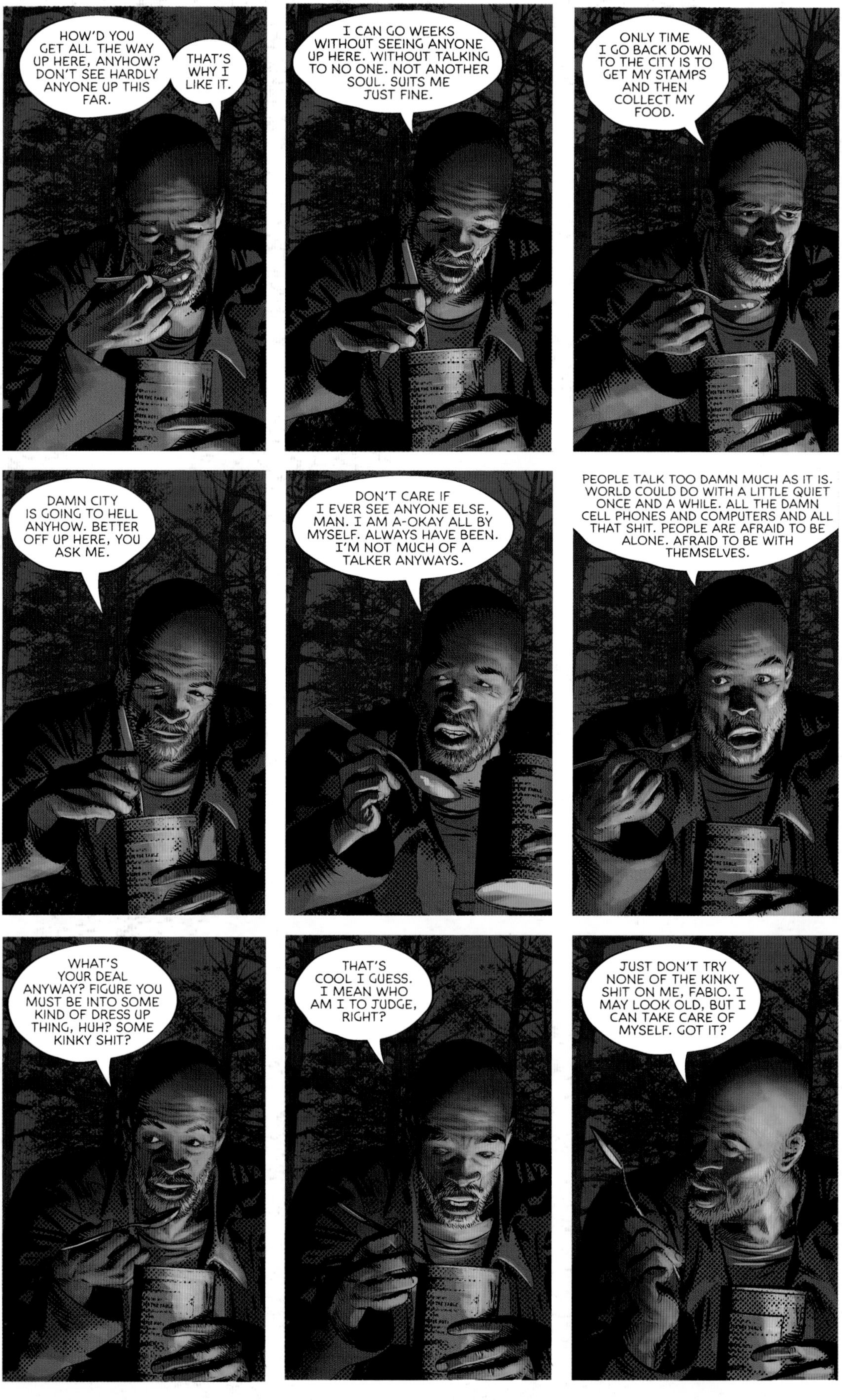
HOW'D YOU GET ALL THE WAY UP HERE, ANYHOW? DON'T SEE HARDLY ANYONE UP THIS FAR.
THAT'S WHY I LIKE IT.
I CAN GO WEEKS WITHOUT SEEING ANYONE UP HERE. WITHOUT TALKING TO NO ONE. NOT ANOTHER SOUL. SUITS ME JUST FINE.
ONLY TIME I GO BACK DOWN TO THE CITY IS TO GET MY STAMPS AND THEN COLLECT MY FOOD.
DAMN CITY IS GOING TO HELL ANYHOW. BETTER OFF UP HERE, YOU ASK ME.
DON'T CARE IF I EVER SEE ANYONE ELSE, MAN. I AM A-OKAY ALL BY MYSELF. ALWAYS HAVE BEEN. I'M NOT MUCH OF A TALKER ANYWAYS.
PEOPLE TALK TOO DAMN MUCH AS IT IS. WORLD COULD DO WITH A LITTLE QUIET ONCE AND A WHILE. ALL THE DAMN CELL PHONES AND COMPUTERS AND ALL THAT SHIT. PEOPLE ARE AFRAID TO BE ALONE. AFRAID TO BE WITH THEMSELVES.
WHAT'S YOUR DEAL ANYWAY? FIGURE YOU MUST BE INTO SOME KIND OF DRESS UP THING, HUH? SOME KINKY SHIT?
THAT'S COOL I GUESS. I MEAN WHO AM I TO JUDGE, RIGHT?
JUST DON'T TRY NONE OF THE KINKY SHIT ON ME, FABIO. I MAY LOOK OLD, BUT I CAN TAKE CARE OF MYSELF. GOT IT?

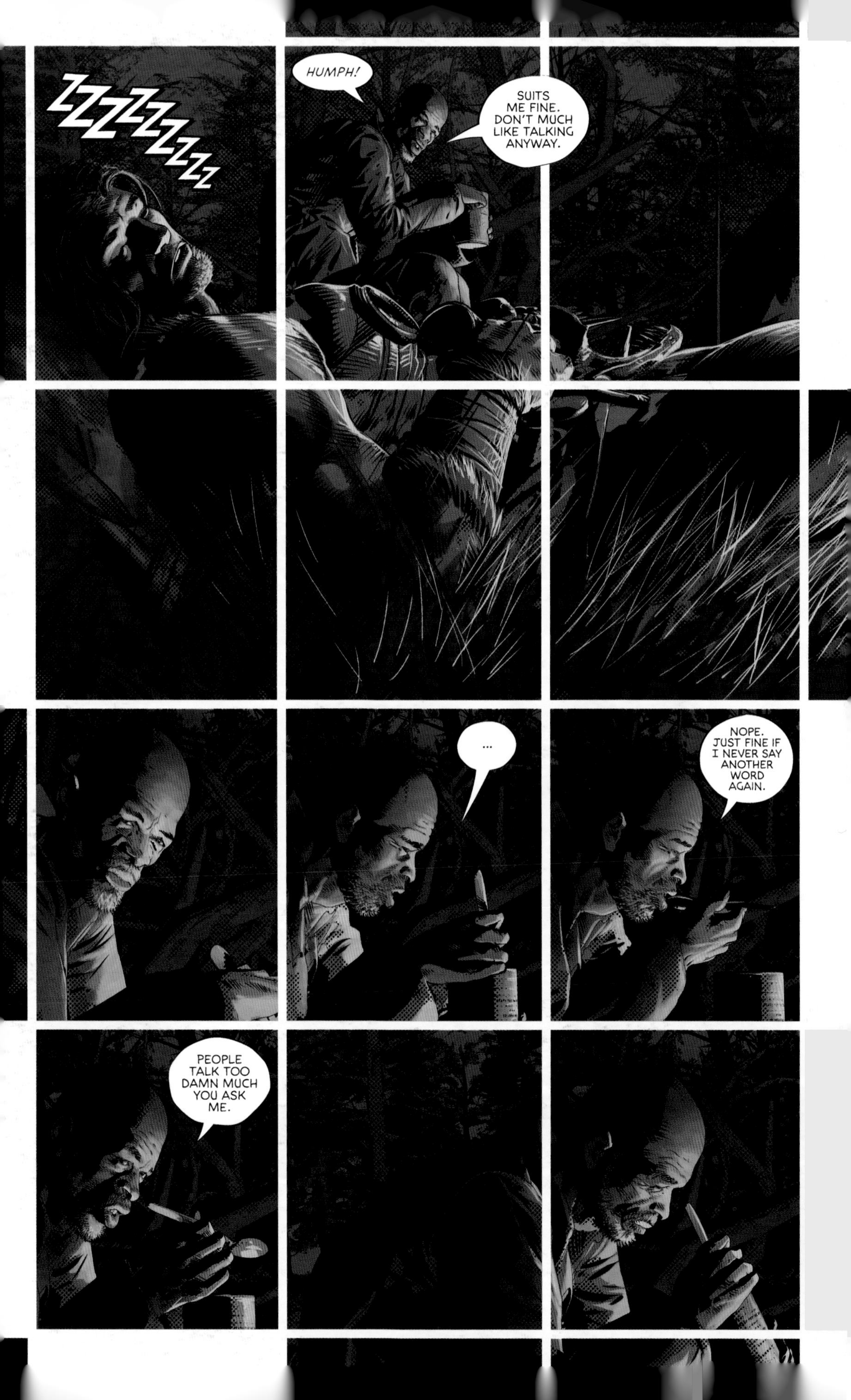
ZZZZZZZZZ
HUMPH!
SUITS ME FINE. DON'T MUCH LIKE TALKING ANYWAY.
...
NOPE. JUST FINE IF I NEVER SAY ANOTHER WORD AGAIN.
PEOPLE TALK TOO DAMN MUCH YOU ASK ME.

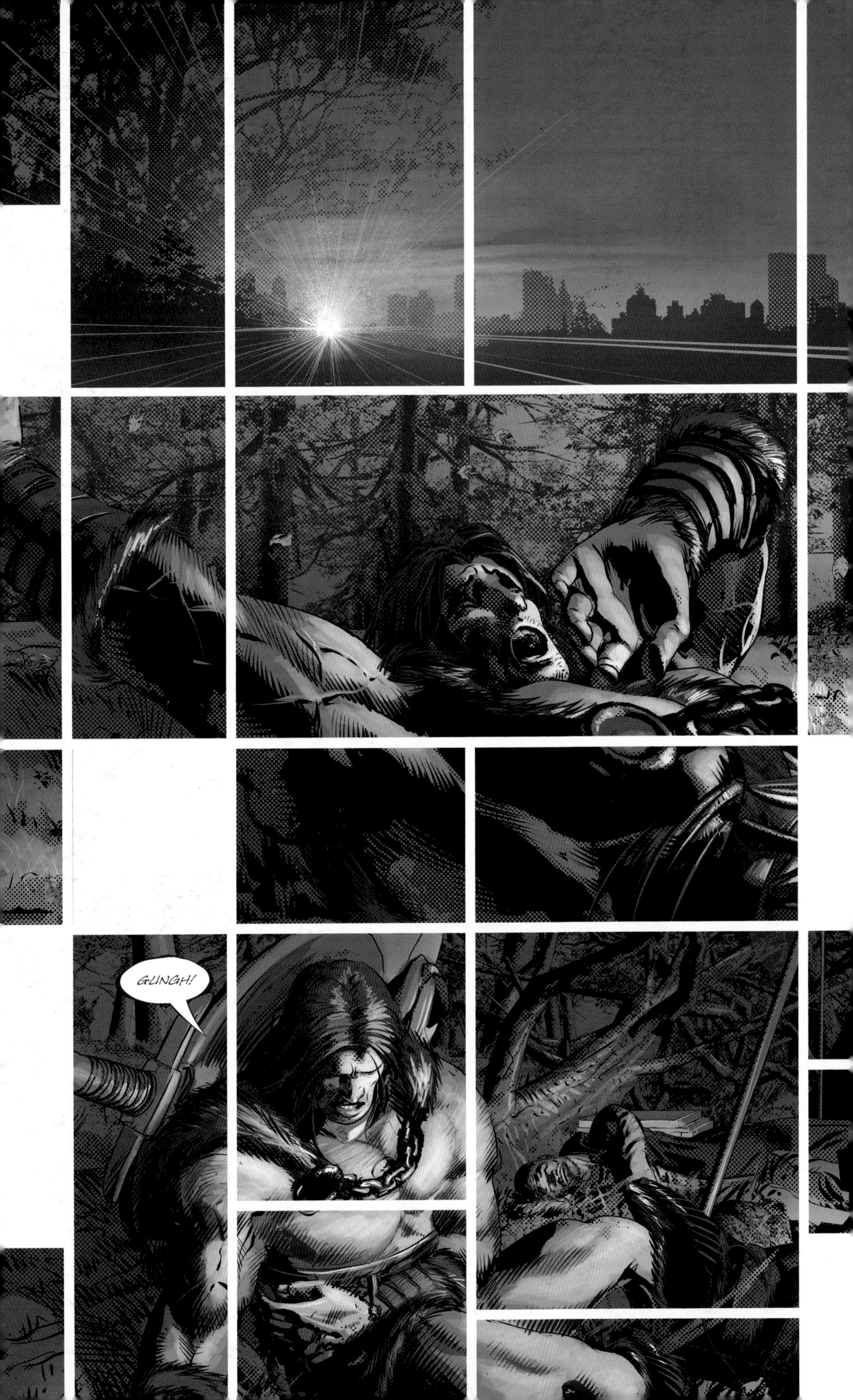
GUNGH!

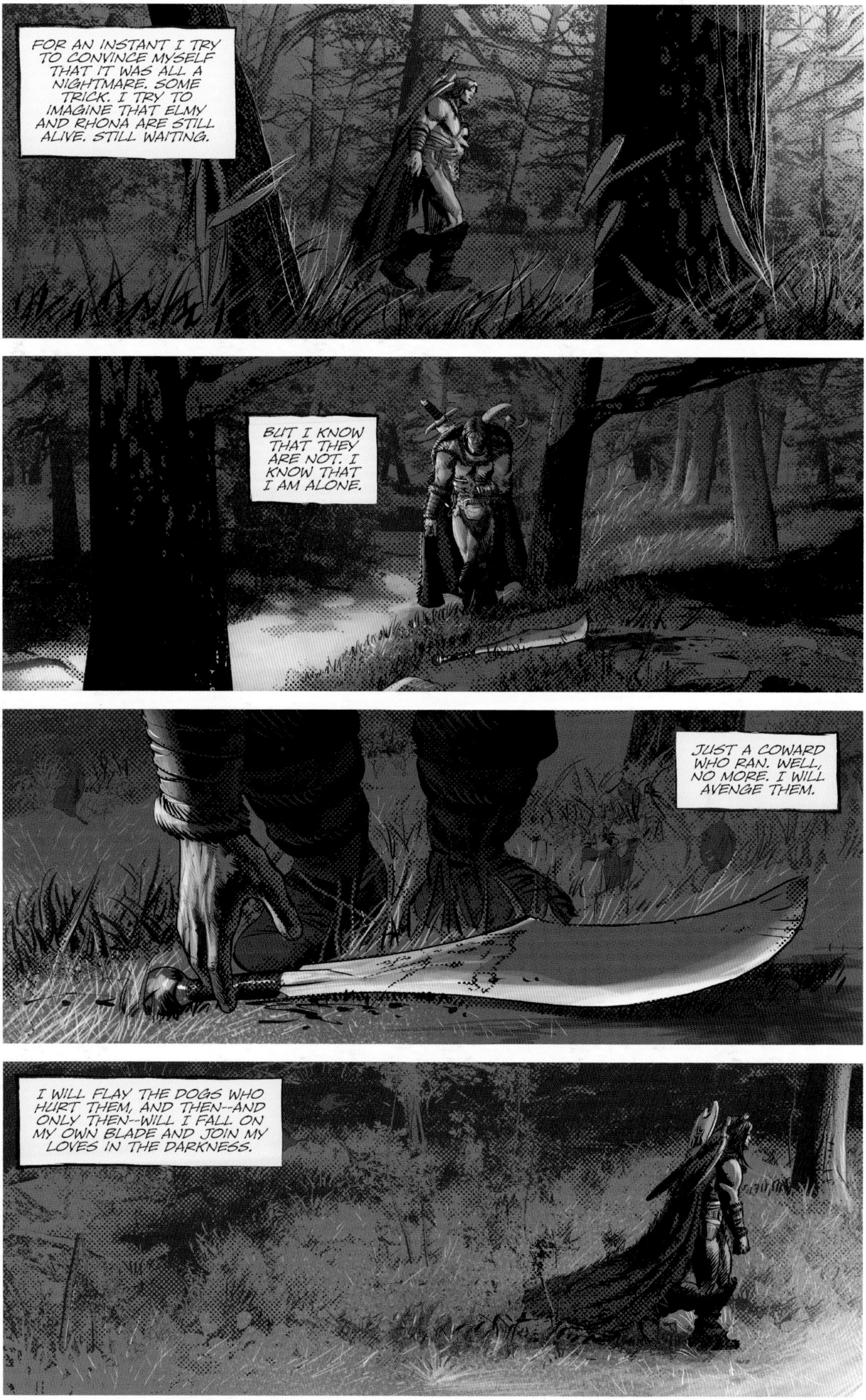
FOR AN INSTANT I TRY TO CONVINCE MYSELF THAT IT WAS ALL A NIGHTMARE. SOME TRICK. I TRY TO IMAGINE THAT ELMY AND RHONA ARE STILL ALIVE. STILL WAITING.
BUT I KNOW THAT THEY ARE NOT. I KNOW THAT I AM ALONE.
JUST A COWARD WHO RAN. WELL, NO MORE. I WILL AVENGE THEM.
I WILL FLAY THE DOGS WHO HURT THEM, AND THEN--AND ONLY THEN--WILL I FALL ON MY OWN BLADE AND JOIN MY LOVES IN THE DARKNESS.

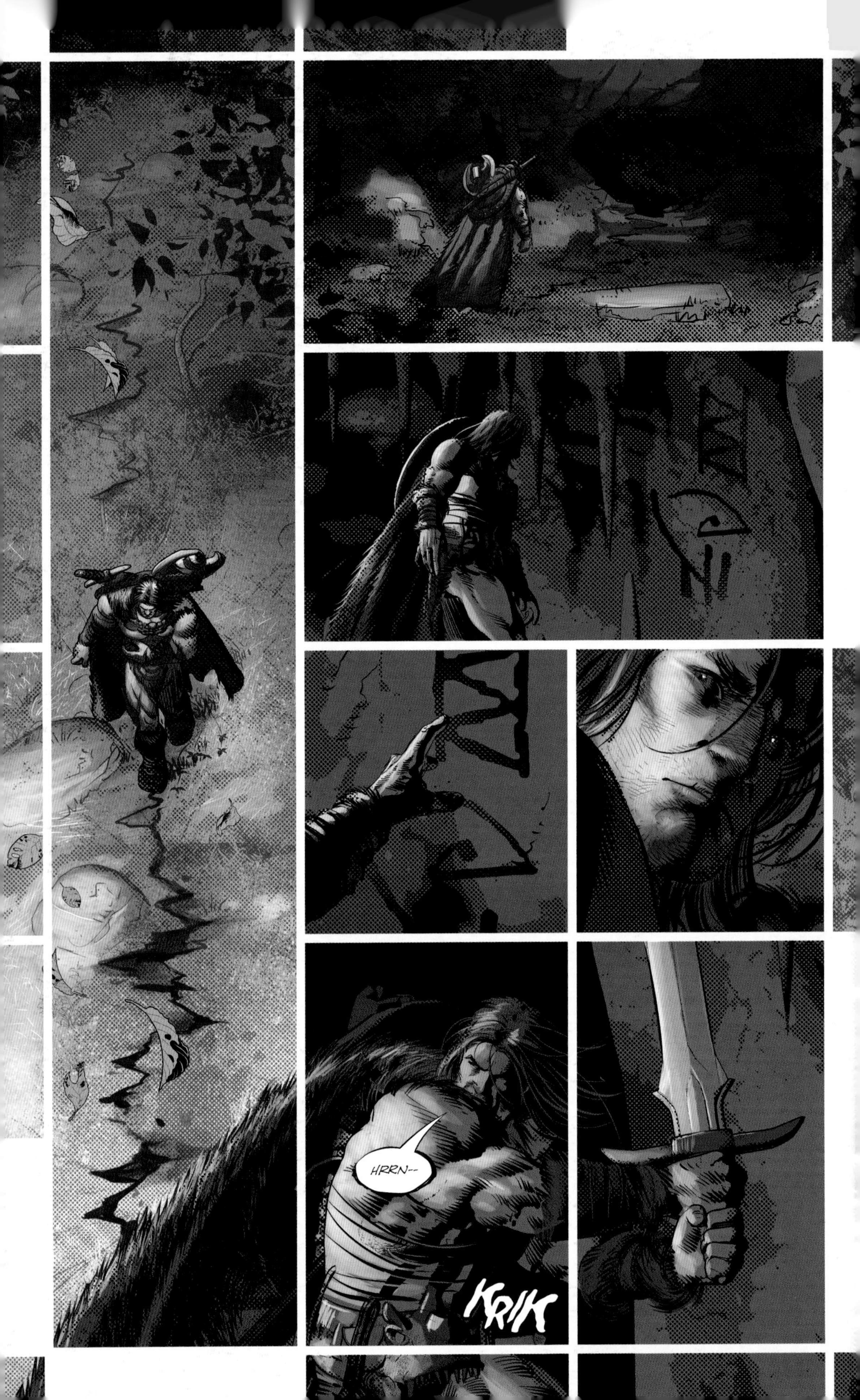
HRRN--
KRIK

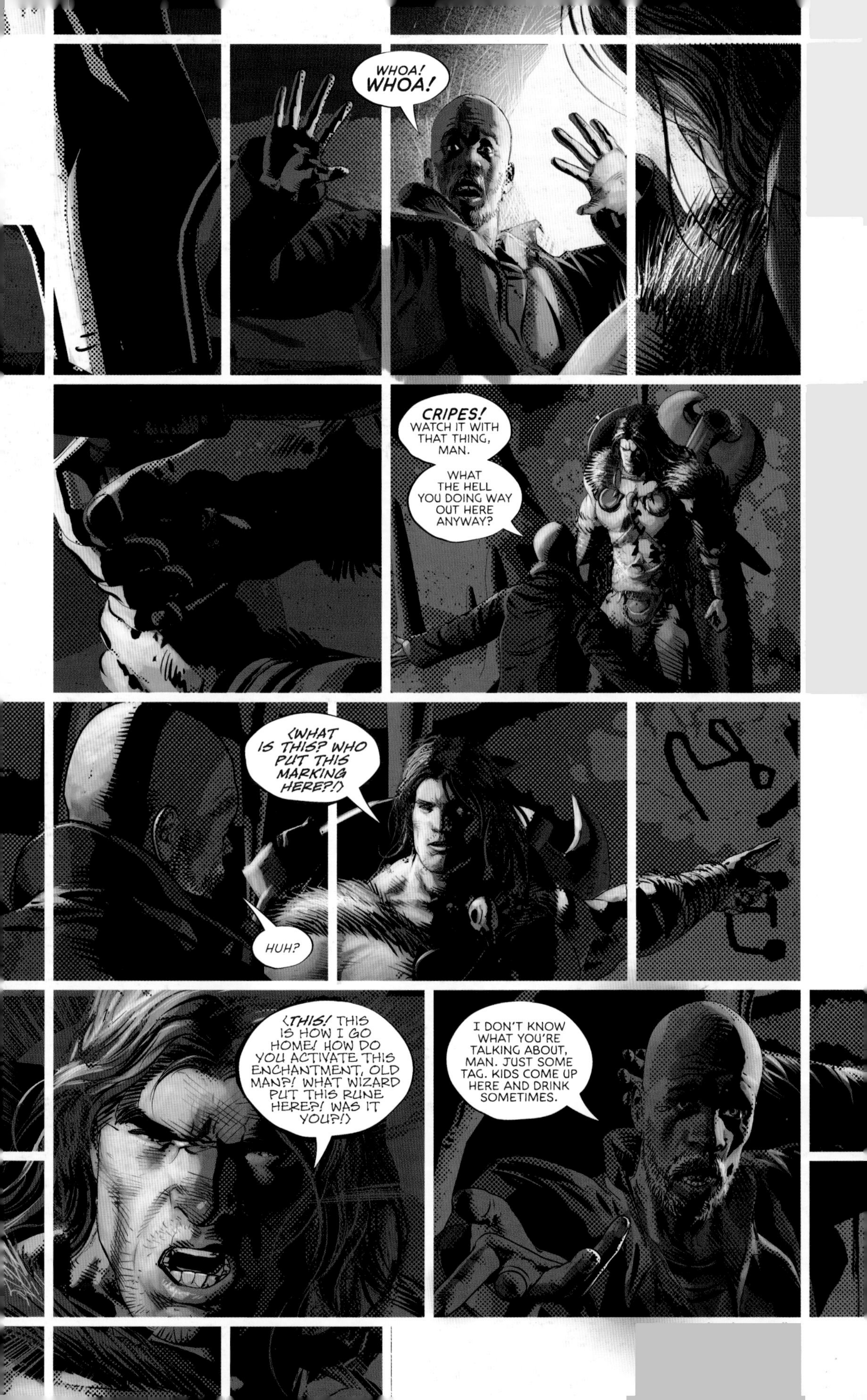
WHOA! WHOA!
CRIPES! WATCH IT WITH THAT THING, MAN.
WHAT THE HELL YOU DOING WAY OUT HERE ANYWAY?
<WHAT IS THIS? WHO PUT THIS MARKING HERE?!>
HUH?
<THIS! THIS IS HOW I GO HOME! HOW DO YOU ACTIVATE THIS ENCHANTMENT, OLD MAN?! WHAT WIZARD PUT THIS RUNE HERE?! WAS IT YOU?!>
I DON'T KNOW WHAT YOU'RE TALKING ABOUT, MAN. JUST SOME TAG. KIDS COME UP HERE AND DRINK SOMETIMES.

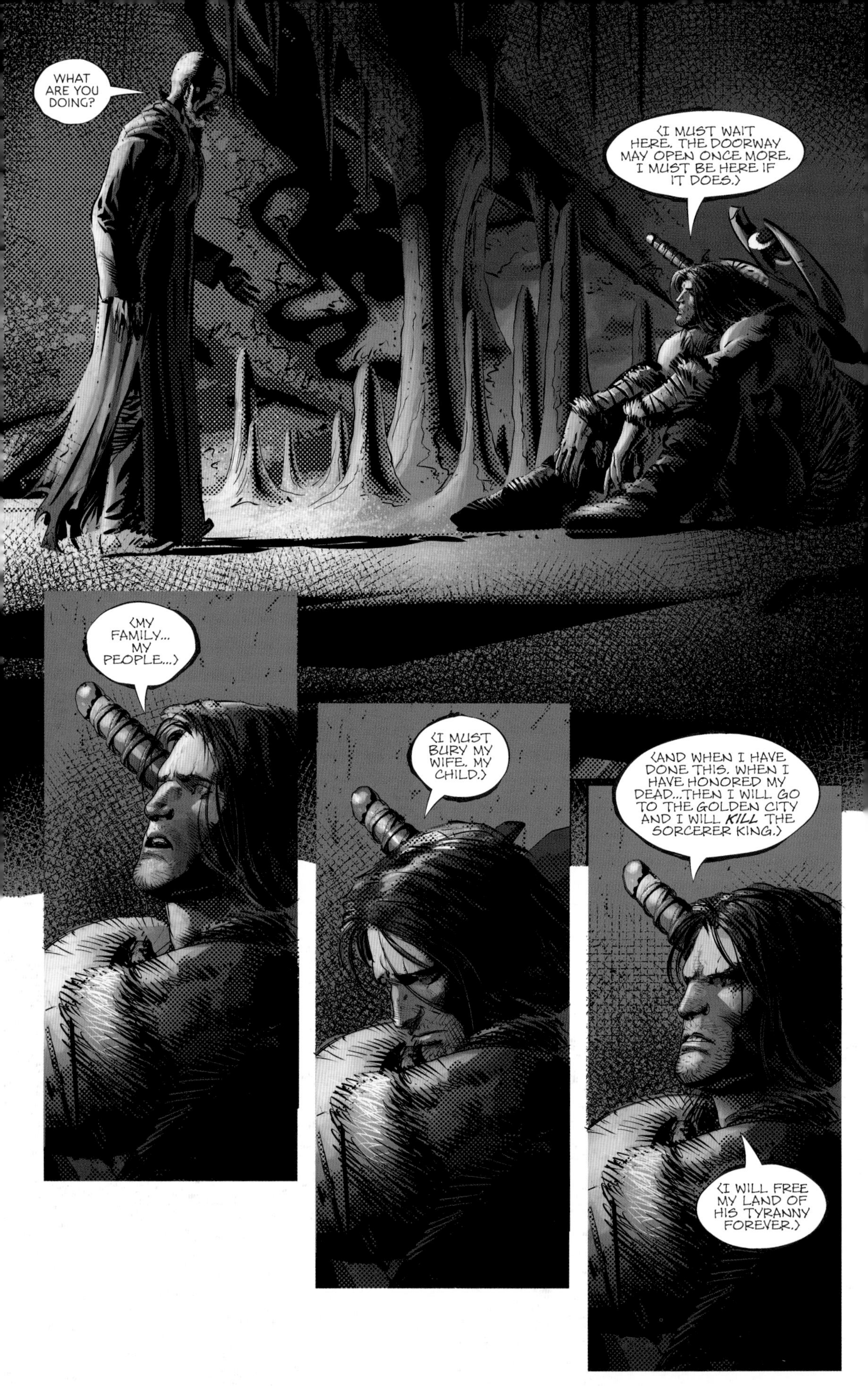
WHAT ARE YOU DOING?
<I MUST WAIT HERE. THE DOORWAY MAY OPEN ONCE MORE. I MUST BE HERE IF IT DOES.>
<MY FAMILY... MY PEOPLE...>
<I MUST BURY MY WIFE. MY CHILD.>
<AND WHEN I HAVE DONE THIS. WHEN I HAVE HONORED MY DEAD...THEN I WILL GO TO THE GOLDEN CITY AND I WILL KILL THE SORCERER KING.>
<I WILL FREE MY LAND OF HIS TYRANNY FOREVER.>

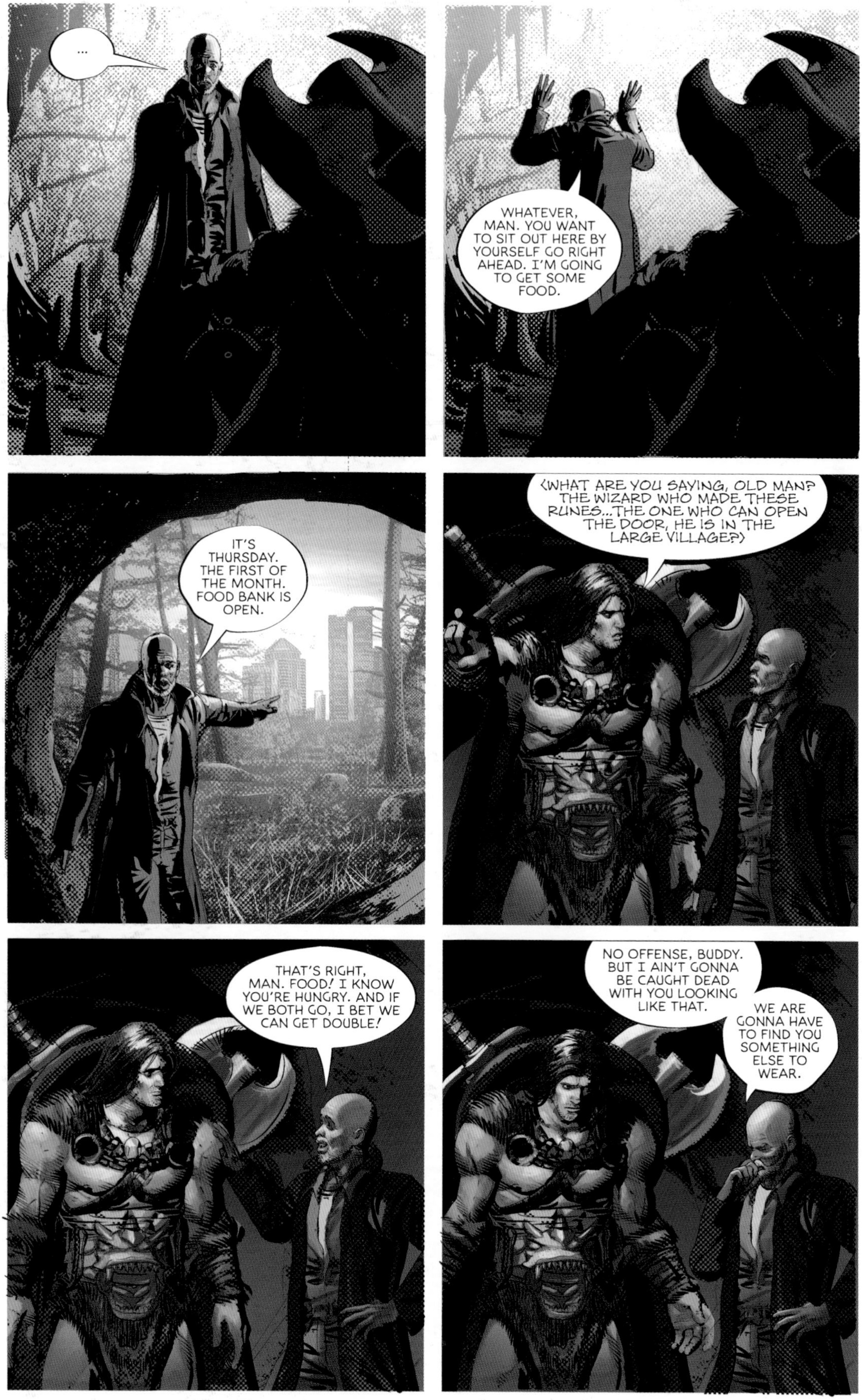
...
WHATEVER, MAN. YOU WANT TO SIT OUT HERE BY YOURSELF GO RIGHT AHEAD. I'M GOING TO GET SOME FOOD.
IT'S THURSDAY. THE FIRST OF THE MONTH. FOOD BANK IS OPEN.
<WHAT ARE YOU SAYING, OLD MAN? THE WIZARD WHO MADE THESE RUNES...THE ONE WHO CAN OPEN THE DOOR, HE IS IN THE LARGE VILLAGE?>
THAT'S RIGHT, MAN. FOOD! I KNOW YOU'RE HUNGRY. AND IF WE BOTH GO, I BET WE CAN GET DOUBLE!
NO OFFENSE, BUDDY. BUT I AIN'T GONNA BE CAUGHT DEAD WITH YOU LOOKING LIKE THAT.
WE ARE GONNA HAVE TO FIND YOU SOMETHING ELSE TO WEAR.

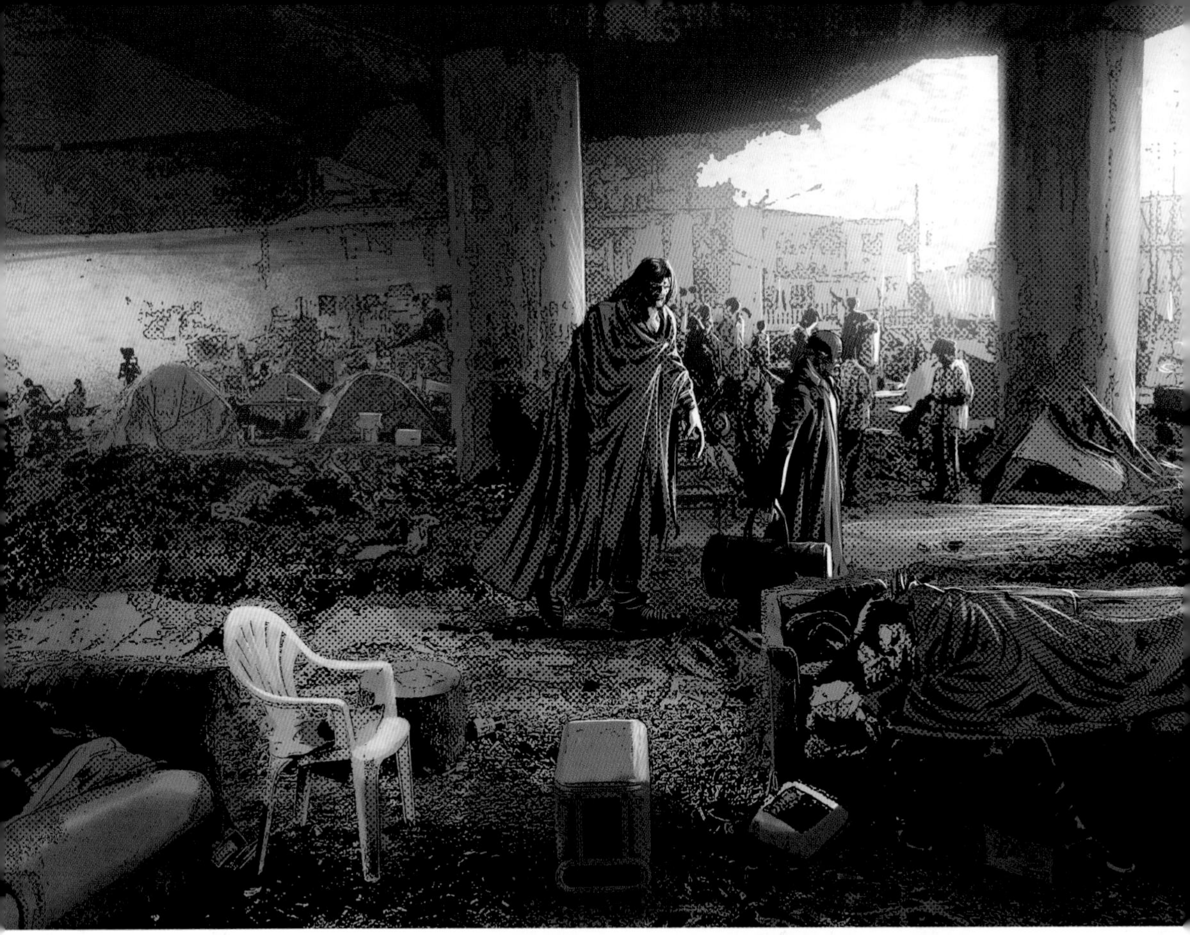

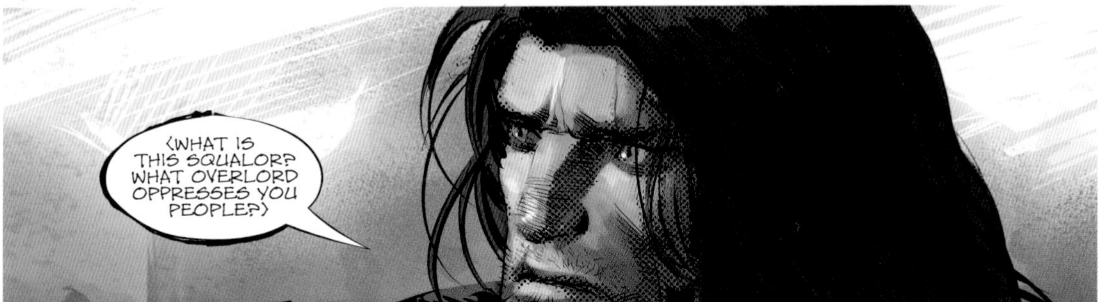

<WHAT IS THIS SQUALOR? WHAT OVERLORD OPPRESSES YOU PEOPLE?>

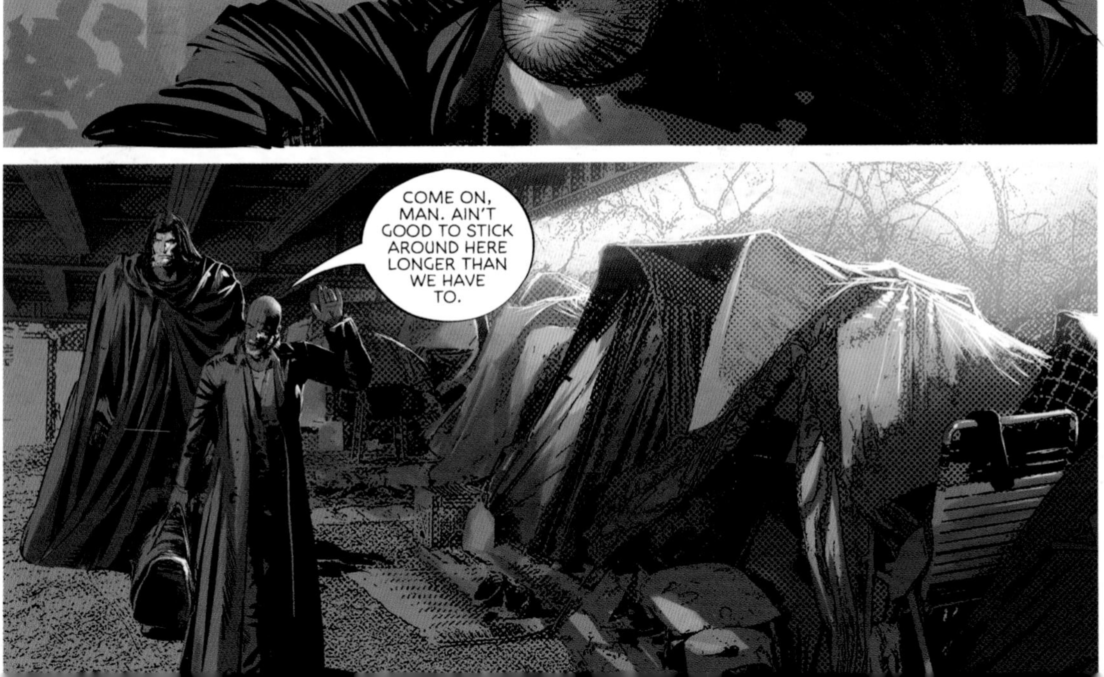

COME ON, MAN. AIN'T GOOD TO STICK AROUND HERE LONGER THAN WE HAVE TO.

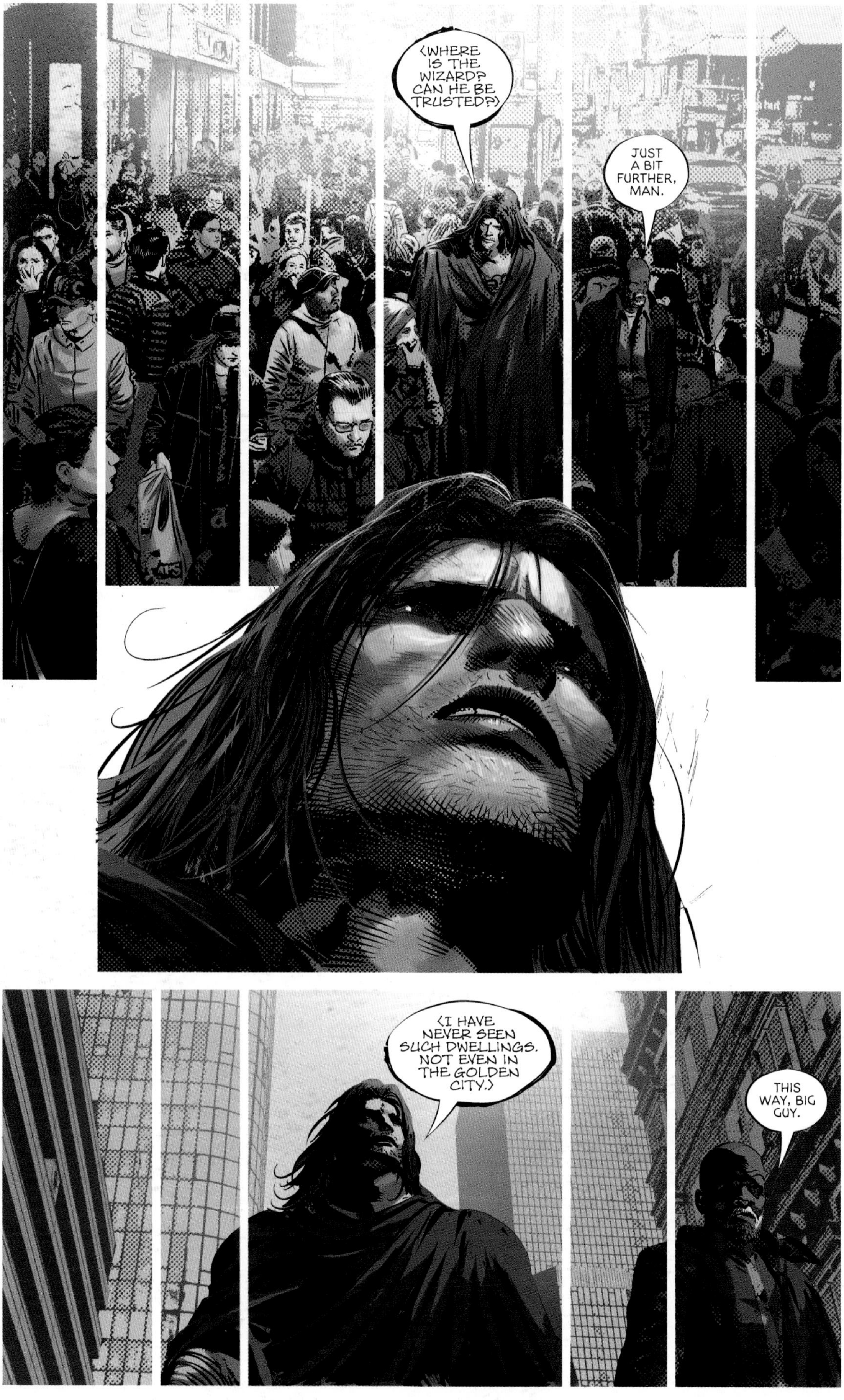
⟨WHERE IS THE WIZARD? CAN HE BE TRUSTED?⟩
JUST A BIT FURTHER, MAN.
⟨I HAVE NEVER SEEN SUCH DWELLINGS. NOT EVEN IN THE GOLDEN CITY.⟩
THIS WAY, BIG GUY.

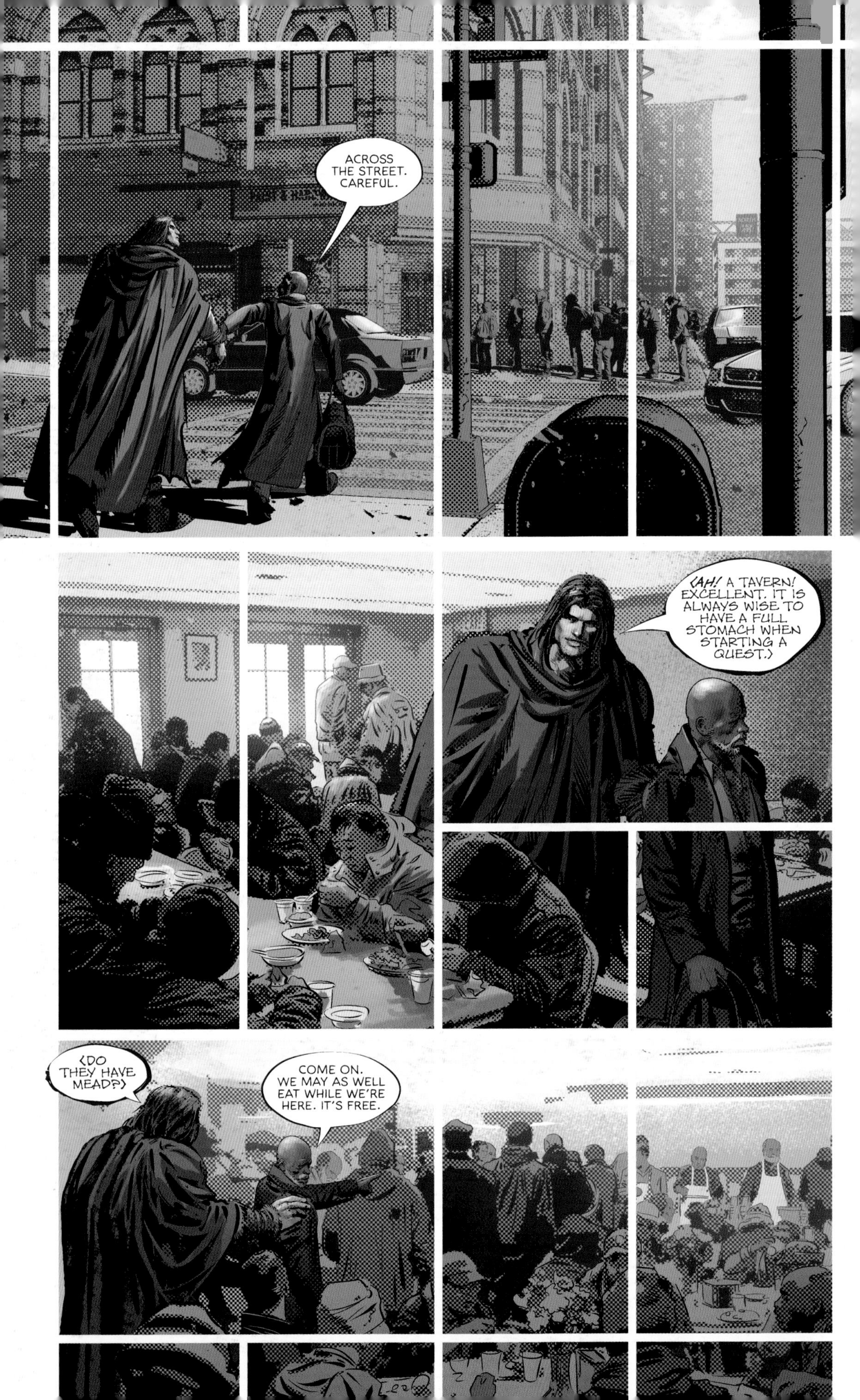
ACROSS THE STREET. CAREFUL.
‹AH! A TAVERN! EXCELLENT. IT IS ALWAYS WISE TO HAVE A FULL STOMACH WHEN STARTING A QUEST.›
‹DO THEY HAVE MEAD?›
COME ON. WE MAY AS WELL EAT WHILE WE'RE HERE. IT'S FREE.

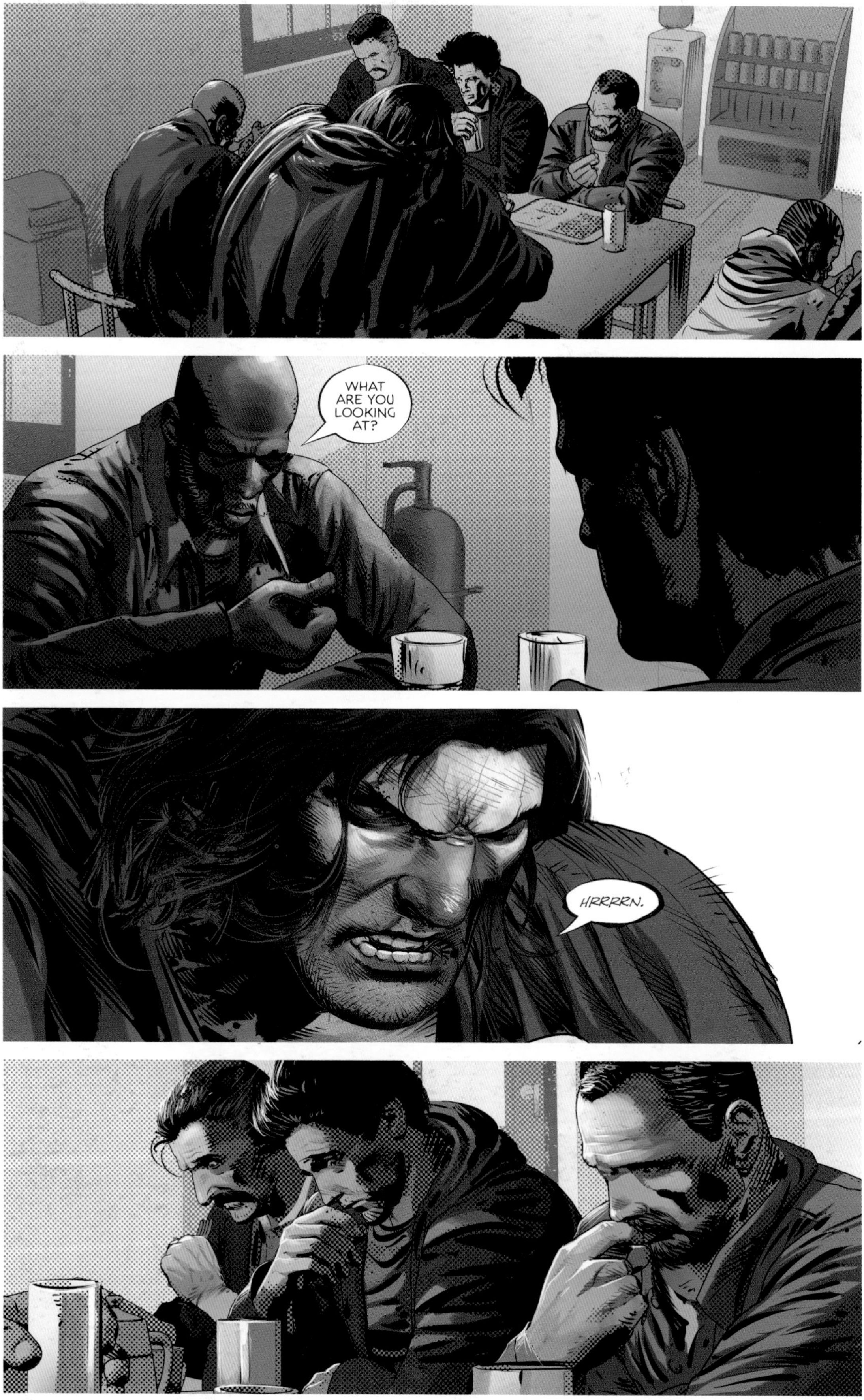
WHAT ARE YOU LOOKING AT?
HRRRRN.

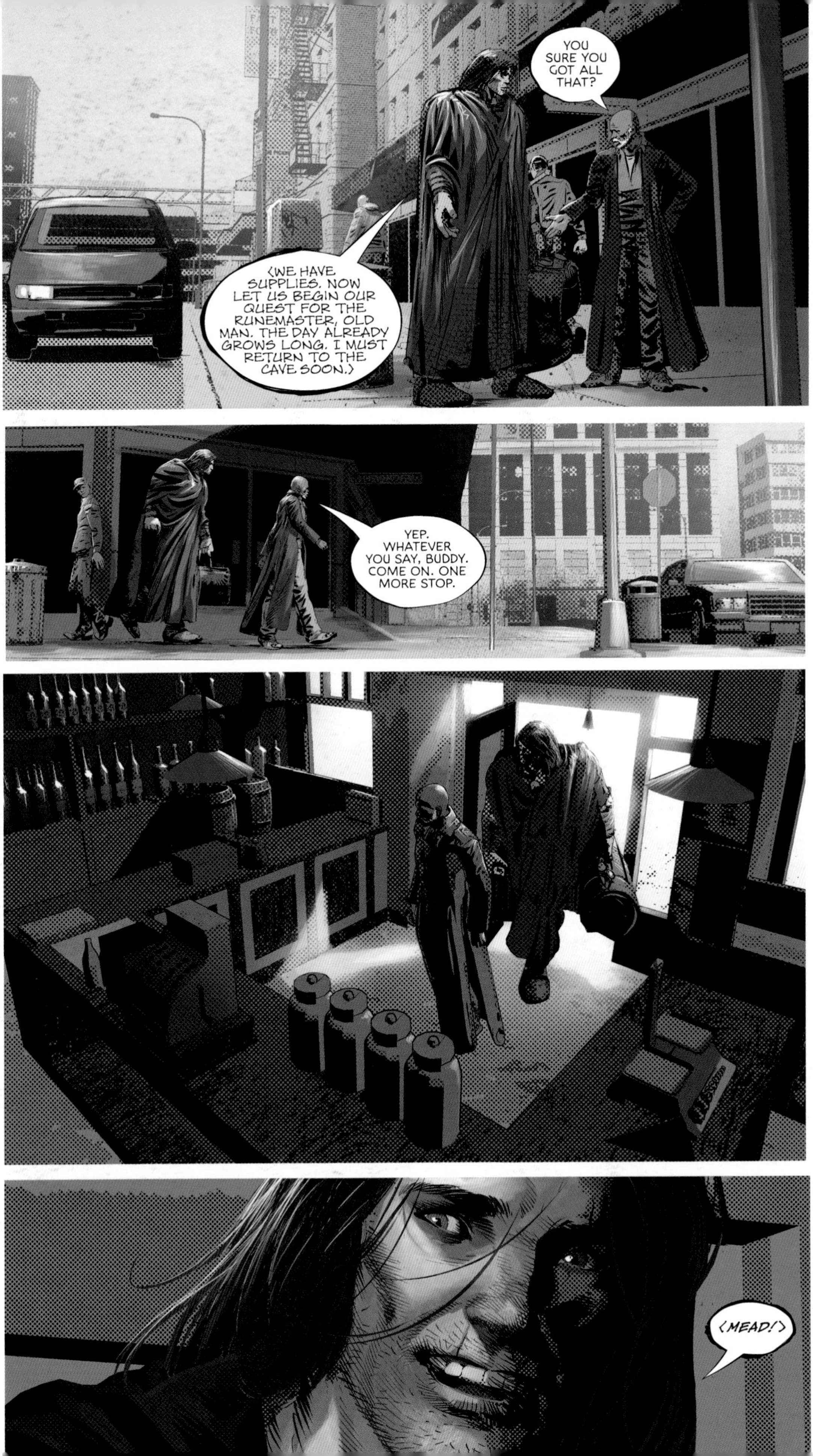
YOU SURE YOU GOT ALL THAT?
<WE HAVE SUPPLIES. NOW LET US BEGIN OUR QUEST FOR THE RUNEMASTER, OLD MAN. THE DAY ALREADY GROWS LONG. I MUST RETURN TO THE CAVE SOON.>
YEP. WHATEVER YOU SAY, BUDDY. COME ON. ONE MORE STOP.
<MEAD!>

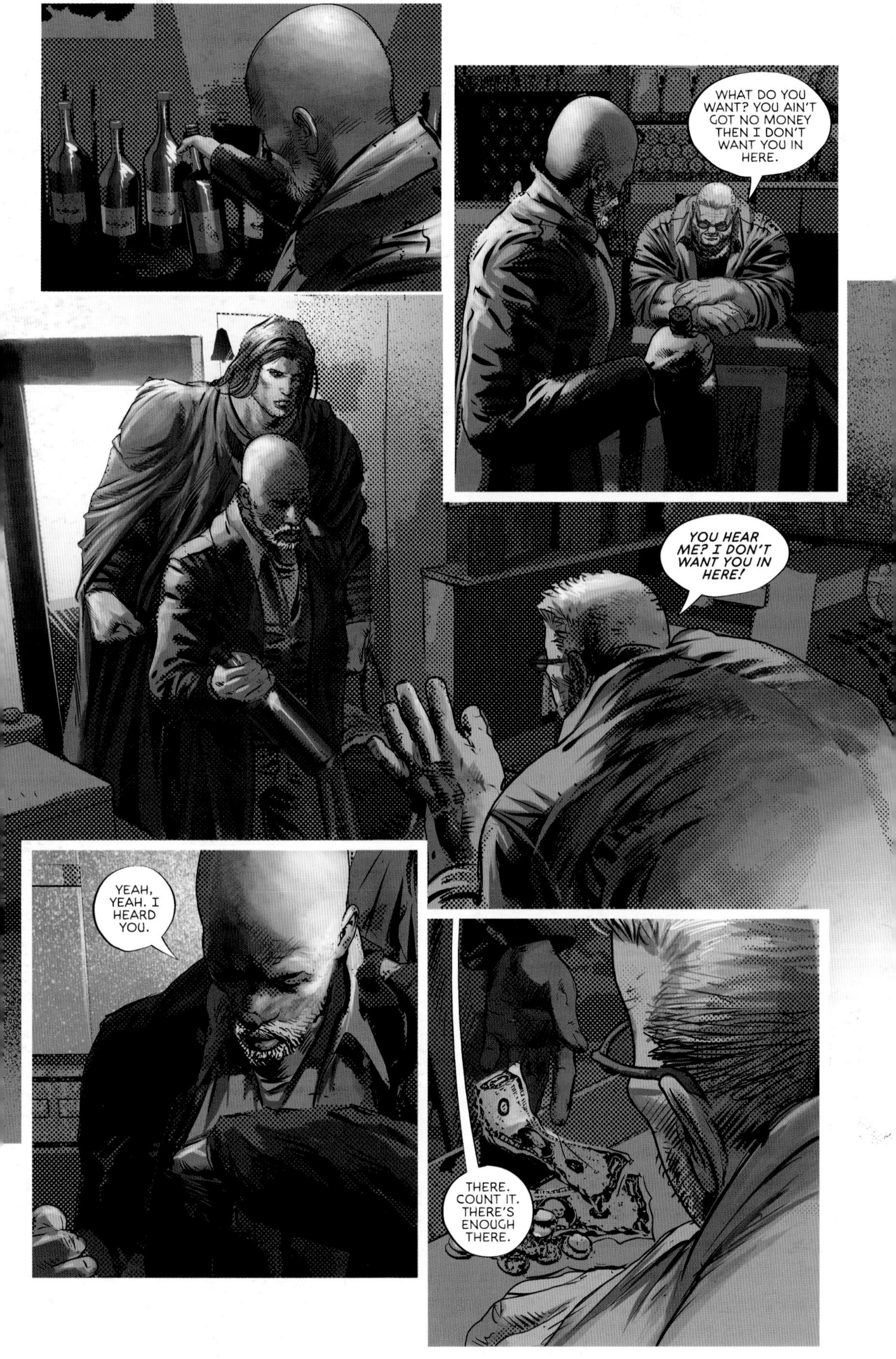
WHAT DO YOU WANT? YOU AIN'T GOT NO MONEY THEN I DON'T WANT YOU IN HERE.
YOU HEAR ME? I DON'T WANT YOU IN HERE!
YEAH, YEAH. I HEARD YOU.
THERE. COUNT IT. THERE'S ENOUGH THERE.

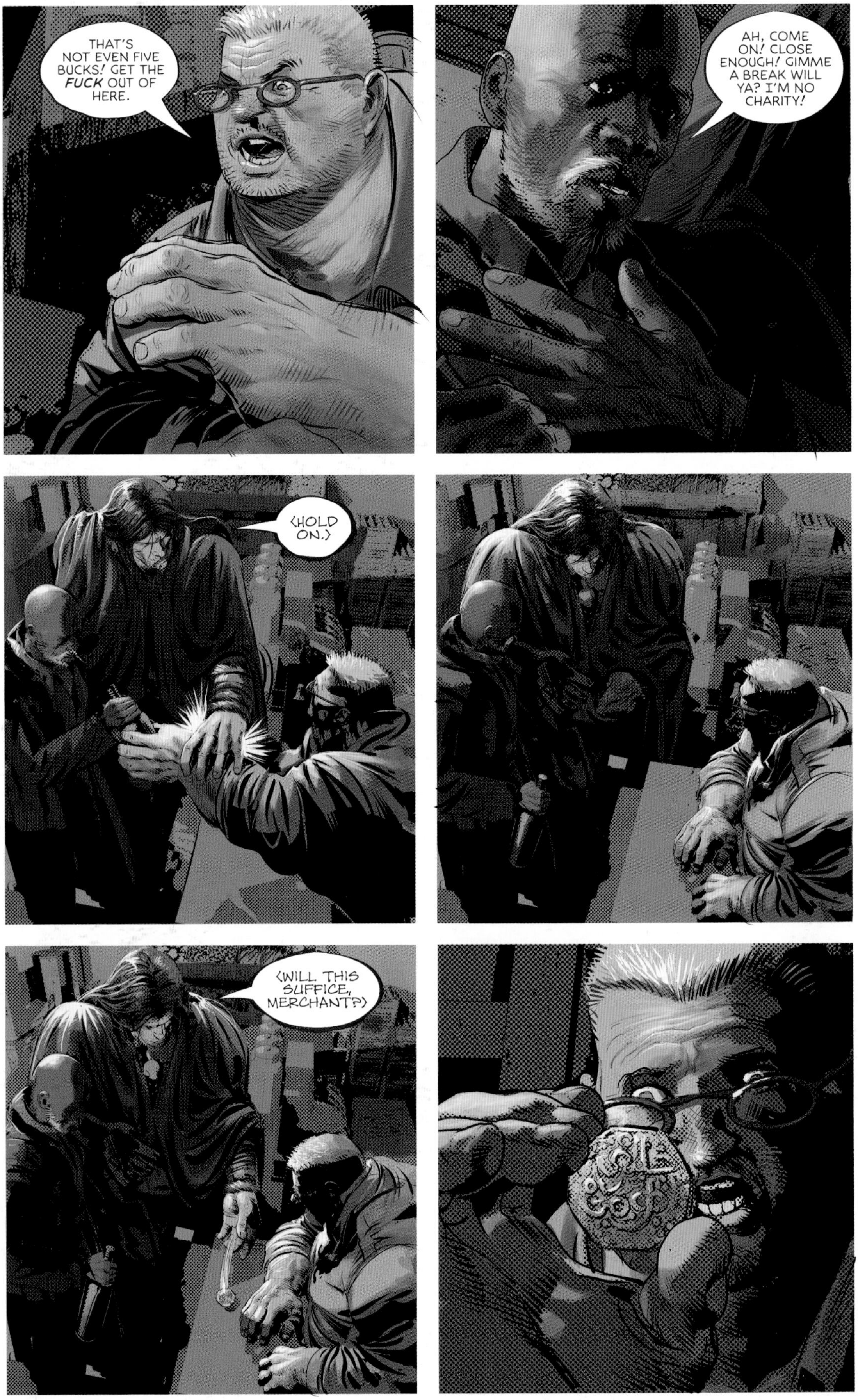
THAT'S NOT EVEN FIVE BUCKS! GET THE FUCK OUT OF HERE.
AH, COME ON! CLOSE ENOUGH! GIMME A BREAK WILL YA? I'M NO CHARITY!
‹HOLD ON.›
‹WILL THIS SUFFICE, MERCHANT?›

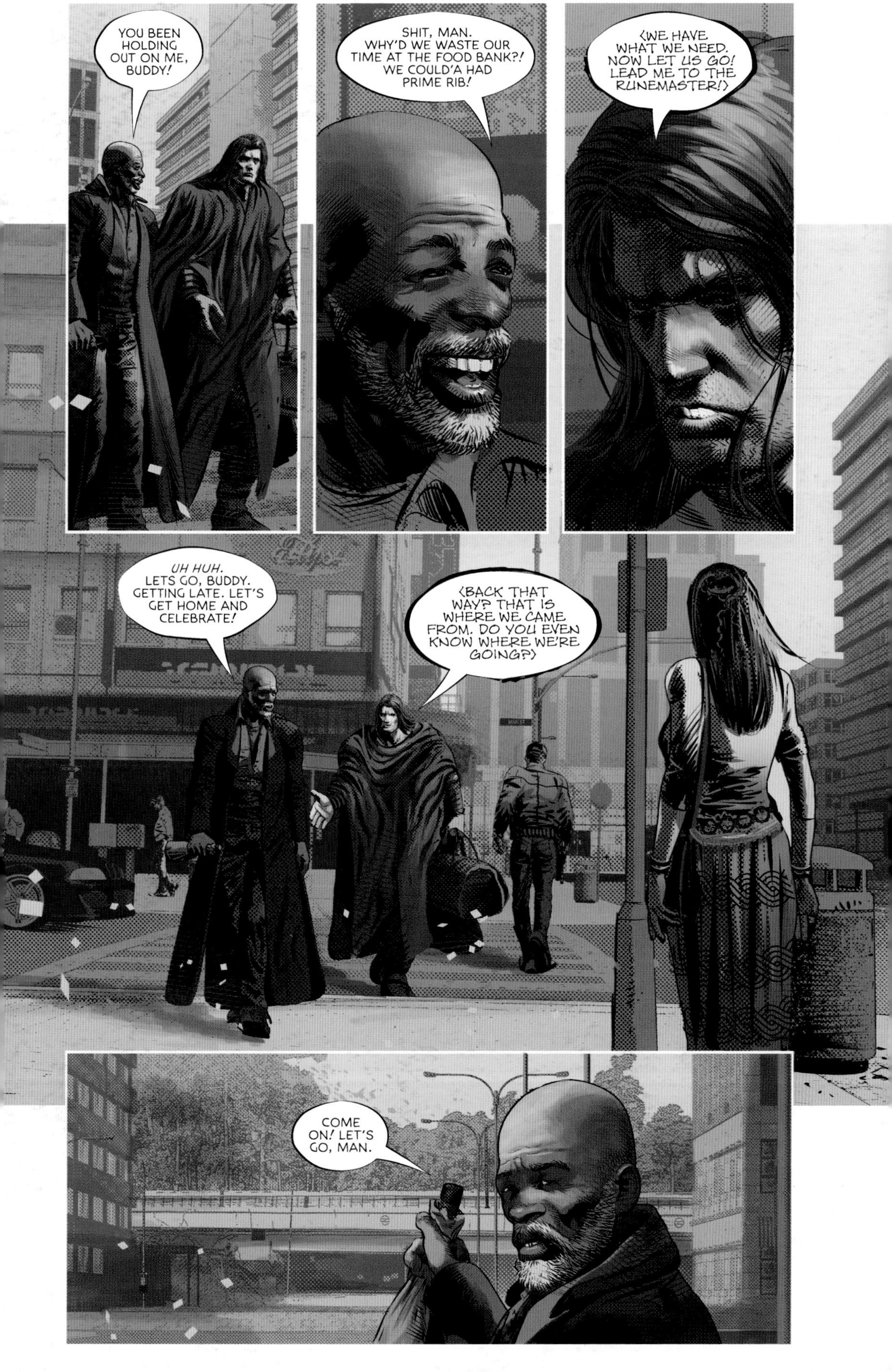
YOU BEEN HOLDING OUT ON ME, BUDDY!
SHIT, MAN. WHY'D WE WASTE OUR TIME AT THE FOOD BANK?! WE COULD'A HAD PRIME RIB!
<WE HAVE WHAT WE NEED. NOW LET US GO! LEAD ME TO THE RUNEMASTER!>
UH HUH. LETS GO, BUDDY. GETTING LATE. LET'S GET HOME AND CELEBRATE!
<BACK THAT WAY? THAT IS WHERE WE CAME FROM. DO YOU EVEN KNOW WHERE WE'RE GOING?>
COME ON! LET'S GO, MAN.

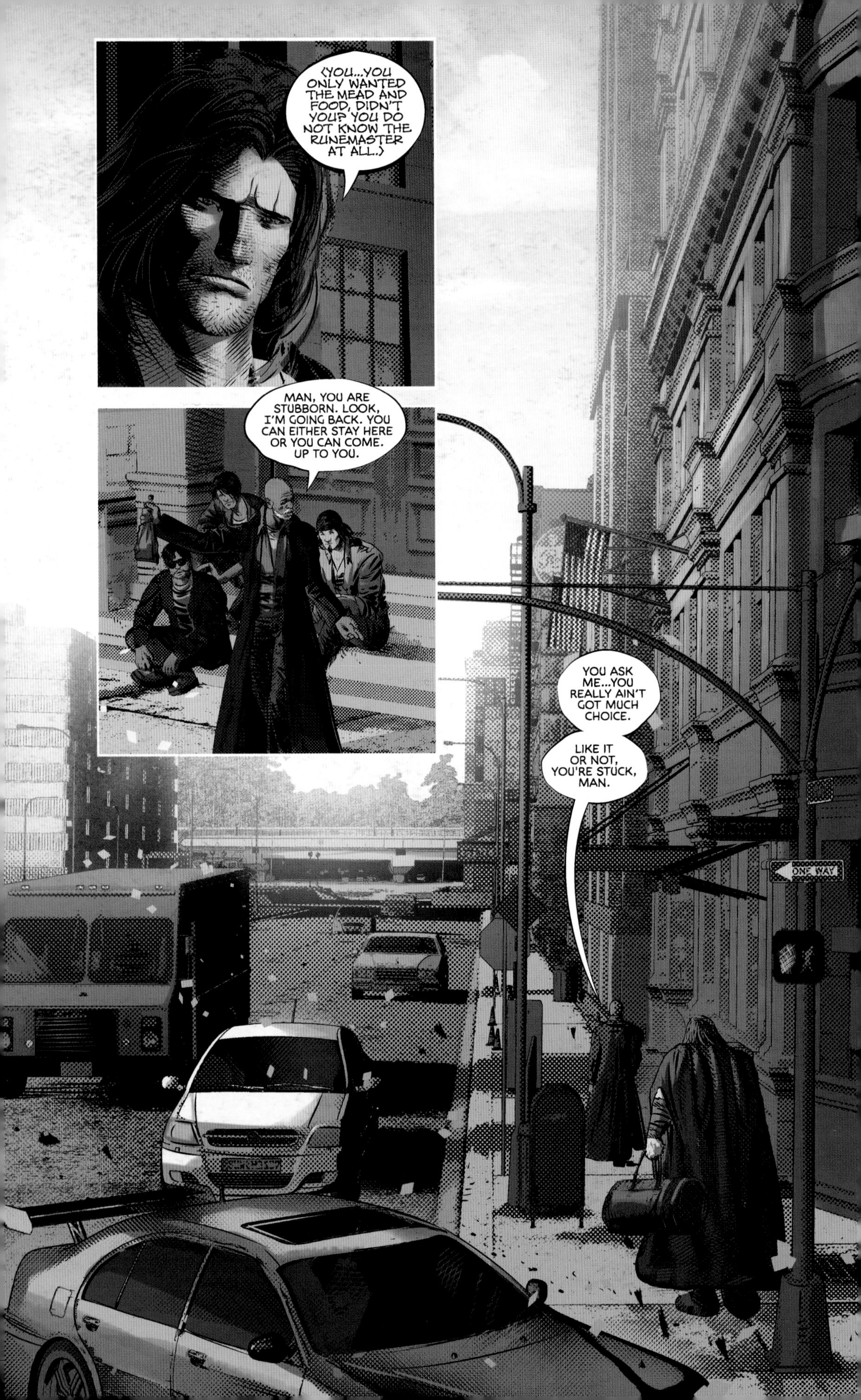
<YOU...YOU ONLY WANTED THE MEAD AND FOOD, DIDN'T YOU? YOU DO NOT KNOW THE RUNEMASTER AT ALL.>
MAN, YOU ARE STUBBORN. LOOK, I'M GOING BACK. YOU CAN EITHER STAY HERE OR YOU CAN COME. UP TO YOU.
YOU ASK ME...YOU REALLY AIN'T GOT MUCH CHOICE.
LIKE IT OR NOT, YOU'RE STUCK, MAN.
ONE WAY

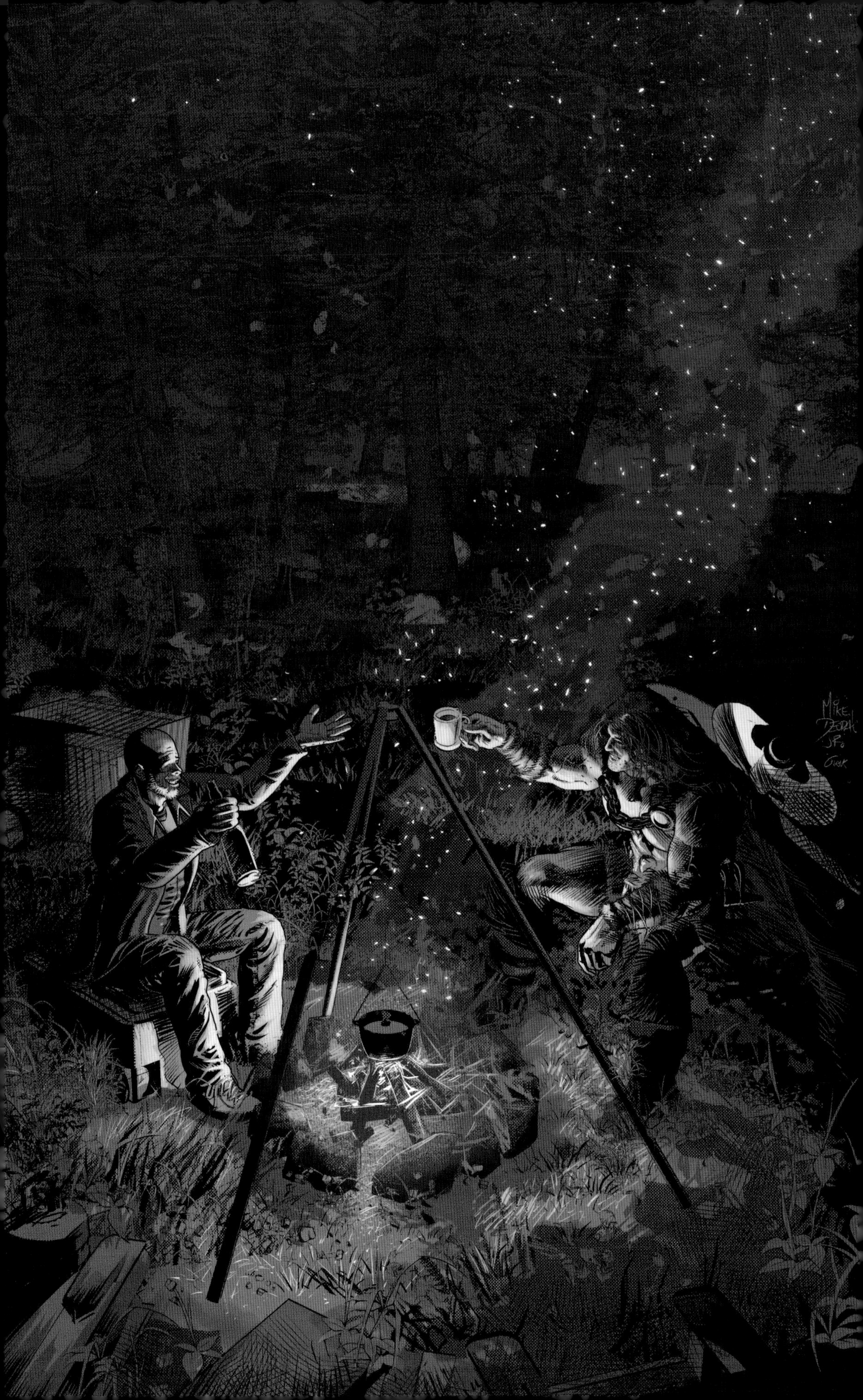

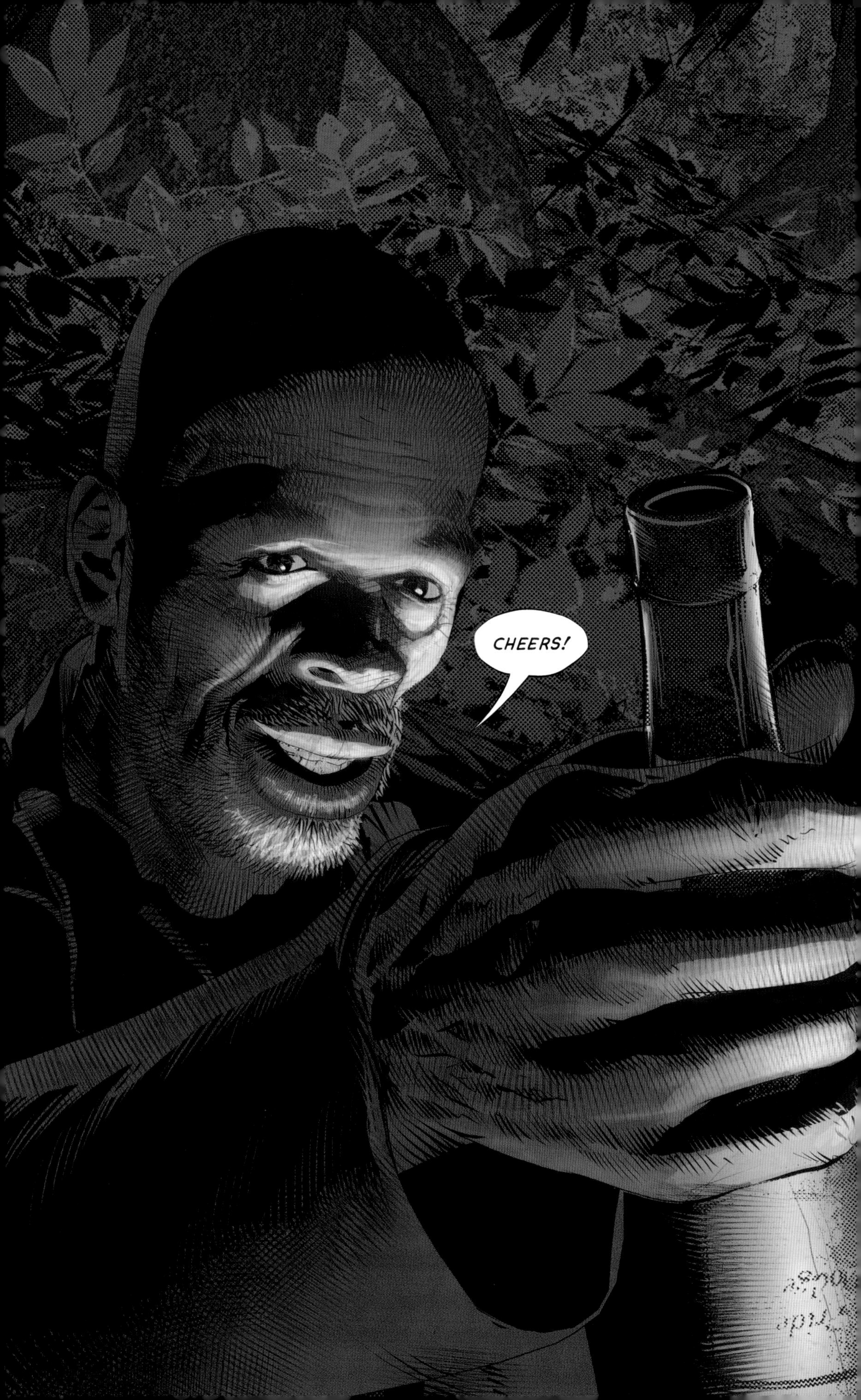
CHEERS!

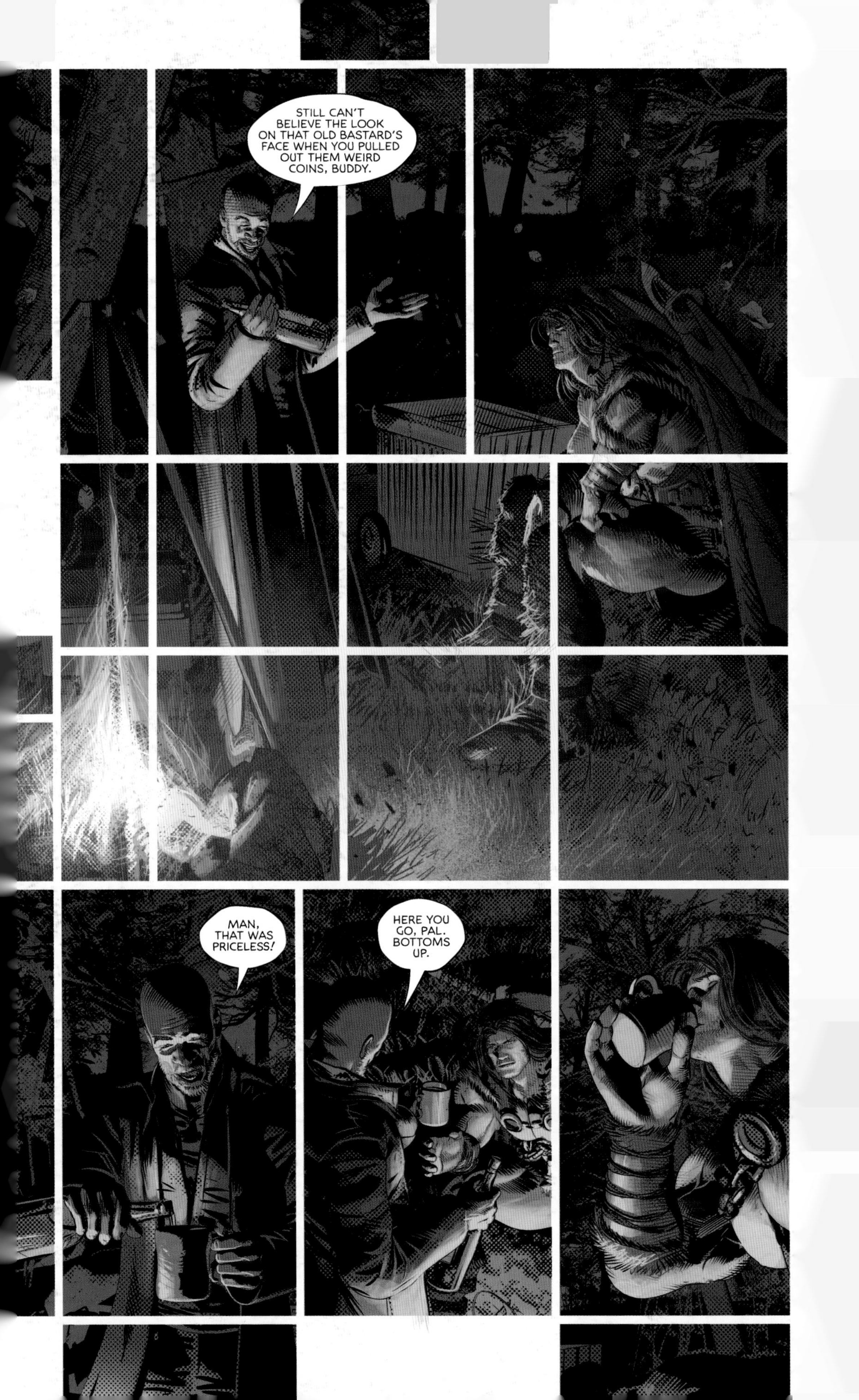
STILL CAN'T BELIEVE THE LOOK ON THAT OLD BASTARD'S FACE WHEN YOU PULLED OUT THEM WEIRD COINS, BUDDY.
MAN, THAT WAS PRICELESS!
HERE YOU GO, PAL. BOTTOMS UP.

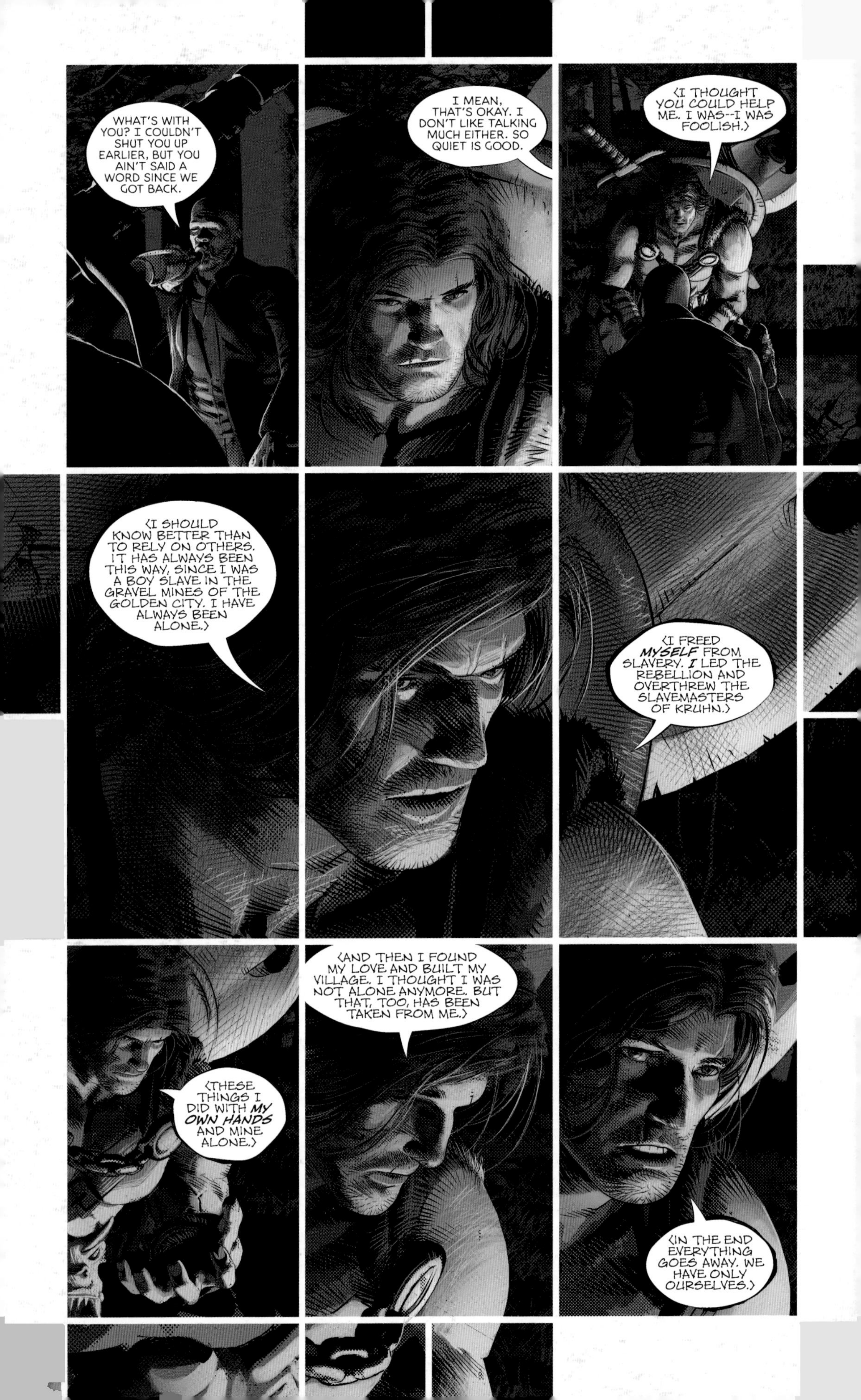
WHAT'S WITH YOU? I COULDN'T SHUT YOU UP EARLIER, BUT YOU AIN'T SAID A WORD SINCE WE GOT BACK.
I MEAN, THAT'S OKAY. I DON'T LIKE TALKING MUCH EITHER. SO QUIET IS GOOD.
‹I THOUGHT YOU COULD HELP ME. I WAS--I WAS FOOLISH.›
‹I SHOULD KNOW BETTER THAN TO RELY ON OTHERS. IT HAS ALWAYS BEEN THIS WAY, SINCE I WAS A BOY SLAVE IN THE GRAVEL MINES OF THE GOLDEN CITY. I HAVE ALWAYS BEEN ALONE.›
‹I FREED *MYSELF* FROM SLAVERY. *I* LED THE REBELLION AND OVERTHREW THE SLAVEMASTERS OF KRUHN.›
‹THESE THINGS I DID WITH *MY OWN HANDS* AND MINE ALONE.›
‹AND THEN I FOUND MY LOVE AND BUILT MY VILLAGE. I THOUGHT I WAS NOT ALONE ANYMORE. BUT THAT, TOO, HAS BEEN TAKEN FROM ME.›
‹IN THE END EVERYTHING GOES AWAY. WE HAVE ONLY OURSELVES.›

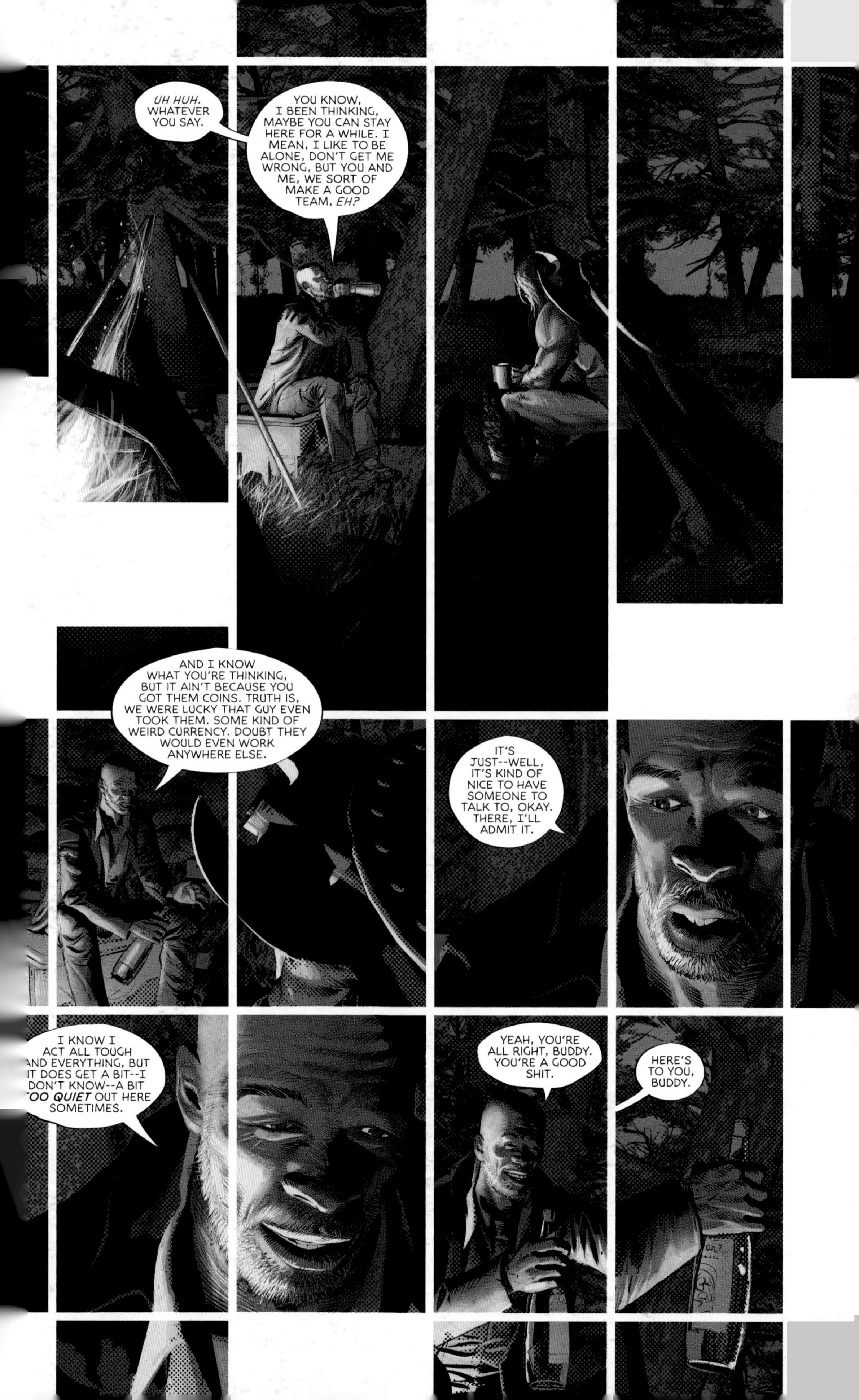
UH HUH. WHATEVER YOU SAY.
YOU KNOW, I BEEN THINKING, MAYBE YOU CAN STAY HERE FOR A WHILE. I MEAN, I LIKE TO BE ALONE, DON'T GET ME WRONG, BUT YOU AND ME, WE SORT OF MAKE A GOOD TEAM, EH?
AND I KNOW WHAT YOU'RE THINKING, BUT IT AIN'T BECAUSE YOU GOT THEM COINS. TRUTH IS, WE WERE LUCKY THAT GUY EVEN TOOK THEM. SOME KIND OF WEIRD CURRENCY. DOUBT THEY WOULD EVEN WORK ANYWHERE ELSE.
IT'S JUST--WELL, IT'S KIND OF NICE TO HAVE SOMEONE TO TALK TO, OKAY. THERE, I'LL ADMIT IT.
I KNOW I ACT ALL TOUGH AND EVERYTHING, BUT IT DOES GET A BIT--I DON'T KNOW--A BIT TOO QUIET OUT HERE SOMETIMES.
YEAH, YOU'RE ALL RIGHT, BUDDY. YOU'RE A GOOD SHIT.
HERE'S TO YOU, BUDDY.

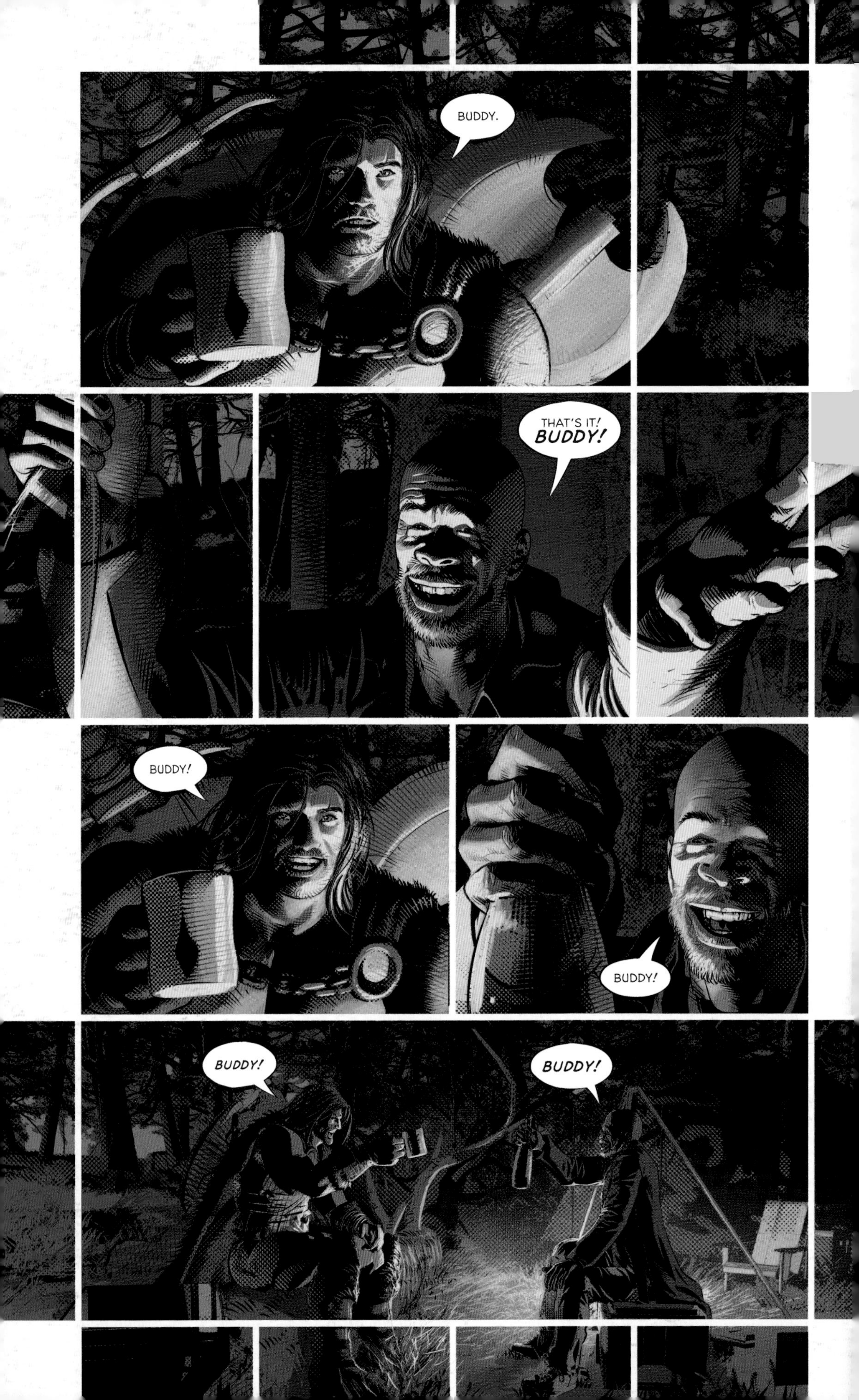
BUDDY.
THAT'S IT! BUDDY!
BUDDY!
BUDDY!
BUDDY!
BUDDY!

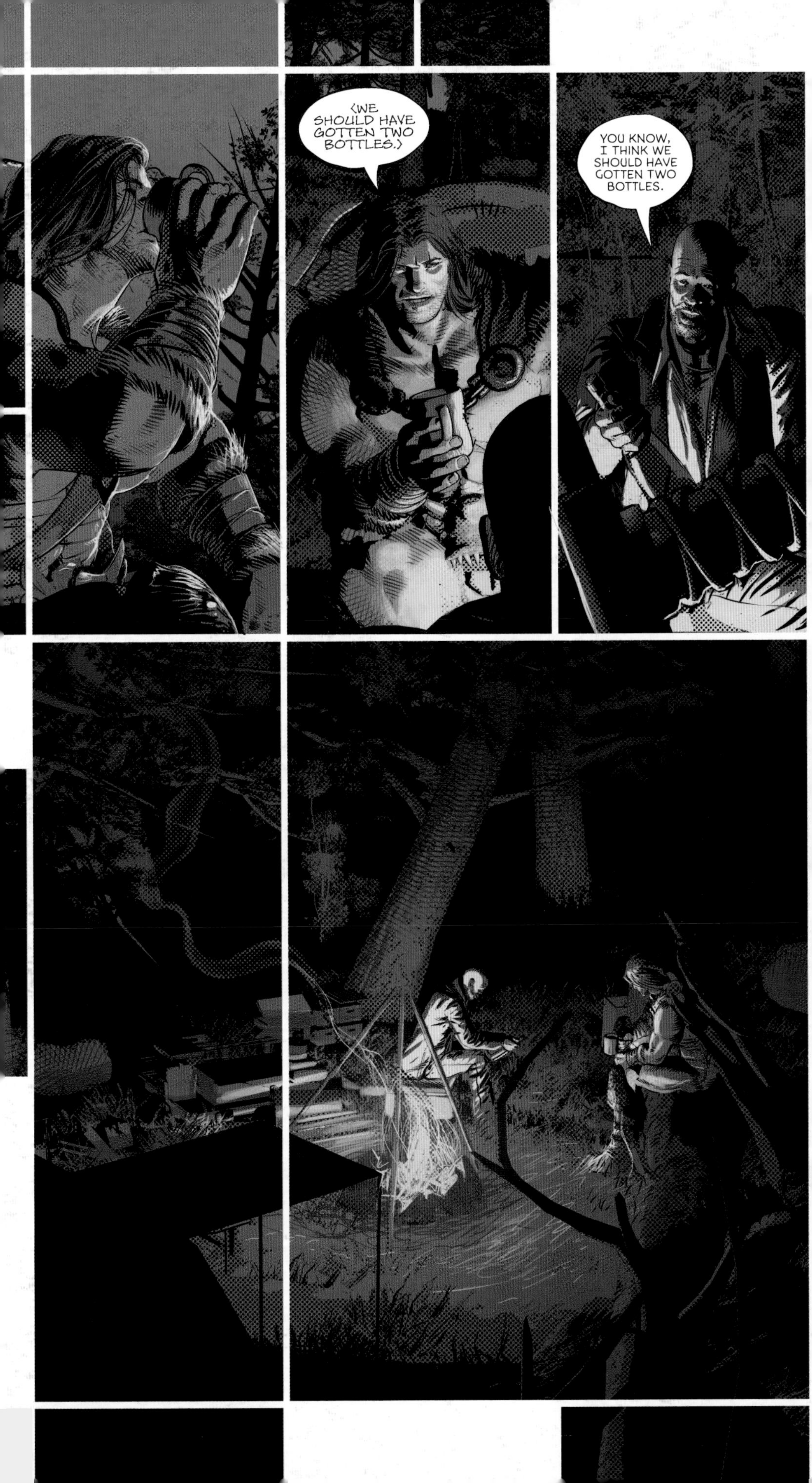
⟨WE SHOULD HAVE GOTTEN TWO BOTTLES.⟩
YOU KNOW, I THINK WE SHOULD HAVE GOTTEN TWO BOTTLES.

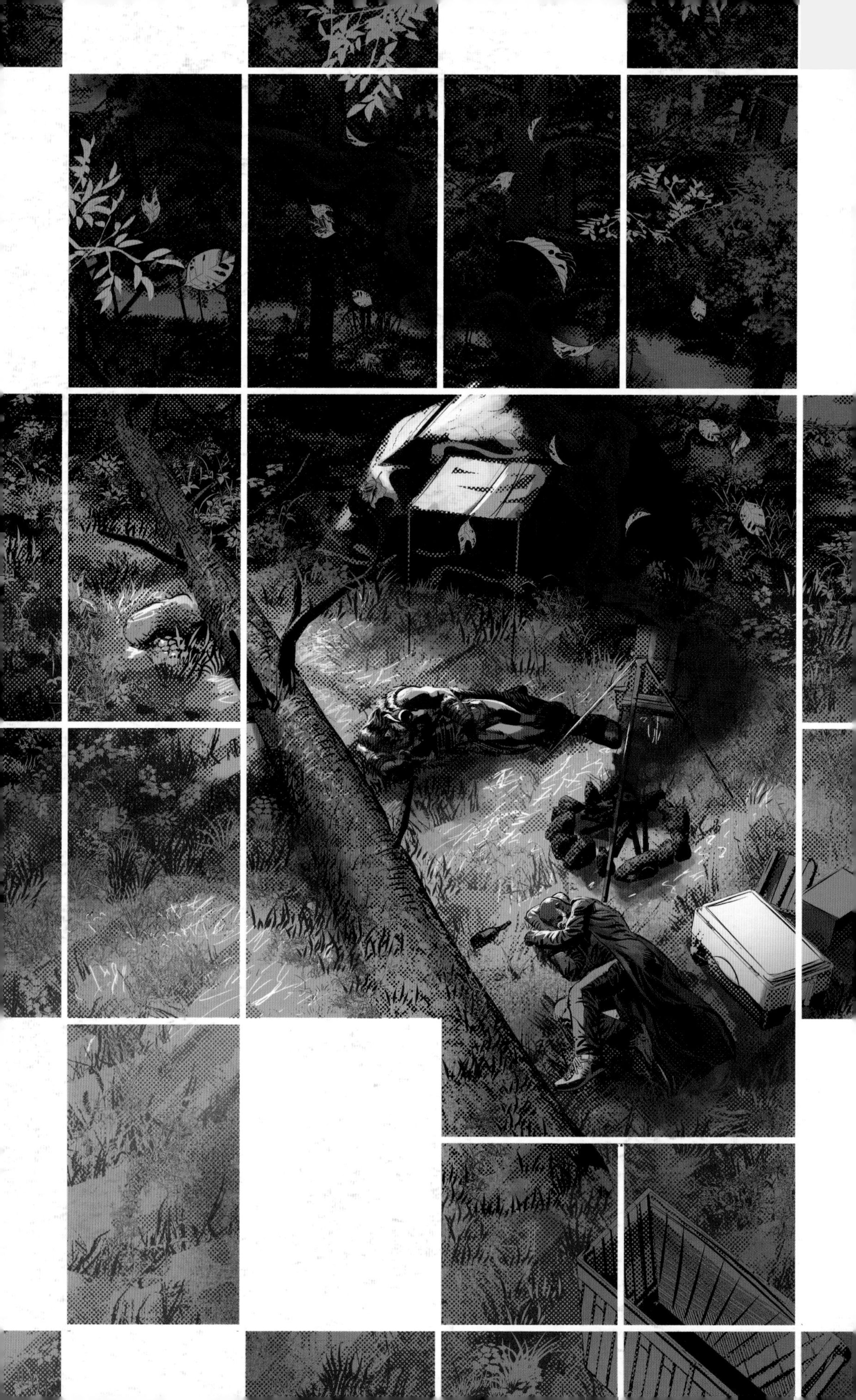

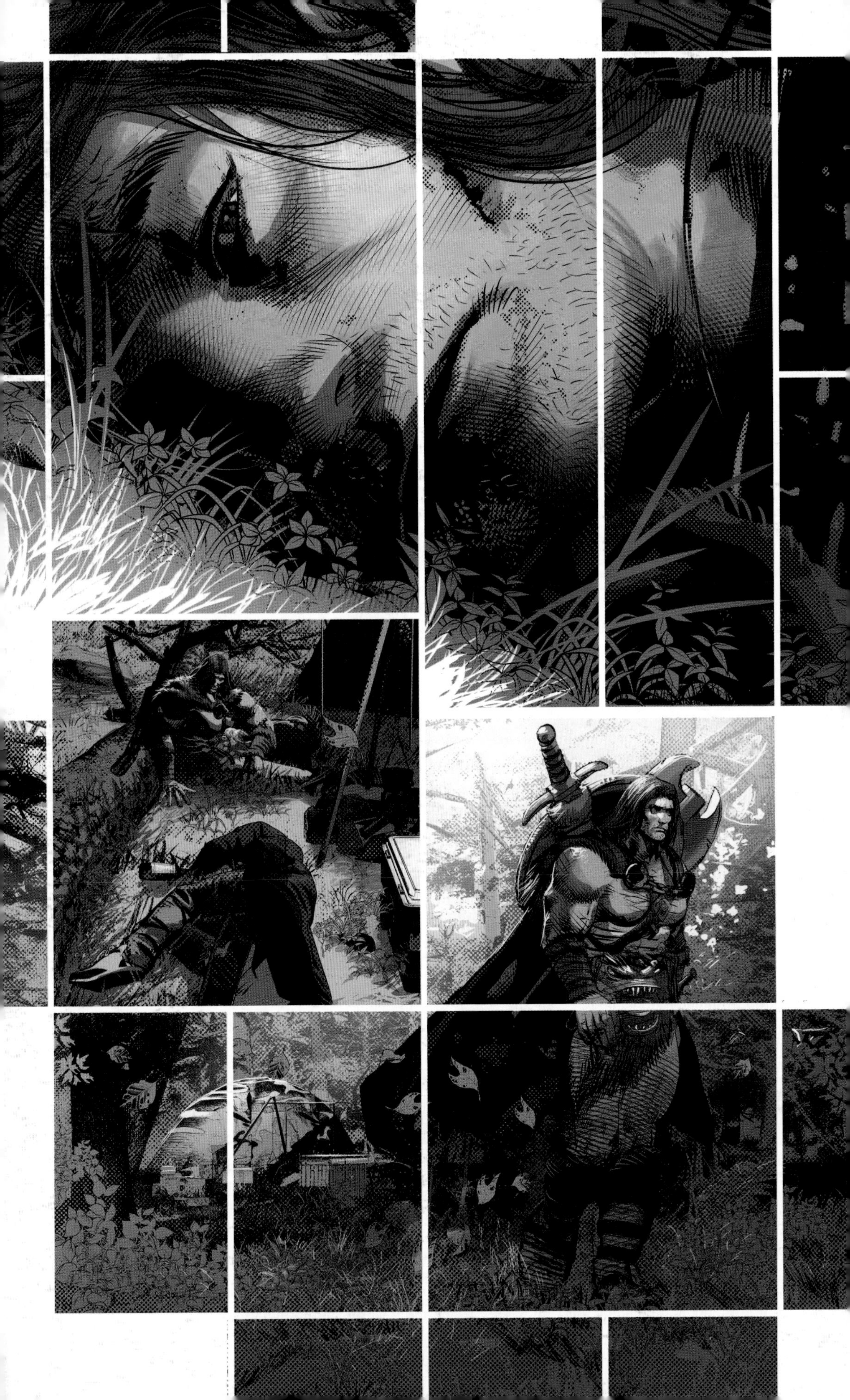

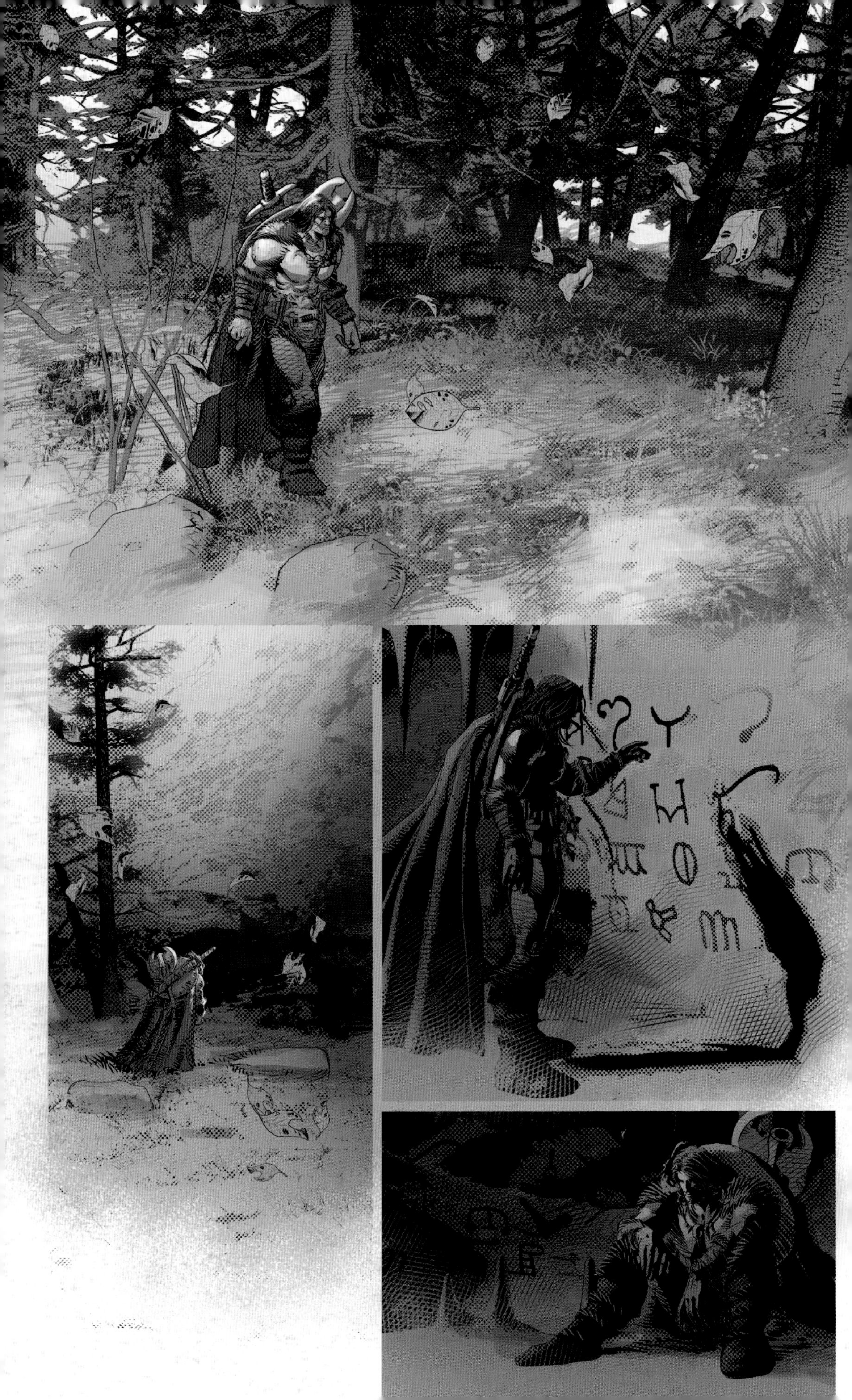

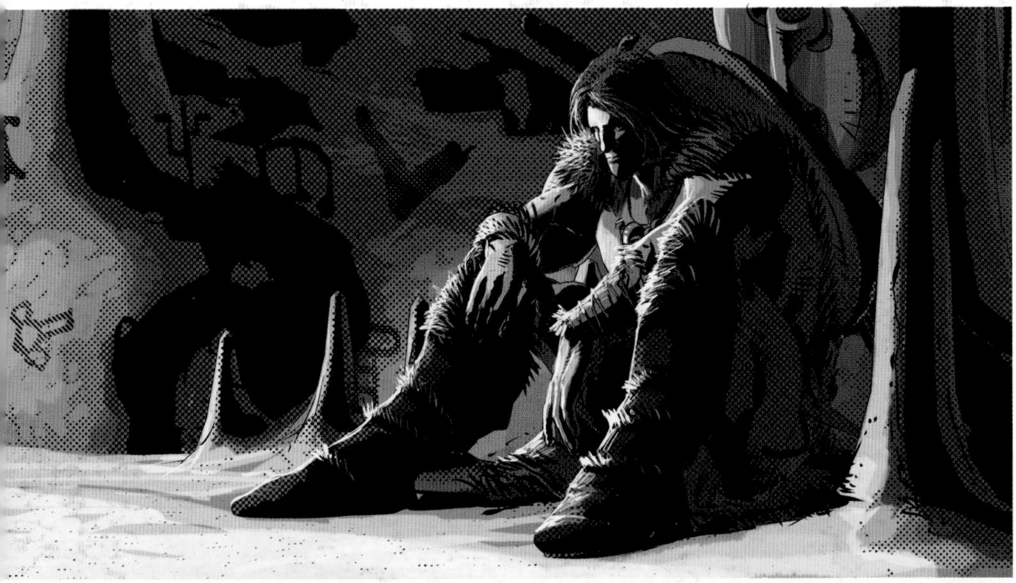

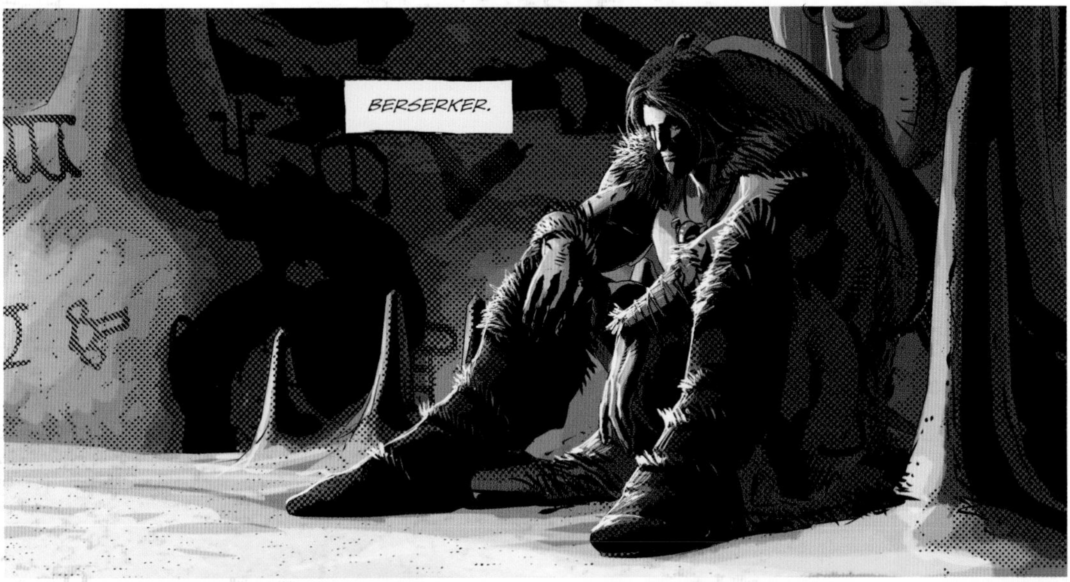
BERSERKER.

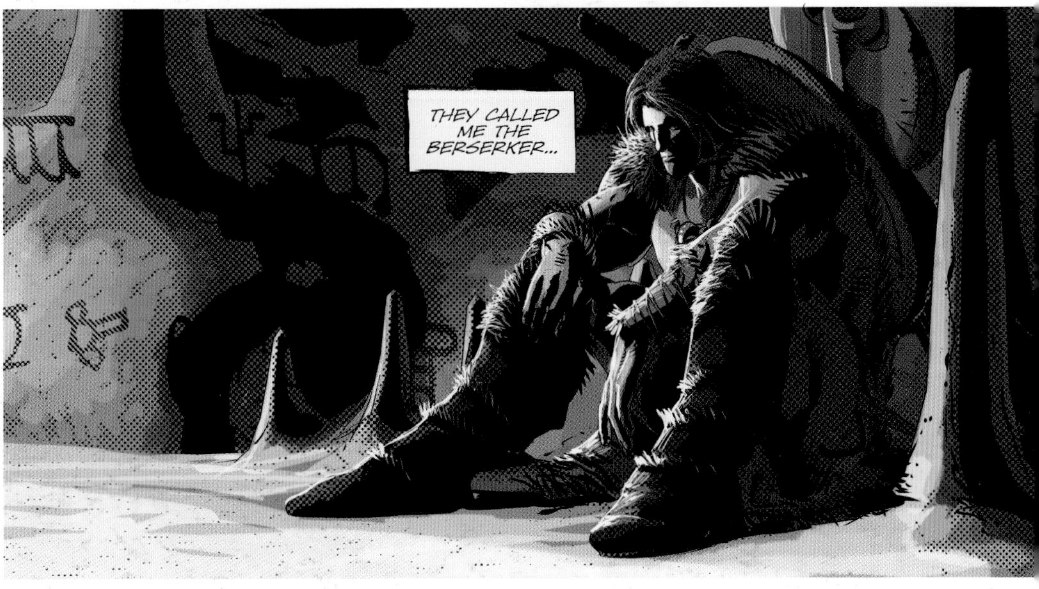
THEY CALLED ME THE BERSERKER...

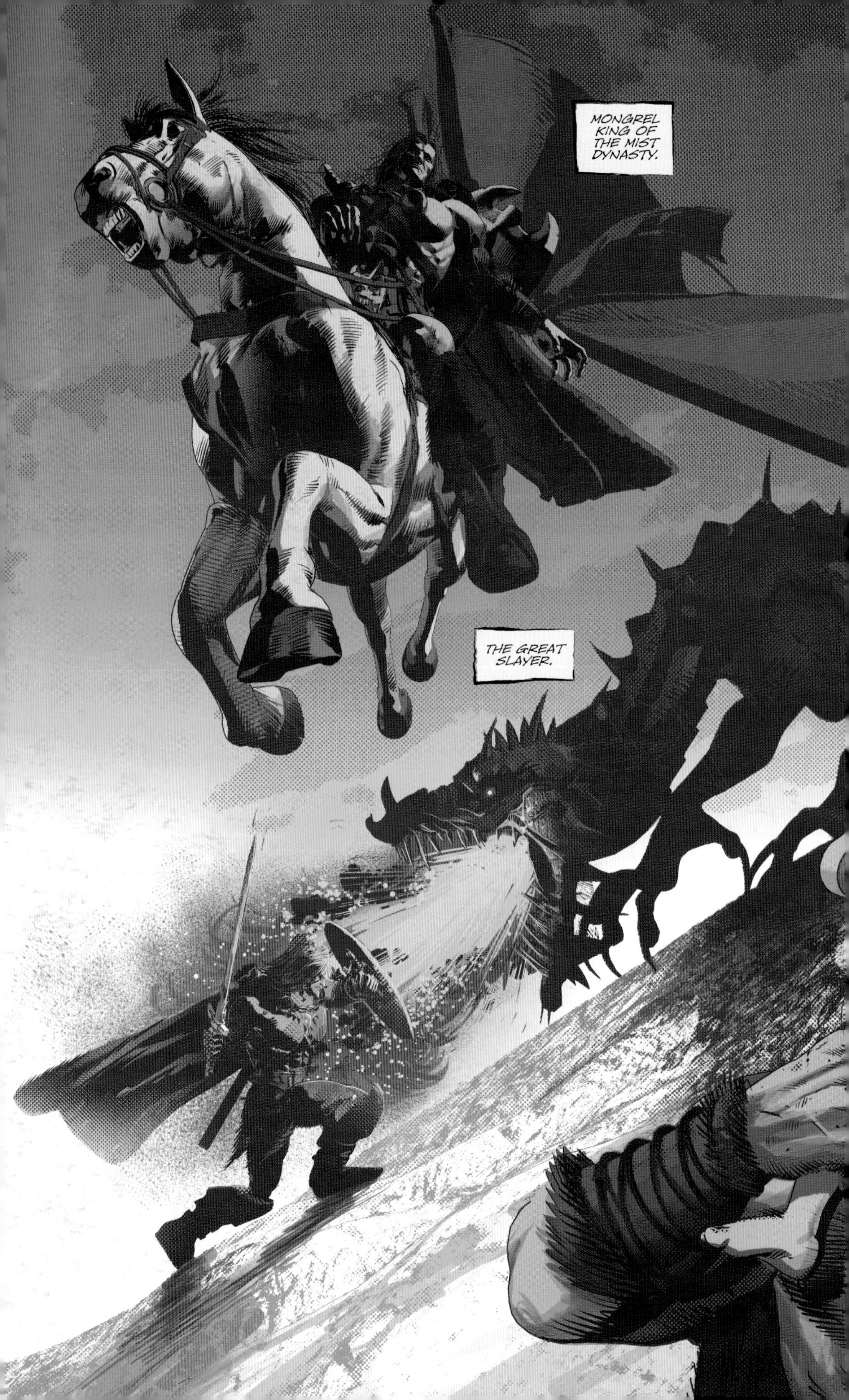
MONGREL KING OF THE MIST DYNASTY.
THE GREAT SLAYER.

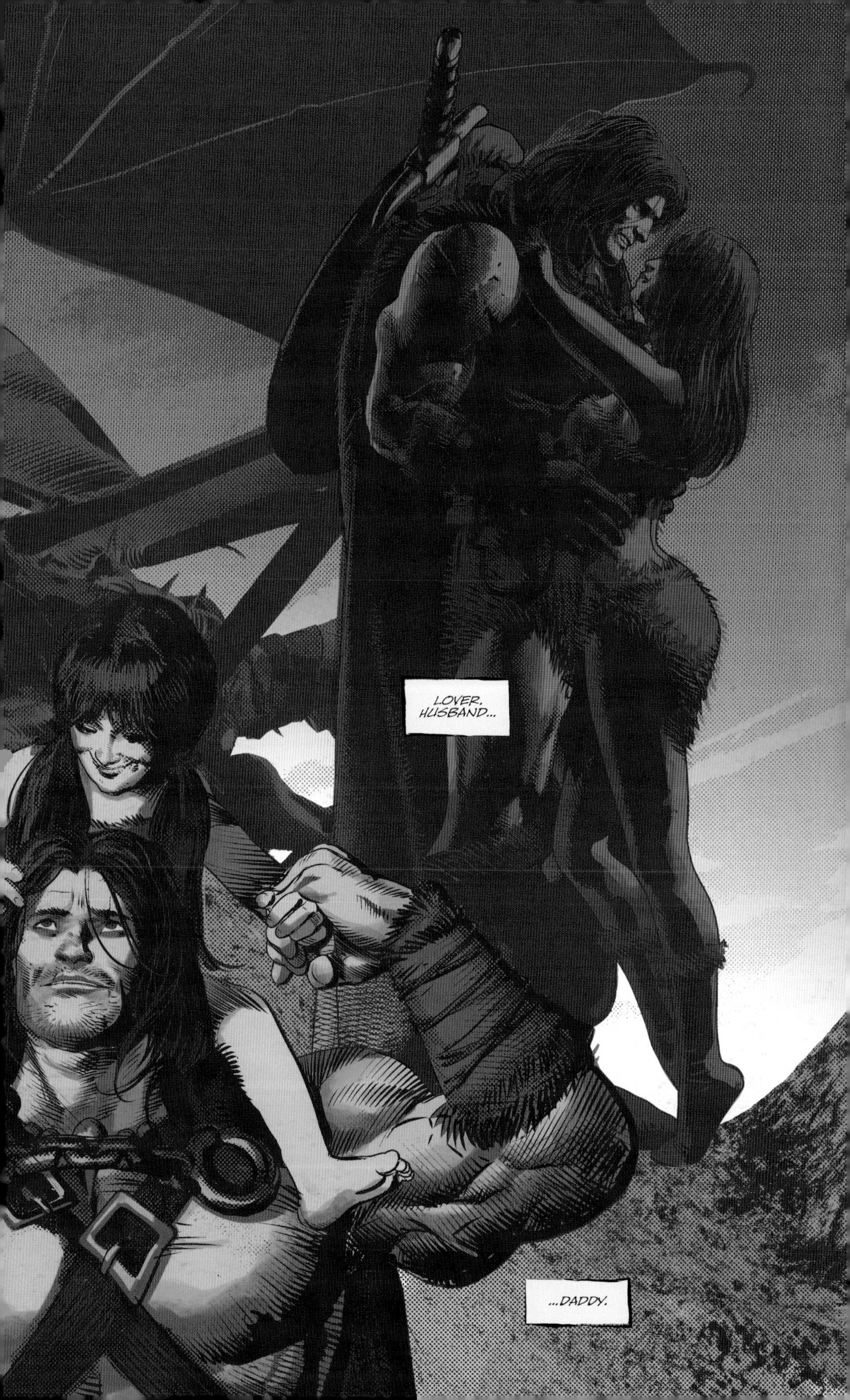
LOVER. HUSBAND...
...DADDY.

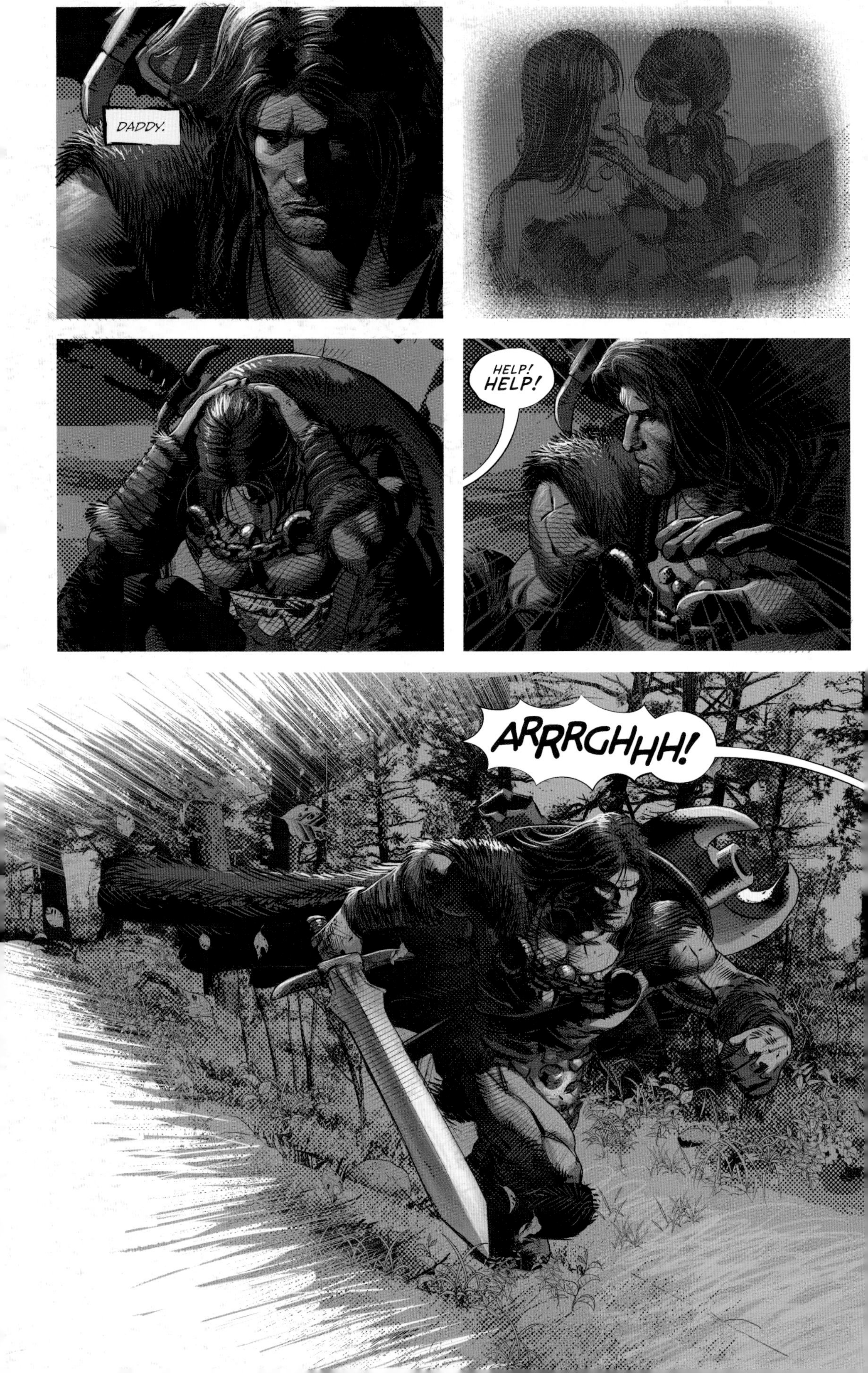
DADDY.
HELP! HELP!
ARRRGHHH!

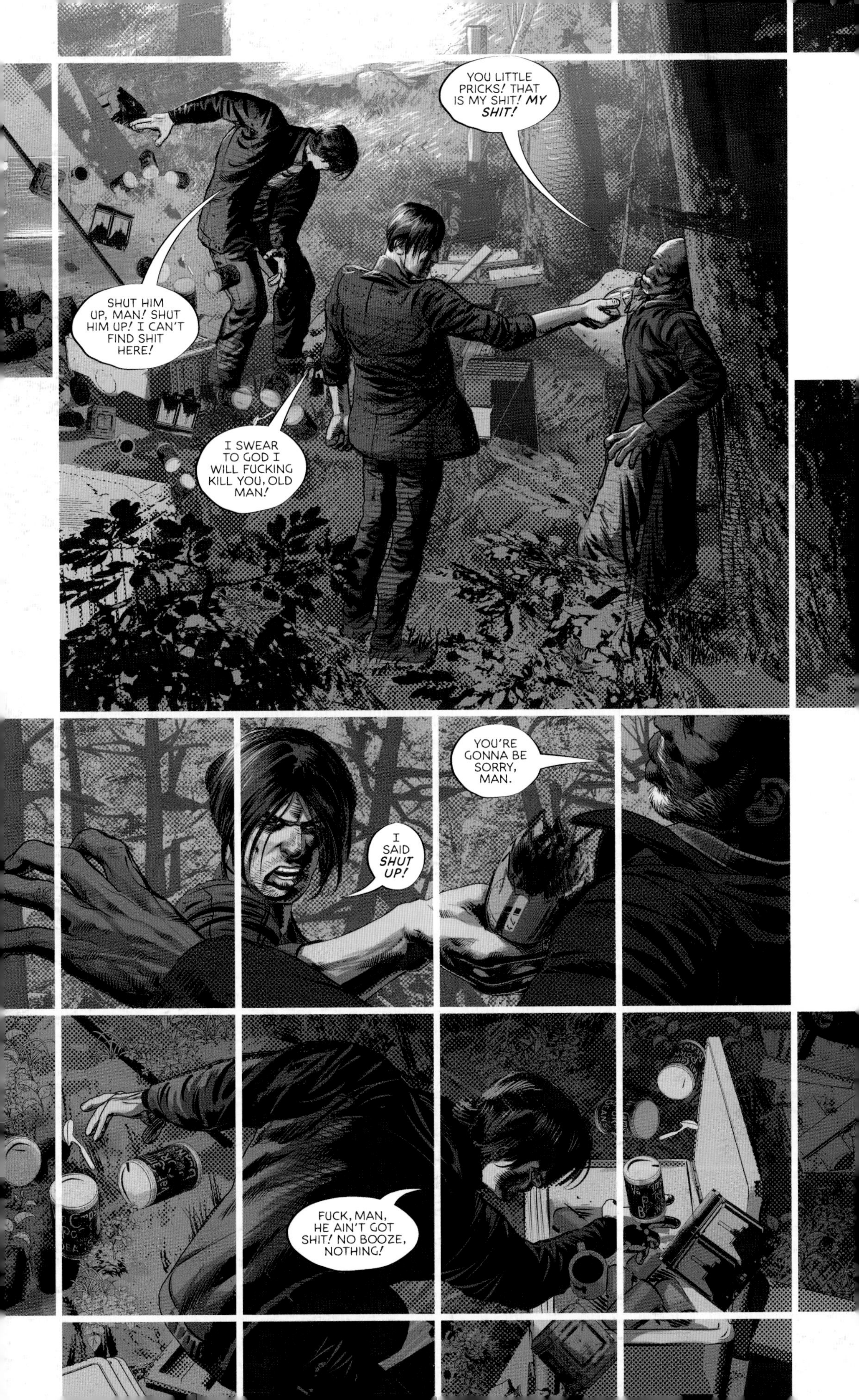
YOU LITTLE PRICKS! THAT IS MY SHIT! MY SHIT!
SHUT HIM UP, MAN! SHUT HIM UP! I CAN'T FIND SHIT HERE!
I SWEAR TO GOD I WILL FUCKING KILL YOU, OLD MAN!
YOU'RE GONNA BE SORRY, MAN.
I SAID SHUT UP!
FUCK, MAN, HE AIN'T GOT SHIT! NO BOOZE, NOTHING!

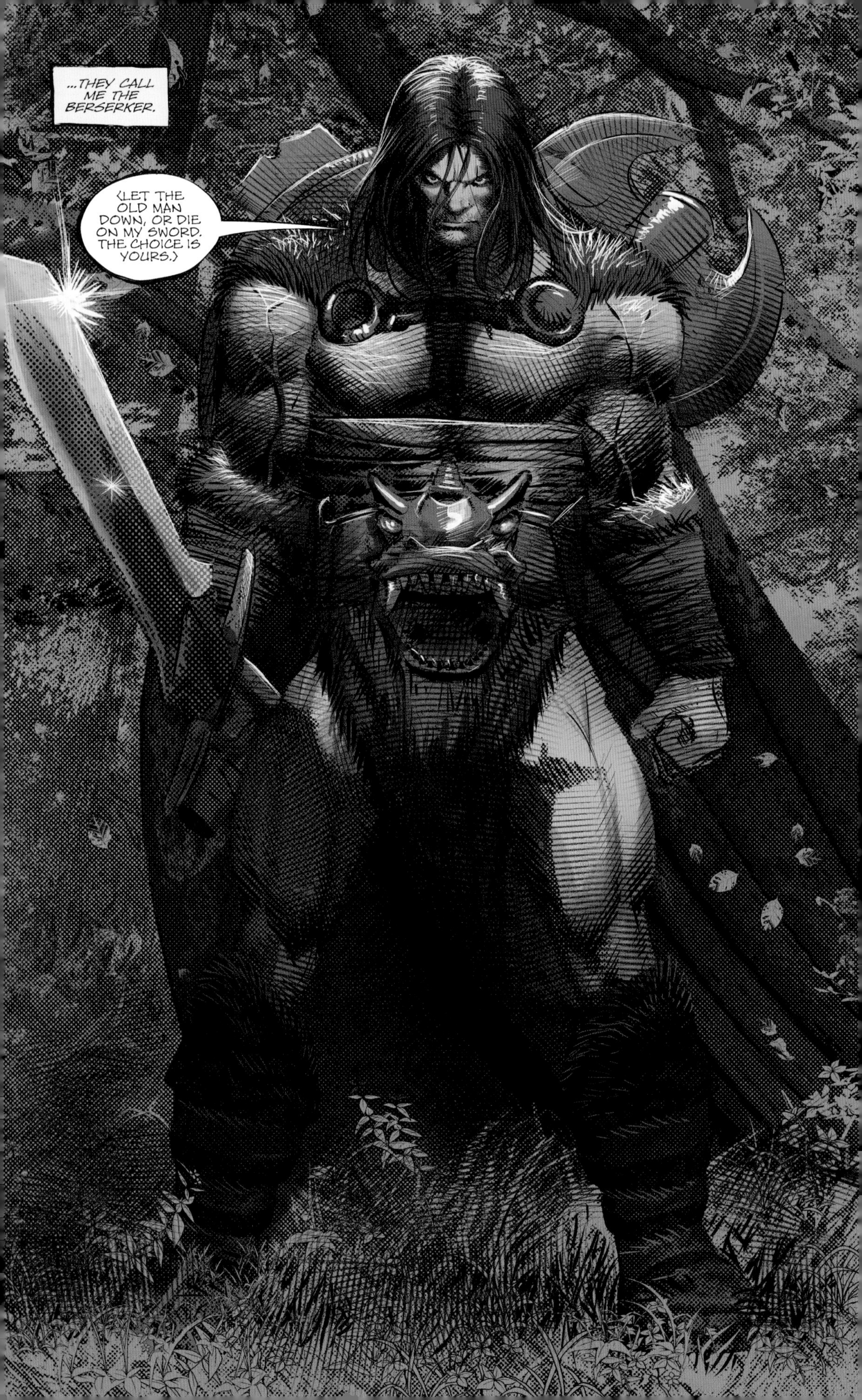
...THEY CALL ME THE BERSERKER.
‹LET THE OLD MAN DOWN, OR DIE ON MY SWORD. THE CHOICE IS YOURS.›

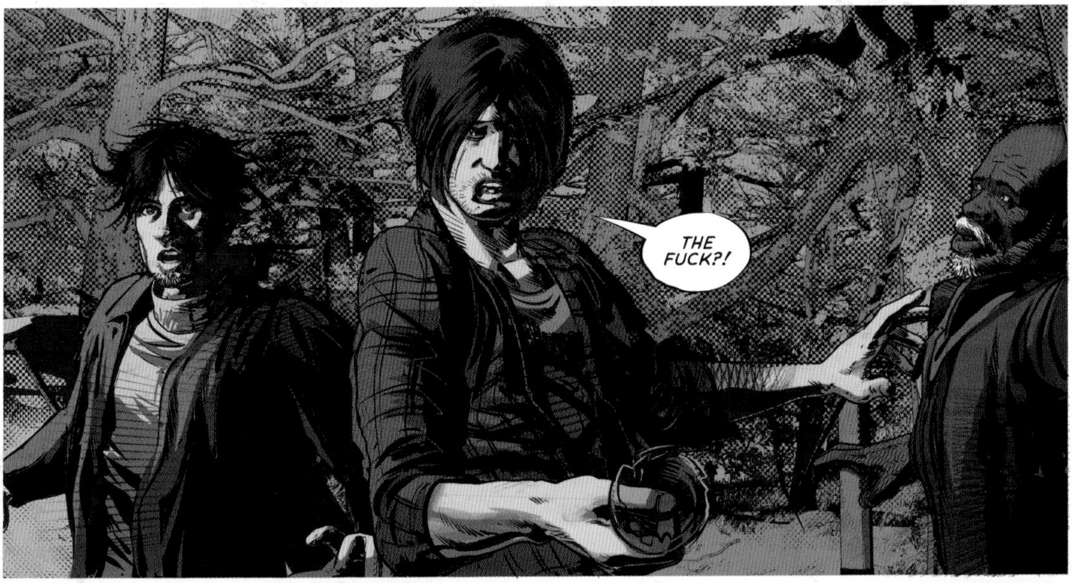
THE FUCK?!

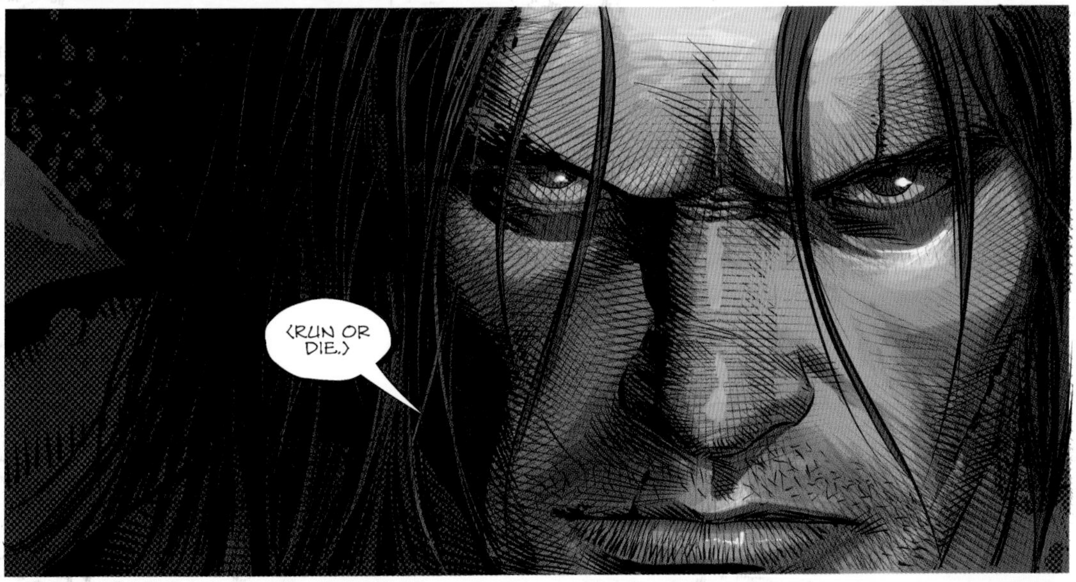
<RUN OR DIE.>

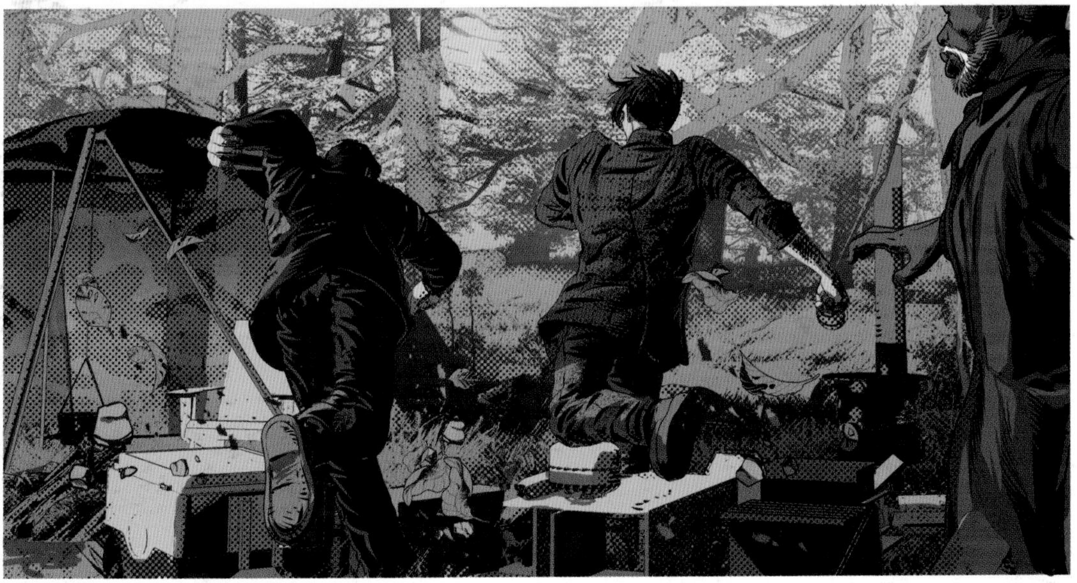

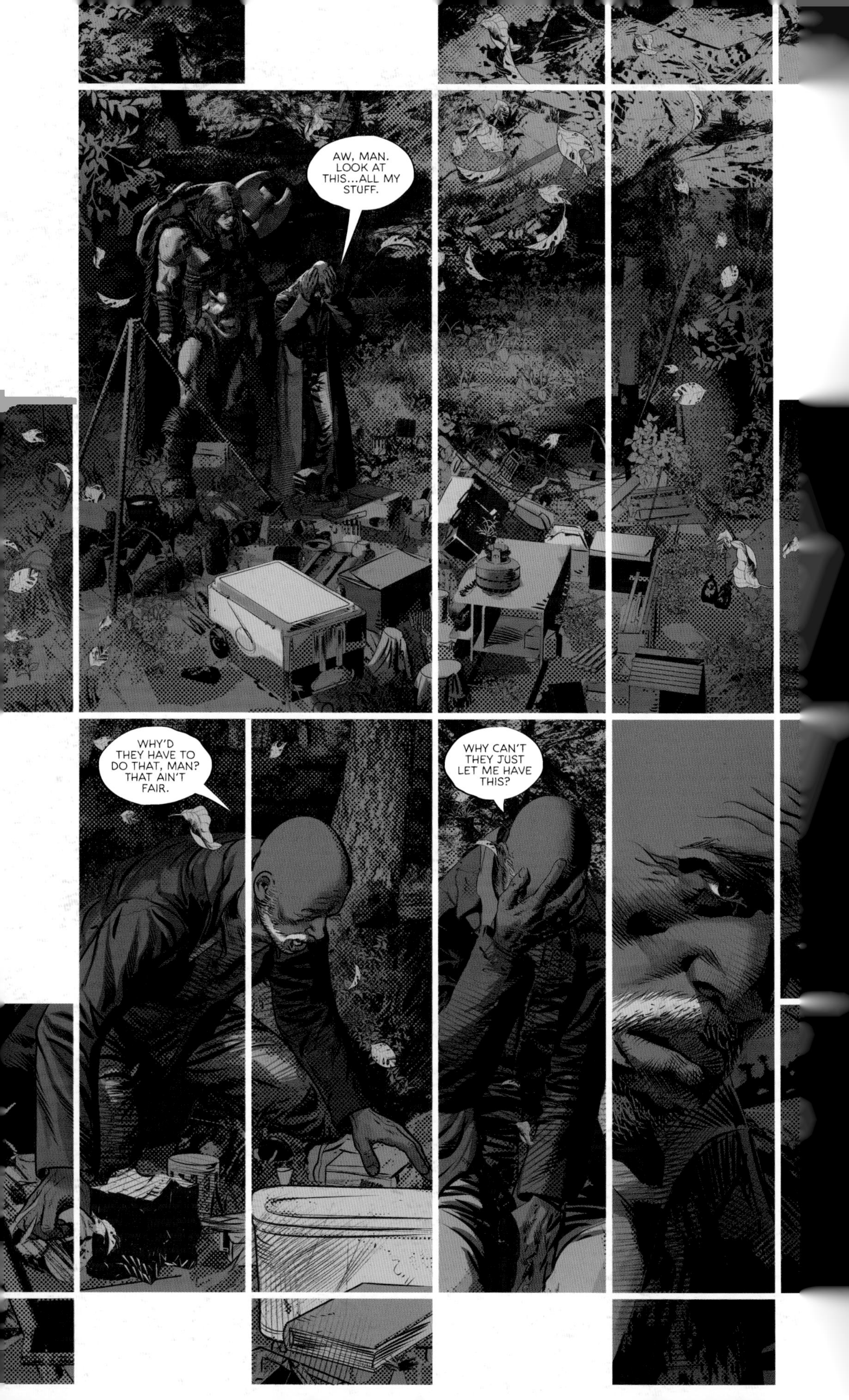
AW, MAN. LOOK AT THIS...ALL MY STUFF.
WHY'D THEY HAVE TO DO THAT, MAN? THAT AIN'T FAIR.
WHY CAN'T THEY JUST LET ME HAVE THIS?

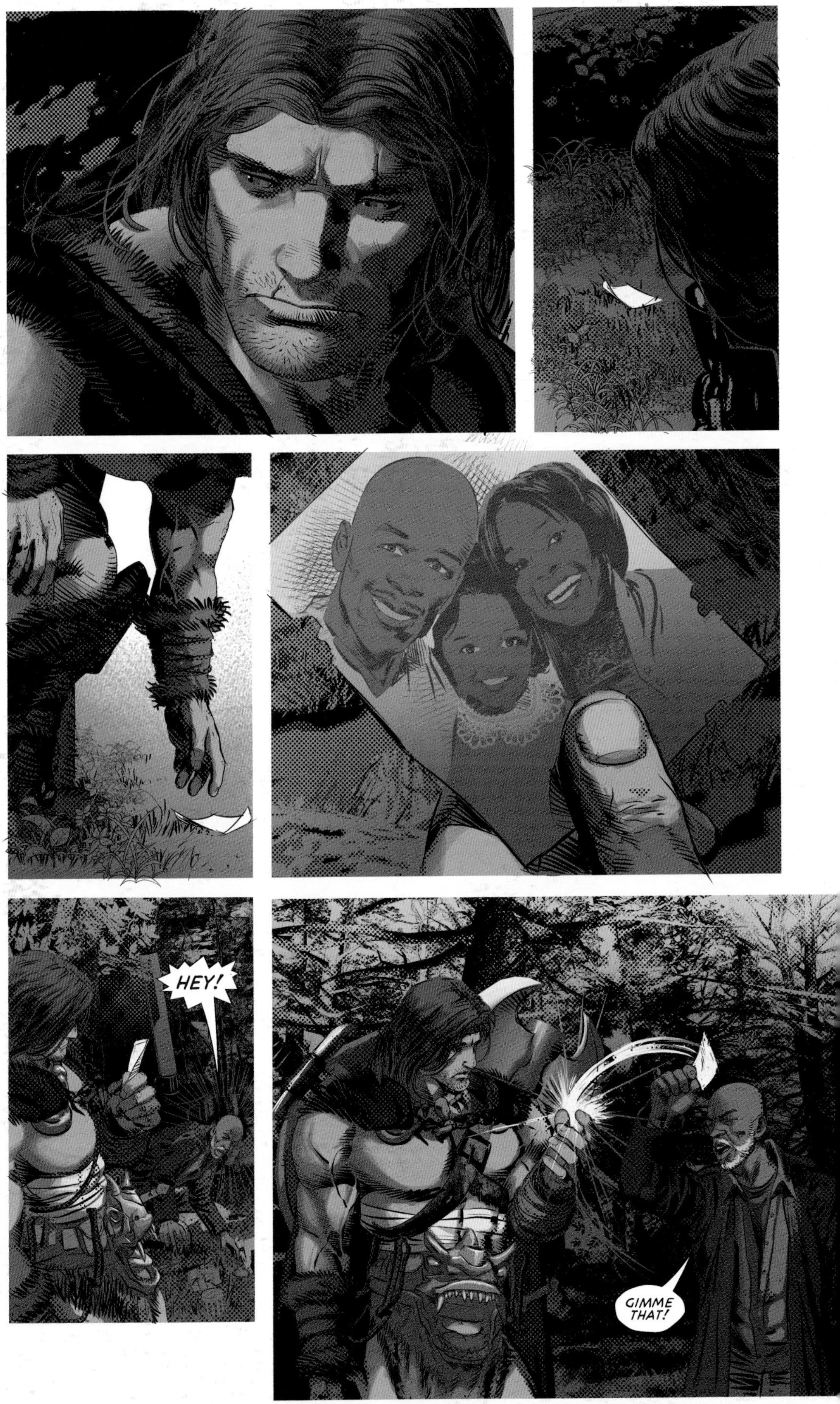

HEY!
GIMME THAT!

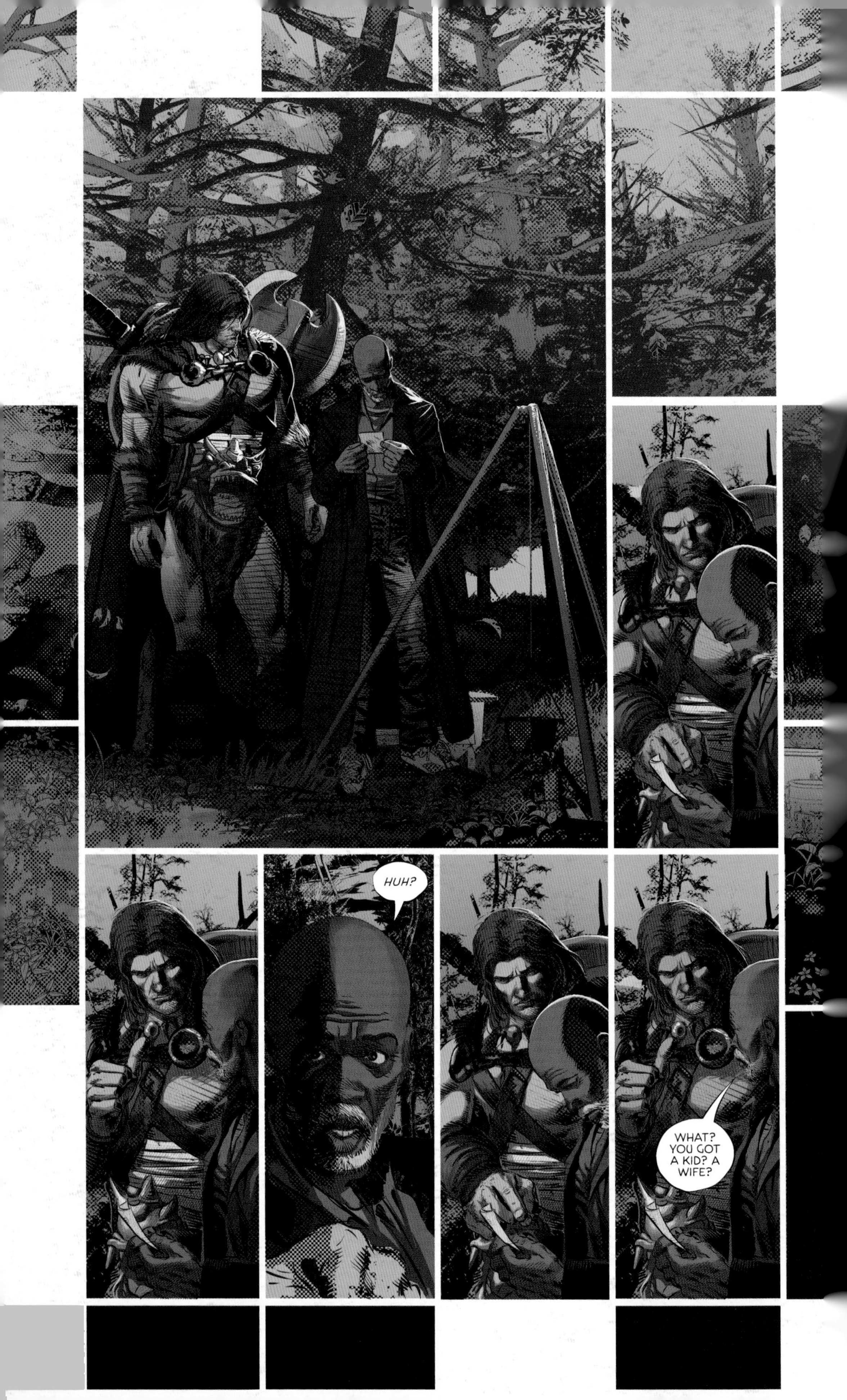
HUH?
WHAT? YOU GOT A KID? A WIFE?

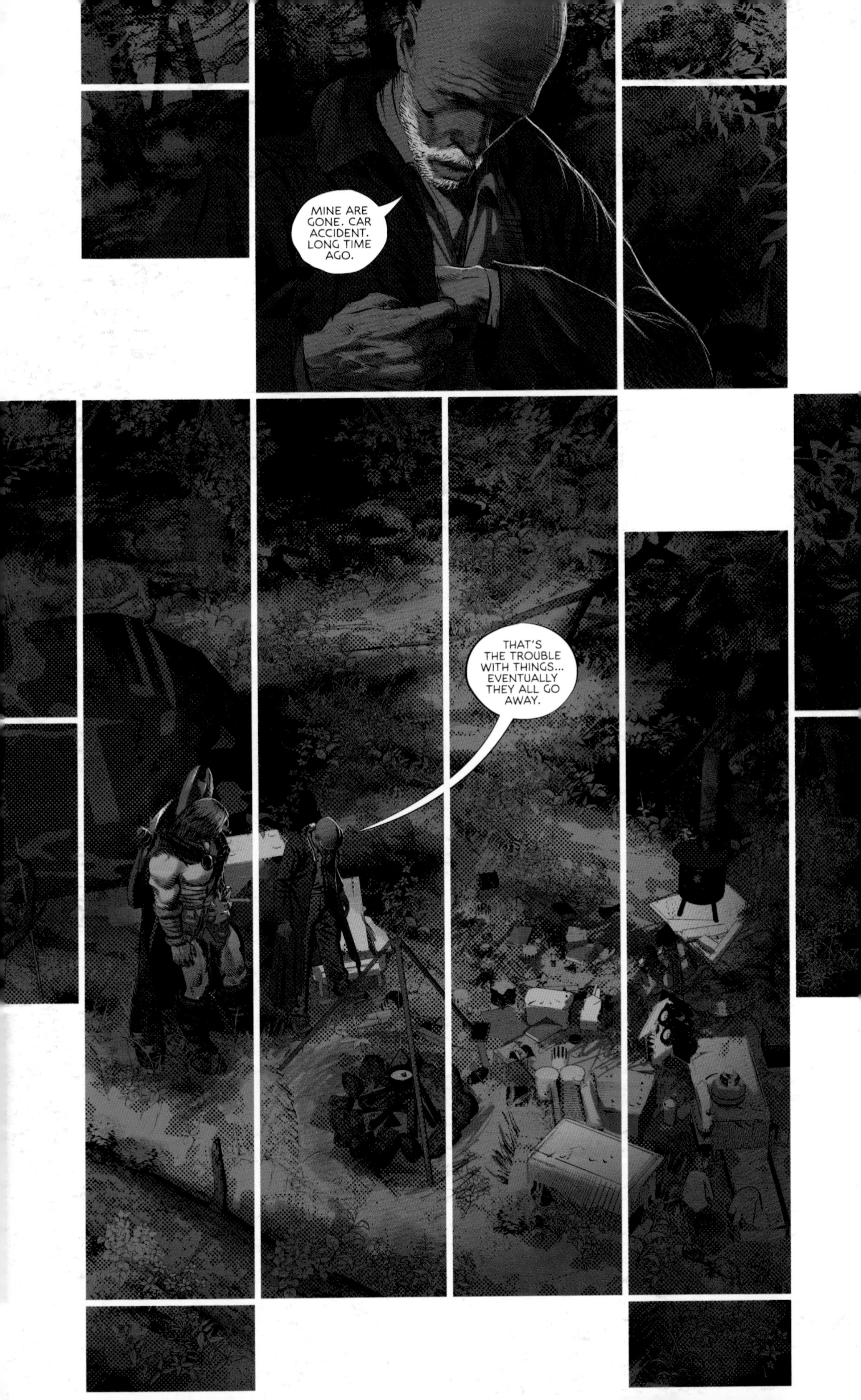
MINE ARE GONE. CAR ACCIDENT. LONG TIME AGO.
THAT'S THE TROUBLE WITH THINGS... EVENTUALLY THEY ALL GO AWAY.

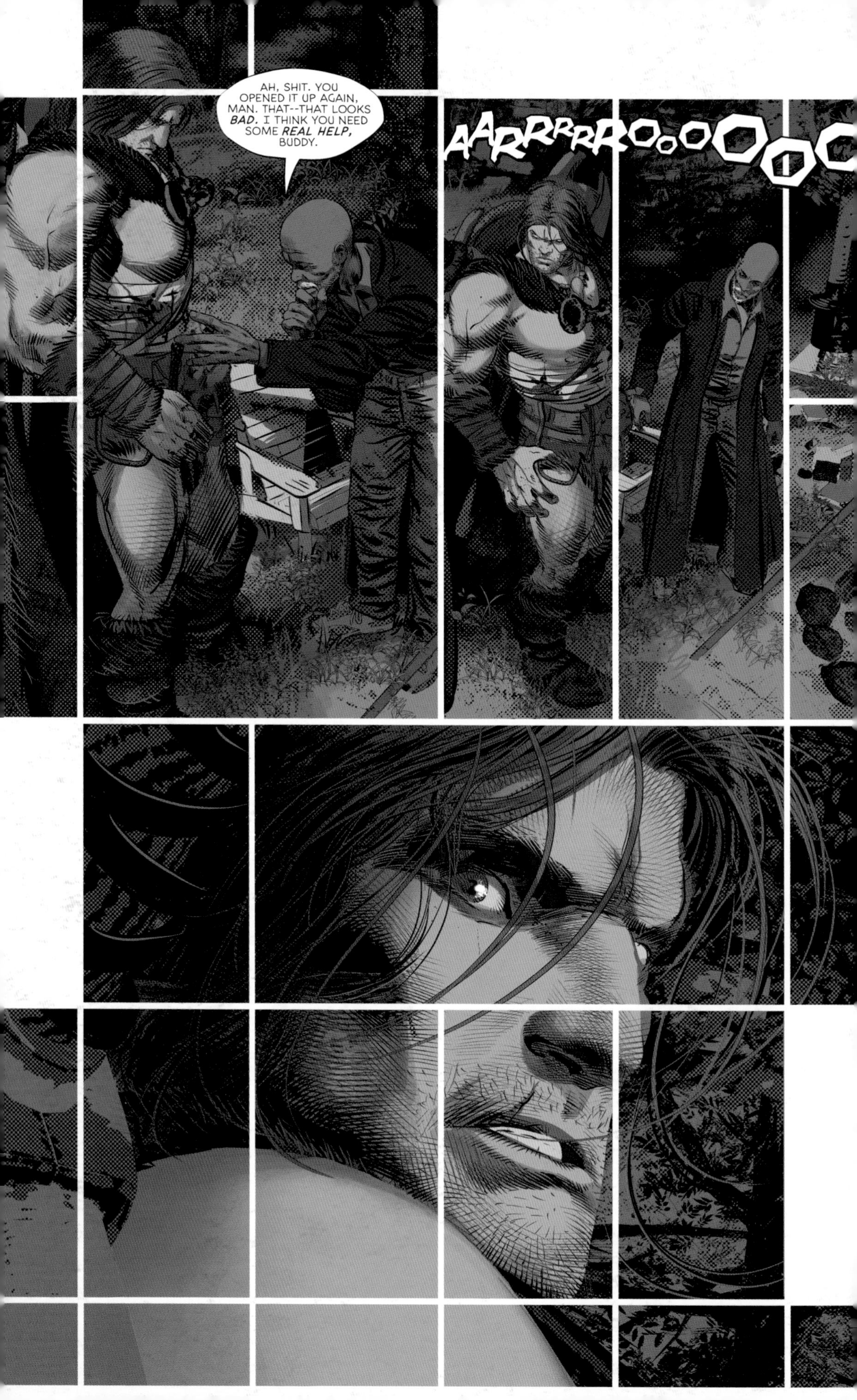
AH, SHIT. YOU OPENED IT UP AGAIN, MAN. THAT--THAT LOOKS BAD. I THINK YOU NEED SOME REAL HELP, BUDDY.
AARRRRROOOOOOO

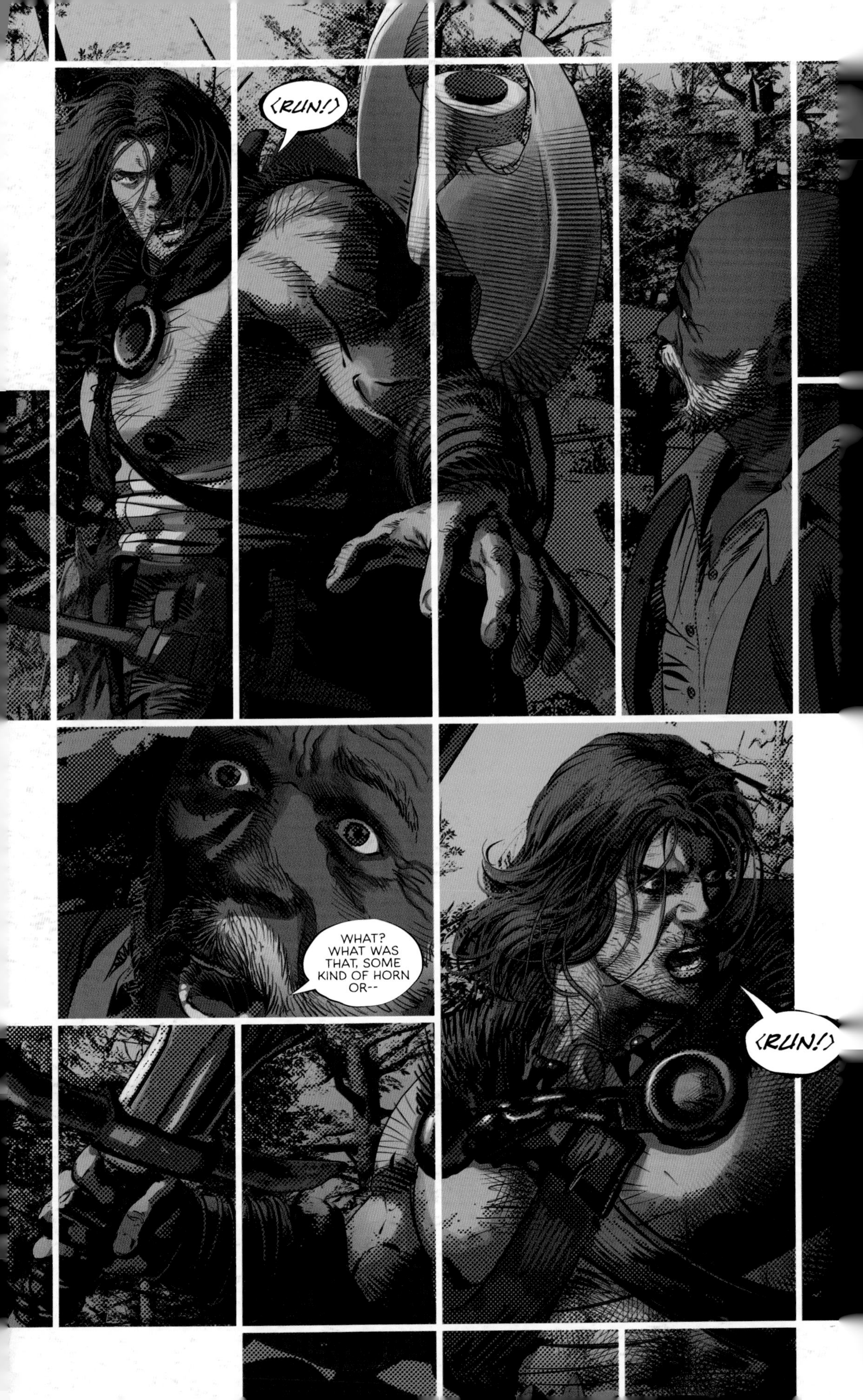

⟨RUN!⟩
WHAT? WHAT WAS THAT, SOME KIND OF HORN OR--
⟨RUN!⟩

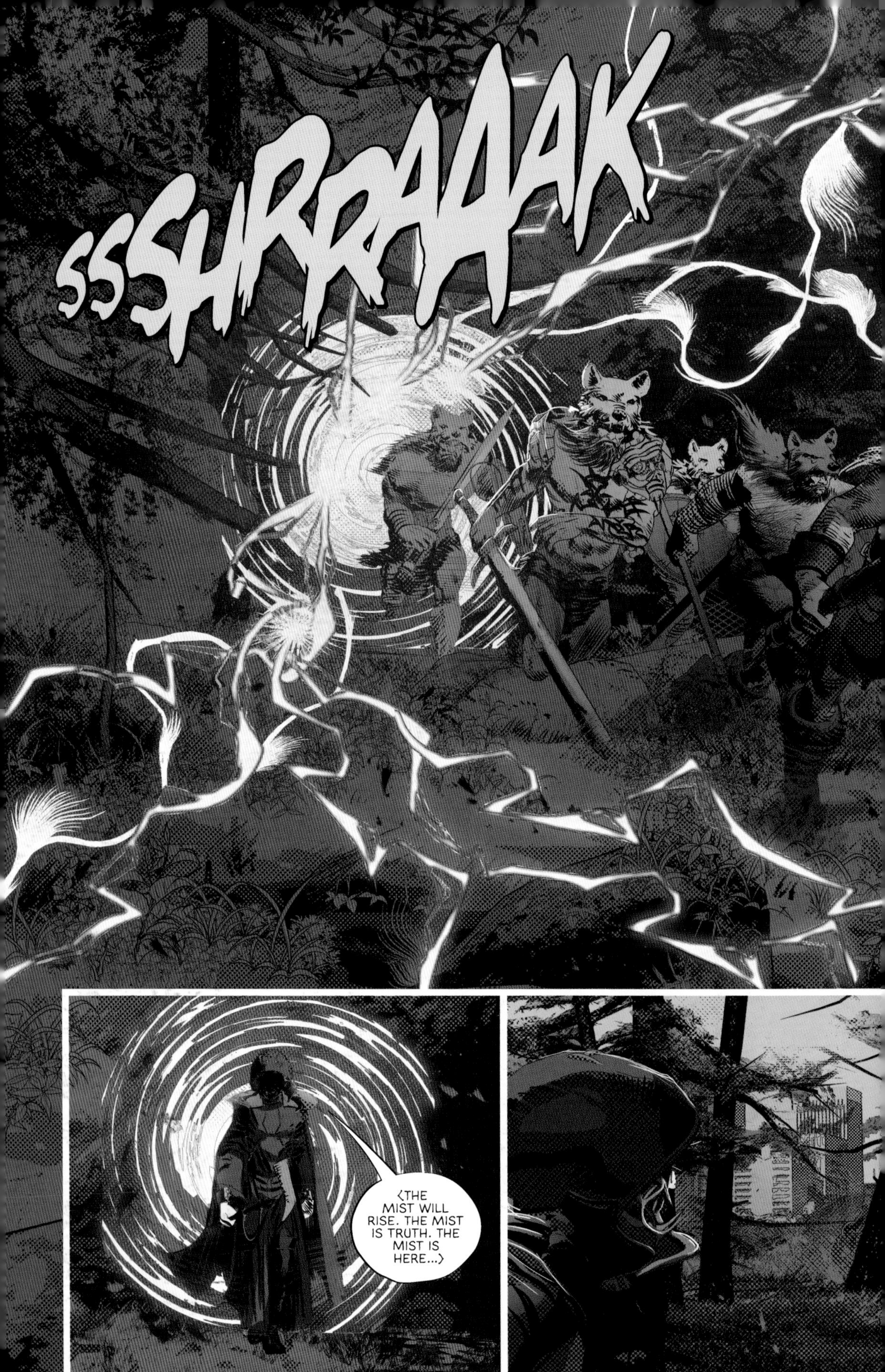
SSSHRRAAAK
⟨THE MIST WILL RISE. THE MIST IS TRUTH. THE MIST IS HERE...⟩

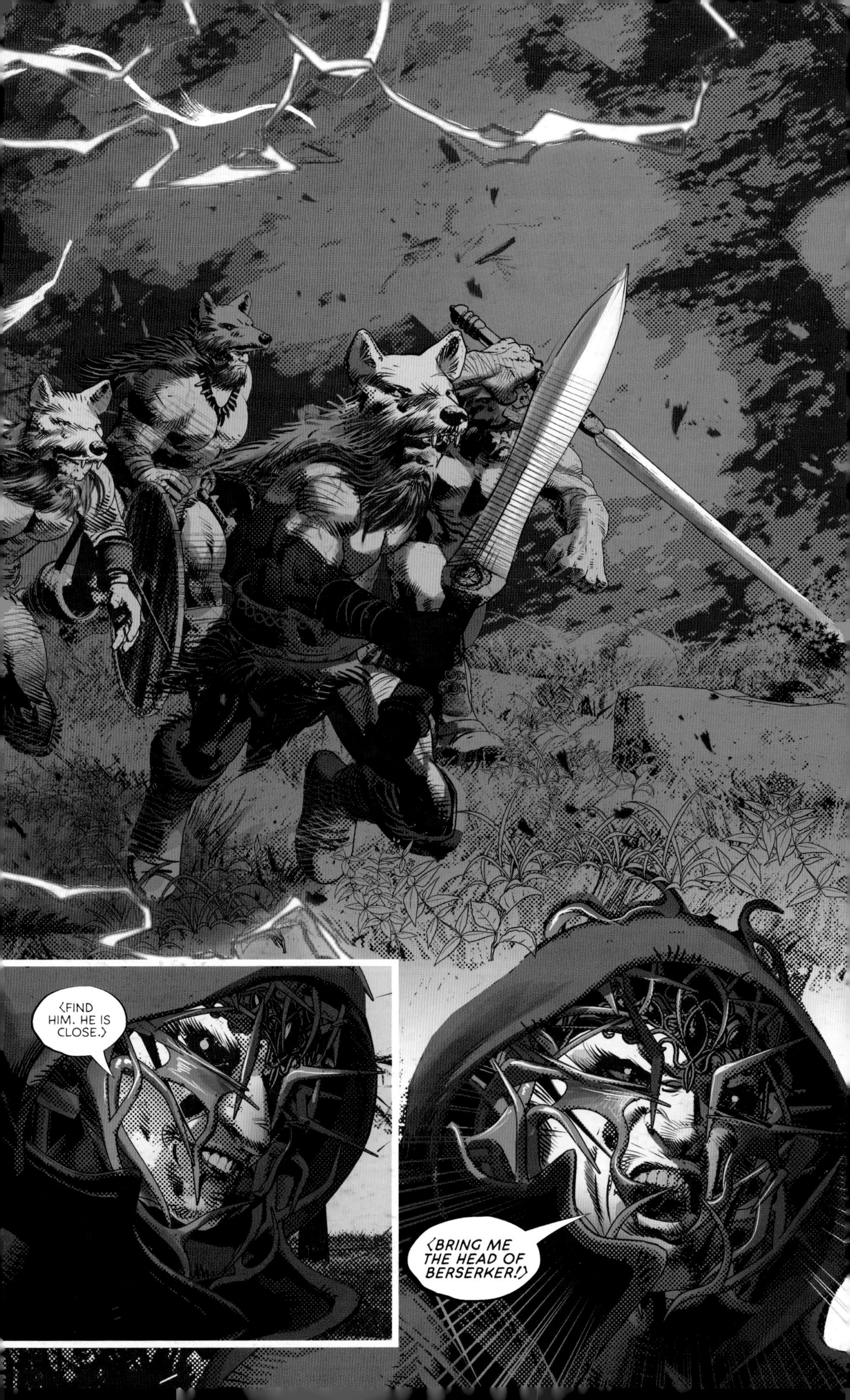
‹FIND HIM. HE IS CLOSE.›
‹BRING ME THE HEAD OF BERSERKER!›

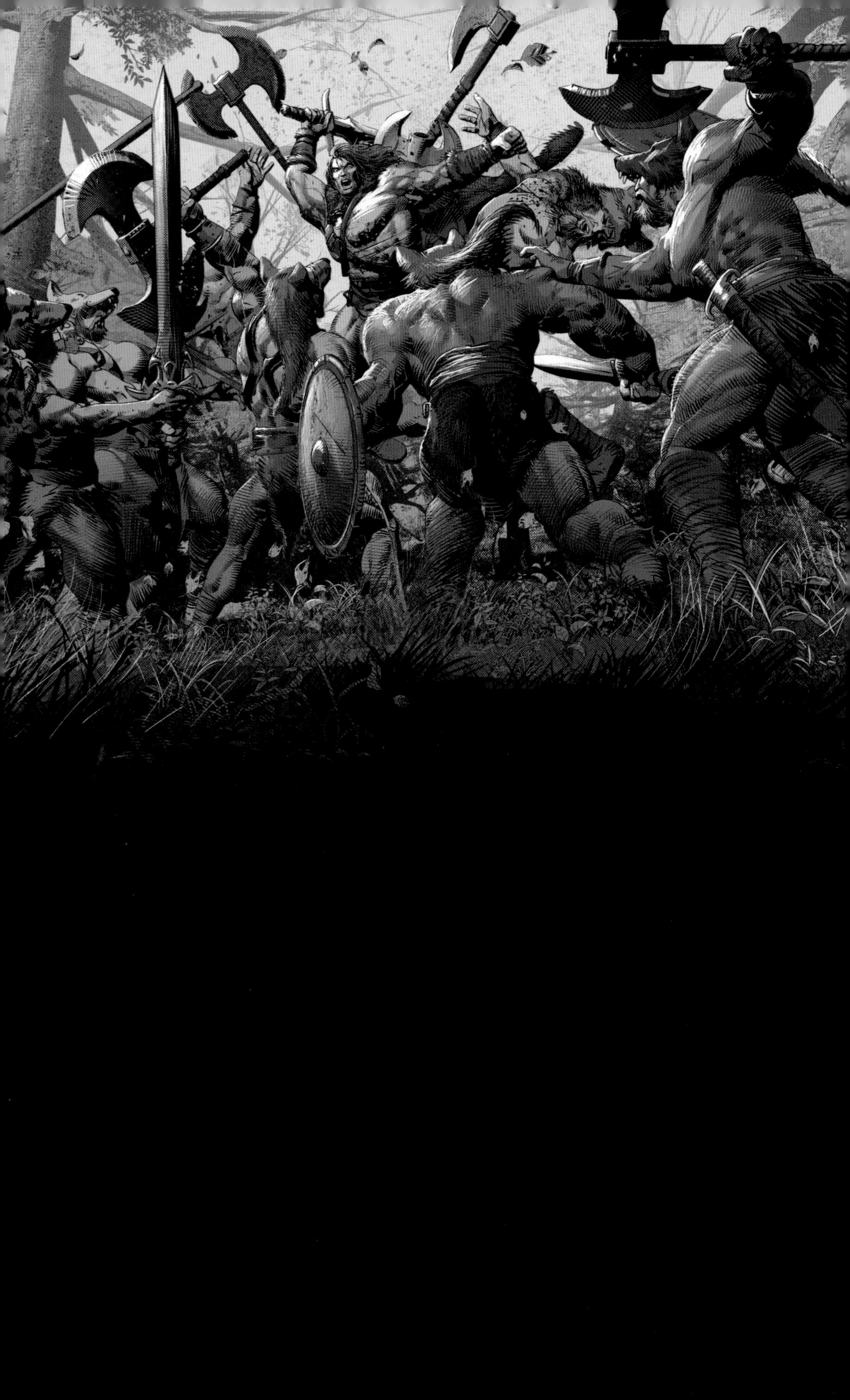

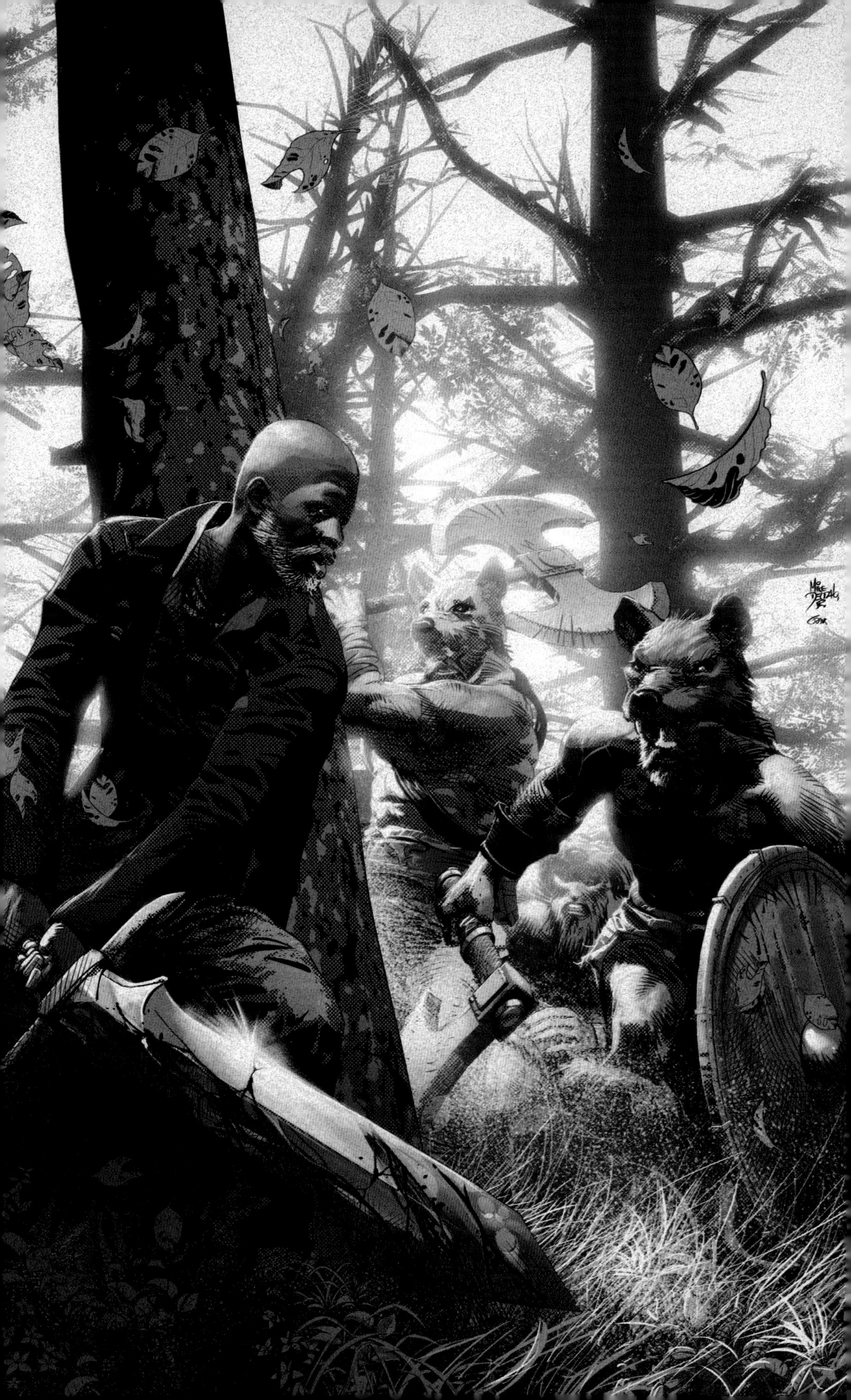

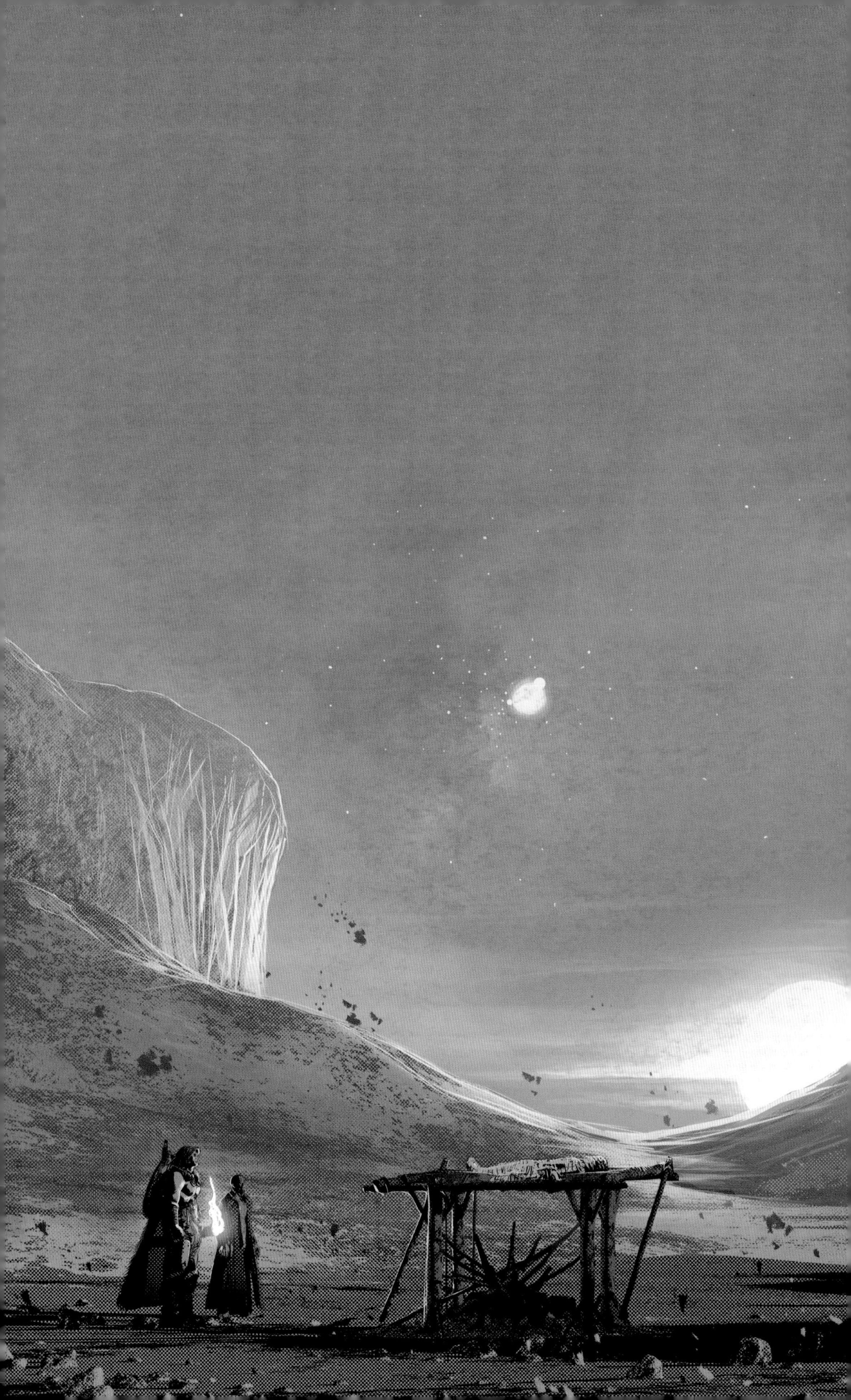

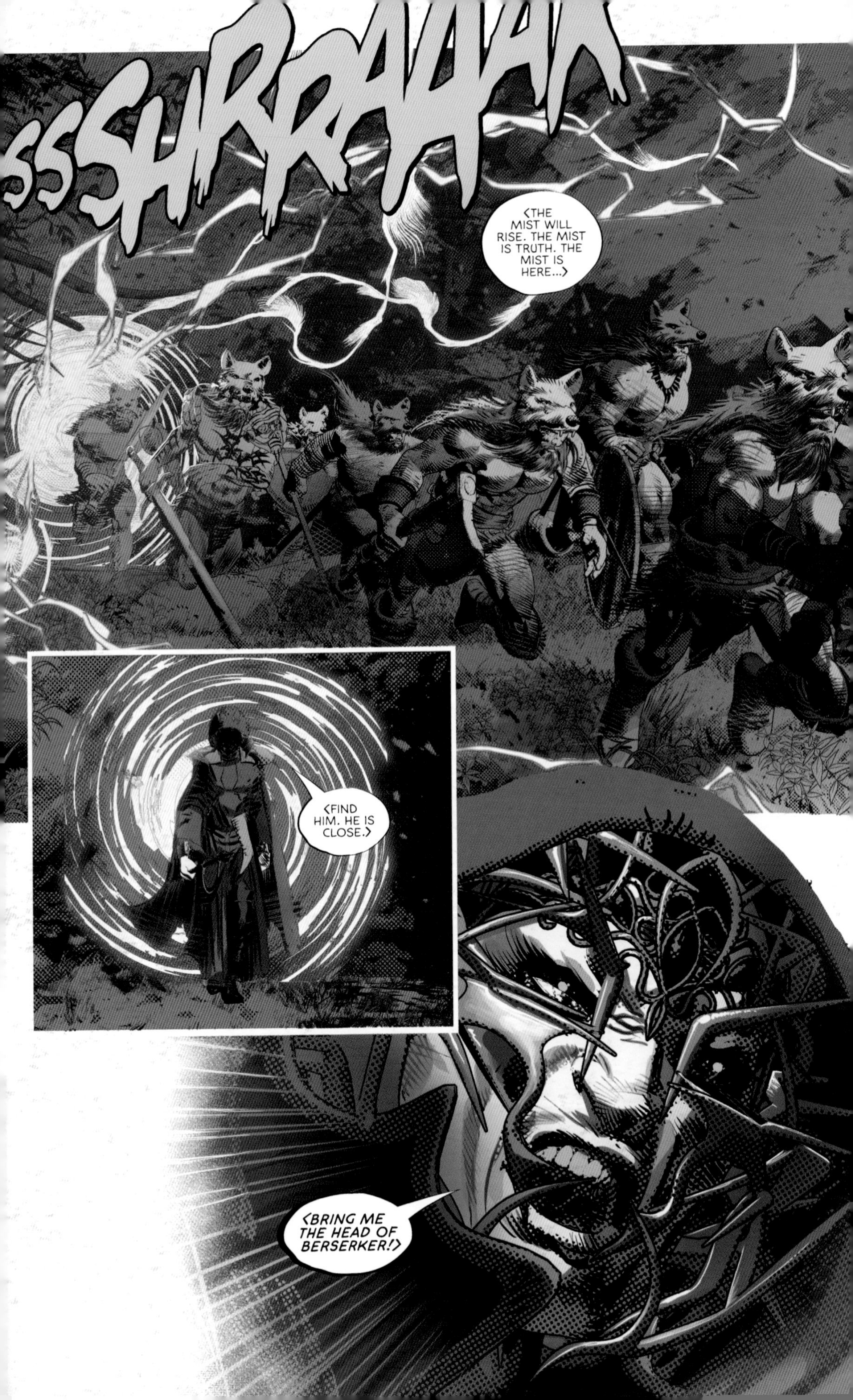
SSSHRAAAAA
<THE MIST WILL RISE. THE MIST IS TRUTH. THE MIST IS HERE...>
<FIND HIM. HE IS CLOSE.>
<BRING ME THE HEAD OF BERSERKER!>

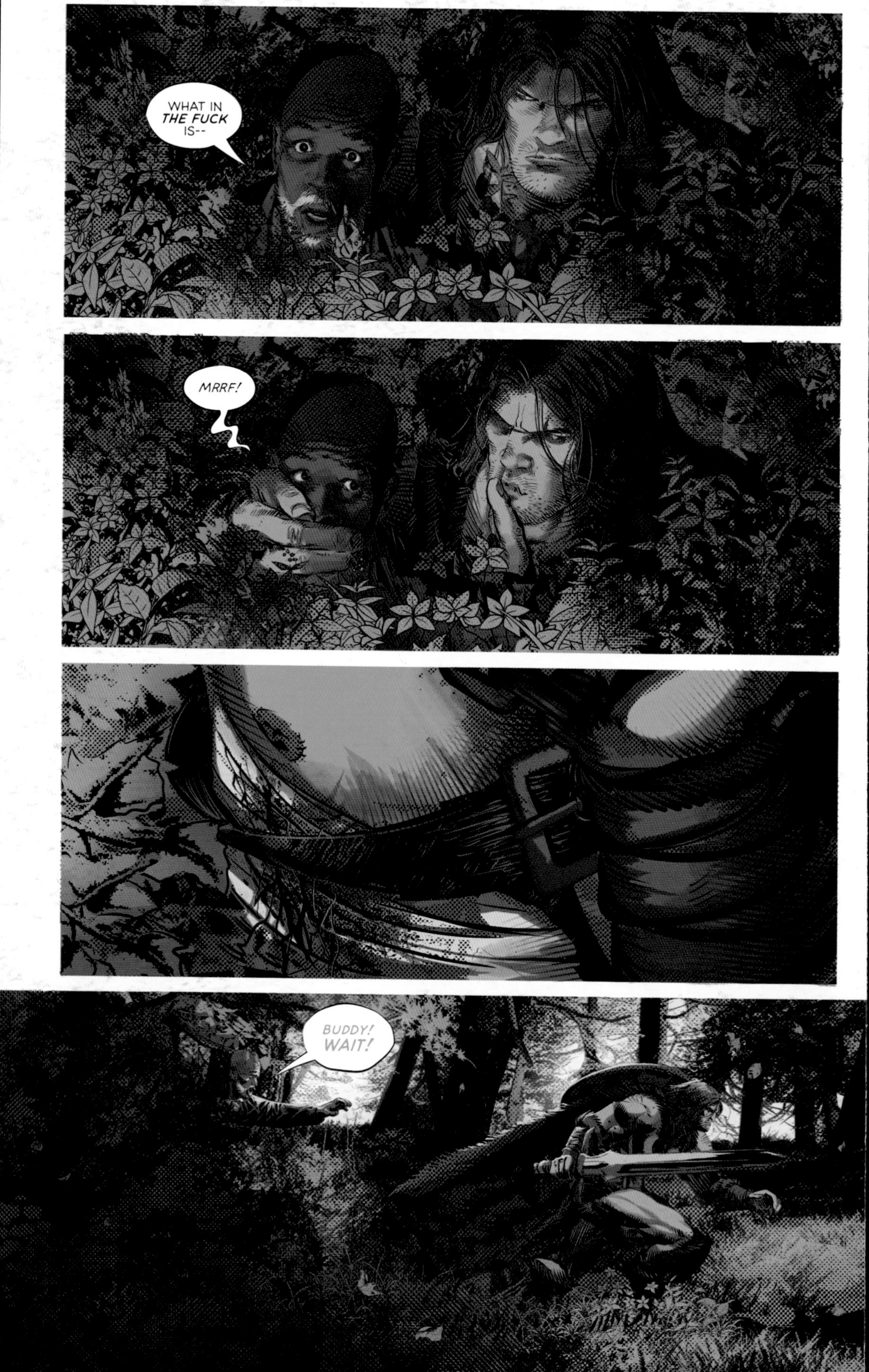
WHAT IN THE FUCK IS--
MRRF!
BUDDY! WAIT!

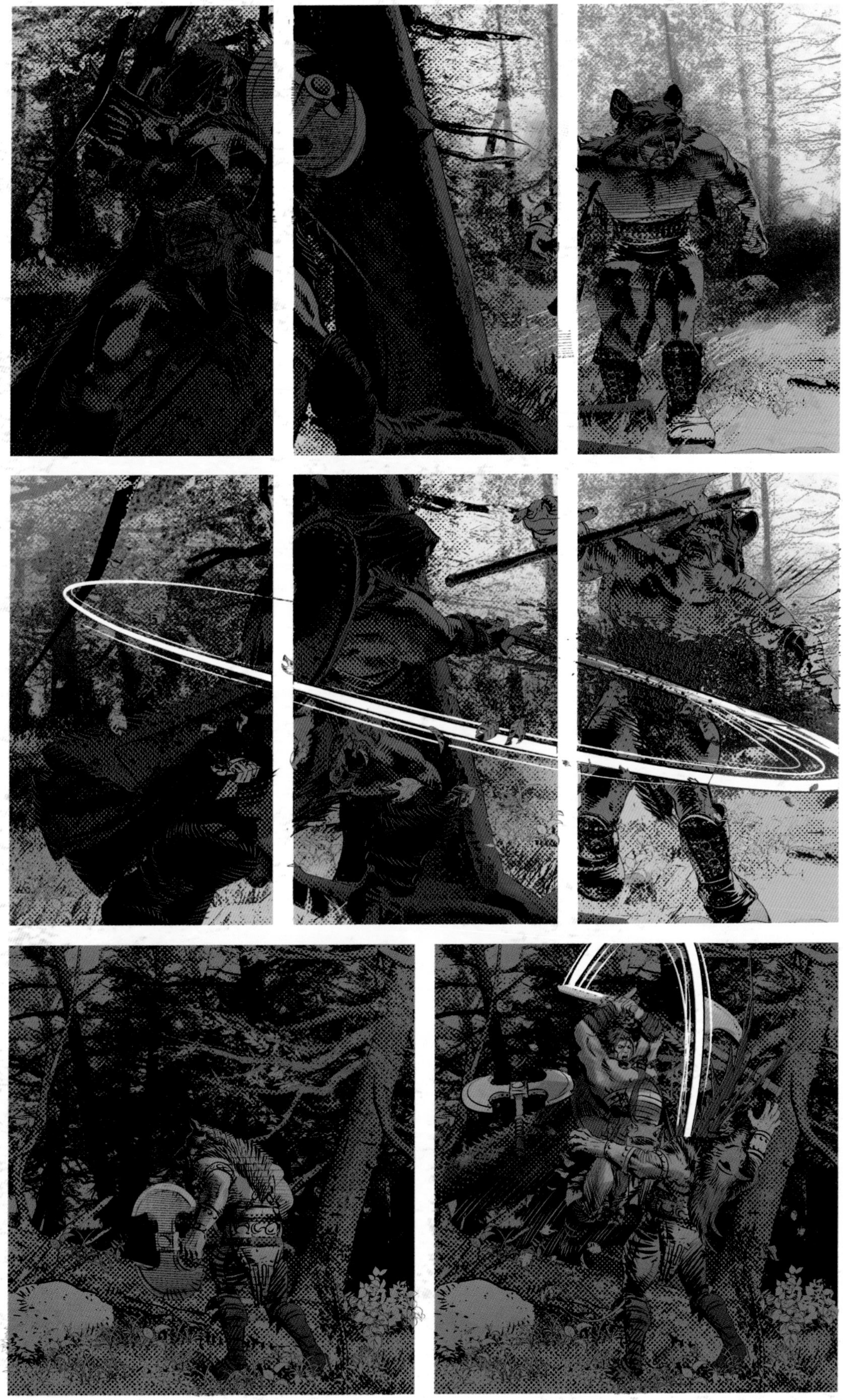

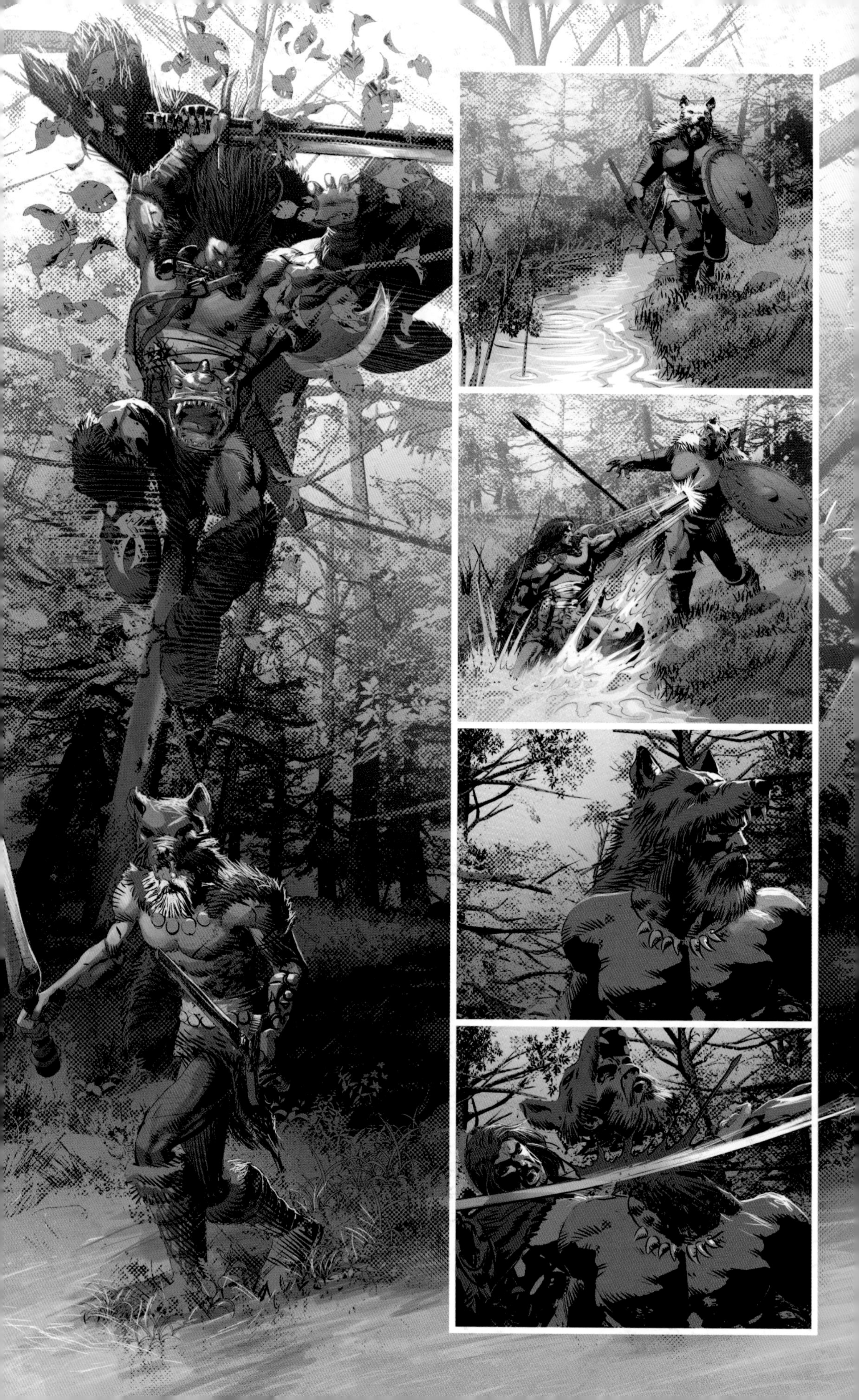

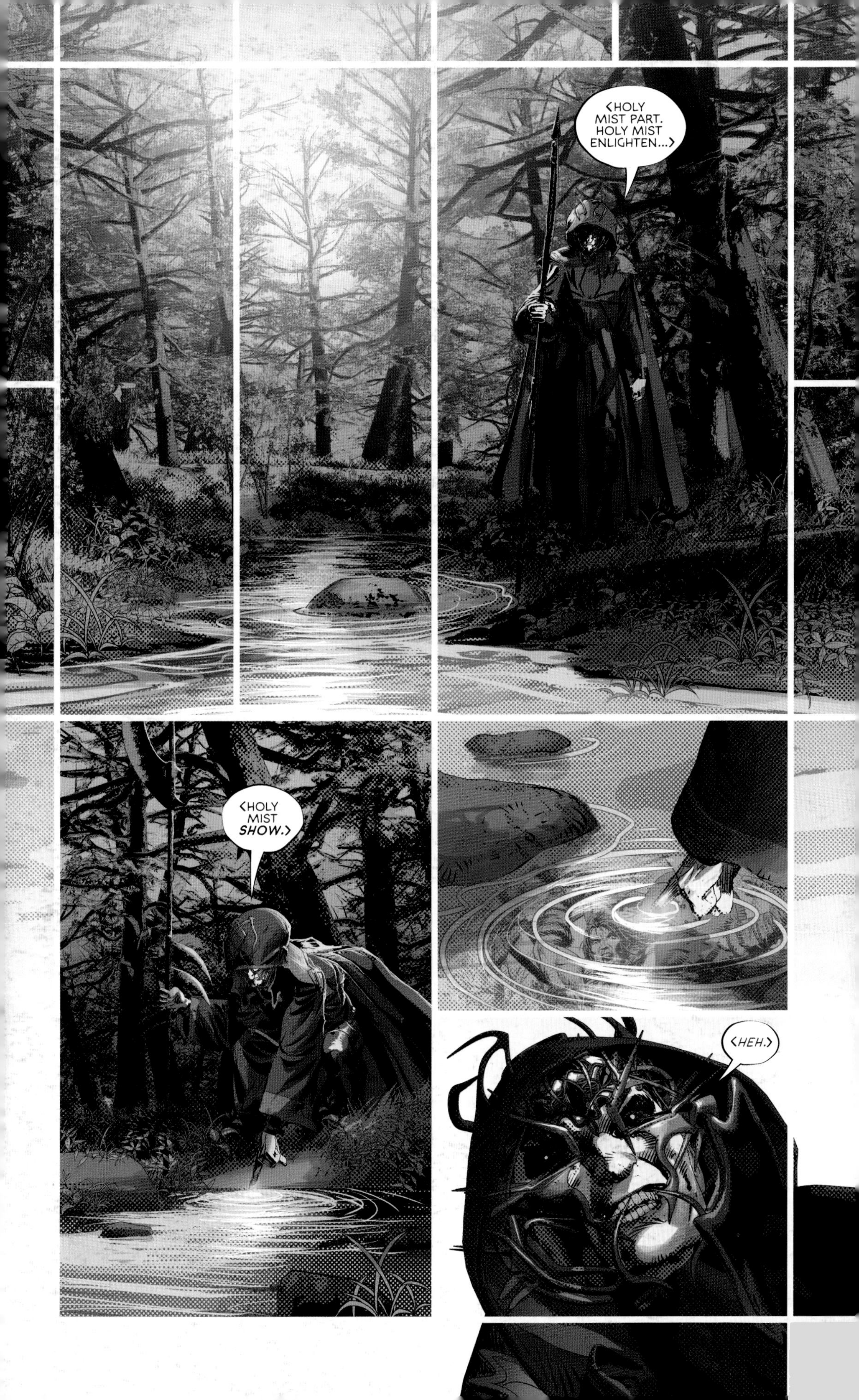
<HOLY MIST PART. HOLY MIST ENLIGHTEN...>
<HOLY MIST SHOW.>
<HEH.>

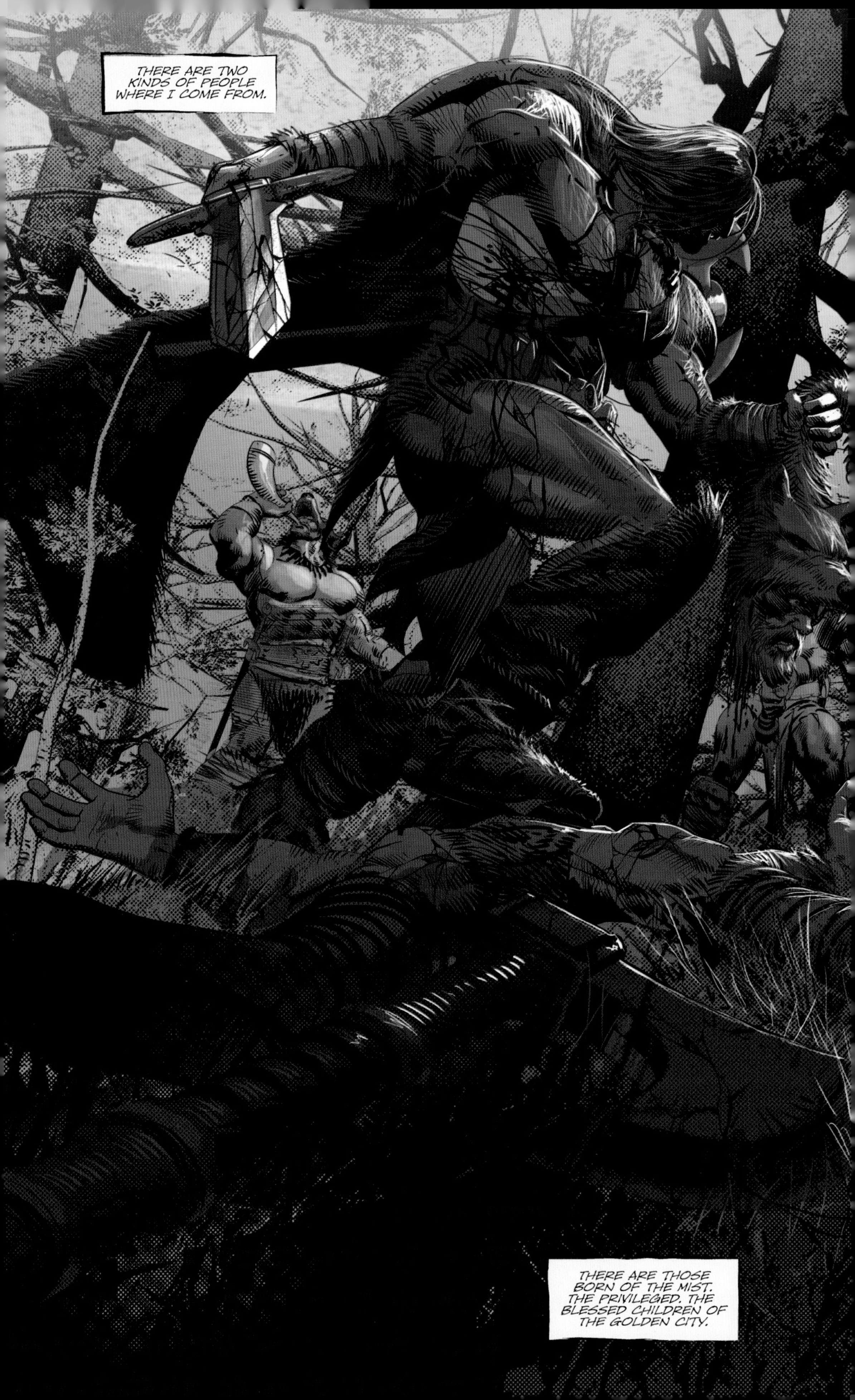
THERE ARE TWO KINDS OF PEOPLE WHERE I COME FROM.
THERE ARE THOSE BORN OF THE MIST. THE PRIVILEGED. THE BLESSED CHILDREN OF THE GOLDEN CITY.

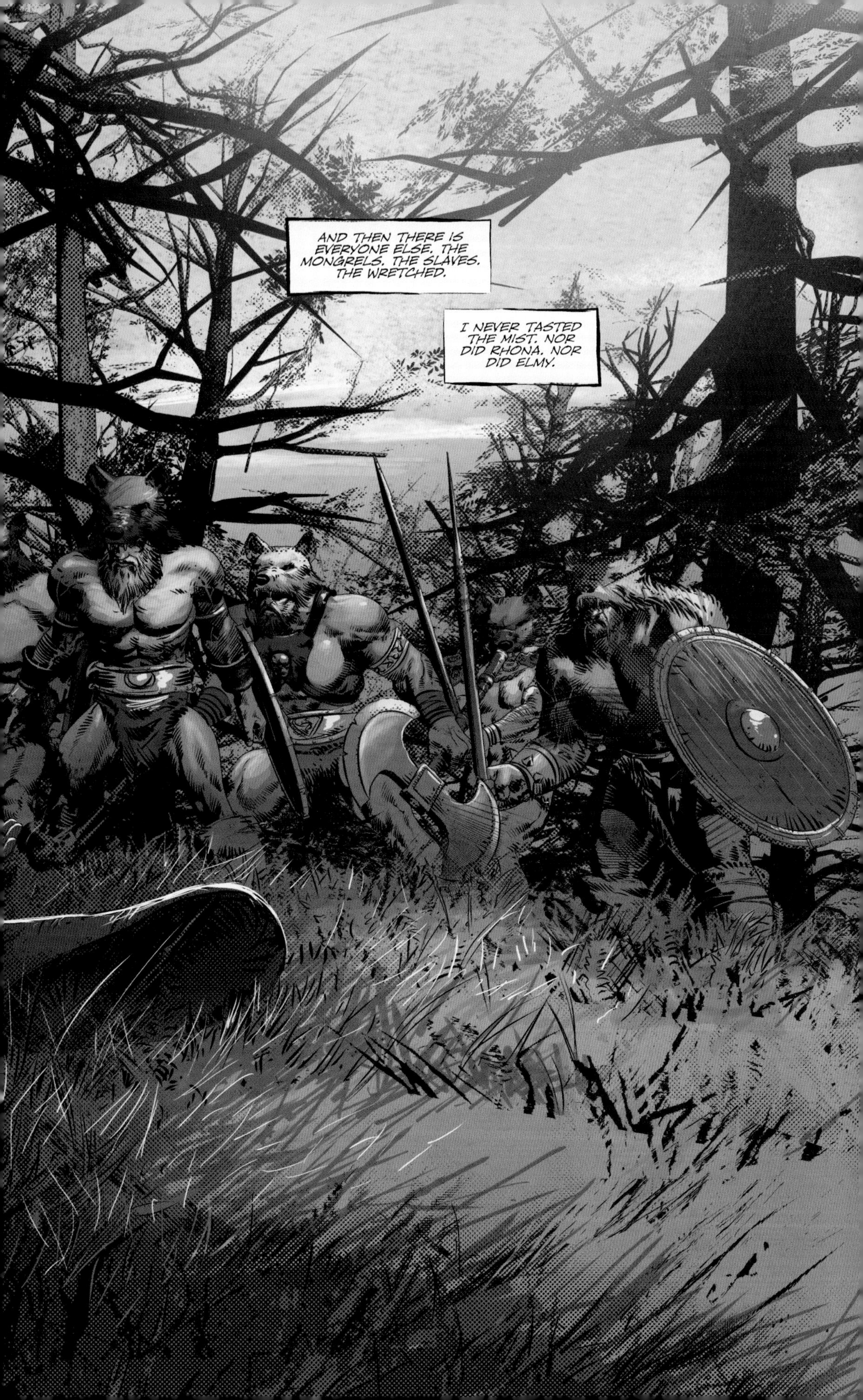
AND THEN THERE IS EVERYONE ELSE. THE MONGRELS. THE SLAVES. THE WRETCHED.
I NEVER TASTED THE MIST. NOR DID RHONA. NOR DID ELMY.

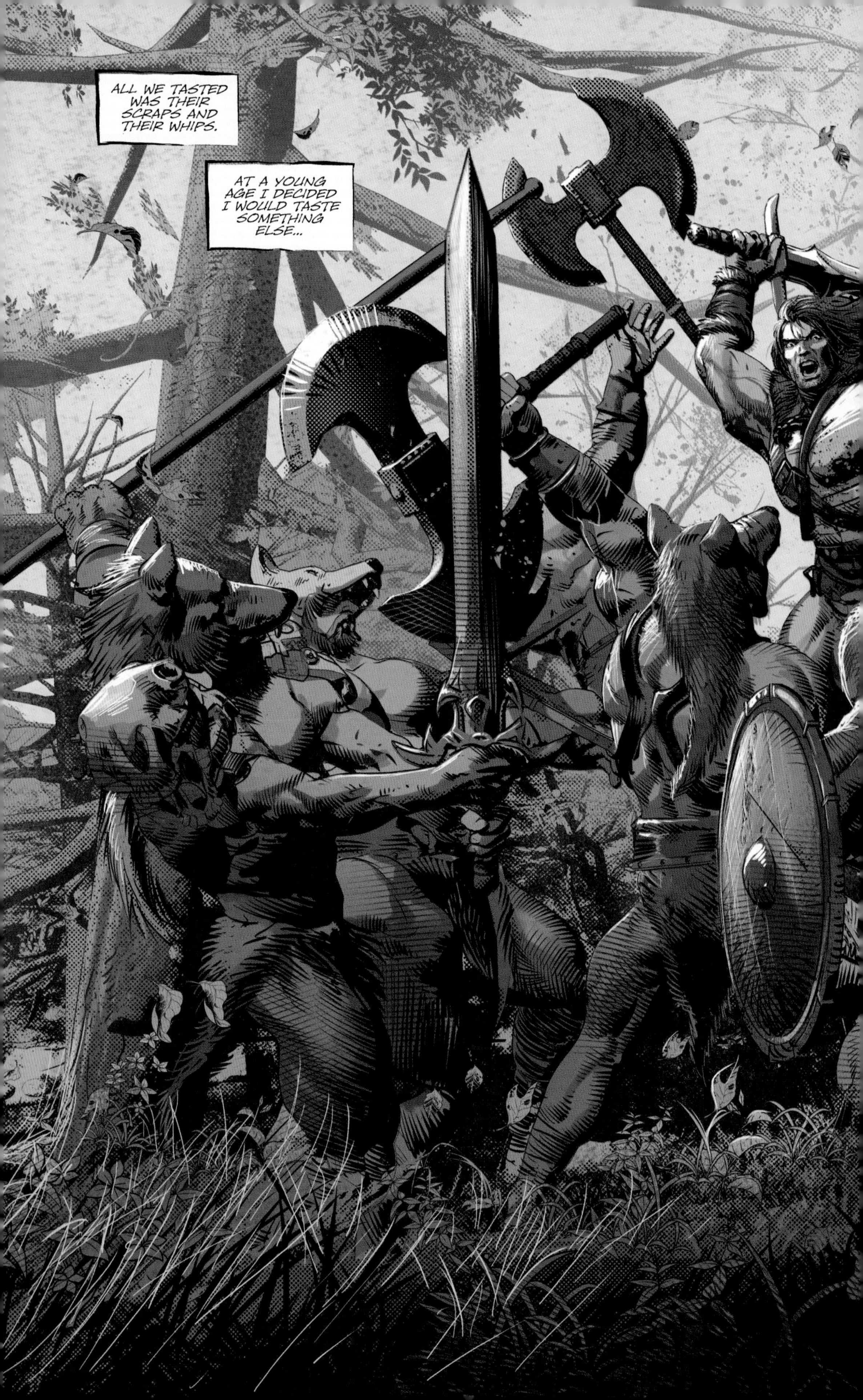
ALL WE TASTED WAS THEIR SCRAPS AND THEIR WHIPS.
AT A YOUNG AGE I DECIDED I WOULD TASTE SOMETHING ELSE...

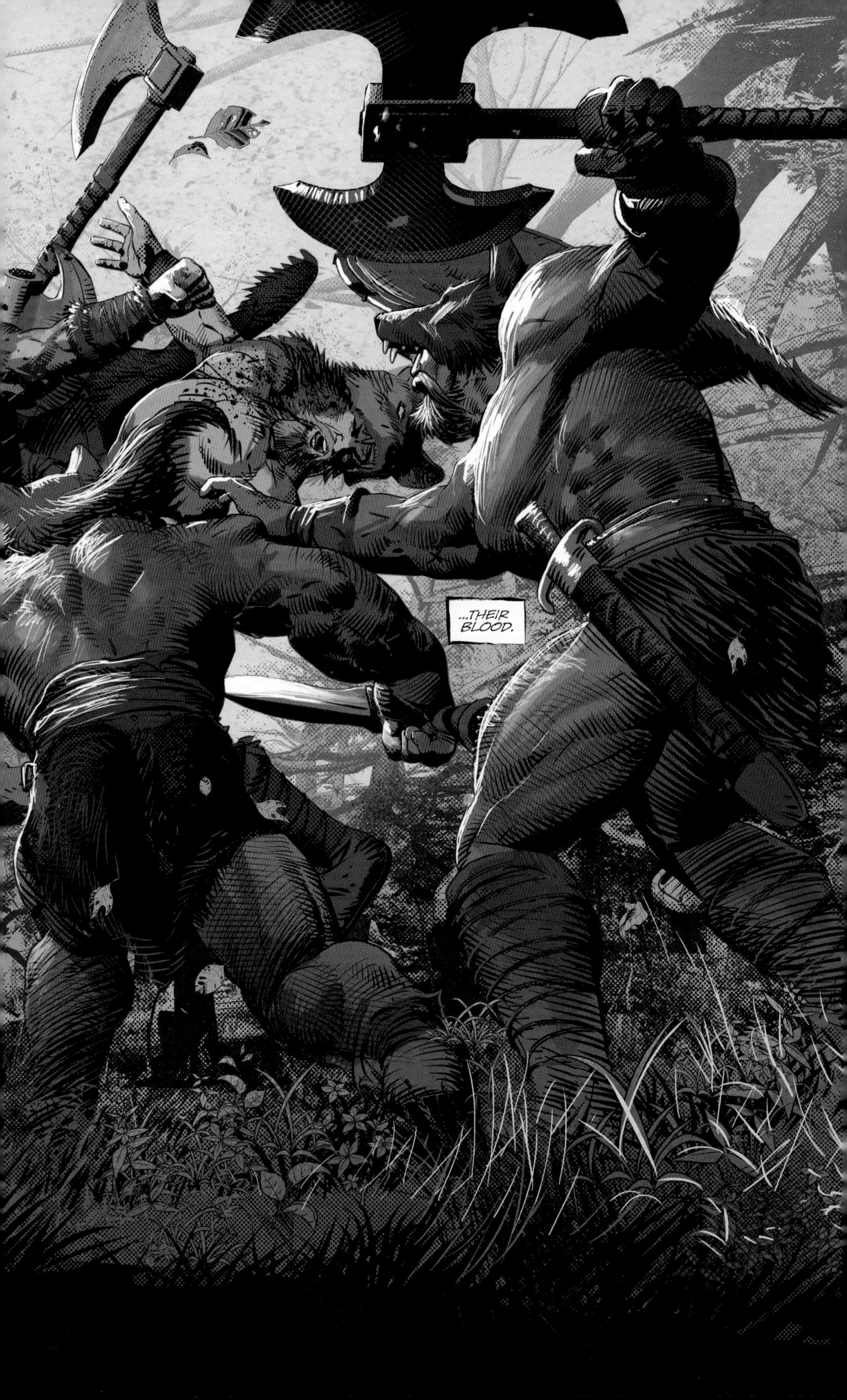
...THEIR BLOOD.

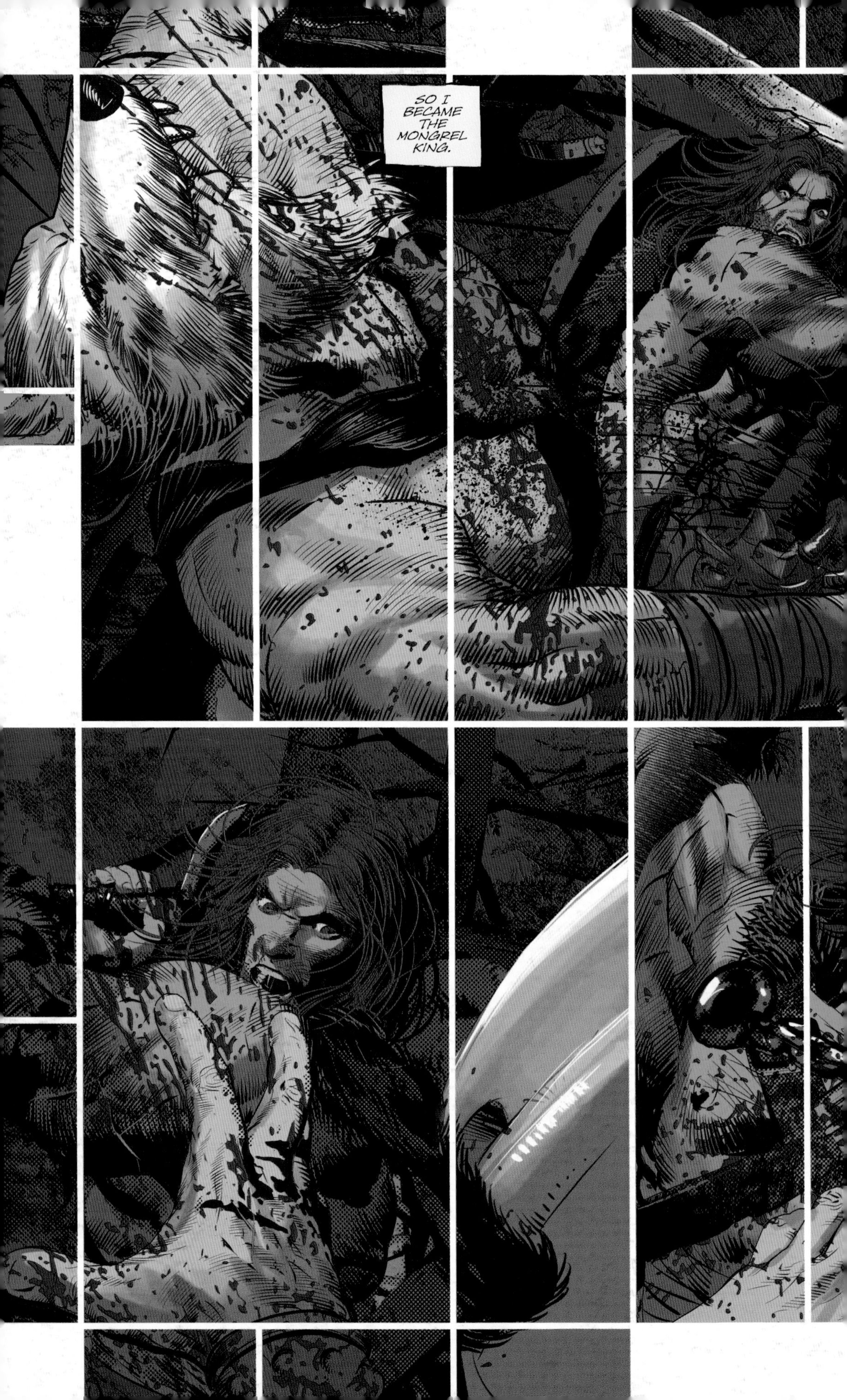
SO I BECAME THE MONGREL KING.

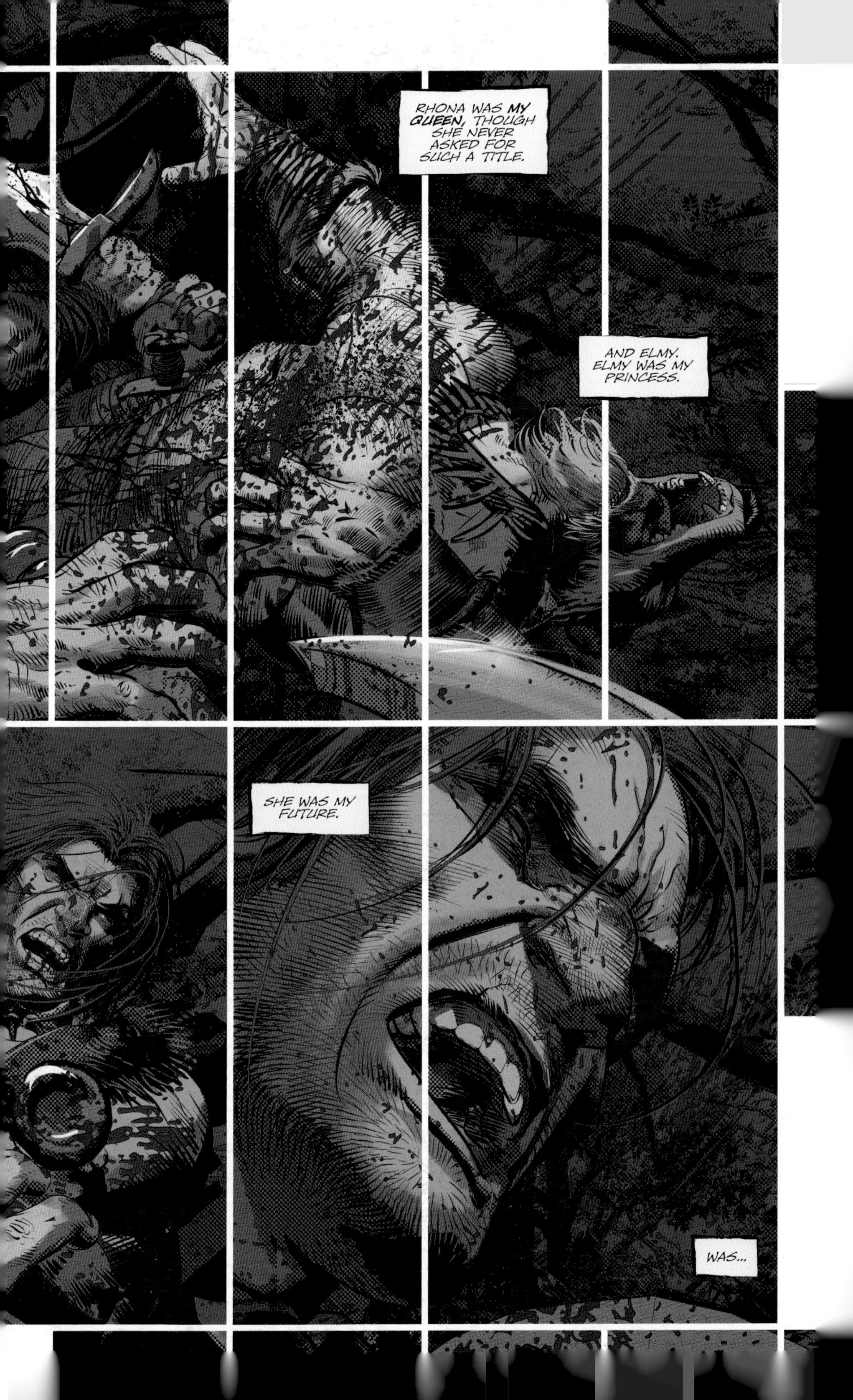
RHONA WAS MY QUEEN, THOUGH SHE NEVER ASKED FOR SUCH A TITLE.
AND ELMY. ELMY WAS MY PRINCESS.
SHE WAS MY FUTURE.
WAS...

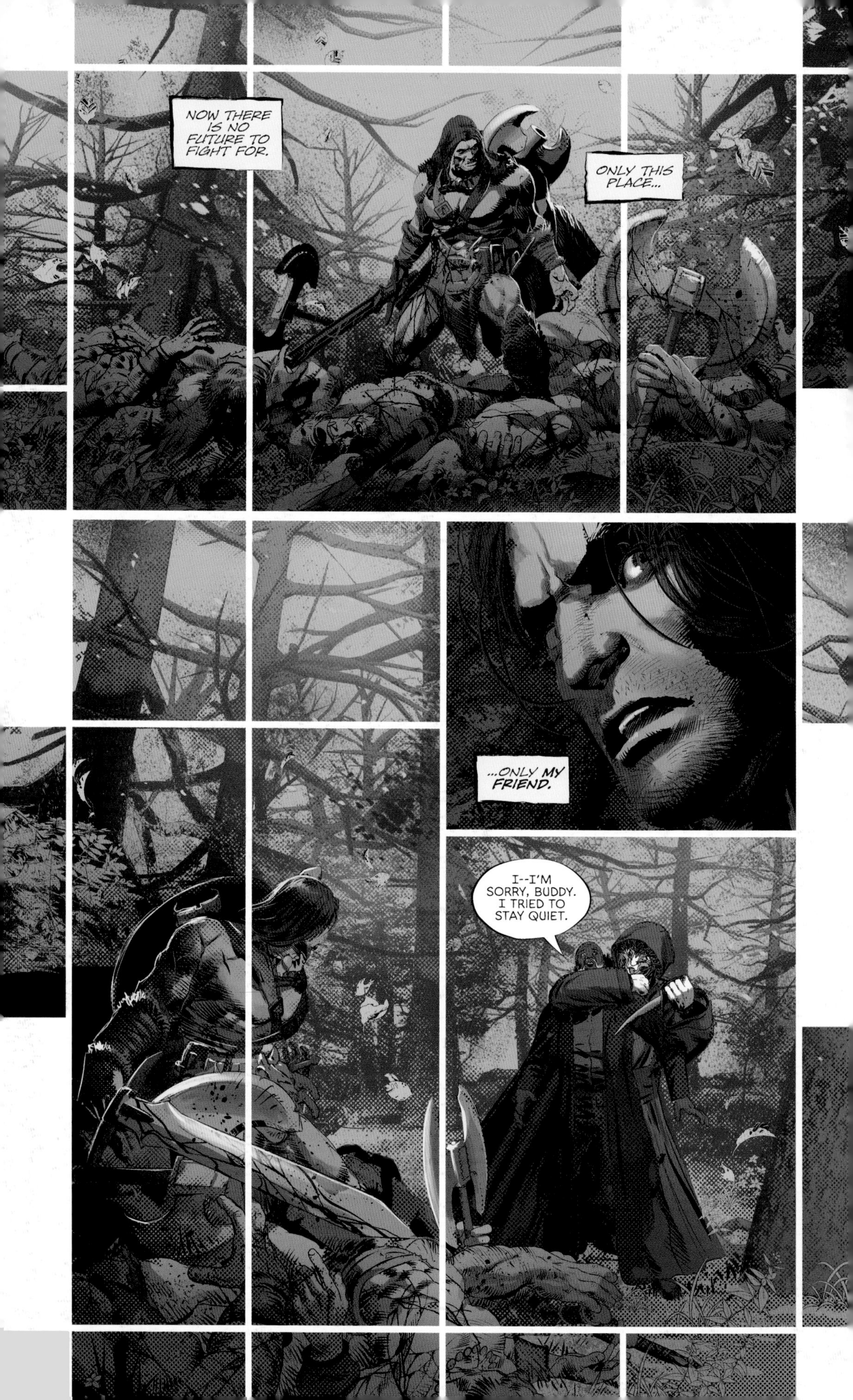
NOW THERE IS NO FUTURE TO FIGHT FOR.
ONLY THIS PLACE...
...ONLY MY FRIEND.
I--I'M SORRY, BUDDY. I TRIED TO STAY QUIET.

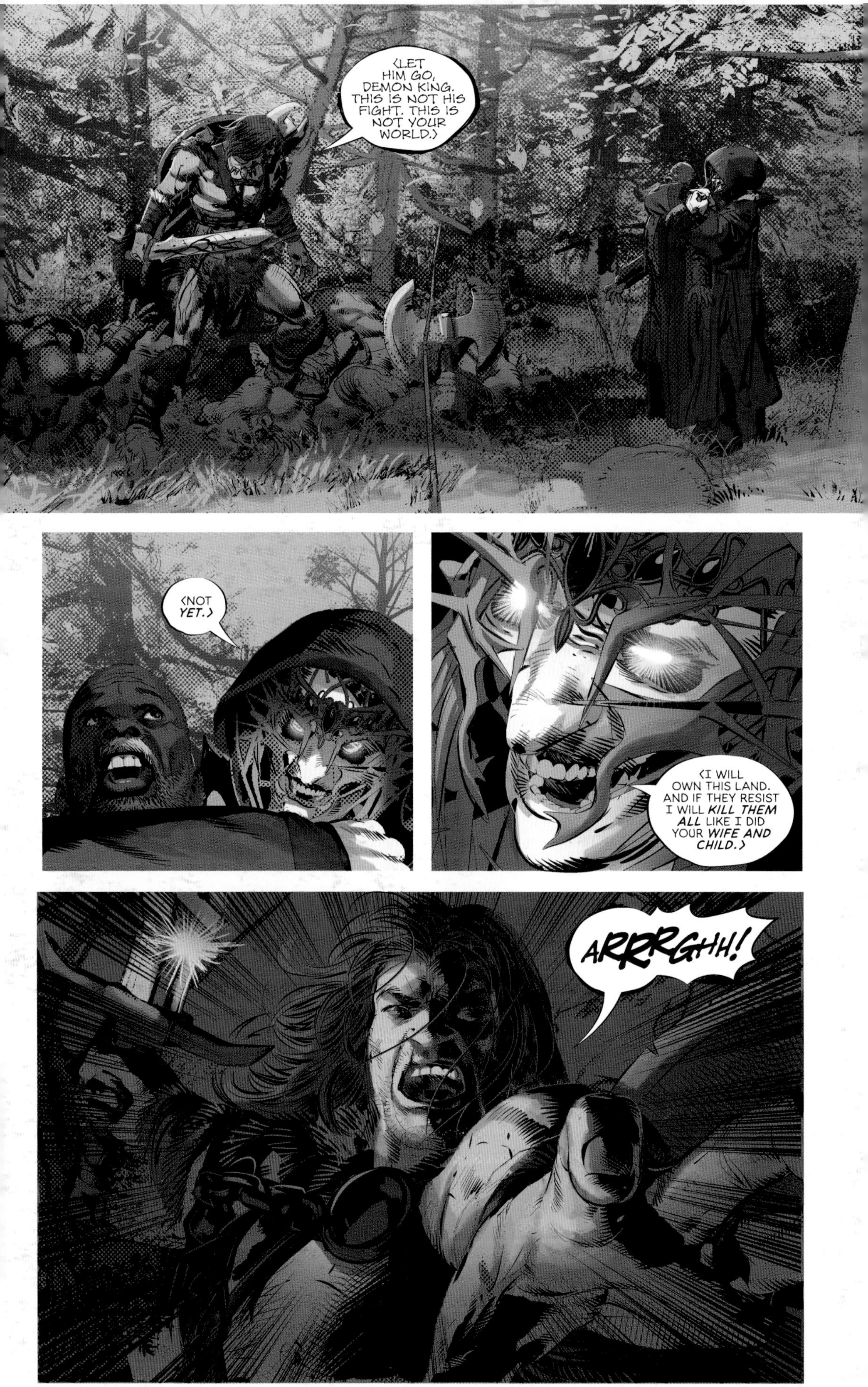
<LET HIM GO, DEMON KING. THIS IS NOT HIS FIGHT. THIS IS NOT YOUR WORLD.>
<NOT *YET.*>
<I WILL OWN THIS LAND. AND IF THEY RESIST I WILL ***KILL THEM ALL*** LIKE I DID YOUR ***WIFE AND CHILD.***>
ARRRGHH!

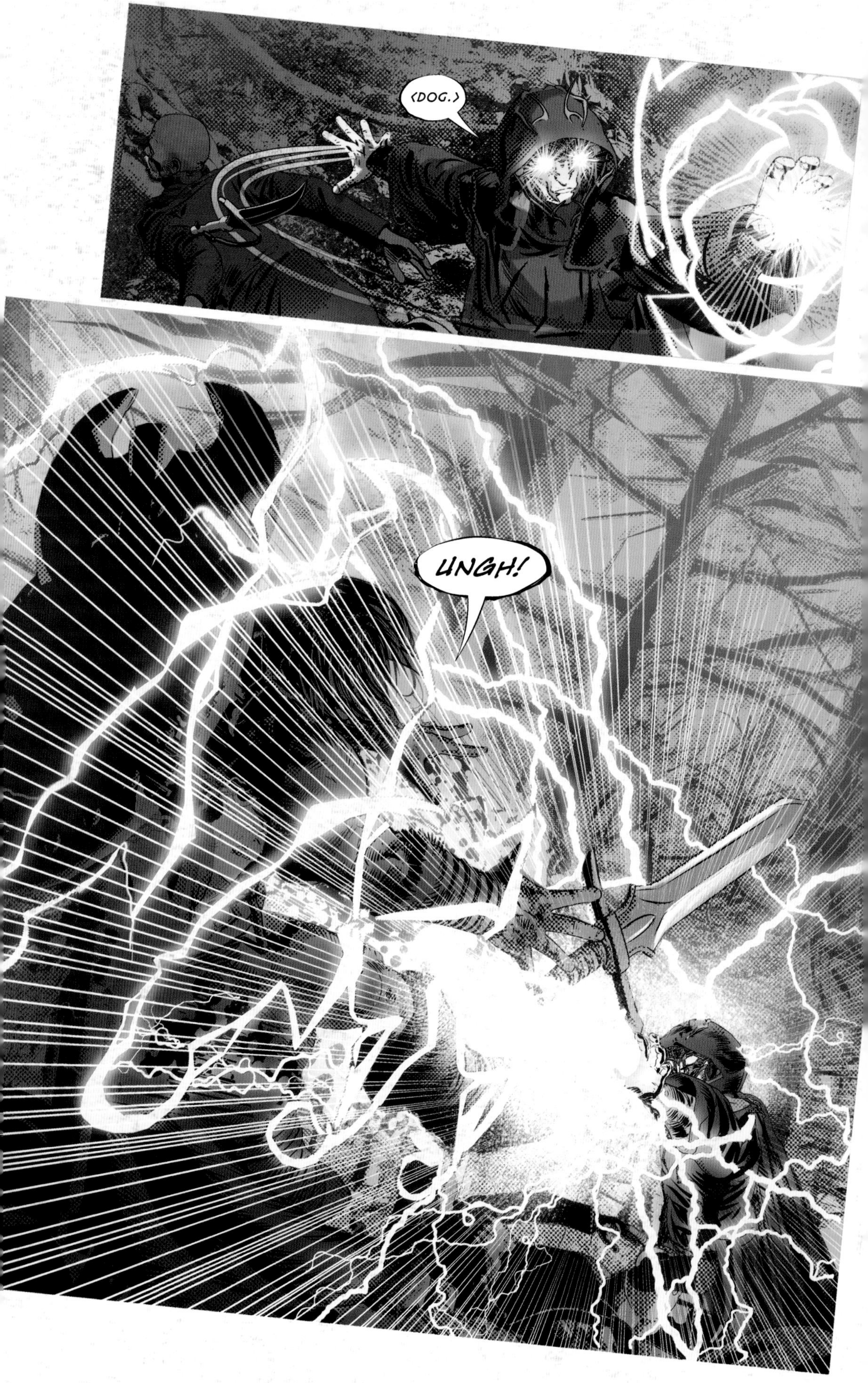
<DOG.>
UNGH!

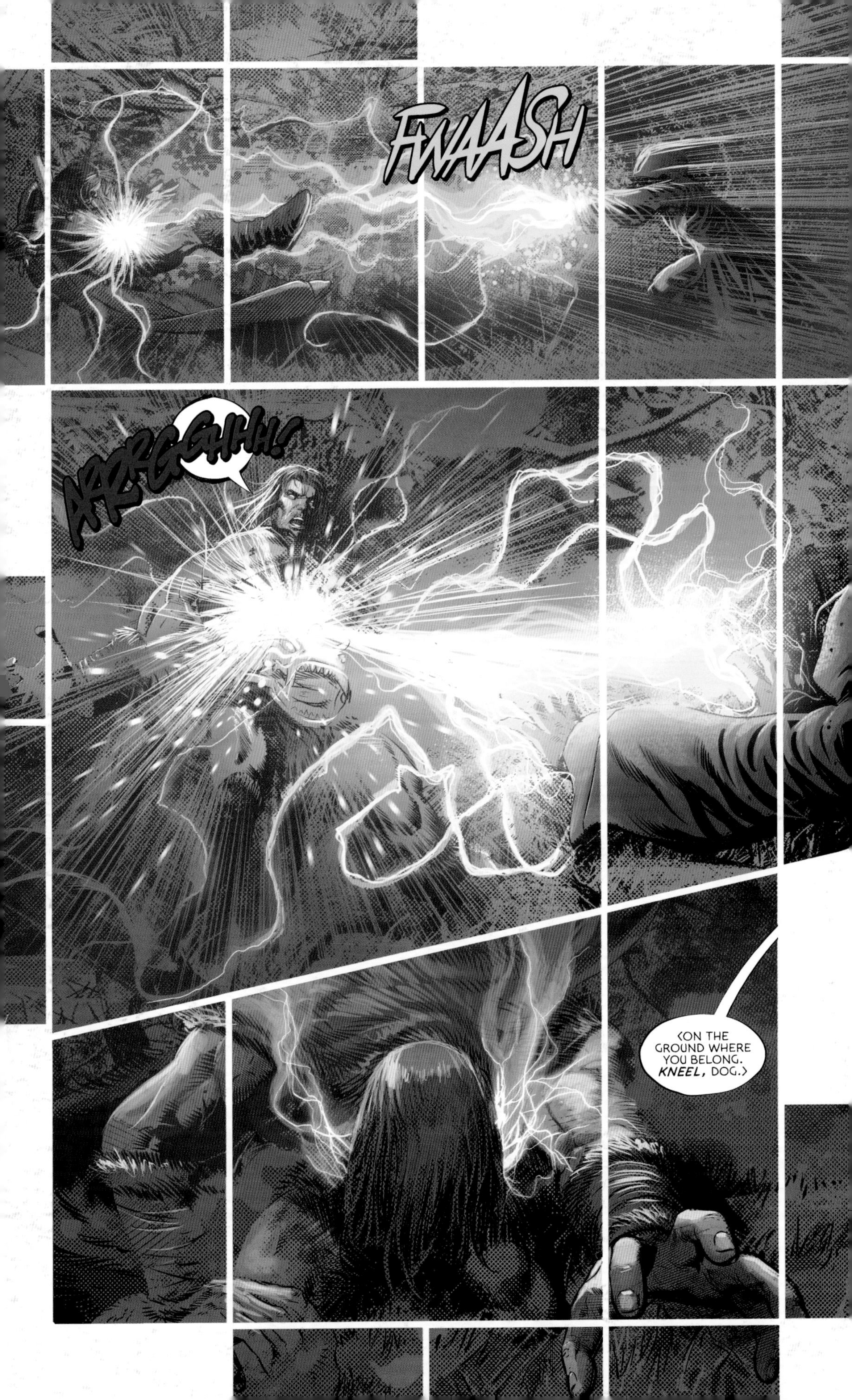
FWAASH
ARRRGGHHH!
<ON THE GROUND WHERE YOU BELONG. KNEEL, DOG.>

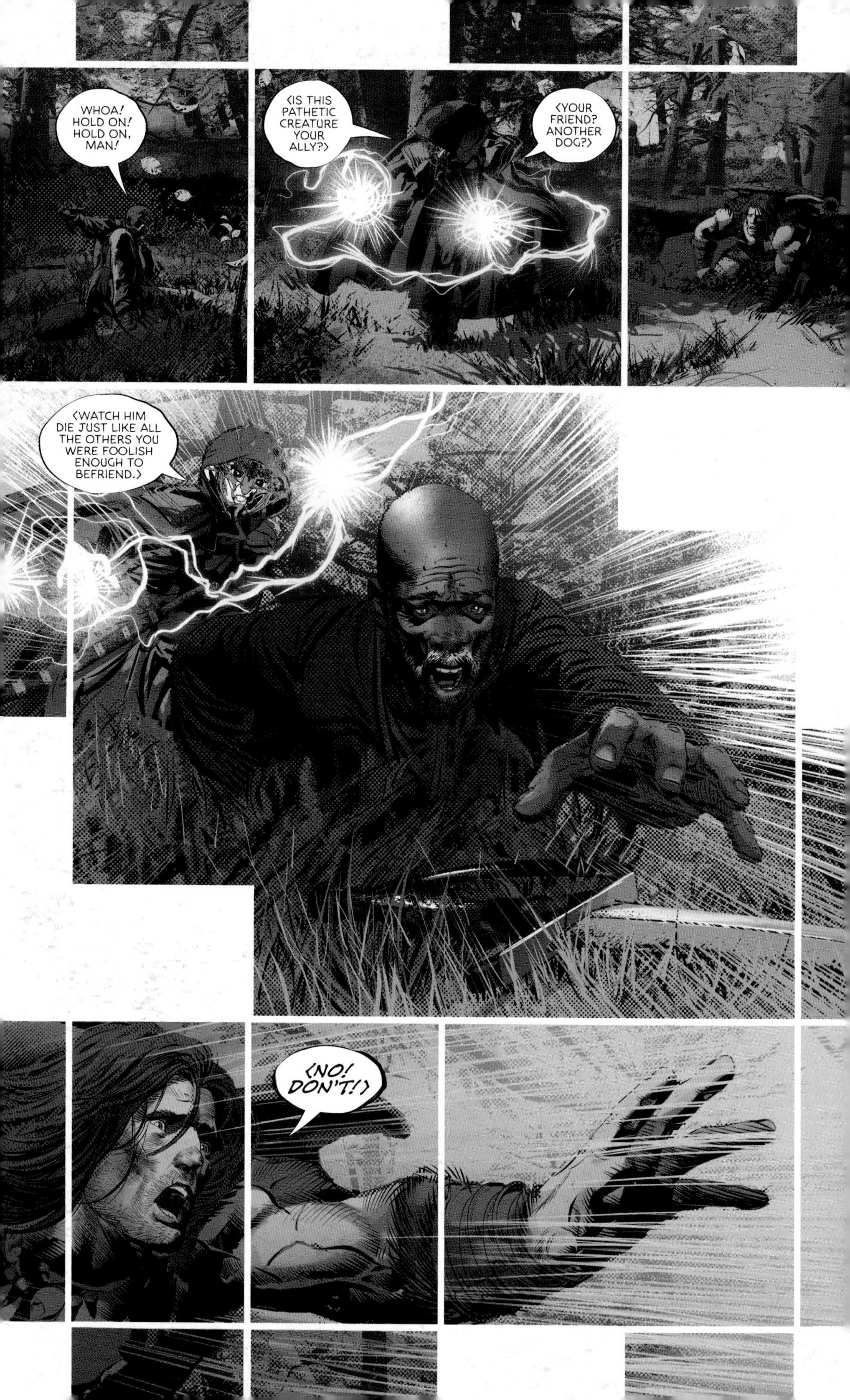
WHOA! HOLD ON! HOLD ON, MAN!
<IS THIS PATHETIC CREATURE YOUR ALLY?>
<YOUR FRIEND? ANOTHER DOG?>
<WATCH HIM DIE JUST LIKE ALL THE OTHERS YOU WERE FOOLISH ENOUGH TO BEFRIEND.>
<NO! DON'T!>

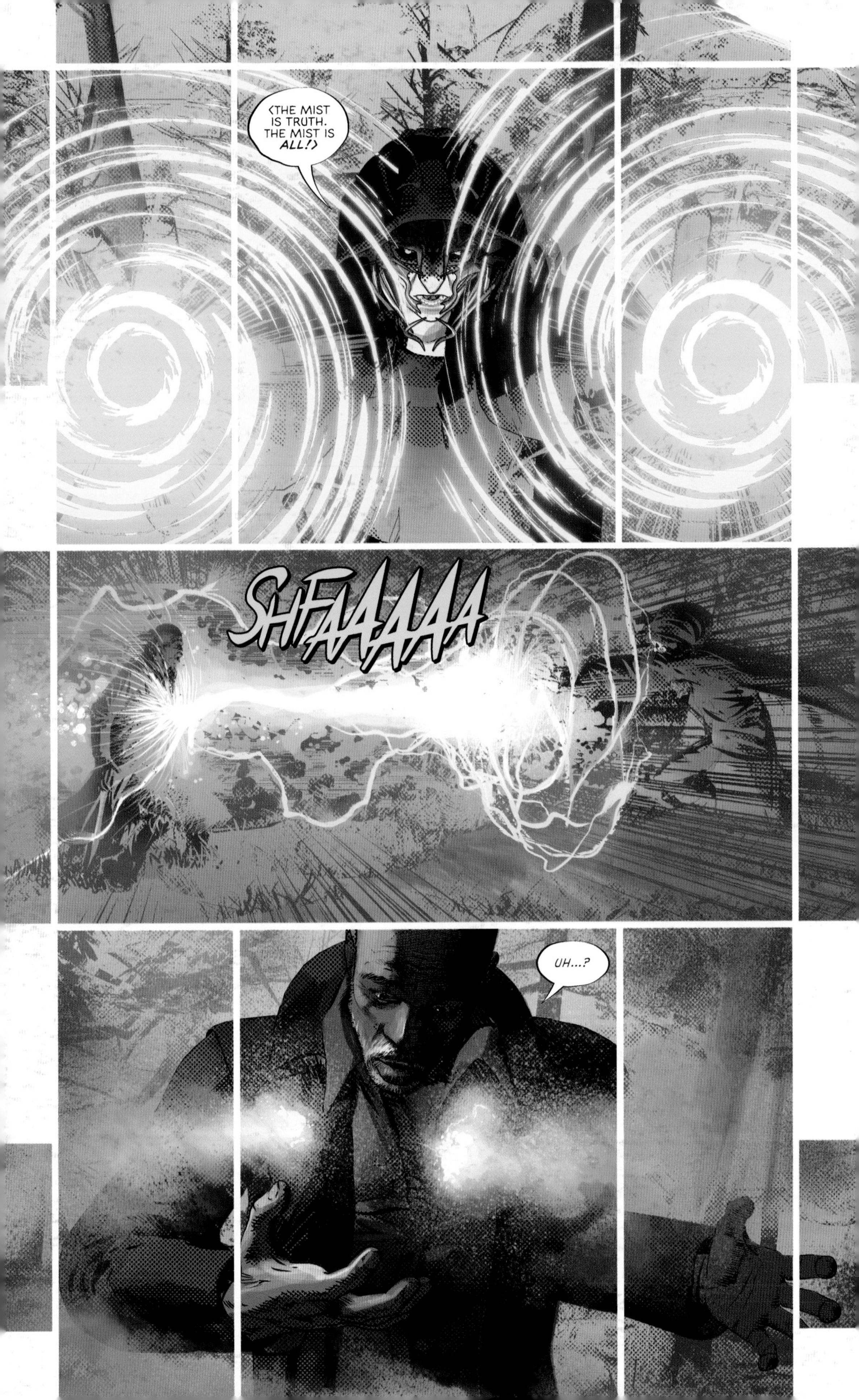
<THE MIST IS TRUTH. THE MIST IS ALL!>
SHFAAAAAA
UH...?

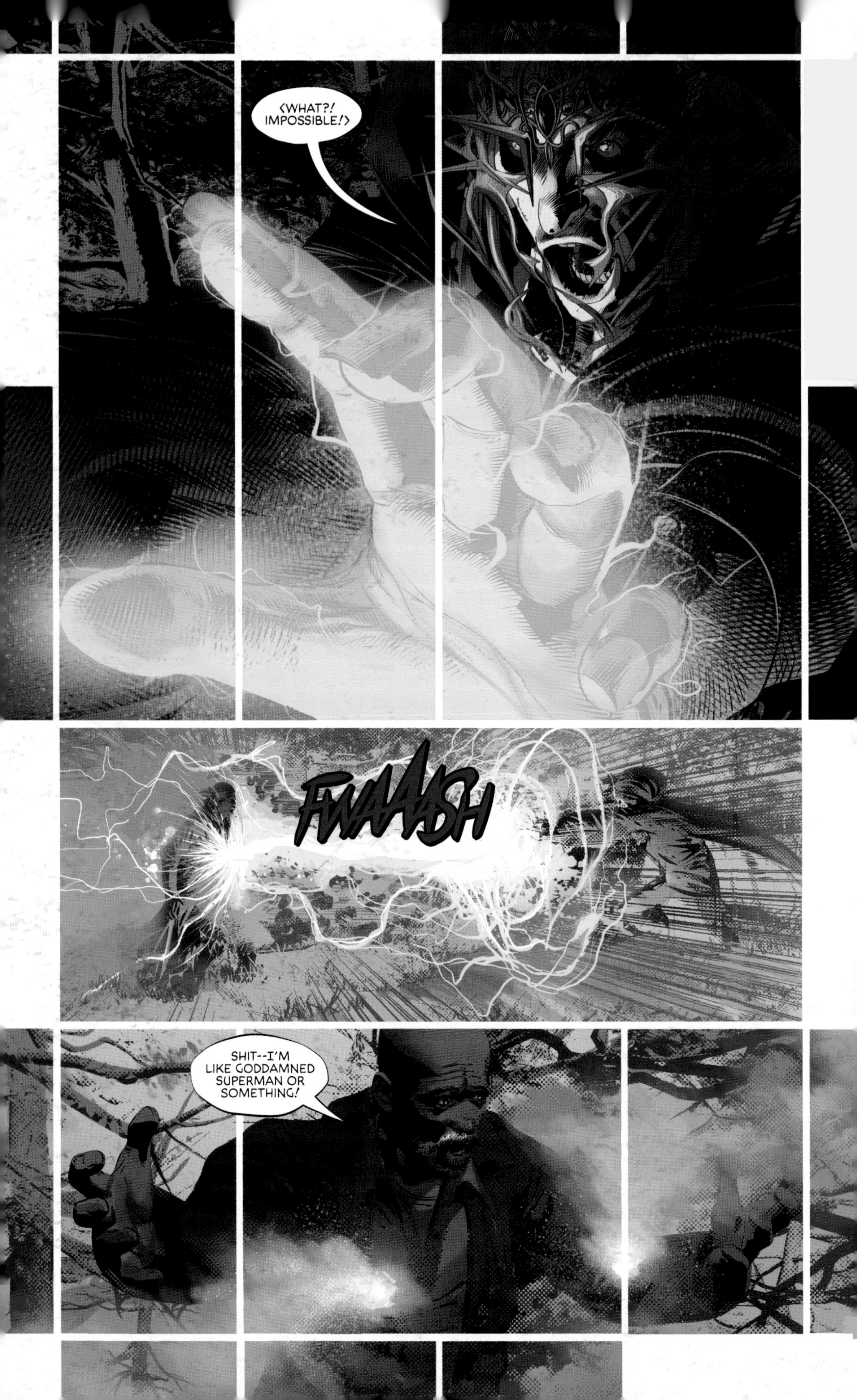
⟨WHAT?! IMPOSSIBLE!⟩
FWAAASH
SHIT--I'M LIKE GODDAMNED SUPERMAN OR SOMETHING!

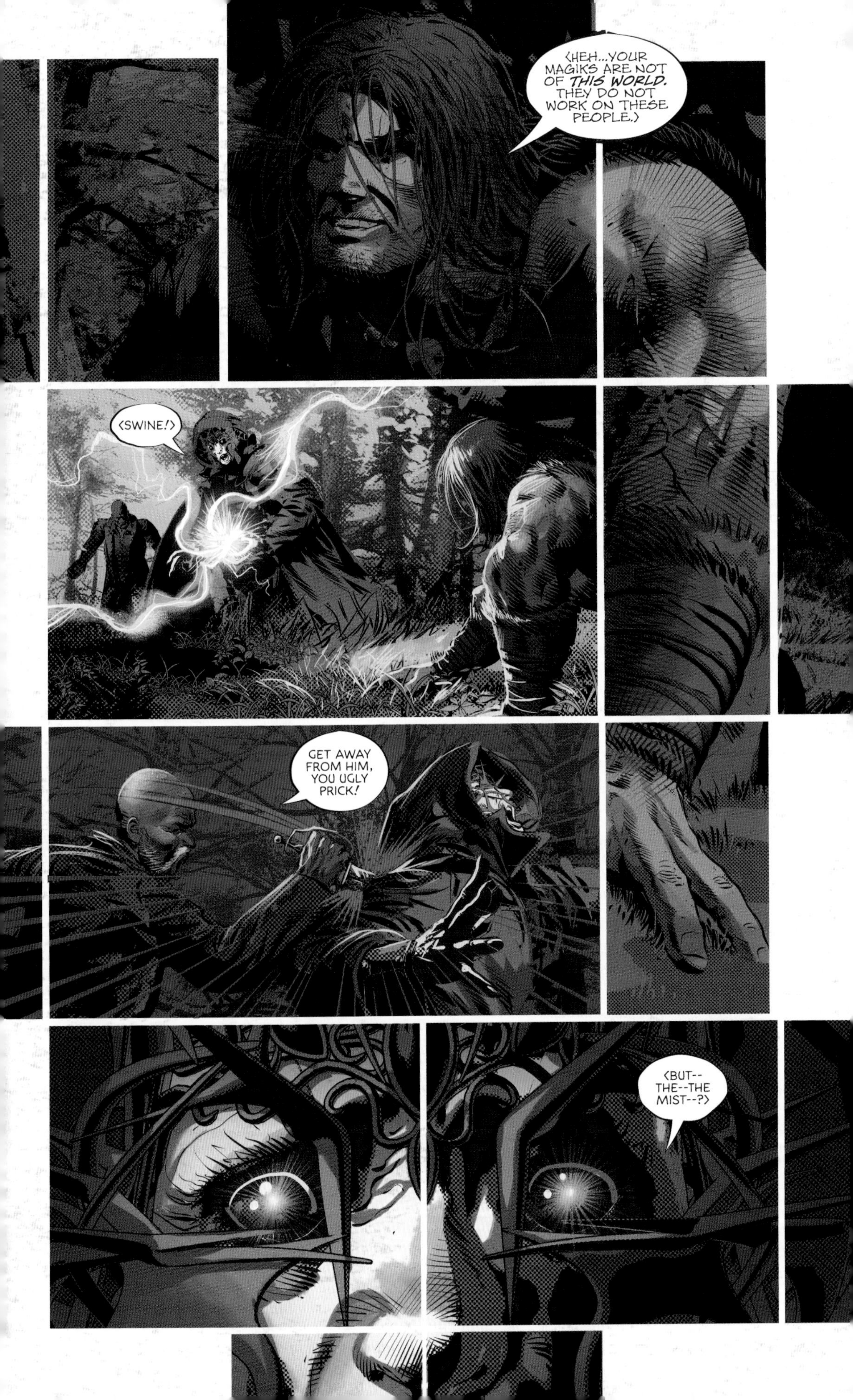

‹HEH...YOUR MAGIKS ARE NOT OF THIS WORLD. THEY DO NOT WORK ON THESE PEOPLE.›
‹SWINE!›
GET AWAY FROM HIM, YOU UGLY PRICK!
‹BUT-- THE--THE MIST--?›

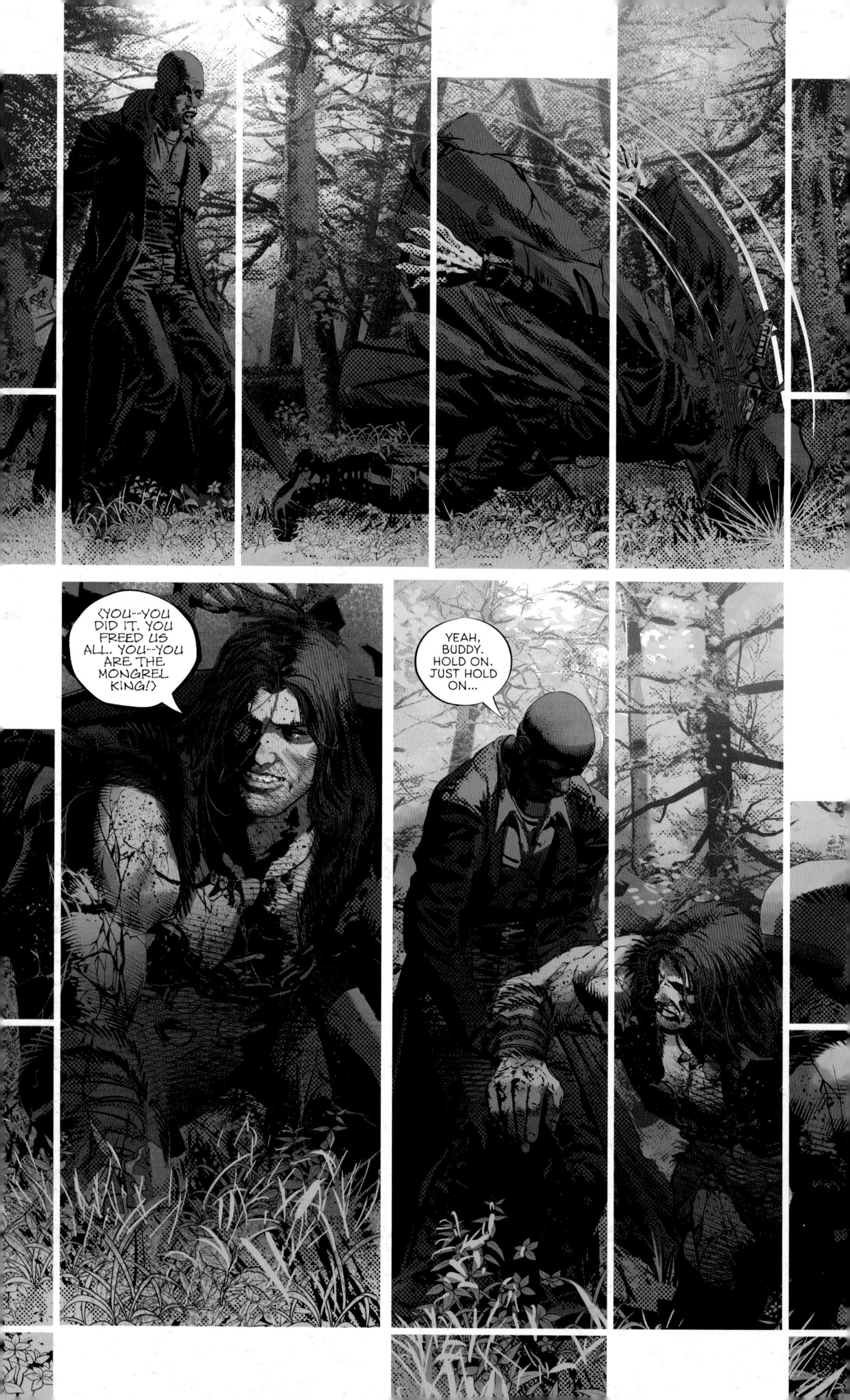
<YOU--YOU DID IT. YOU FREED US ALL. YOU--YOU ARE THE MONGREL KING!>
YEAH, BUDDY. HOLD ON. JUST HOLD ON...

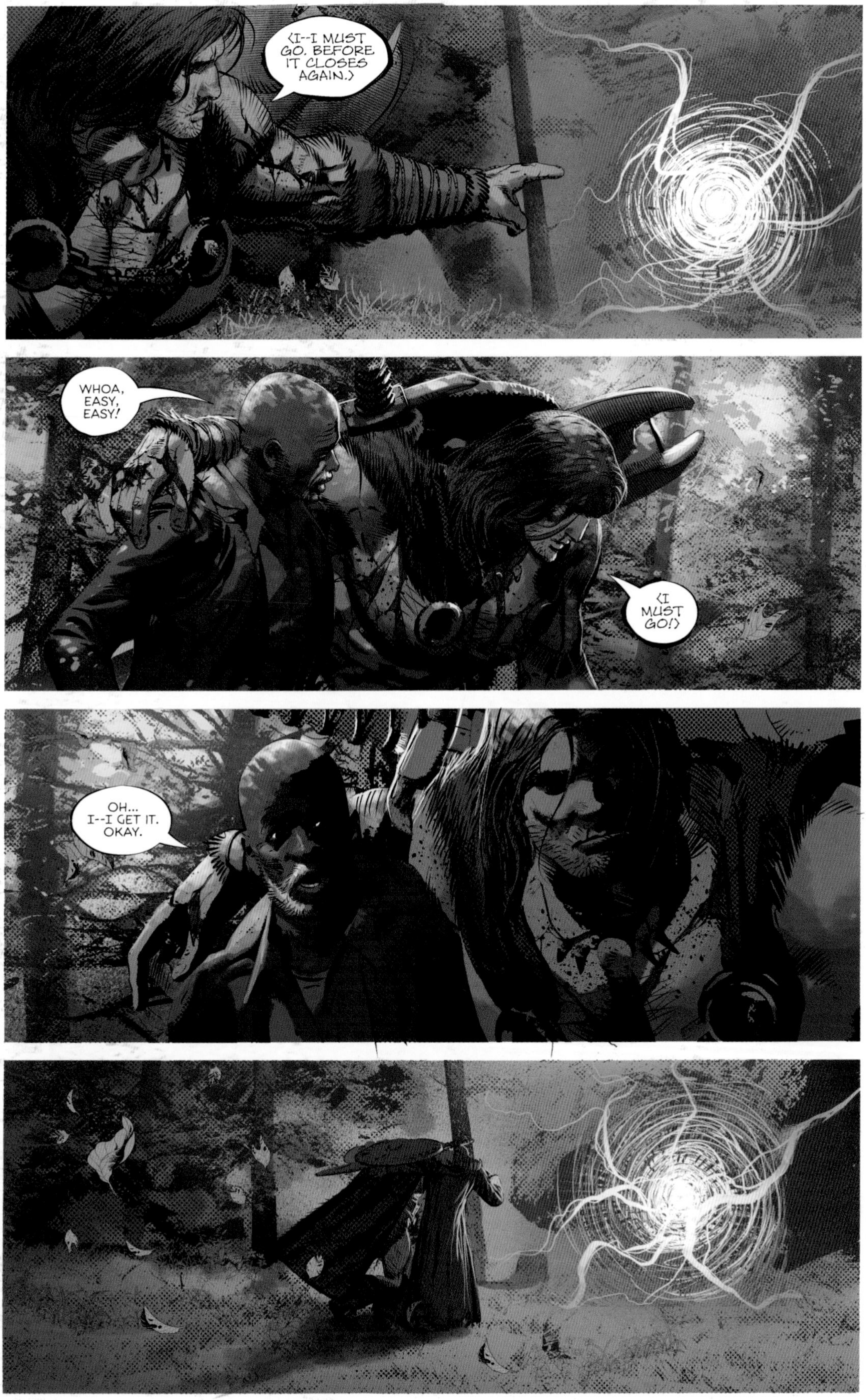
⟨I--I MUST GO. BEFORE IT CLOSES AGAIN.⟩
WHOA, EASY, EASY!
⟨I MUST GO!⟩
OH... I--I GET IT. OKAY.

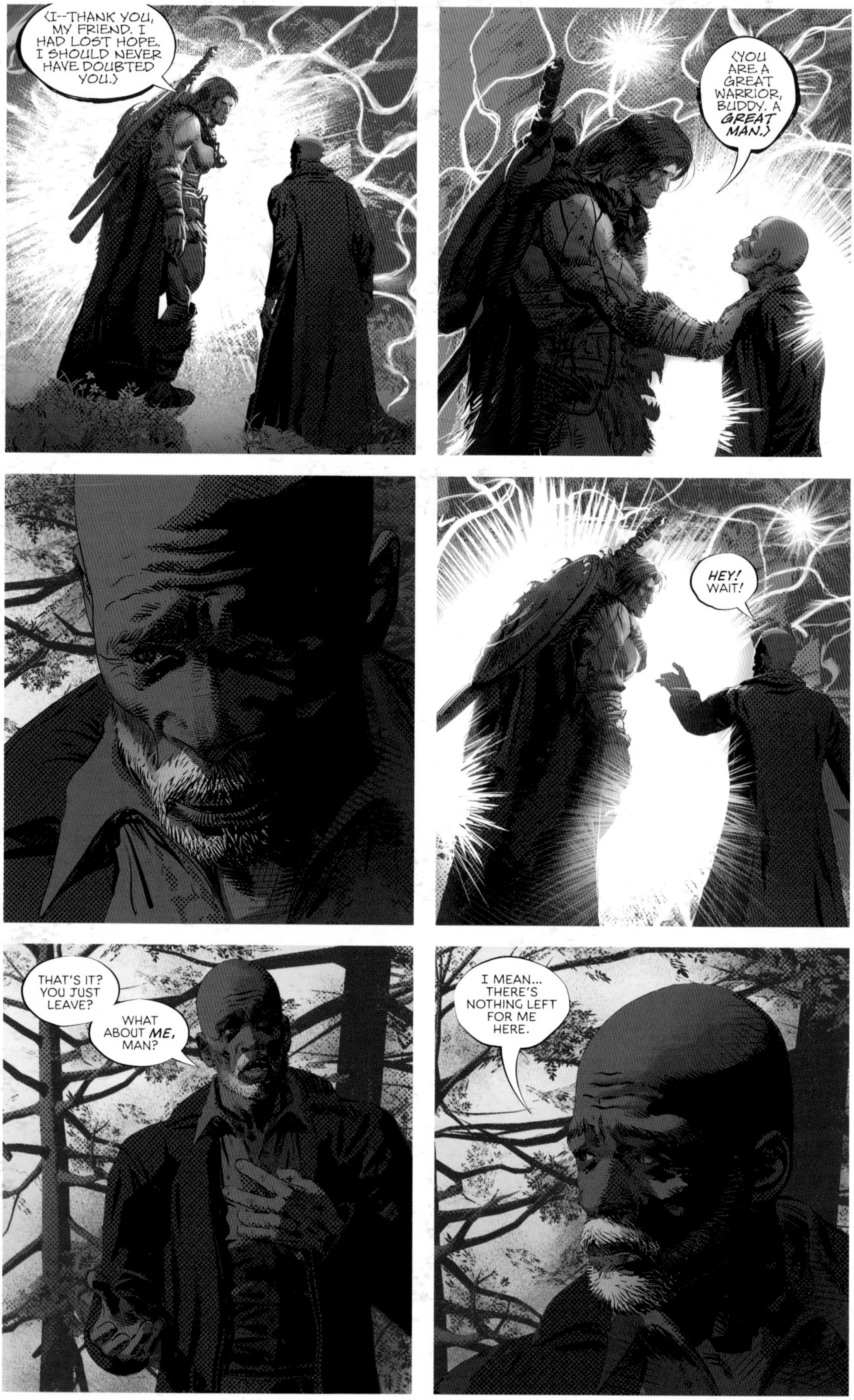

<I--THANK YOU, MY FRIEND. I HAD LOST HOPE. I SHOULD NEVER HAVE DOUBTED YOU.>
<YOU ARE A GREAT WARRIOR, BUDDY. A *GREAT* MAN.>
HEY! WAIT!
THAT'S IT? YOU JUST LEAVE?
WHAT ABOUT *ME,* MAN?
I MEAN... THERE'S NOTHING LEFT FOR ME HERE.

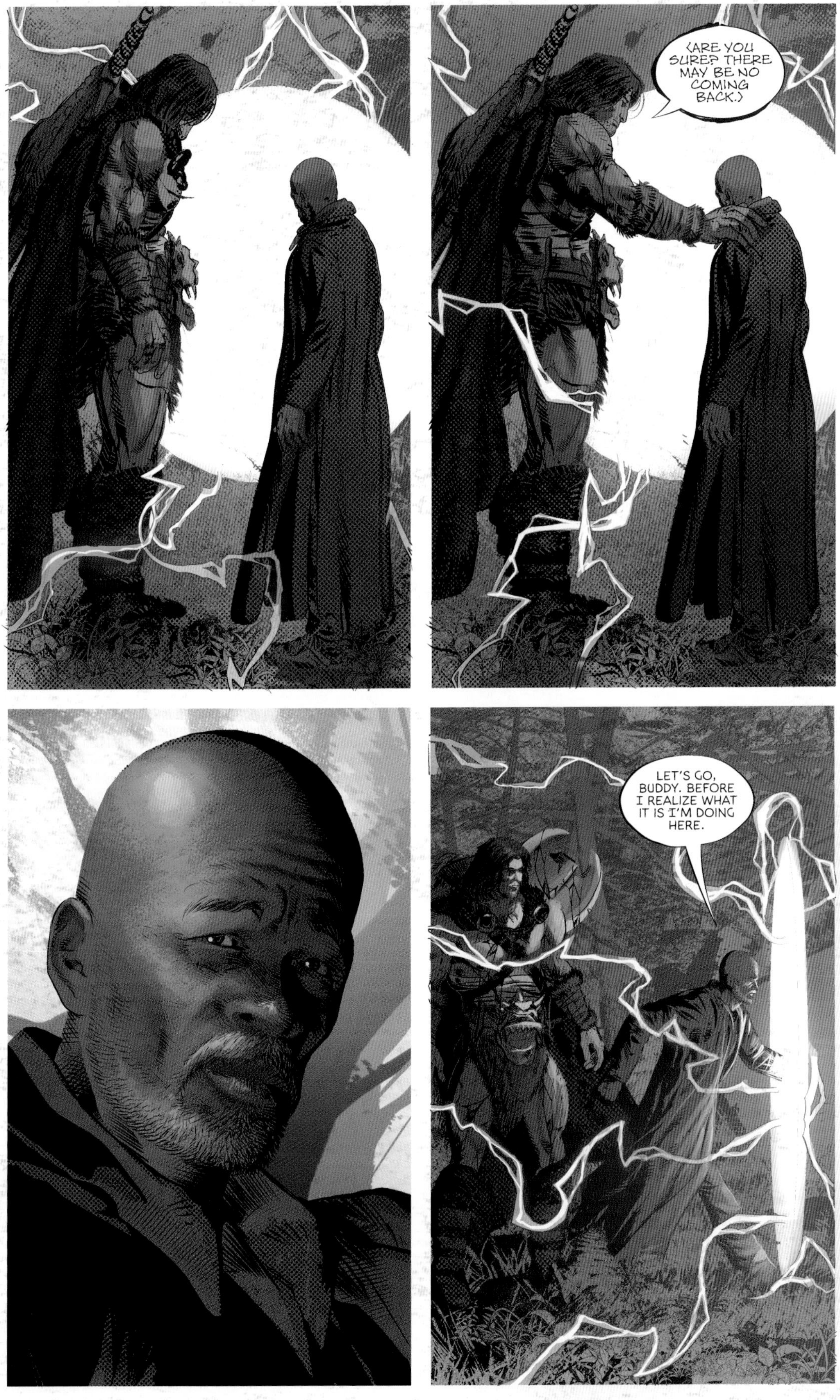
<ARE YOU SURE? THERE MAY BE NO COMING BACK.>
LET'S GO, BUDDY. BEFORE I REALIZE WHAT IT IS I'M DOING HERE.

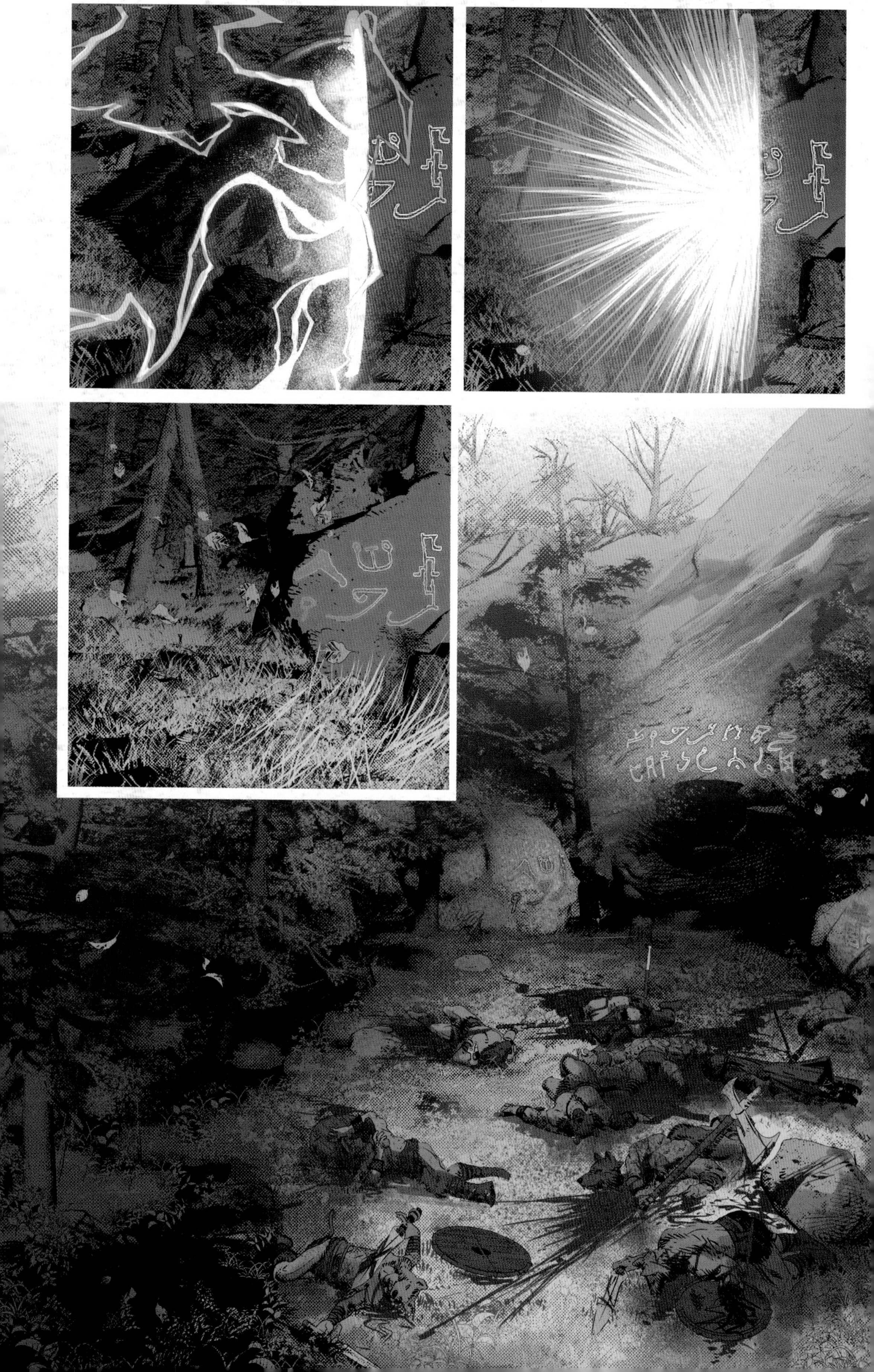

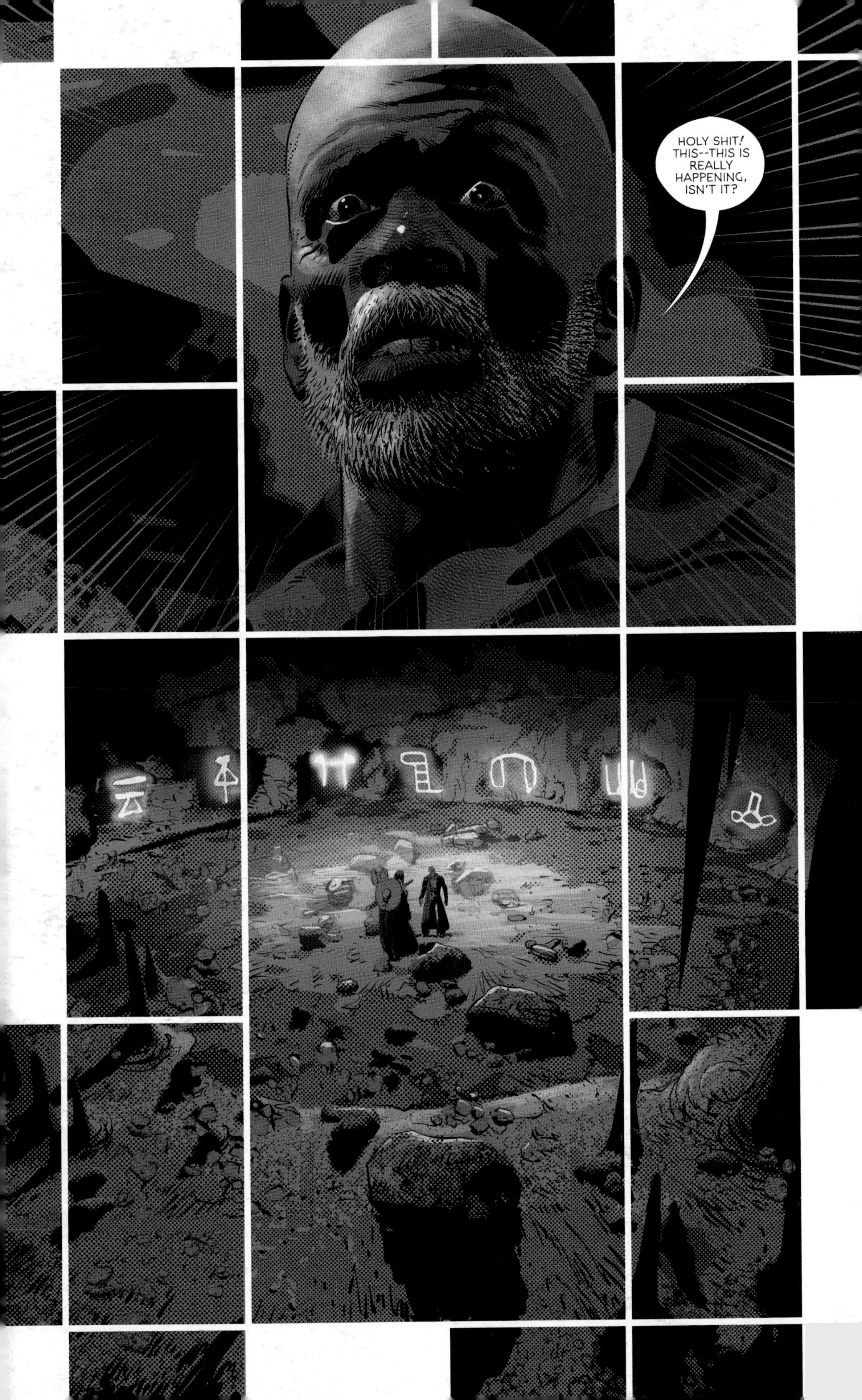
HOLY SHIT! THIS--THIS IS REALLY HAPPENING, ISN'T IT?

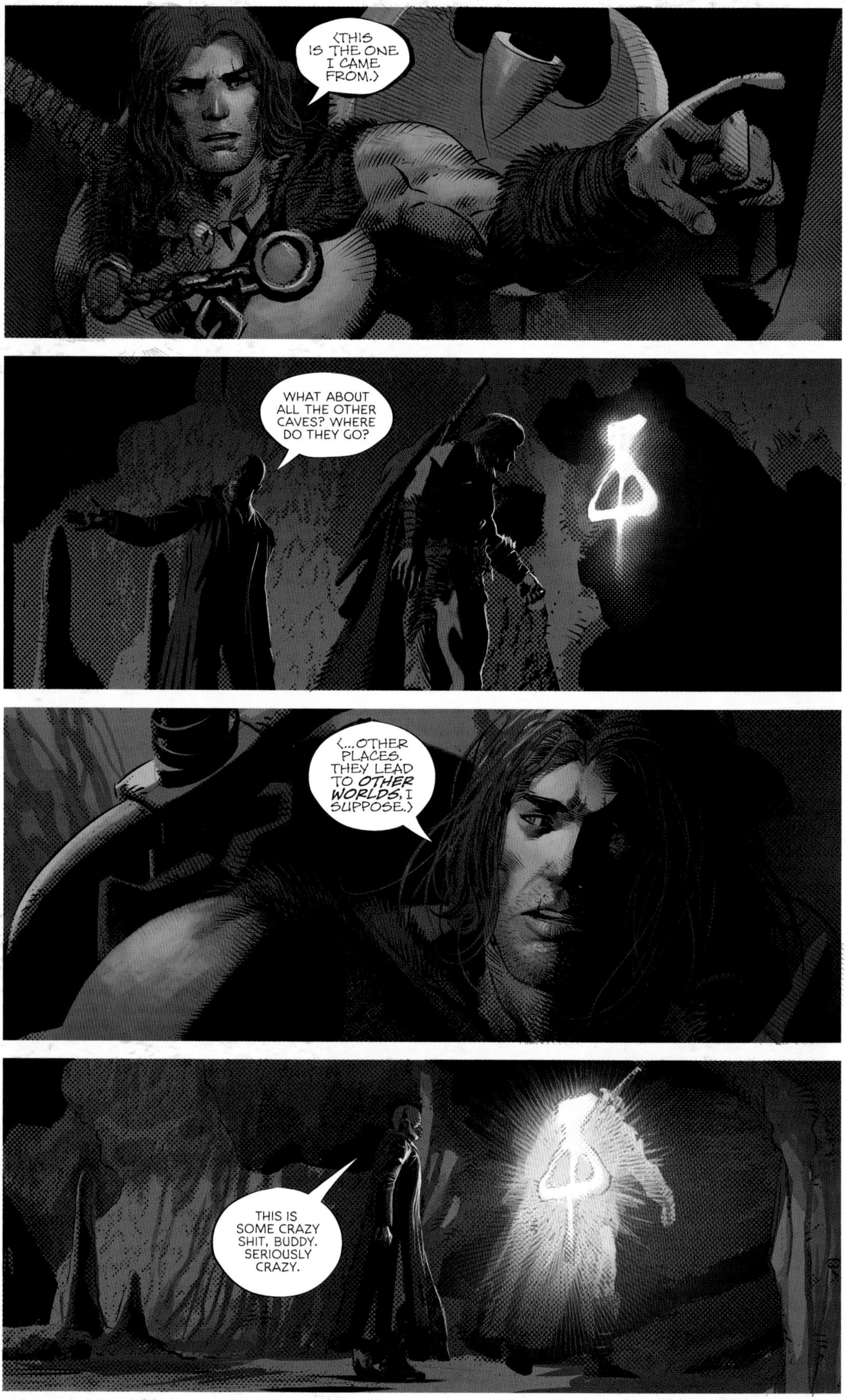
<THIS IS THE ONE I CAME FROM.>
WHAT ABOUT ALL THE OTHER CAVES? WHERE DO THEY GO?
<...OTHER PLACES. THEY LEAD TO *OTHER WORLDS*, I SUPPOSE.>
THIS IS SOME CRAZY SHIT, BUDDY. SERIOUSLY CRAZY.

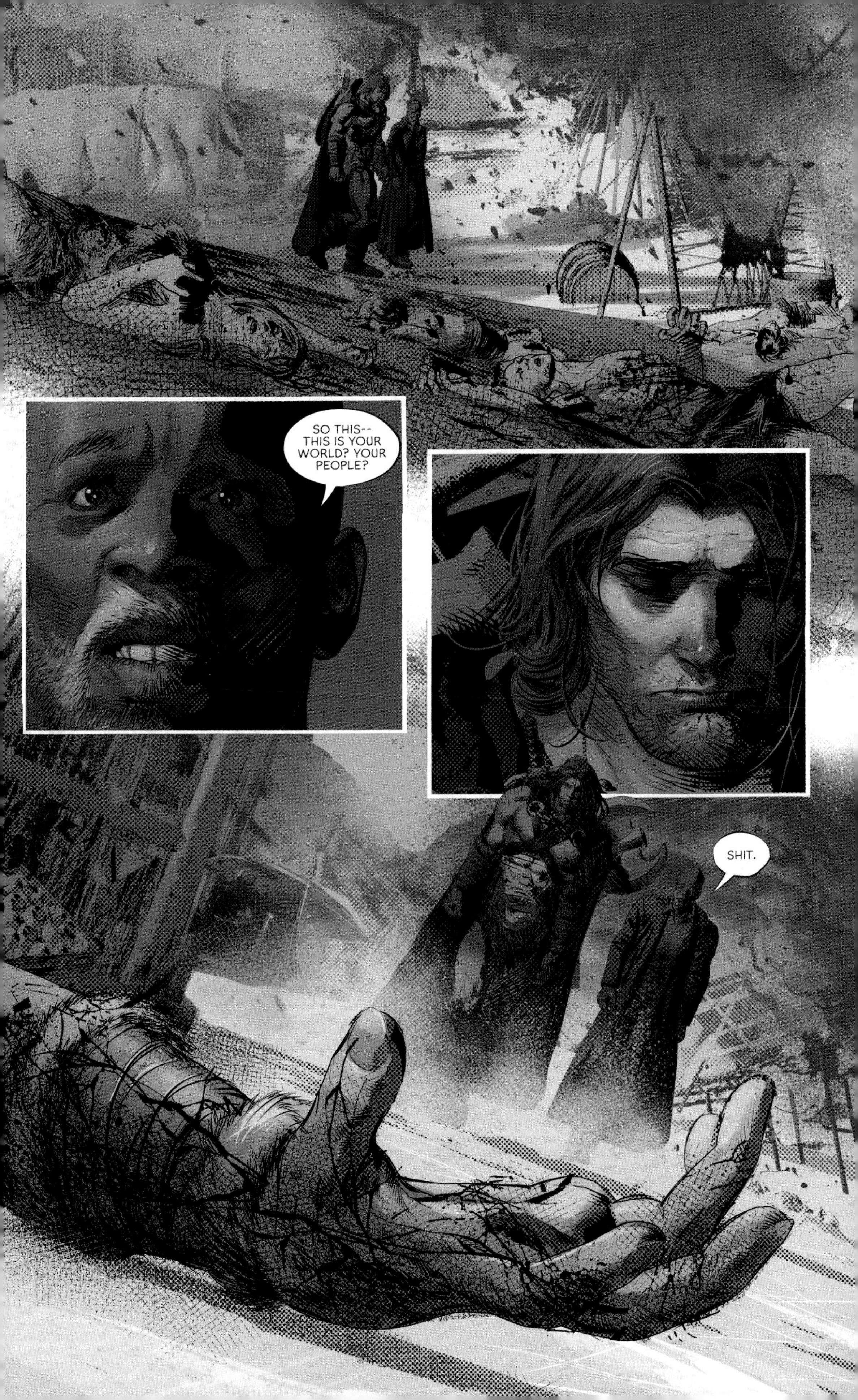
SO THIS--
THIS IS YOUR
WORLD? YOUR
PEOPLE?
SHIT.

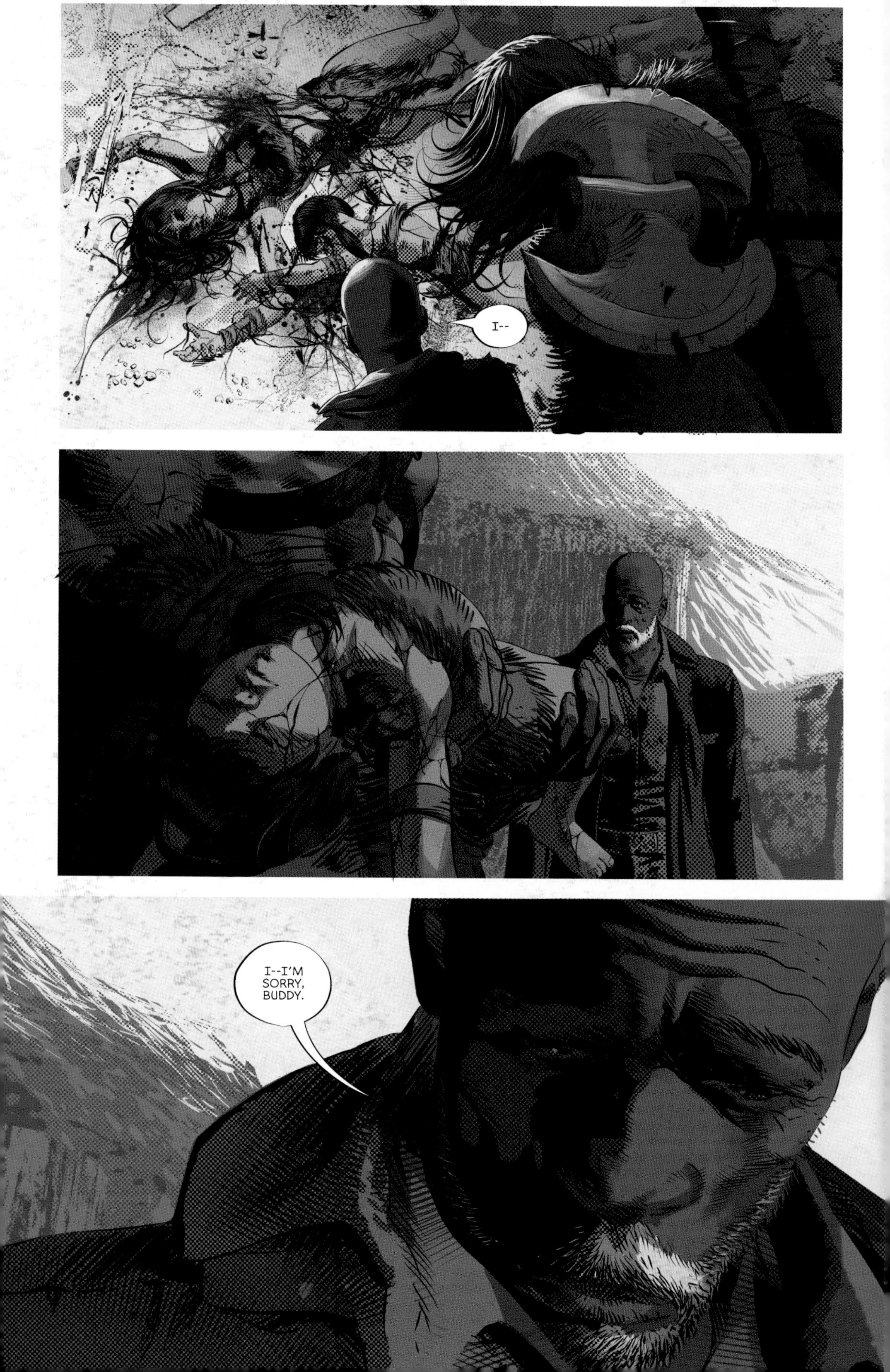
I--
I--I'M SORRY, BUDDY.

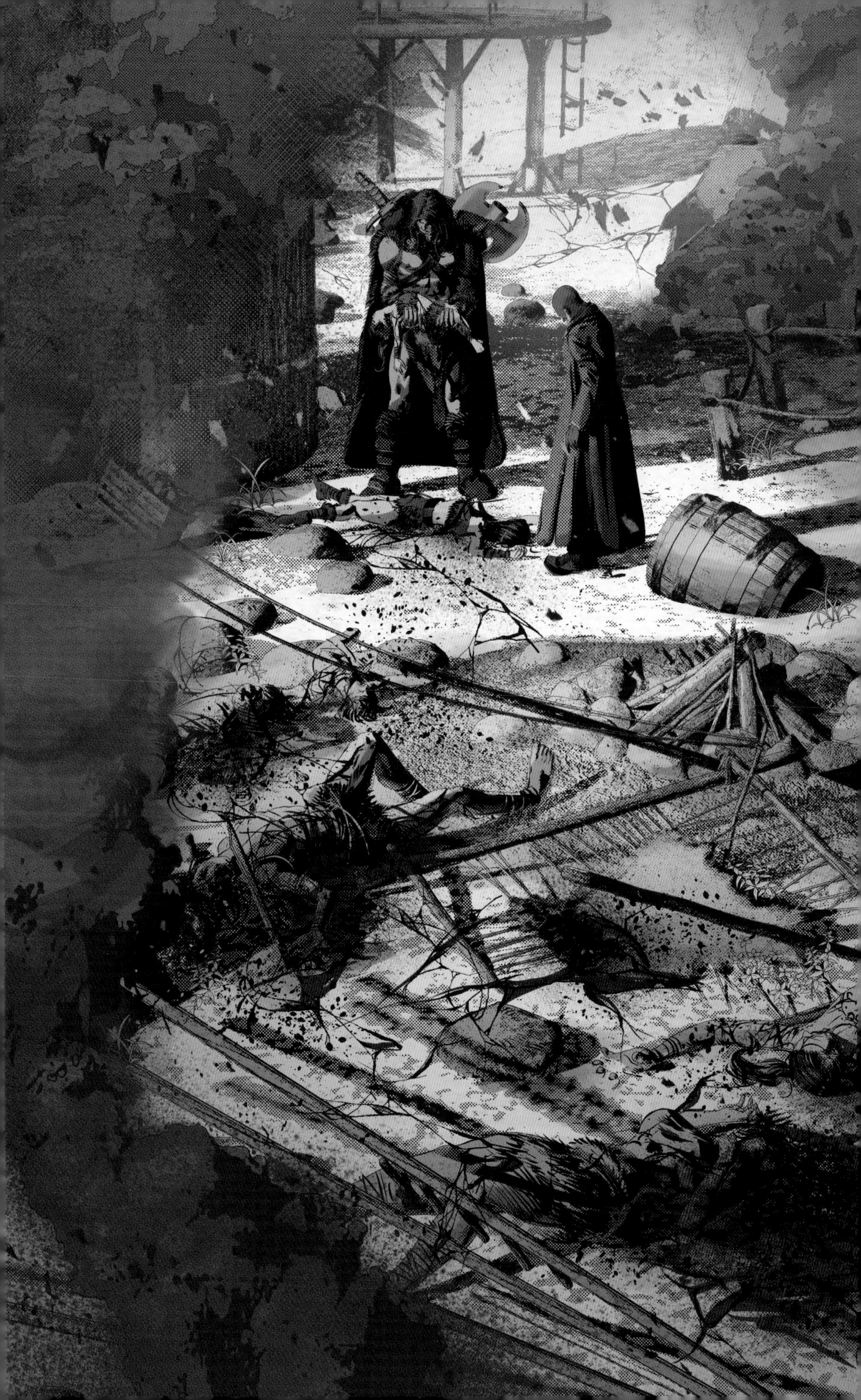

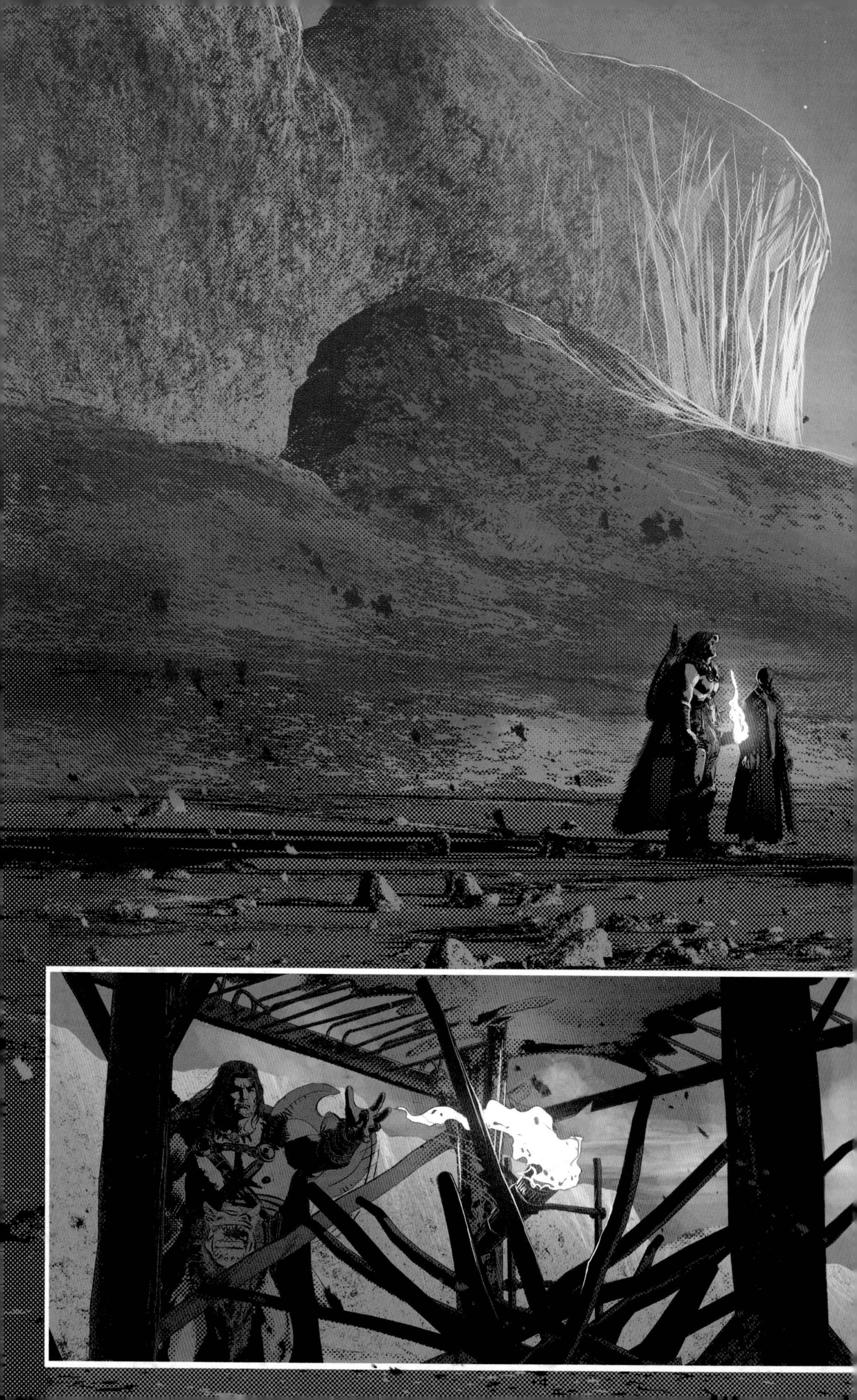

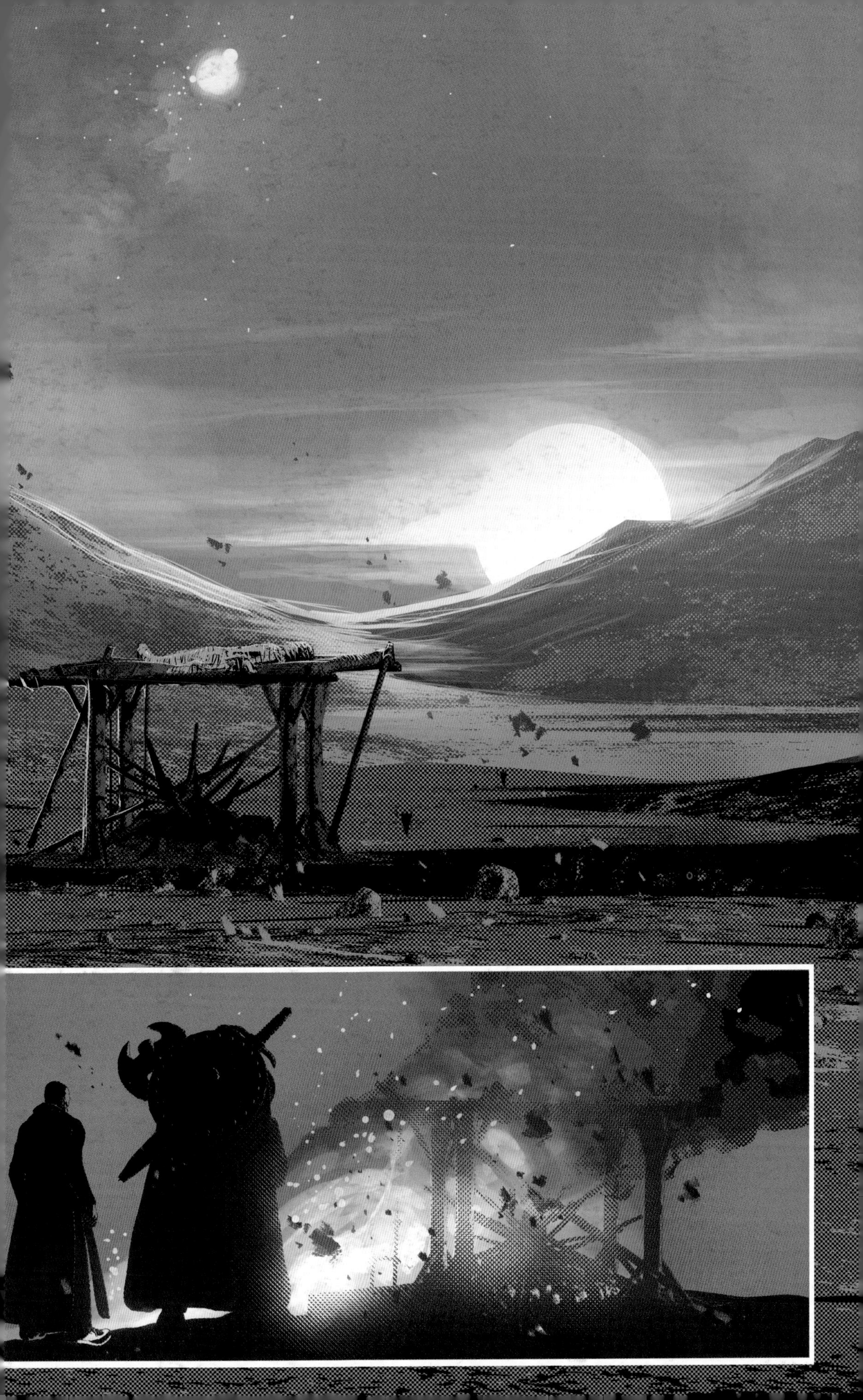

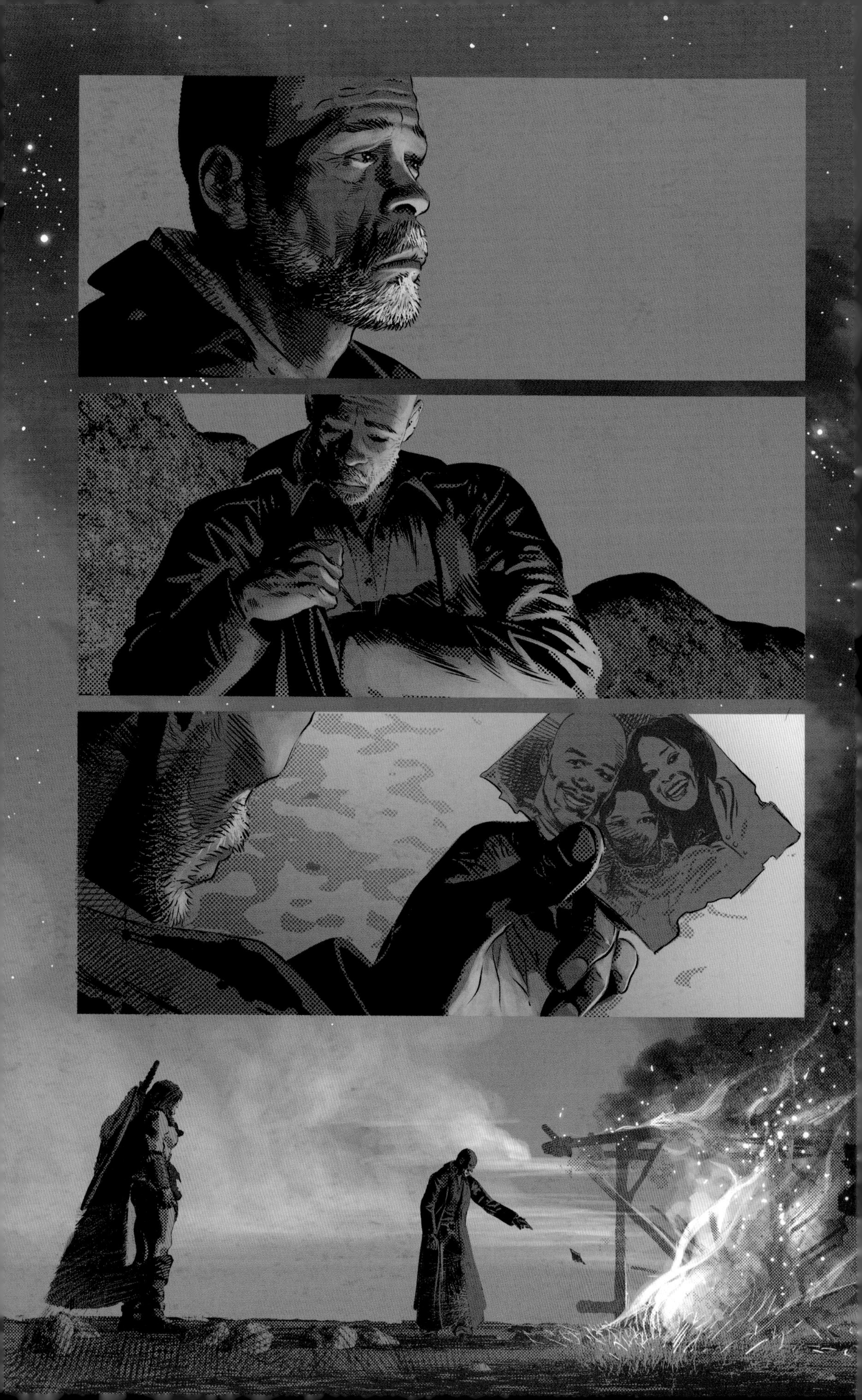

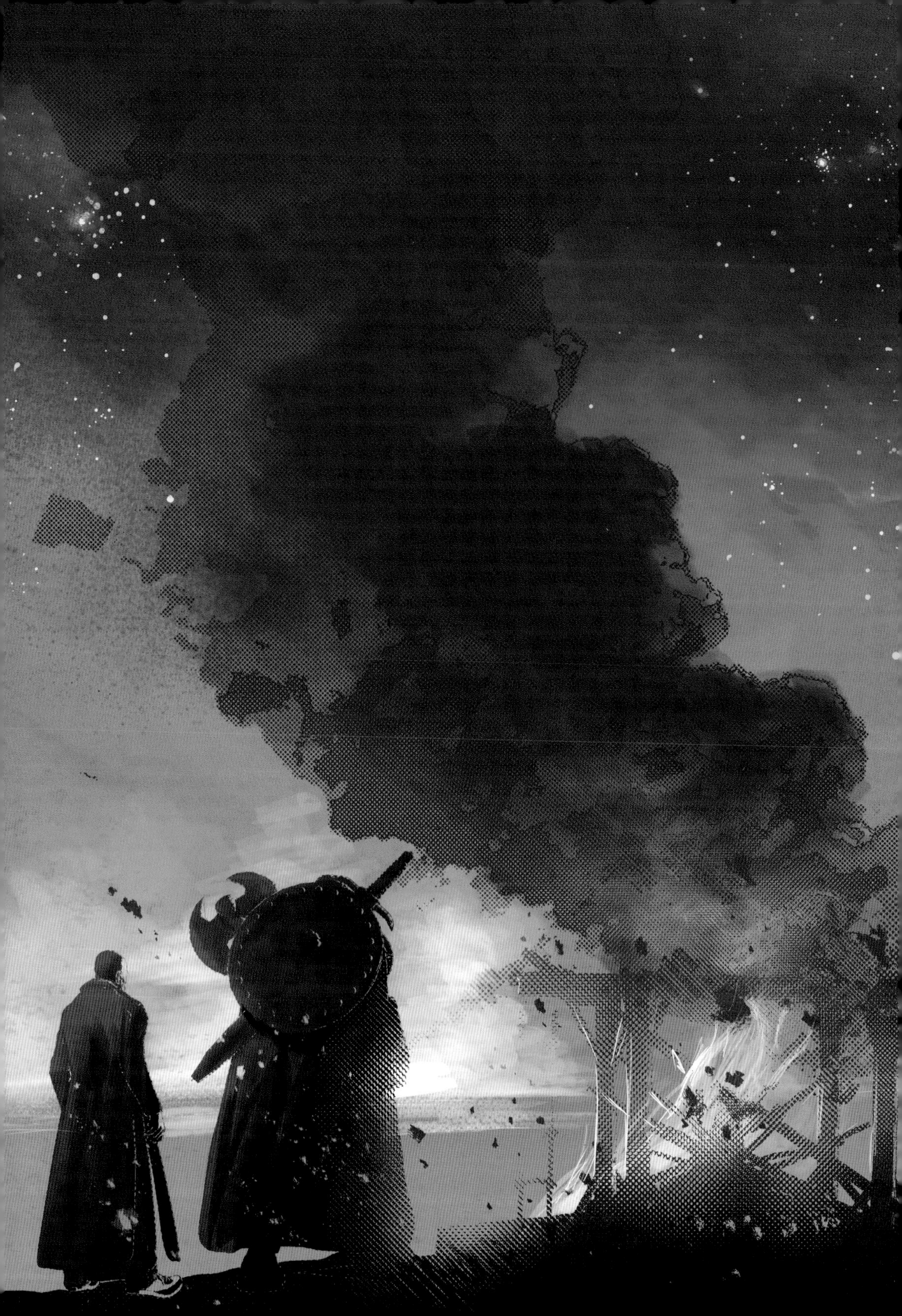

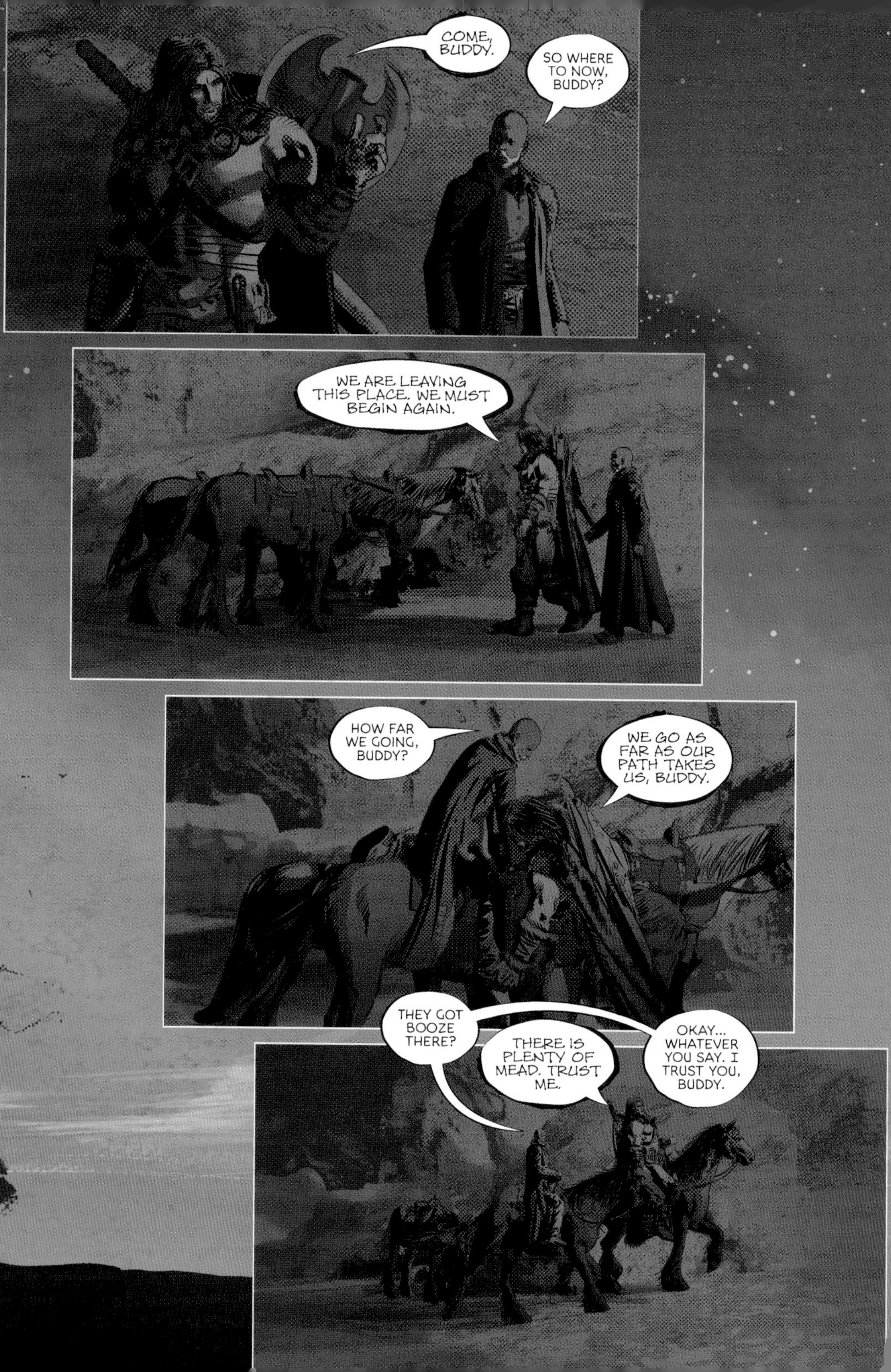
COME, BUDDY.
SO WHERE TO NOW, BUDDY?
WE ARE LEAVING THIS PLACE. WE MUST BEGIN AGAIN.
HOW FAR WE GOING, BUDDY?
WE GO AS FAR AS OUR PATH TAKES US, BUDDY.
THEY GOT BOOZE THERE?
THERE IS PLENTY OF MEAD. TRUST ME.
OKAY... WHATEVER YOU SAY. I TRUST YOU, BUDDY.

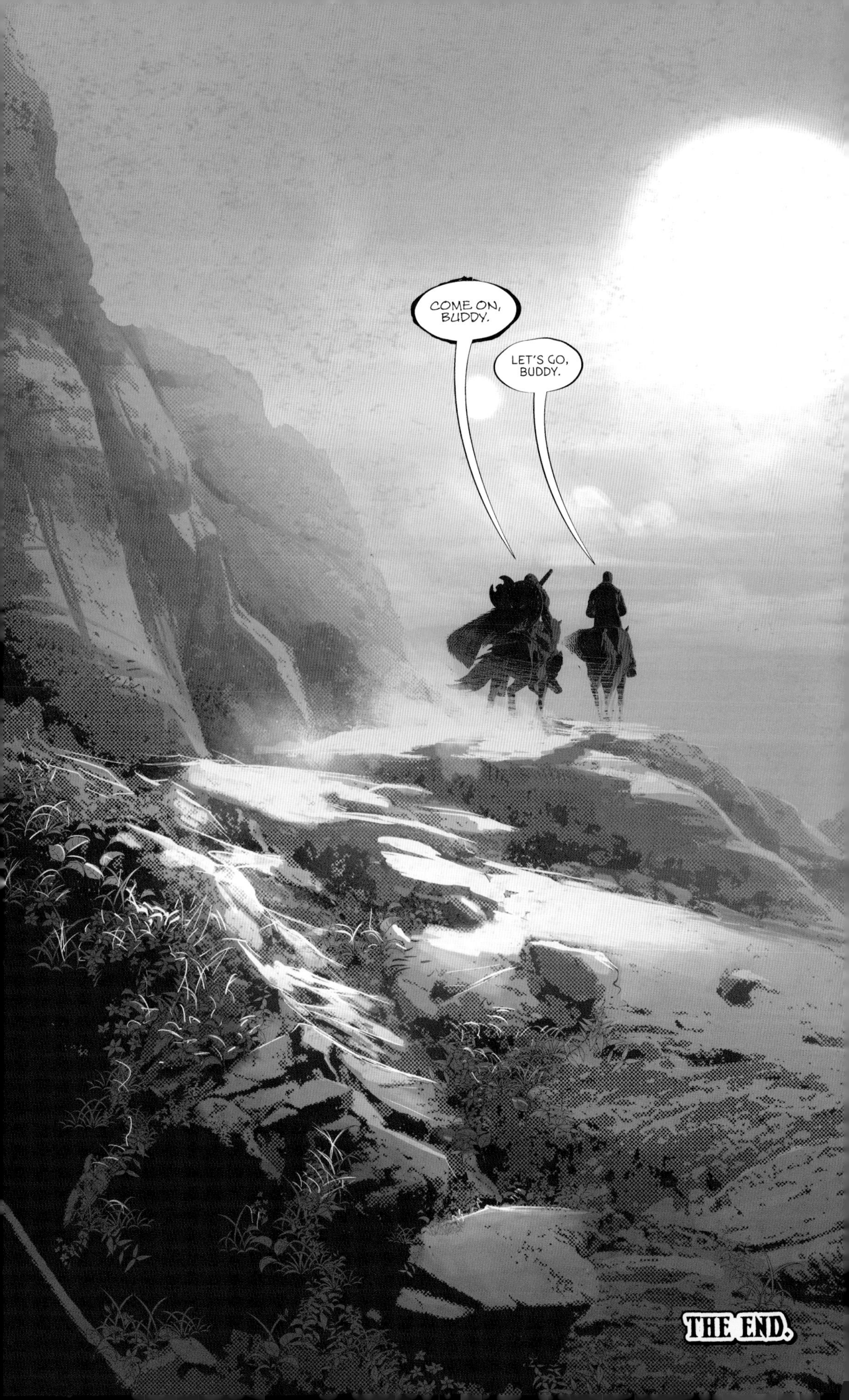
COME ON, BUDDY.
LET'S GO, BUDDY.
THE END.

Variant cover for *Berserker Unbound* #1 by Mike Mignola with Dave Stewart

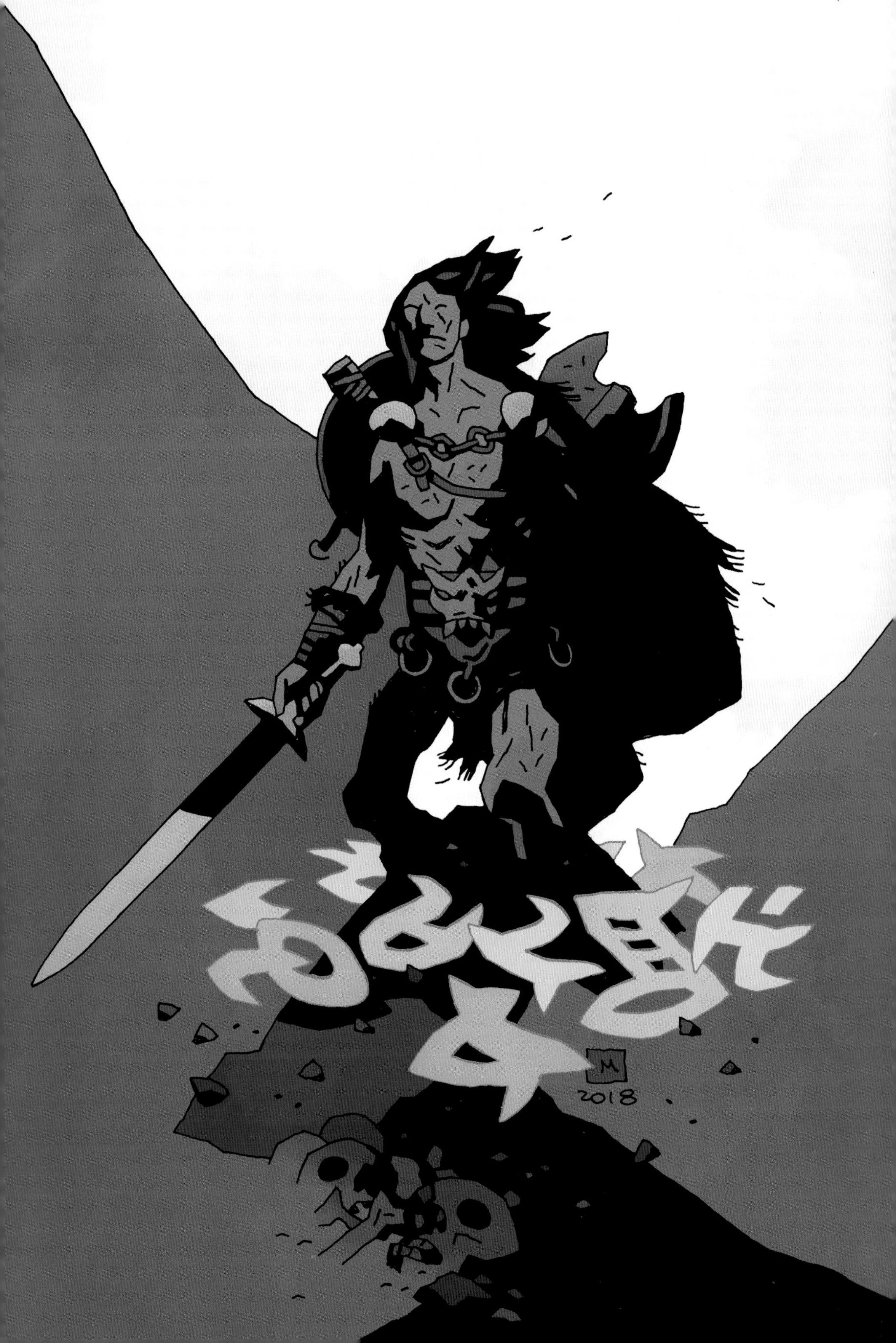
2018

Variant cover for *Berserker Unbound* #2 by Andrea Sorrentino

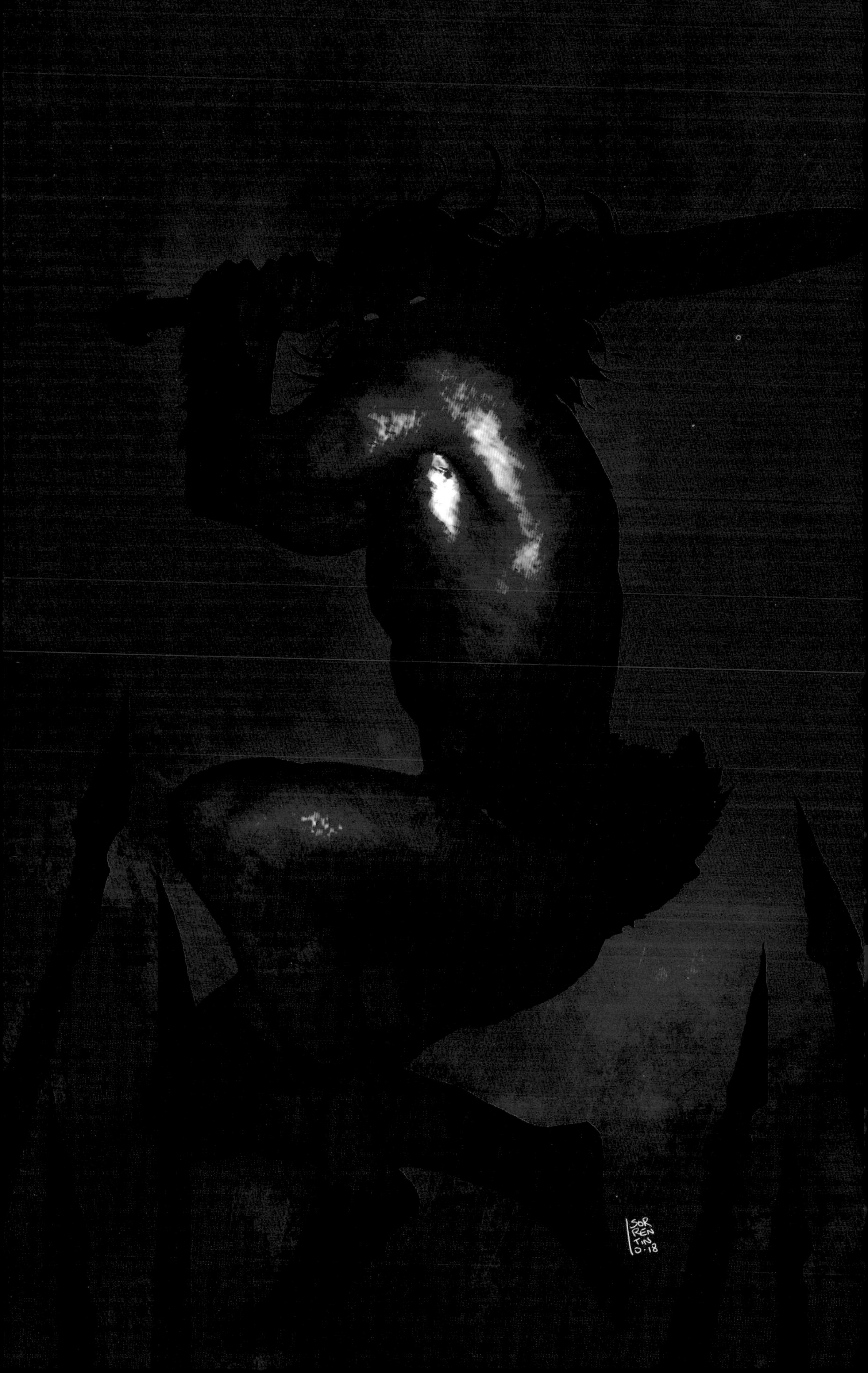
SOR
REN
TIN
O·18

Variant cover for *Berserker Unbound* #3 by Dustin Nguyen

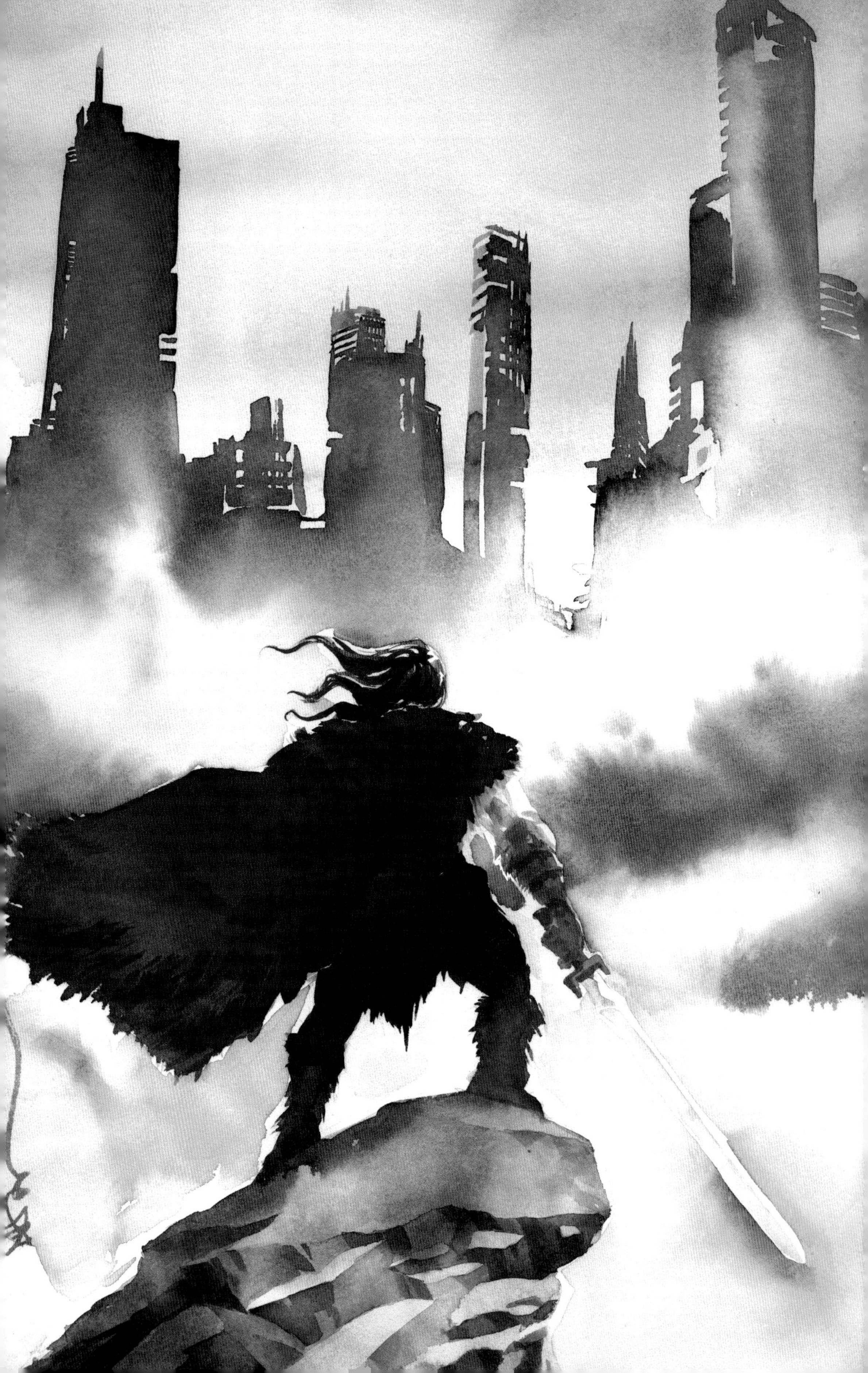

Variant cover for *Berserker Unbound* #4 by Christian Ward

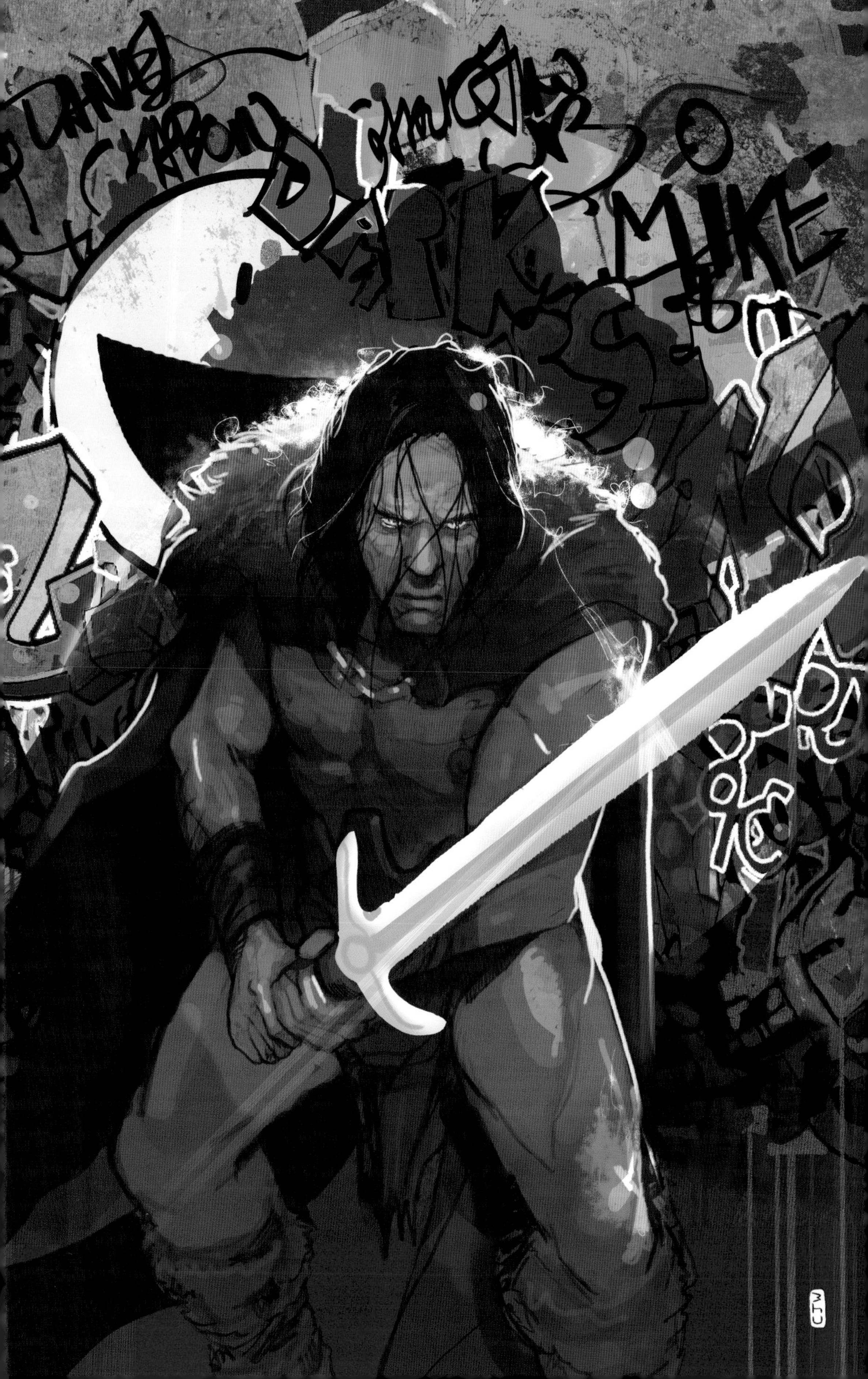
MIKE

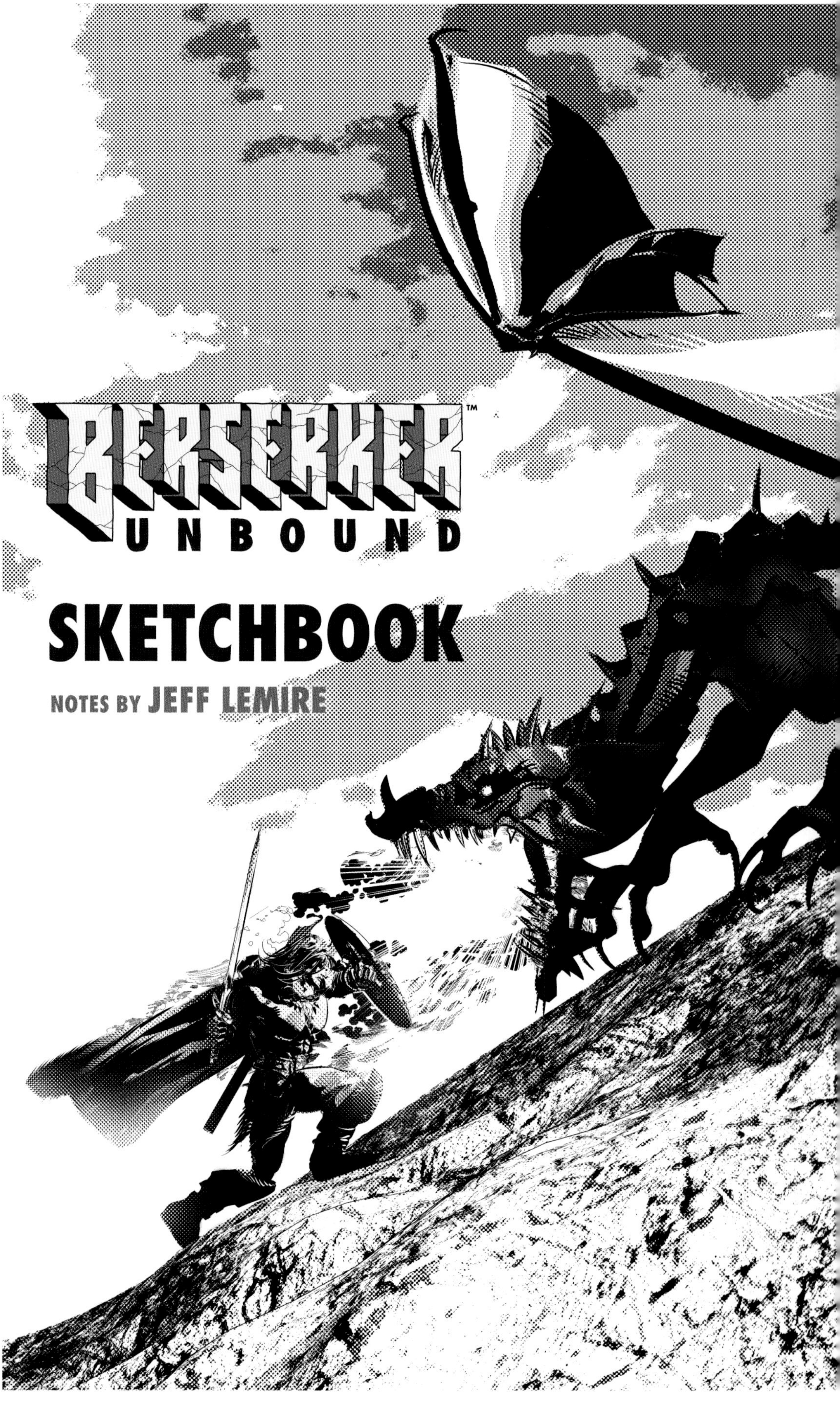

BERSERKER™ UNBOUND

SKETCHBOOK

NOTES BY JEFF LEMIRE

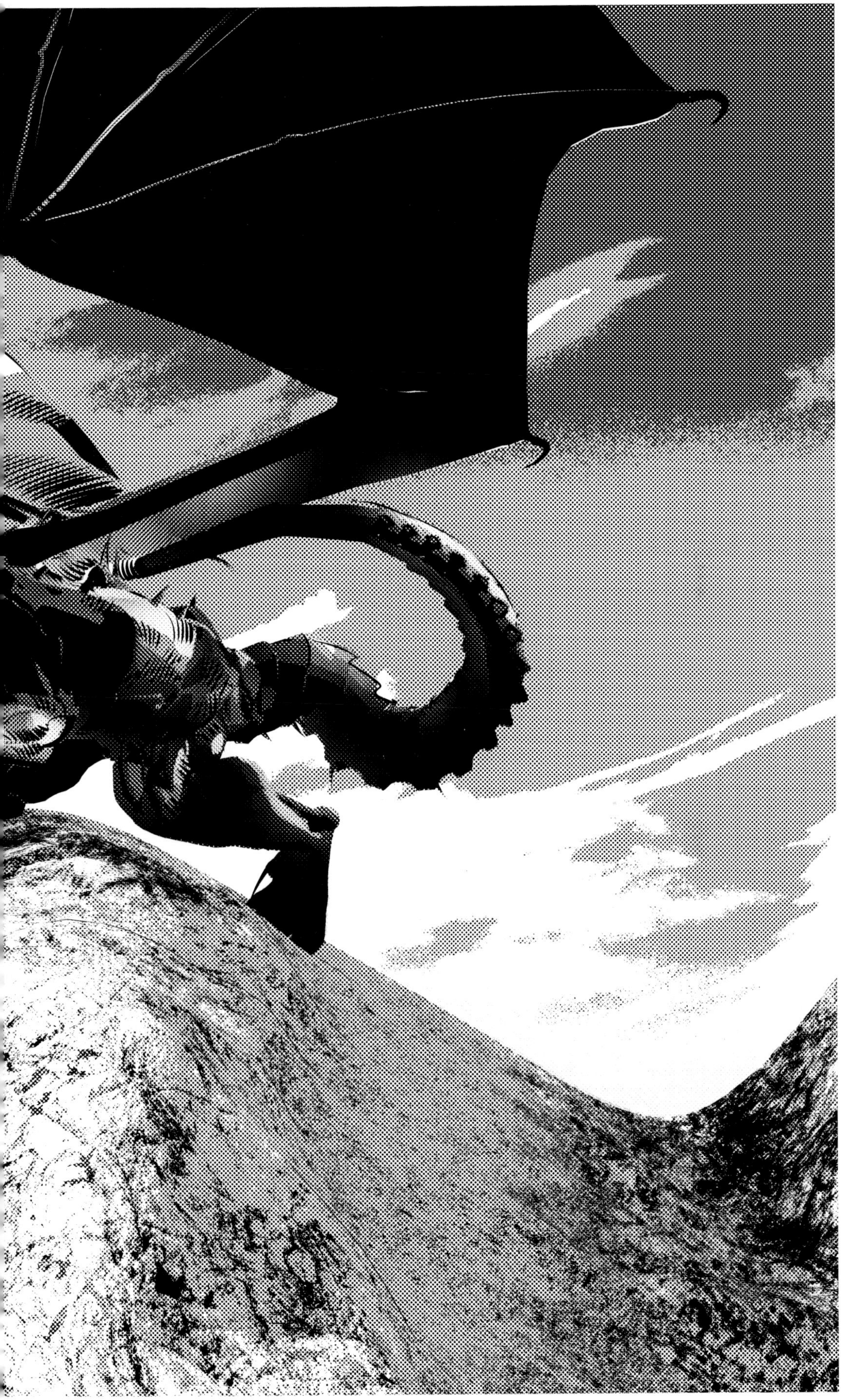

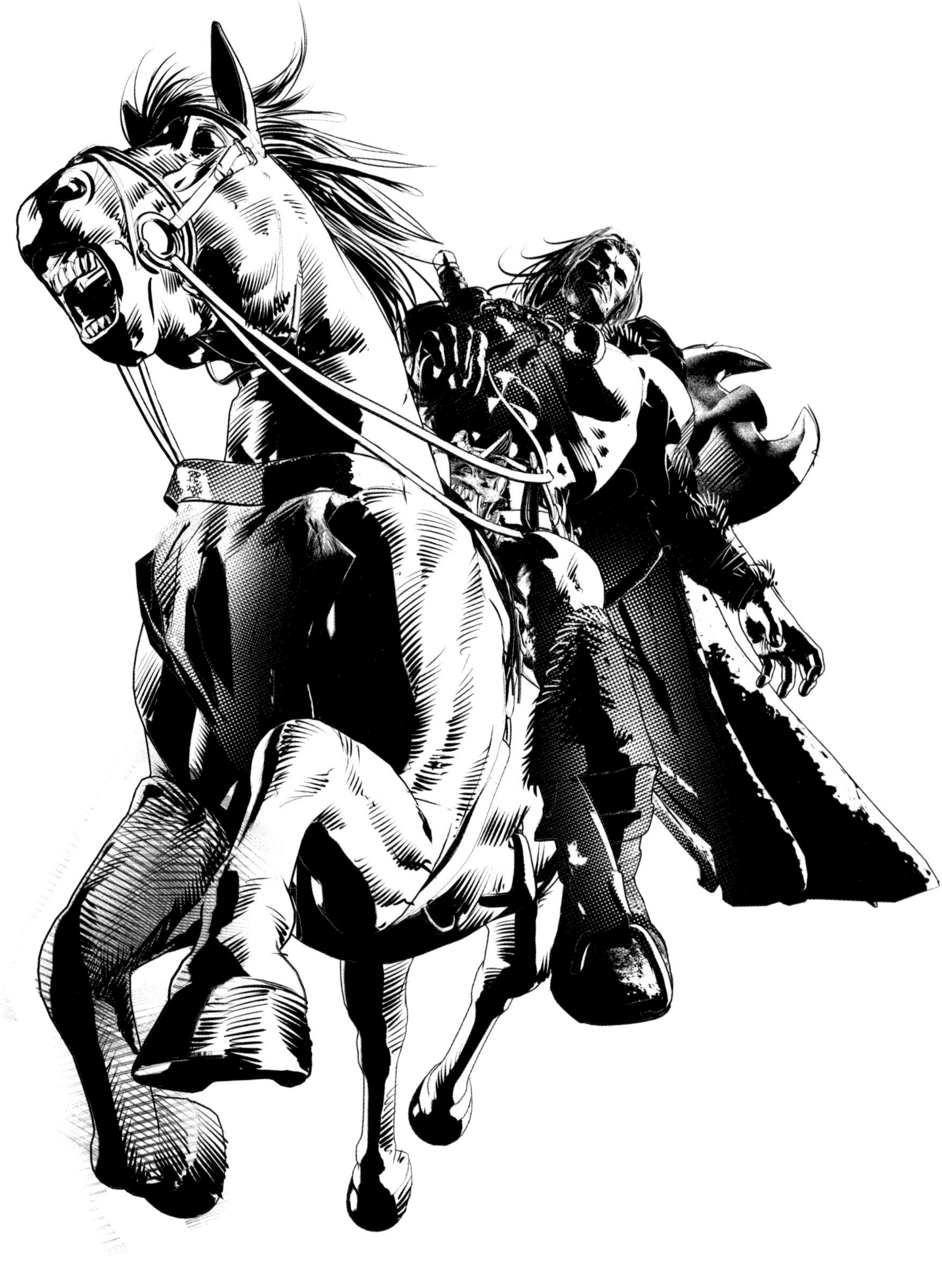

BERSERKER

I was lucky enough to get paired with Mike Deodato Jr. on a short-lived *Thanos* series at Marvel a few years back. We hit it off right away and soon after started talking about possible creator-owned stories we could do together. I asked Mike what kinds of stories or genres he would be interested in and he immediately said his dream was to do a barbarian story. As soon as he said that, I knew Mike would draw an incredible "sword and sandal" story and I was right. Calling his pages on *Berserker* "epic" would be an understatement. Mike Deodato was the true berserker here. And it all starts with his initial designs for Bez. They were instantly iconic and powerful and he created the kind of character that inspires legends.

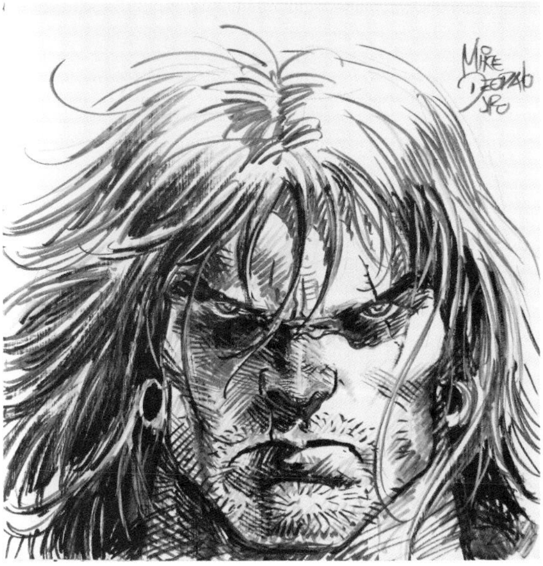

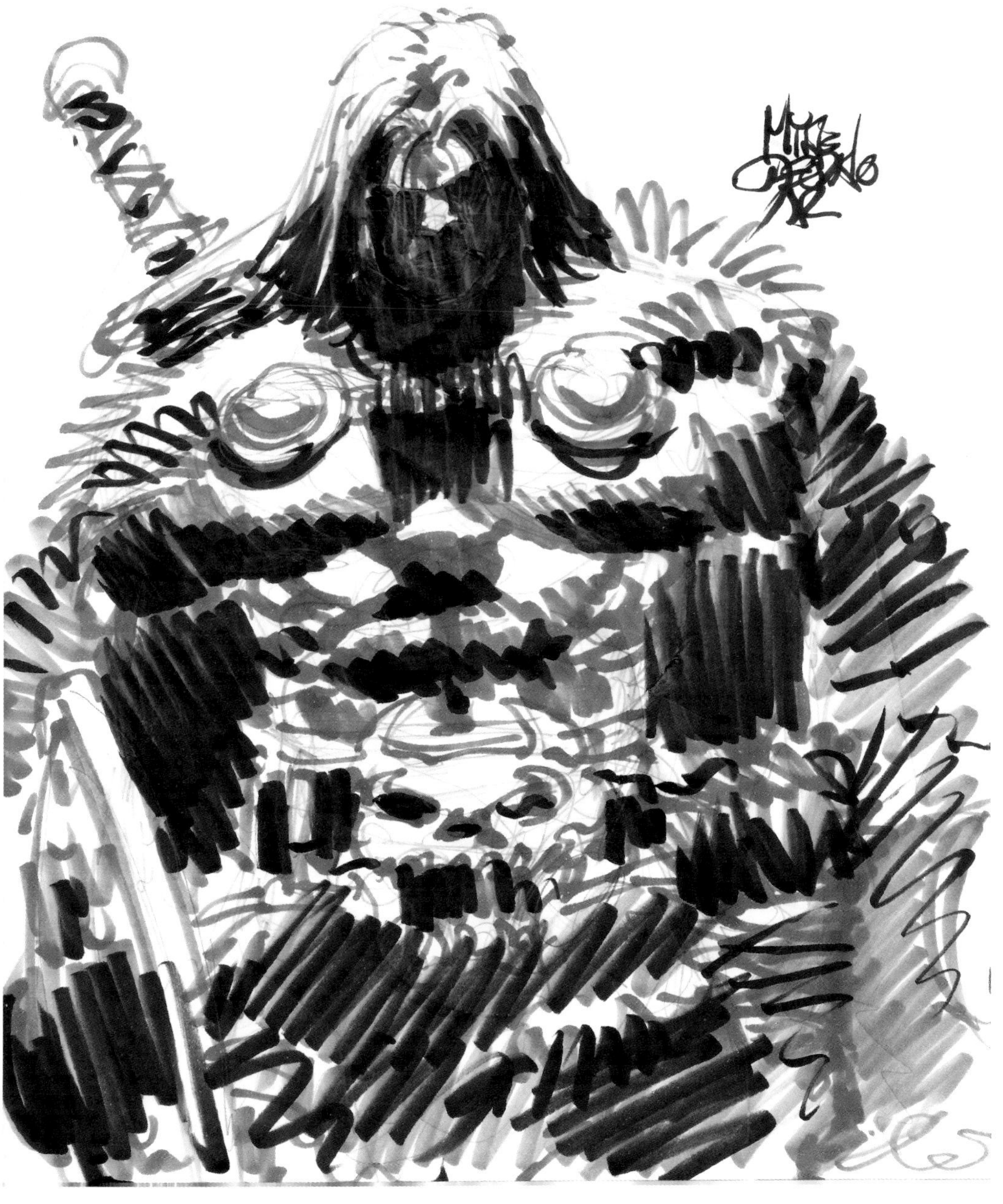

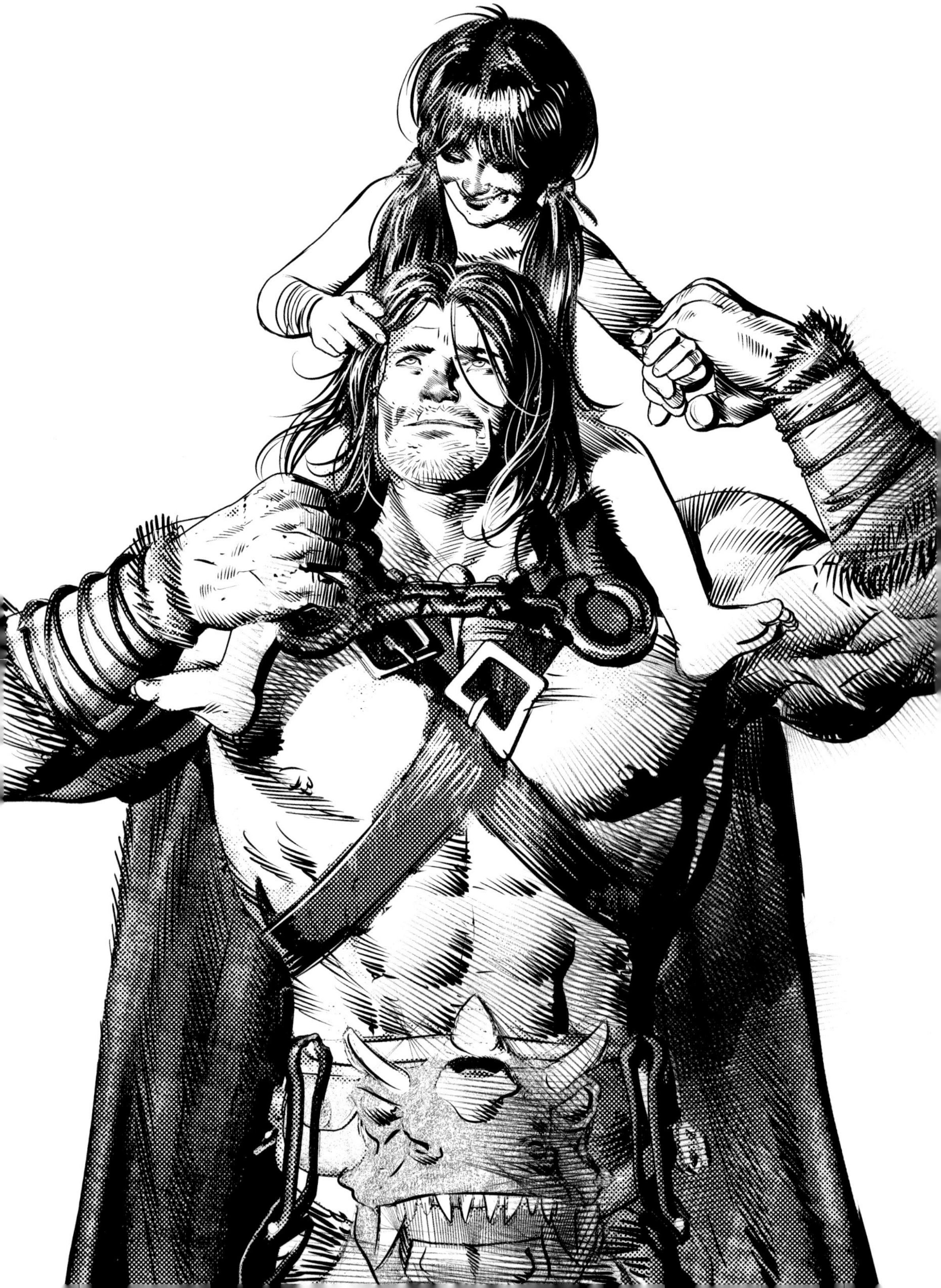

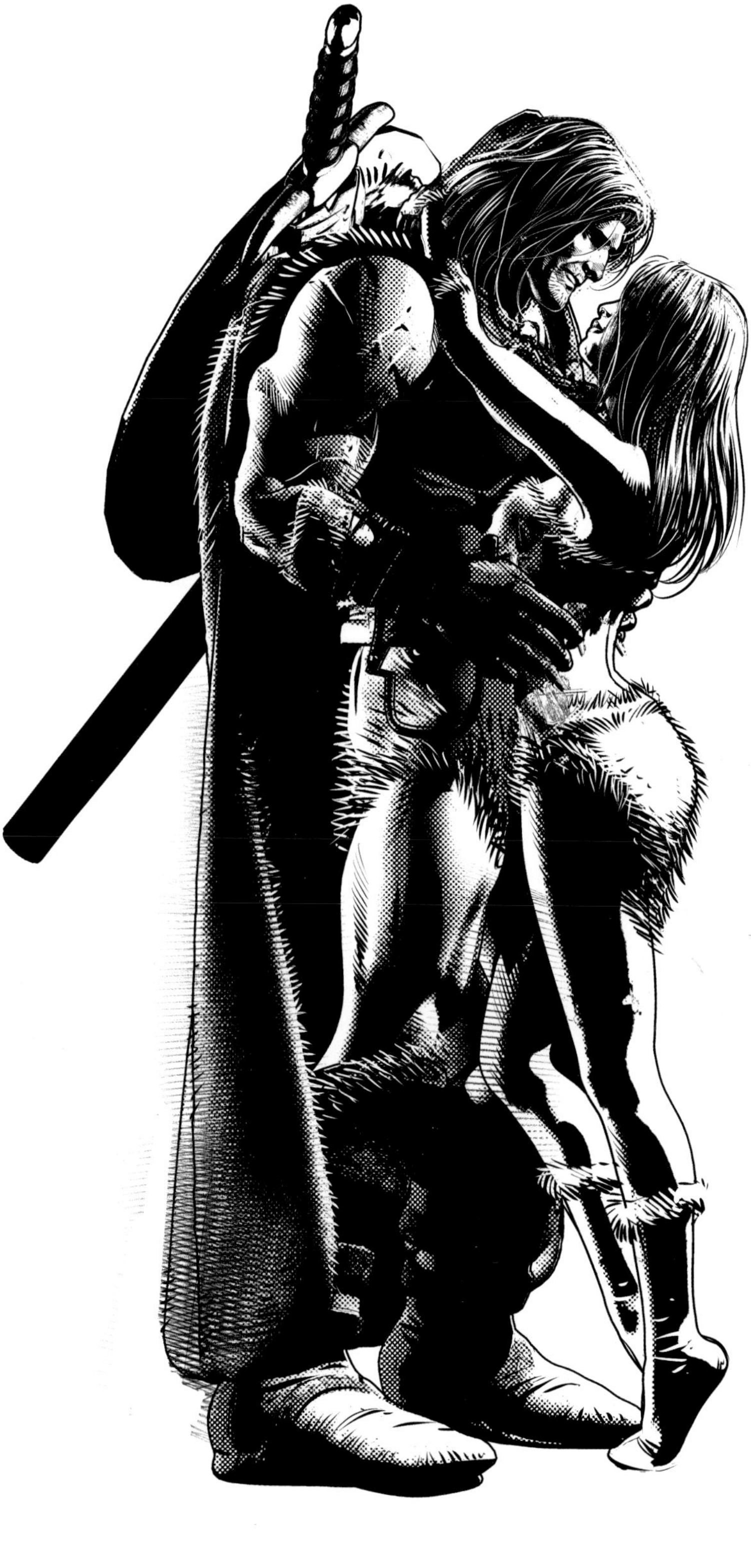

While the action-packed barbarian aspects of this series are certainly important, it's the humanity of Bez and Cobb that really lie at the heart of the story. And this is where you see Mike's true genius. He can create these almost monolithic figures like Bez, but also imbue them with real heart and humanity. This dual nature in Berserker epitomizes the dual nature of the story itself. The scene with Bez and his family are particularly heart-warming and Mike put as much thought and power into those scenes as he did the fight scenes.